What the critics are saying...

Diamond Assets by Ruth D. Kerce

4 Cups! "The love scenes are hot enough to cause steam to rise from the pages. There are a few moments in them that actually left me gasping for breath. Ms. Kerce is a talented author who has written a hot story of lust and love that I enjoyed very much. I am certain that I will re-read Diamond Assets repeatedly." ~ *Susan White, Coffee Time Romance*

Diamond in the Snow by Diana Hunter

4 Cups! "Well-rounded characters... The sex scenes are graphically detailed and hotter than a firecracker. Ms. Hunter has penned a very interesting tale of two individuals who are perfect for each other. Diamond in the Snow is a very hot story that I enjoyed reading very much." ~ *Susan White, Coffee Time Romance*

Diamond in the Rough by Ruby Storm

5 Stars! "This is a masterfully woven tale of two inexperienced and overzealous fairies and their laugh out loud hilarious antics... While reading this phenomenal story, I found myself laughing so hard one minute and the next wanting to cry for the heartache these two wonderfully tenderhearted people have gone through." ~ *Christine, eCataRomance Reviews*

4 Hearts!" DIAMOND STUDS was not only a lot of fun to read, but it has plenty of erotic sexual encounters... Get your hands on a copy of this story as soon as you can." ~ *Sarah W, The Romance Studio*

5 Blue Ribbons! "DIAMOND STUDS was amazing and is a recommended read. Definitely a keeper." ~ *Phyllis Ingram, Romance Junkies*

Diamond Studs

Ruth D. Kerce
Diana Hunter
Ruby Storm

Ellora's Cave
Romantica Publishing

An Ellora's Cave Romantica Publication

www.ellorascave.com

Diamond Studs

ISBN # 1419952242

Edited by: Pamela Campbell
Cover art by: Syneca

Electronic book Publication: January, 2005
Trade paperback Publication: October, 2005

Warning:

The following material contains graphic sexual content meant for mature readers. *Diamond Studs* has been rated *E-rotic* by a minimum of three independent reviewers.

Ellora's Cave Publishing offers three levels of Romantica™ reading entertainment: S (S-ensuous), E (E-rotic), and X (X-treme).

S-*ensuous* love scenes are explicit and leave nothing to the imagination.

E-*rotic* love scenes are explicit, leave nothing to the imagination, and are high in volume per the overall word count. In addition, some E-rated titles might contain fantasy material that some readers find objectionable, such as bondage, submission, same sex encounters, forced seductions, etc. E-rated titles are the most graphic titles we carry; it is common, for instance, for an author to use words such as "fucking", "cock", "pussy", etc., within their work of literature.

X-*treme* titles differ from E-rated titles only in plot premise and storyline execution. Unlike E-rated titles, stories designated with the letter X tend to contain controversial subject matter not for the faint of heart.

Contents

Diamond Assets
Ruth D. Kerce
~11~

Diamond in the Snow
Diana Hunter
~103~

Diamond in the Rough
Ruby Storm
~195~

Diamond Assets

Ruth D. Kerce

Chapter One

Headquarters of Everlasting Love, Inc.
Chicago, Illinois

"Get between my legs already!" Ronni grunted. Mounting frustration shot her blood pressure to sweat level. With her luck, she'd have pits under her arms by the time she got out of here. She tugged on her twisted pantyhose, trying to get them crotch-height, an almost impossibility with the new pair. Her elbow banged against the large, round toilet-paper dispenser, and pain vibrated up her arm. "Ow. Shoot!" She hated cramped spaces.

She pulled again and punched her thumbnail right through the nylon. "Dang it!" At that moment, she heard the bathroom door swish open, and voices filtered inside. She froze in the stall, hoping nobody had heard her outburst.

"I saw Hunter Dunlap in the company sauna yesterday with only a skimpy towel on and nothing else. That man is a major hunk. If he even once glanced in my direction, with a modicum of interest, I'd jump his bones and stay strapped on like a bronc rider at a rodeo."

"Ooo, baby! Yee-ha!"

"You can bet the ranch I'd be screaming more than that. I wonder if he talks dirty when he fucks. I'd sure love to say a few dirty things to him. Hell, I'd love to *do* a few dirty things to him."

"You always wonder that about guys. And you'd better watch what you say. You've already been reprimanded twice this week for language."

"Like I'm scared. My cousin is head of personnel. He'll just put me in another department if need be. Maybe the erotic toy division. The people working over there probably aren't so lame."

"Maybe, but I wouldn't count on it. How did you get into the sauna anyway? Only keyholders can get in."

Ronni recognized the voices as belonging to two clerks in the lingerie sales division—Jess and whatever-the-other-was-named—she couldn't remember.

"An important call came in for Mr. Elroy during lunch. I went to get him, and he was standing right outside the sauna area. The door opened, and there Hunter was. I swear, I thought I was going to cream my panties when he strolled into view, all hot and sweaty."

"Jess! Good grief!" The woman's laughter echoed off the tiled walls. "The way you put things..."

"Well, it's true. You'd react the same, so don't act all innocent. Besides, I'd bet his cock could use a good workout. From what I hear, no one's seen him with a woman in months. He's probably ready to spew."

"I can't believe his wife ran off with his personal assistant. She had to be nuts to give up that man's body, not to mention all his money."

"I'm sure she got a wad of a settlement. Can you imagine how much he must be worth as co-owner of *Everlasting Love*?"

The sound of a faucet turning on and water rushing into a basin drowned out their suddenly lowered voices. Ronni adjusted her hose one last time and lowered her skirt. It sure hadn't taken them long to find out Hunter's marital history. They'd worked for the company less time than she had. Gossip traveled fast.

The faucet shut off. "Maybe he's not as hunky in bed as he is out of bed, and that's why she left," Jess whispered, as if afraid to criticize Hunter in a normal tone. Even so, now without the rushing water, the words filtered into the stall.

The women's ensuing giggles grated on Ronni's nerves worse than fingernails on a chalkboard. She tugged on her skirt to get it straight and prepared to interrupt their fun. She'd heard enough. She reached for the door latch, but the mention of her name by motormouth Jess stopped her.

"If Ronni had worked for Hunter back then, it never would have happened."

"You said it. Who picks out her wardrobe anyway? She dresses like my spinster aunt. And those glasses…"

"Oh, they're the worst! She looks like an owl."

Tears misted Ronni's eyes, and her chest tightened.

Well, it's not as if she hadn't heard similar comments before. Always from catty women. She felt like calling them worse, but refrained. Still, it hurt.

So what, if she dressed conservatively? This was a place of business, not the *Ho to Go* club. She took a deep breath, felt her cheeks to make sure no tears had escaped, and buried her feelings as best she could. Before she heard any more trash about herself or her boss, she pushed her way out of the stall.

The two young women jumped in surprise. Under different circumstances, Ronni would have laughed at the comical look on their faces.

"O-Oh! Ms. Strickland," whatever-the-other-was-named stuttered. "We didn't know you were in here. Umm…we didn't mean anything. We just—"

"Get back to work, ladies, and I'll forget everything I heard. This time." She put on her best business face, and said nothing further, though she really wanted to dole out some medieval-type discipline. Maybe make them walk around with a toilet seat cover hanging out over their asses.

Her nose twitched. Sheesh. One of them had bathed in exceptionally cheap perfume today. She'd love to dunk the offender in the toilet. A commode smell had to be better than the sharp odor presently attacking her sinuses.

Hopefully, the fact that she'd caught them gossiping would be enough to make the two think twice before letting their tongues wag so freely in the future. She didn't actually have the power to do much else. The women worked in Dextor Elroy's area—the co-owner of the company—not Hunter's area, where she held at least some authority. She gave them her fiercest scowl, hoping to intimidate them into compliance.

With flushed faces, and lips at least temporarily sealed, they rushed out the door.

Ronni examined her still moist eyes in the mirror. They were right. She did look like an owl. She lowered her utilitarian glasses and perched them on the tip of her nose. Squinting into the mirror, she tried to remember what she used to look like with contacts. It didn't matter, she supposed. Contacts irritated her eyes now, and she hadn't been able to wear a pair in years. She pushed the glasses back into position. Maybe she *should* check into getting something more fashionable. Or redo her makeup. She had good skin. She could play that up. She needed to lose about ten pounds to show off her cheekbones better, but overall she was happy with who she was. She'd never be a ravishing beauty, but that was okay. She liked herself.

And no matter how she looked, she had a secure position at *Everlasting Love* as the personal assistant to one of the co-owners, Hunter Dunlap. That's what really mattered. She'd worked hard, gaining experience at smaller companies until she acquired the skills and experience to get a position here. Her next goal was to attain a leadership role in the research area, and eventually run the whole division. She doubted the Board of Directors would appoint some "eye candy" for that particular responsibility, so she'd always concentrated her efforts on growing her knowledge base rather than tweaking her appearance. She wanted to gain respect and know that the respect was due to her brain size, not her bra size. Her looks certainly wouldn't crack any mirrors, but that's not how she wanted to define her success.

Switching her gaze from the mirror to the sink, she turned on the faucet to wash her hands.

As she thought about her position in the company and her boss, she acknowledged that the two women had been right about something else. Hunter was a major hunk with a major body. Tall, fit, with just enough muscle to make any woman weak in the knees.

His eyes were what really drew her though. Deep brown like rich, thick chocolate. They showed a hint of mischief when he smiled, as if he held a wealth of sexual secrets that he'd love to share. Or maybe that was just wishful on her part.

She'd had many a fantasy about the man. She turned off the water and tore a paper towel from the dispenser.

Even though she knew Hunter must have been devastated and embarrassed by his wife's betrayal, she would have thought a man partially responsible for forming one of the largest romance-related companies in the country would be more interested in having romance in his personal life. Since she'd been with him six months now, he'd never given a woman a second look that she'd noticed. Such a waste.

She tossed the towel in the trash and took one last look in the mirror, wondering what Hunter thought of her as a *woman*, not simply an employee.

Despite what the giggle-twins had speculated, Ronni was certain that Hunter would be just as hunky in bed. Her female intuition told her so. Something about the way he moved, and the confidence he exuded, convinced her that those abilities would transfer to the bedroom. She doubted he'd be the type to trip out of his underwear or try to fold her into some impossible sexual position he'd seen in a book, like her last lover. She rubbed her lower back and cringed, the memory still vivid, though almost two years had passed since the uncomfortable incident. She should have sent the jerk her chiropractic bills.

No, Hunter would be different. She warmed at the thought of his strong, thick fingers exploring her body…inside and out.

Suddenly her pantyhose felt exceedingly hot and scratchy against her skin.

* * * * *

From across the extra-large oak desk, Hunter Dunlap pushed a financial report toward his business partner. "Here's the first spreadsheet, Dex. The numbers look good for next quarter. I'll have the other projections for you in the morning."

"Great." Dextor Elroy slid his hip onto the desk and sat on the edge, his leg dangling off the side. He picked up the report and studied the figures. "It's almost Valentine's Day. Do you have any decadent plans with some company babe?"

"Hardly." Maybe if his wife hadn't run off with his personal assistant—another woman, no less—three years ago on Valentine's, he'd have a different attitude. His life had fallen apart, and as far as he was concerned, Valentine's Day sucked.

Dex looked up as if surprised. "No?" His eyes narrowed. "Why not?"

"Why not?" The man had to be kidding.

Barely a beat passed before Dex cleared his throat, and a coat of red crept up his neck. "Oh, yeah." He plucked at some invisible piece of lint on his pant leg. "Sorry, man. I keep forgetting."

"I wish I could."

Dex looked over at him. "You can't avoid Valentine's Day forever, you know. Eventually, you're going to have to get past what happened."

"Eventually is in the future. I'm not interested yet."

"You're just rusty about asking out chicks."

"Chicks? What are you? Fourteen? Besides, I've had a few relationships." Dex was a sharp businessman, but Hunter wasn't about to take love advice from his partner. The man had never quite outgrown his adolescence where women were concerned.

"Yeah, I can count your 'relationships' on one hand. And say what you will about me—I've got a woman." A conspiratorial smile eased across his face, and he leaned forward. "Why don't you ask out Ronni? She has the hots for you."

The hots? Ronni? His new personal assistant. Well, not so new. She'd been with him almost six months now. He'd gone through eight assistants before her. He liked Ronni and really hoped she'd be around for a long time. "That's ridiculous, Dex. Where do you get these crazy ideas? Besides, mixing business with pleasure is not good."

"Worked for me. Or did you forget that my lovely wife used to be one of my personal, research assistants?"

"You lucked out with Jill. She's the only woman I know with enough patience to put up with you." Generally, he trusted Dex's opinion, at least in business, but he was way off base on this one. Ronni was efficient, dependable, and a good listener. That was all. Yeah, maybe he'd had a sexual fantasy or two about her, but he'd never seriously considered her an option as a bed partner. And she'd never flirted or shown an interest in him. He wasn't so dense as to not know when a female was attracted to him.

"Yeah, yeah, yeah. Maybe so. However, we're talking about you now. I know Ronni's no great beauty, but hey, you have to start somewhere. You haven't laid anyone in months. She'd do you in a hot second and be grateful for the attention. If it doesn't work out, you can arrange a transfer or fire her."

"Geez." Hunter scrubbed a hand down his face. "Don't let the women in the office hear you say stuff like that. They'll string you up by your balls, then sue the pants off you and me both. And how would you know the last time I got laid?"

"Word gets around."

Hunter frowned, and anger built up inside him at Dex's comments. So what if it had been several months since he'd had sex? And sure, maybe Ronni wasn't model material. She sported large, black-framed glasses instead of something more fashionable, kept her brownish hair in a bun so tight that he couldn't tell whether she had naturally straight or wavy strands, and she wore clothing that was always professional, but hid her figure. What did it matter? She was extremely skilled in office procedures and protocol, and had been his best assistant. He didn't like anyone, even his partner, saying bad things about her. "Don't you and Jill have a dinner reservation or something?" he snapped, hoping to get Dex out of there before he said something he'd regret.

"Okay, okay. I can take a hint. I'll see you in the morning. I'll look over the complete set of reports, after you get the other projections together." Dex dropped the spreadsheet on the desk and strolled from the office, whistling a familiar tune.

"A love song," Hunter muttered in disgust. "I hate freakin' love songs."

Love was for fools, and Valentine's Day was strictly for saps. He sighed, knowing that was a crappy attitude to have, considering he dealt with romance all day long—romantic gifts, cards, books, novelties, lingerie, and soon fantasy vacations, if Dex could get the numbers to jive, as needed. But *romance* was just work, and that's how he'd viewed it since his wife decided she preferred a woman's tongue stroking her pussy, instead of his.

Romance in his personal life was just too painful, so he'd officially taken himself off the serious relationship market. And lately, he hadn't even looked at a set of boobs. Well, maybe he'd looked, but that's as far as it went.

Turning his attention back to work, he faced the computer and began pounding the keys, taking out his frustration on the electronic equipment and repeating his mantra—*work is good.*

* * * * *

Ronni stepped into the doorway and watched Hunter typing furiously on the keyboard. Only his profile was in view, but his face showed a mask of concentration. Power and barely leashed passion seemed to emanate off him in waves. He was so different from most of the other executives. More like a man who worked with his hands, instead of behind a desk all day.

"Hunter?"

He stopped immediately, almost as if he'd been waiting for the sound of her voice. *That's silly, Ronni.* But a tantalizing thought.

Hunter swiveled his chair toward her, and a lock of wavy brown hair fell across his forehead. Her fingers itched to caress the soft-looking strands and push them back into place. He didn't say anything, just stared at her with a look on his face that she couldn't discern.

"I found those figures you wanted." His eyes dipped to the papers in her hand. At least, that's where she thought he was staring.

Even so, her nipples hardened—almost painfully. Thank goodness the blouse she wore was loose enough to hide her body's reaction.

He cleared his throat and adjusted his gaze to meet hers. "Thanks. Set them on the conference table with the other reports. I'll go over them later."

She nodded and walked across the room, hoping she wouldn't trip over her own feet and embarrass herself. She could feel his eyes watching her. It was unnerving. Something about him was different today. She had the strangest sensation that he was checking out her butt, which was ridiculous. Even so, a sexual thrill raced down her spine at the thought.

After she placed the papers on the table, she turned, and her gaze locked with his incredible, chocolate-brown eyes. "Do you need coffee or…anything?"

The side of his mouth hitched up. He rolled a pen between his palms. "I'm satisfied with what I have. For now."

"I'll go then." She chewed at the corner of her lip and rushed out to her cubicle, feeling as if he'd just assessed her in some manner that she couldn't quite figure out.

* * * * *

Her just-below-the-knee, business-suit skirt hid her legs and ass…as usual. Too bad, because now he was really curious to know what she looked like under all those clothes.

Hunter stared at the empty doorway, and Dex's words returned to haunt him. *She's no great beauty*. It brought back the truth to hit him squarely in the face. If he were honest with himself, he'd have to admit that was the main reason he'd hired Ronni.

Most of his assistants before her had been wet T-shirt type, contest-winning beauties. Like some hormone-challenged adolescent jerk, he'd wanted a trophy to display to the other executives. Then after his wife left him for long-legged, 38DD Shannon, he'd done a total one-eighty.

Okay, so it was kind of late after that.

But he hadn't been thinking clearly for a long time when it came to women. Whenever he'd let an assistant go, he'd hired a less attractive woman, not wanting to be reminded of the hell Kara had put him through when she moved out of their condo and in with Shannon. Smart, beautiful women, in positions of power, meant trouble. Or so was his thinking.

He felt bad, like a lowly slug, for judging Ronni mostly on looks, not ability, at the time. He'd criticized Dex for his words and attitude, but he wasn't much better when it came to women.

With Ronni, he'd lucked out. She had proven her worth time and again by flawlessly organizing his busy schedule, fielding problems for him, and finding all the statistics and handwritten notes to himself that he was always misplacing, like she knew his mind and actions better than he did. He glanced over at the conference table where she'd placed the figures.

He had made her nervous with his scrutiny. He couldn't remember the last time he'd affected a woman like that. The women he normally associated with were sexual predators in their aggressiveness for his body…and his money. Nervous wasn't part of their portfolio. He knew their motivations, and he made sure they knew where he stood. He'd loved his wife. But after she left and sued him for a considerable stash—saying he was always working, so it was his fault that she had to find affection elsewhere—he'd protected his heart and pocketbook by only dating women who wouldn't be long-termers. After the sex got stale, they parted ways. No muss, no fuss.

Devious thoughts of sexually tempting Ronni, in real life, not just his fantasies, entered his mind, and he wondered how nervous he could actually make her. He shook his head. "What the hell am I thinking?" He wasn't even attracted to her in that way. Not really. His fantasies were only normal guy stuff, nothing serious. She simply intrigued him now, after his conversation with Dex.

The boss/secretary fantasy was a common one. It was about control—imagining Ronni naked, bent over the conference table, her hair loose, with his hand gripping the brown strands tightly, as he plunged into her wet pussy from behind. Her allowing him to do anything he wanted to her body and enjoying it, begging for it. He shifted uncomfortably, then scrubbed his hands down his face. Damn. Maybe he *was* attracted to her. At least, a little.

Well, he wasn't about to analyze his erotic fantasies. It might get him into trouble.

Ronni was a bright light around here, in his opinion. He genuinely liked her as a friend. She was a nice person who didn't deserve Dex's unkind words. Or his own suddenly lascivious thoughts. If she knew that he was imagining her on her knees, sucking his dick until he came long and hard in her mouth, she'd run screaming from the building.

He needed to finish going over the company data, not spend time thinking up 101 ways to fuck his assistant. He turned back to the computer and continued working on the projection reports.

Everlasting Love was doing well, and he was pleased with what he and Dex had been able to accomplish. Each year they achieved additional growth. He was careful not to move the company too fast. As one of his old, baseball buddies said at their last reunion, *You've hit a homerun, Hunter. Don't screw it up by stumbling over the bases.* Sound advice, he'd thought. So he made sure that he always covered all the bases.

"It's five-fifteen, Hunter."

His body tightened, and he turned to see Ronni standing inside the door. "Thanks." She hated to leave the office before he did. Normally, he liked that in case he needed her for something. Tonight it would have been better if she'd simply gone. He might need her for something that she didn't want to give, and he could end up saying or doing something stupid. Not that he'd ever take advantage of her, but the thought of them locked together, fucking wildly, was an enticing idea that he couldn't now seem to get out of his head.

He didn't know what Ronni was like away from the office, but at work, the woman was too nice for her own good. The one exception he'd noticed was when someone tried to get past her to see him without an appointment. Then she turned, like a she-wolf protecting the den. He smiled. He had to admire her dedication to him and the company. A lot of passion existed in the woman, under all her protective layers. "I'll be working late tonight, Ronni. I need to get these reports done. Go on home and have a nice evening."

He'd seen flowers delivered to her desk earlier and wondered if she had plans for Valentine's Day. Ronni spending a romantic Valentine's with her current guy, whoever the man might be, flashed across his weary brain like a neon sign, causing a throb between his eyebrows. His smile faded, and a muscle in his jaw ticked, as it used to when some sleaze flirted with his wife.

Strange reaction—and all because Dex had said Ronni was hot for him. His partner had to be messing with his mind. Or was he?

Hunter cocked his head, wondering if Dex's words could possibly be true. He'd been working so hard lately, and his thoughts were in such a jumble that he didn't know what to believe.

He needed to take some time off and go somewhere exotic and warm, with lots of beautiful, naked, and willing women. No romance, mind you. Just pure monkey sex with no strings attached. One of Dex's fantasy vacations sounded exceedingly good right now. He could clear the pipes, so to speak. And his thoughts, too.

"Damn." Without realizing it, he'd totally dismissed Ronni. Disappointment flooded through him. He could be such a bastard sometimes. Whether she'd noticed his rudeness or not, he didn't know. All he knew was that she was gone.

Chapter Two

On her way out, Ronni grabbed the roses off her desk and deposited them in the nearest trash receptacle. She'd waited until after work so she wouldn't have an audience. Someone was always nosy enough to ask questions. She'd received enough raised eyebrows and inquiries this afternoon when the deliveryman showed up with the small bouquet.

She wished Howard would just leave her alone. She'd gone out with him a couple of times, then discovered he was only interested in a promotion and thought she could put in a good word for him with Hunter. She hoped he stayed down in Data Processing until Mr. Happy—as he'd referred to his penis on their second date—blech—shriveled up and fell off. Which it might as well do. He'd grabbed her hand and pressed it to his groin in the movie theater that night. The man's "Mr. Happy" was smaller than a mini-wiener.

She stepped inside the empty elevator, clutching her handbag under her arm so tightly that she felt the gold decorator studs dig into her skin. She relaxed her hold before she ended up squashing her spare glasses.

The image of Hunter sitting at his desk, lost in thought, came to mind. Something was bothering him. She hadn't wanted to pry, so she didn't ask him about it. But she was concerned.

Much as he seemed to be, she'd also been distracted. But she knew the cause of her distraction. Her thoughts couldn't let go of the offer Dex had made her right after lunch. It had come unexpectedly, and she hadn't thought of much else since.

She hit the wrong button and the half-closed elevator door slid back open. With a sigh, she punched the correct button for the lobby.

Dex was trying to arrange fantasy vacations with some special resort, for *Everlasting Love.* He'd asked her to go check it out for him. He'd already cleared it with Hunter, he'd said. She was surprised that Hunter hadn't mentioned it to her this afternoon. Dex had said they both trusted her to bring back the needed information, and her impressions of the resort, from a female perspective. They feared another assistant would simply use it as an excuse to take time off and not be concerned with doing the job right.

She hadn't given him her answer yet. He'd said to let him know soon, since he needed to make a room arrangement. Plane reservations wouldn't be a problem. The company had its own jet ready to go.

Too bad she didn't have some special man to take with her. Even though it was a business trip, she probably could have finagled it. And if she had a man even half as sexy as Hunter... She'd bet he didn't have a mini-wiener.

Her body grew warm and achy at the thought of him feeding her fruit on some private beach, the two of them strolling together under the stars, maybe even sharing a goodnight kiss. Her hand slid down her stomach as more intimate images flooded her thoughts. She shook her head and pulled her hand back. Anything more, she didn't dare fantasize. No need to work herself up in the elevator. She'd wait until she got home where she could pull out the Dunlap Dildo and pretend it was more than just the company's newest sex novelty.

A sigh escaped her. She so needed to get a life. All work, and no play, was making her pathetically dull.

After this trip, things were going to change.

First, she had to make certain that Hunter didn't mind her doing this for Dex. Even though he had already cleared it, she needed to talk to Hunter herself and free up her schedule. Then, she intended to carve out some personal time for herself and start socializing more. She didn't consider that a selfish move since success in business included being able to schmooze clients. She needed to learn how to interact better.

Maybe she could pick up some guy at the resort and have a little fun while she was there, so she didn't get too bored. Not for sex, of course. That was too dangerous with a stranger. But just someone to keep her company. "I guess I've really made the decision to go. This will do me good, I'm sure."

The elevator jerked, and she reached for the side. "I hate this blasted thing." She would take the stairs if the offices weren't on the top floor. She needed to talk to Hunter about installing a new lift system. It's not as if the company couldn't afford it.

Unfortunately, Hunter was already working himself to death on numerous other projects, and he shouldn't be. He needed to delegate more. And he should be the one checking out the fantasy vacation resort, if only to get out of the office for a couple of days. She would bring it up to him, but she already knew his work habits. He'd probably never take the time off to visit the facility himself. Not unless the money involved had a higher percentage payout. He'd view it all in business terms, instead of a chance to enjoy himself.

The elevator opened, and she stepped out. "Finally." She pulled her coat closed, in anticipation of the cold night, and headed for the exit.

"Hey, Ronni!" a security guard called out.

She turned, and a smile spread across her face. She'd forgotten her friend was working tonight. She headed for the side door. "Jake. How's Kimberly?"

"Ready to pop out the twins any day. Say, I haven't seen Mr. Dunlap come down yet."

"He's working late."

"Again?"

"Again."

Jake shook his head. "That man needs to find himself a playmate."

Ronni laughed. "I'll pass along the message." She'd love to apply for the position. Decadent ideas flowed through her mind.

Hunter was such a good boss and a considerate man. Everyone in the company liked him, even the security guards.

Last month, he'd had a bouquet of wildflowers and white balloons, with multi-colored streamers, delivered to the office on her birthday. How could she not like a man who would do that? Unfortunately, she knew, *like* wasn't all she felt for him. She was not only attracted to the man, she was falling hard for his kindness. She feared she was headed straight for heartache where Hunter was concerned.

"Ronni?"

"Um, what? Sorry. It's been a long day, Jake. My mind was elsewhere. You were saying?"

"I've had many of those days myself. I was just saying that I hope you have a nice, quiet evening." He pushed open the door for her.

"Thanks. You too. Give my best to Kim. Tell her I'll call next week to set up a lunch. It's been too long since we've spoken." She stepped outside, and a gust of wind hit her, whipping up her skirt, as if it had a purpose. She shivered and headed for her car.

She hoped Hunter didn't work too late. When he was past due on a deadline and didn't sleep, he ran around so wired the next morning that it was hard to keep up with him. If he didn't finish those projections tonight, even the Steroid Bunny wouldn't be able to keep up with him tomorrow.

She stopped in the middle of the sidewalk. "Hmm. Why not?" In the end, it would just make her day easier…and tonight something to look forward to. She turned and headed toward the crosswalk, new determination in her stride.

* * * * *

The door to the office flew open.

Hunter's heart leapt in his chest, and his chair tipped backward, almost dumping him on the floor. He righted himself and swiveled around, eyes wide.

"Geez!" When he spoke, his voice came out louder than intended, but *damn*. "You scared me to death."

Especially since he'd just been enjoying a particularly nasty fantasy of Ronni stripped naked, sitting on top of him and riding him hard, while he sat in the desk chair, sucking her nipples and having the time of his life. "What are you doing back here?"

"Food." Ronni lifted two white sacks. A tentative look crossed her face, then she smiled apologetically. "Sorry. I didn't mean to surprise you like that." She walked across the room and set the sacks on the small conference table in front of the window. "If we're going to work all night, I thought I'd better bring in dinner."

"We?" Hunter's voice lowered. A jolt of pleasure shot through him and those darn erotic thoughts hit full force. The images flickered through his mind like a late night, adult film. Intellectually, he knew that she hadn't returned to entice him into sex, but the scenario of *Secretary Seduces Supervisor* wouldn't leave him.

Ronni pushed her glasses up the bridge of her nose—a motion he found particularly cute—and strolled over to the desk. His dick immediately hardened.

"You'll never get done, working all by yourself, Hunter. You can feed me the numbers, and I'll type them in. It'll go much faster that way."

"You don't have to do this, Ronni." The smell of fast food wafted to his nose, and his stomach rumbled. Licking special sauce off her fingers suddenly held appeal.

"I might as well help. I don't have anything else to do tonight. Besides, when you work late and don't get enough sleep, you bounce off the walls the next day and drive me crazy."

"I'm sorry." He chuckled. "I didn't realize." A weight lifted from his chest. His weariness disappeared, and he felt energized. Probably because deep down he was thrilled not to be the only one with nobody to go home to. How pathetic was that attitude?

Hell, it wasn't even that. He just liked the idea of spending time alone with Ronni, even if it was work-related.

He still wondered about those flowers delivered to her. Maybe they hadn't been from a man, after all. Or not a special man. Certainly not one waiting at home for her, or she wouldn't be here, volunteering to work late. Besides, he didn't want anyone sending her flowers. Thoughts of possession grabbed at him and wouldn't let go. His nostrils twitched as he took in her subtle perfume.

He cleared his throat and turned to load the next spreadsheet. Thinking about Ronni, and her possible love life, was doing him no good. He needed to concentrate on work. He scrolled down the template to an empty data cell. At least he'd gotten his body under control. It would have been embarrassing if she'd noticed the boner jutting from his pants. "Let me get organized here."

He might need to take Dex up on his offer to check out that fantasy resort, after all. He'd originally said no, but Dex had asked him to think about it. A couple of days away from the office would do him good. It would get his thoughts off Ronni and back into perspective. Or at least give him time to figure out if he was interested in more than a quick fuck with her. She deserved a real relationship, not just some horny guy out to get laid.

Maybe he should consider taking a woman with him. Erase Ronni from his mind completely for a while. He shuffled through some papers.

He really should keep his concentration on the business aspect of the trip though, he supposed. No distractions. And he couldn't think of a woman that he was excited enough about to invite anyway. No one in his black book held appeal all of a sudden.

He wondered what Ronni's reaction would be if he asked her to go with him. Not to have sex. Just to take notes.

Right... If they went away together, he knew his goal would be to seduce Ronni so thoroughly that she'd never want any other man in her life—or between her legs.

So much for keeping his mind off the woman and getting perspective.

Ronni's heart tumbled in her chest. She hadn't been sure about coming back and interrupting, but Hunter seemed genuinely glad to see her. Of course, why wouldn't he be? They'd finish the reports faster, and he could go home to his current flavor of the week. Ugh! That was a depressing thought.

Earlier, while waiting in line for the food at the restaurant across the street, she'd decided that just because she hadn't seen him with any particular woman, and he worked a lot of overtime, that didn't necessarily mean he was spending his nights alone.

She wanted Hunter to be happy. But thoughts of him with another woman made her agitated, somehow. She knew her feelings weren't rational, given their boss-employee relationship, but there it was. She sighed. Certainly, she could somehow turn off her desire for him. Even if she took a chance and tried to entice the man, the whole thing might turn into a disaster...or the best sex of her life. Dang. She didn't know what to do.

She'd better keep her thoughts on work. Anything else was counterproductive. She was here to help. Nothing more. "Come on. Get up." She tugged at his arm. "You're a horrible typist. You make too many mistakes."

"Just getting things set up for you. And, hey, I'm not that bad," he muttered, vacating the seat. "At least I use all my fingers, which is more than I can say about most of the other executives around here."

He waggled his fingers at her, and Ronni remembered her bathroom fantasy about those fingers moving in and out of her pussy. Her pulse raced way too fast and perspiration dotted her skin.

Stop it!

She couldn't keep thinking about Hunter, the boss, in those terms. At least, not while in the office and standing right next to him. It would just lead to trouble.

Too bad the light stubble on his cheeks and chin made him look exceptionally sexy tonight. That didn't help. She wondered how that stubble would feel nuzzling her neck, her breasts, her inner thighs. She'd better pick up some fresh batteries before she went home. She had a feeling she'd be giving her favorite vibrator a good workout later.

She licked her suddenly dry lips. "All of you guys have been spoiled by your secretaries and assistants and would be useless without us," she somehow managed to respond.

Hunter grew silent. He stared at her mouth, as if he'd never seen a woman moisten her lips.

At the intensity of his gaze, Ronni swallowed hard. That look—it couldn't mean what she thought she saw in his eyes. She was simply overstimulated by all her thoughts of sex and was imagining things.

He raised his gaze, grinned, and scratched his chin. "Well, you're probably right about that. I know I would be." He winked.

Ronni felt a blush tinge her cheeks, and Hunter smiled at her with that sexy look that always caused a buzz from the women in the office. Oh, my! He *was*. He was flirting with her! He'd never flirted with her before. But then, they'd never worked alone, late like this. Maybe…

She moved past him, and her arm brushed his. Their eyes locked, this time in what was definitely a heated stare. He towered above her, making her feel small and fragile. Vulnerable.

The cologne he wore teased her nose. She inhaled deeply, savoring the woodsy scent of him. Just enough to make her want to lean closer, but not so much as to bother her sinuses. She wondered how much of the aroma was cologne and how much was pure Hunter. Dare she take a chance?

No. She'd better backtrack fast, before she ended up saying or doing something embarrassing. Like begging him to toss her on the desk and take her right here and now. Her panties grew moist at the thought. Ronni pulled her gaze away, sat down, and adjusted the chair. "Okay." She cleared her throat. "I-I'm ready." She was ready, all right. More ready than Hunter would ever know.

When she'd licked her lips, Hunter had almost groaned aloud. Such a simple thing. Something he'd seen hundreds of women do. Today, with Ronni, the movement threatened to turn his dick rock-hard once again. Rarely did he lose control of his body, so the fact that he was reacting like some horny teenager, surprised him. When her voice turned shaky, he'd gotten even more hot and bothered. And repeating his normal *work is good* mantra was not helping to quell the desire.

He recited the figures for her to input, but found it hard to focus on the numbers.

Hunter kept admiring her hands. Ronni's slim fingers fluttered across the keyboard effortlessly. He wondered what those long, delicate fingers would feel like moving across his body, her short nails grazing his skin, trailing lightly over his balls. *Damn.*

If Dex had kept his mouth shut, erotic thoughts about Ronni would never have entered his mind. At least, he didn't think so. She wasn't anywhere near his type, which might be what fueled the current attraction. And it wasn't just a physical attraction, so that made it even harder to ignore.

He liked Ronni's outlook on life, and the way she lit up a room when she entered. He couldn't imagine coming to the office and her not being here.

But now, other thoughts also entered his mind. He wanted to know how a woman like Ronni would react in bed. Did she like simple sex or something hot, wild, and dangerous? It would be interesting to find out what brought her pleasure, and just how far she would go if given the proper stimulation.

An image of him languidly kissing her inner thighs came to mind. Or maybe she'd simply prefer him to get right to it and fuck her long and hard. The eager monster in his pants twitched.

He paused longer than normal in giving her the numbers, and she looked up at him with a smile that was half-sexy, half-expectant. What would that smile look like on the verge of a climax? He wished he could reach out and caress her breasts, peel off her clothes—one by one, finger her pussy, take his mouth and tongue along the same path, and lick every inch of her. He loved the taste of a woman's skin. And Ronni's looked particularly delectable.

"I'm ready, Hunter."

So was he, dammit. And she had purposely purred those provocative words. No. Probably not. He was reading too much into things. Just because he was having wild, sexual fantasies about her didn't mean that she was fantasizing about him, too. He wished he knew for sure though, one way or the other.

"Sorry. I drifted." Somehow, he wrestled his thoughts back to business and gave her the remaining figures.

She clicked on print, and the machine next to the monitor spit out several pieces of paper. "This report's all done. Unless you want to double-check the figures?"

"Tomorrow. I'll have a clearer head. Thanks, Ronni." The smile she bestowed on him made his heart expand in pleasure. "How about we polish off that food you brought in?" He wanted an opportunity to talk with her about something other than work, something personal, so they could get closer.

"I think the food is probably cold by now."

"Oh." Disappointment filled him. He glanced over at the sacks, then returned his gaze to hers. "Yeah, I guess you're right. We should have eaten it right away." He'd rather eat her, his hunger was so strong, but he didn't think that suggestion would go over well, so he decided to try something else. His voice lowered to a husky tone. "How about a drink then?"

"A drink? As in alcohol?"

The deer-caught-in-headlights look he received wasn't what he'd expected. She looked panicked and so incredibly adorable that he had to smile. "Actually, I meant coffee. Or a soda." The way his voice had come out all low and scratchy, she probably thought he'd meant to get her drunk and go for some action. He definitely wanted her, but she didn't need to know that…yet. And he didn't want her drunk when he took her body, but very much sober and willing.

She hesitated, as if thinking it over, then glanced at her watch. "It's kind of getting late."

His smile faded. Crashed and burned. *Well, shoot.* "Sure. Right. You must be tired. I still have a few more things to do here. You go on home. I'll see you in the morning. Or you can come in after lunch if you want." So she'd turned him down. That was all right. He wasn't ready to give up yet.

"Thanks. That won't be necessary. I didn't mind helping you out." She stood, but avoided his eyes as she brushed past him. "Good night, Hunter."

He touched her before she made it completely past, stopping her progress. His hand slid down her arm to caress the skin just below the sleeve of the blouse she wore. He felt her pulse pounding. Great. That meant she was feeling the attraction, too, even if she wasn't admitting it. "Good night, Ronni." He leaned close and whispered in her ear. "Sleep well." He knew he wasn't going to, not now that he'd changed the way he viewed the woman.

He felt her shiver and released his hold. He didn't want to push too hard. He probably shouldn't have touched her at all, but he couldn't help himself. Her skin was as soft as he'd imagined. Would the hair covering her pussy feel soft too? Or maybe she kept her mound shaved smooth and silky. Damn, he wanted to know!

She turned and looked up at him, lightly touching his arm.

Oh, that's nice. He wanted more. Soon.

A tentative smile graced her face. "I'll see you in the morning, Hunter." Then she stepped away and left him standing in the office alone.

With a groan, he sank down in the desk chair. "That woman has deep-down, sensual secrets. I'd bet on it. And I'm going to uncover every sexual layer of need buried inside her."

A moment of hesitation hit. Things could get awkward if he didn't handle this right. He didn't want to ruin what they already had. Maybe it wasn't a good idea to try to take things further.

"No." He shook his head, and a smile slowly crossed his face. "It'll work. I can make her want me and still preserve our working relationship. I know she feels at least a little something already. We'll burn up the sheets. That's a definite." His hand rubbed the growing hard-on inside his pants, trying to ease his discomfort.

For Ronni, he happily looked forward to tossing out his "no mixing business with pleasure" rule. She was worth it.

Chapter Three

Ronni paused, studying the computer screen. The spreadsheet formulas were giving her hives. She needed to concentrate, but Hunter's presence kept distracting her. She heard him moving around the office, behind the desk where she was working. From time to time, he'd stop, and she could feel him staring at her. She'd give anything to know what he was thinking.

Last night, she'd run from him like a scared virgin and regretted it all the way home. *Someone award me a too-stupid-to-live trophy.*

She should have had that drink. Seen where it led. She still wasn't sure why she'd refused, other than she hadn't been expecting the invite, and it had taken her totally by surprise. Okay, so she'd wimped out.

If he ever asked her again, she wouldn't bypass the opportunity twice.

Of course, she knew he hadn't just been asking for coffee. She'd seen it in his eyes. Heard it in his voice. She might not have a line of men after her, but she was far from naïve. And ninety-five percent sure he'd have dropped his shorts if she'd asked.

The confusing part was why he suddenly seemed interested in her. Not that she was complaining. Just curious. She'd worked for him almost six months. He'd always been friendly toward her, but nothing more. Or at least she'd never noticed anything more. Now, just knowing that he might actually want her made her almost giddy.

The fact that Hunter was her boss could prove problematical. If she were smart, she'd make sure their relationship stayed as it was. Avoid complications developing in the future. But then, she didn't much feel like being smart if she had a possibility of hooking up with someone as hunky, intelligent, successful, kindhearted, and all-around great as Hunter Dunlap.

The image of his cock pushing inside her, his tongue laving her nipples, her legs wrapped tightly around him as he rode her hard... She squirmed in the desk chair. That man corrupted her every thought, and he didn't even know it. Or maybe he did.

Dang. She'd better keep her mind on work or she might orgasm right here, simply from her fantasies.

She'd certainly come hard last night, pleasuring herself over and over again, until her body and mind were so sated that all she could do was lie on the bed like a lump of flesh. She knew that if she and Hunter ever did become physically involved, she'd never get enough of the man.

Hunter watched Ronni out of the corner of his eye. He finished filing some data sheets, then walked over to his desk where she was typing on the computer. The Board of Directors had asked him for some advertising cost projections, and he and Ronni were working hard on the stats. He probably could have done them without her. But where was the fun in that? He sat on the edge of the desk and picked up some reports still warm from the printer.

Last night, he'd barely slept a wink, thinking about all the things he wanted to do to this woman, not only sexually, but also emotionally. She made him feel things that went beyond his physical body. And he wanted her to feel those things, too.

After their encounter, he'd gotten hard enough to break wood. Once home, somehow, he'd resisted jacking off, even though his body protested. The next time he came, he wanted to be deep inside Ronni's pussy. He smiled at the enticing thought.

Never had he obsessed so much over a female. Not even his ex-wife. He felt alive again, like his future held unlimited possibilities.

Ronni was genuine, or so she seemed to be. He couldn't help but want to know her better, inside and out. He wondered what she would look like without the glasses, with her hair down, without all that loose clothing. Did she like a man to take care of her? Or did she prefer more independence and space? What was her favorite color? Her favorite food? Her favorite sex toy?

Hunter rubbed the back of his neck.

He'd decided to take Dex up on his fantasy vacation offer. And he was going to ask Ronni to go with him. They needed privacy, away from the office, if he had any hope of exploring a relationship with her. Or just finding out if she was interested. As long as he presented it as a business trip, she'd probably agree to go. Maybe that was a little underhanded on his part, but he certainly wasn't going to force her into anything she didn't want. And the trip *would* be business, just not only business, if she agreed to something more personal.

Either way, right now, he needed to keep his mind on work. Only, he felt so wiped out that he could barely focus. "How about a break, Ronni? These numbers are one big blur. It's been a long day."

"Okay." She pushed back the chair and stood up.

When she stretched and arched her back, Hunter fumbled the papers in his hand, spilling them across the desk. Ronni had taken off her suit jacket earlier, and her blouse—not as loose-fitting as usual—pulled tightly across full, firm-looking breasts. He quickly scooped the pages back up, hoping she hadn't caught him staring. He'd rather she thought him a klutz than some sort of voyeur. She was hiding quite a set under there. He ached to get his hands and mouth on them. He hadn't realized a blouse could conceal so much. But then, he'd only recently started checking out the woman's body. He supposed too much work had blinded him from noticing sooner.

Ronni slipped off her heels and sighed. "That's better. I hope you don't mind."

"No. Of course not." His gaze locked on her feet as she rotated first one delicate ankle, then the other.

"I hate new shoes." She glanced over at him and a wary look entered her eyes. "Um, you've seemed uncharacteristically distracted, Hunter. Is it anything you want to talk about?" She skirted her gaze away.

The way she wouldn't meet his eyes made him wonder if she suspected his feelings. He swallowed hard, not realizing he'd been so obvious. Though maybe that wasn't a bad thing. Still, he wanted to pursue this carefully. "It's nothing, Ronni. Really."

She squeezed her toes into the carpet.

He stared at her lovely feet, and erotic images ran through his head. Of sucking toes. Running his tongue along her sole until she squirmed. Licking the soft skin between those cute digits. Having her feet stroke his dick. *Geez. I've just developed a damn foot fetish.*

"I need something to drink." She walked over to the small refrigerator in the corner of the office, bent over, and opened the door. "Do you want something?"

Don't look, Hunter warned himself, as he looked. His heart hammered against his ribs at the sight of Ronni leaning over. She had a great ass—full and round. His fingers twitched, and he imagined his hands massaging her soft, bare flesh, pressing against her from behind, pushing deep inside her pussy, or even right up that luscious ass, if she'd let him.

It hit hard, an almost painful need to know what kind of sounds she made when a man entered her, what she'd sound like when *he* entered her, and when she climaxed from what he would do to her body.

Ronni glanced over her shoulder. "What do you want, Hunter?"

He closed his eyes and turned away. "Nothing," he choked out, the lie leaving a stale taste in his mouth. He still didn't know, for sure, if she wanted him, so he had to be careful not to scare her off as he had last night. He walked over to the conference table and looked out the high-rise window at the traffic below. Working too hard and being too long without a woman had turned his brain into mush and his body into a hot poker, ready for action. What he needed was a plan.

Hunter turned as she stepped up beside him to look out the window. She didn't say anything, so he remained silent, too. He watched her open the bottle of pop and lift it to her mouth for a sip.

"Looks to be a nice day," he blurted, unable to keep quiet. He never had been all that comfortable with stillness, not since he was a child. He liked noise and action. And he hated feeling so…insecure…about what to do next.

Lowering the bottle, she arched an eyebrow. "Really? Looks kind of like rain to me."

Ugh! That was stupid. His small-talk skills needed definite work. He felt completely tongue-tied around her. And he never felt tongue-tied around women. Or, he never used to suffer from that affliction.

She raised her drink again and took a long draw of the pop.

He stared at her lips wrapped tightly around the top of the bottle as she sucked down the contents. "Oh, yeah," he literally groaned, then hurried to continue, "but, um, I've always enjoyed the rain." *Stop talking, you sound like a fucking idiot.*

A small smile crossed Ronni's face as she lowered the bottle. "Rain can be nice. But not so much in the winter, I don't think. It tends to turn into ice." She turned away from him, concentrating on a fender-bender down on the street.

He could normally charm a rat from a snake. But Ronni made him a nervous wreck. His palms were even sweating. This was crazy. He wanted her. He just needed to let her know in such a way as to entice her into bed with him, and not in such a way where she'd feel justified in smacking him a good one. How hard could that be?

Hunter noticed her usually tight bun had slipped and was now half up and half down. Unable to resist an opportunity, which he doubted he'd get again, he reached over and pulled two pins from her hair, releasing the rest of the brown tresses. Geez, her hair was soft. If the hair covering her pussy were equally soft, he'd die a happy man, given the opportunity to stroke it.

Her head whipped around, swirling the loose strands around her face. "What are you doing?"

Good question. He'd obviously lost all common sense. "Sorry. It's just that your bun looked beyond repair. As if I'd ravaged you…or something." He actually liked the sound of that. His eyes locked with hers, and the tension in the room escalated. She felt it too. He could tell by the way her eyes dilated.

"Oh," she finally said, not looking away.

Neither of them moved.

Finally, she tucked the loose strands behind her ears. "Um, I guess I better go fix it." She set the half-empty bottle on the conference table.

"No need." His hand covered hers, briefly stroking her skin, before he pulled back. Her long brown strands, with auburn highlights that he now noticed, made her look soft and feminine. The need to touch her, and for more than a simple caress, urged him to move closer. "I like it down."

"You do?"

He nodded.

She slid off her glasses and swiped one remaining strand from her face. She took the pins from his outstretched hand and looked into his eyes from behind slightly lowered lashes. "Thanks. You're acting differently than normal, Hunter. Are you sure you're all right?" She stepped closer and lightly touched his chest.

Her touch and look of concern held him captive, causing his heartbeat to kick up several notches. Why she hid her cocoa-colored eyes behind those glasses and disguised her softness with that tight bun, he'd never understand. She wasn't classically beautiful, but still, everything about her drew him in.

"I will be all right. In a minute." *Here we go.* He couldn't wait any longer. Damn the consequences. Hunter laced his fingers through her hair.

Her sudden gasp barely registered in his brain.

"Ronni..." Her name tasted right on his lips, and sounded warm and sexy to his ears. He had to know how she would react in his arms, to his kiss—if she'd push him away or melt against him in ecstasy. He'd deal with the fallout, if there was any, later.

Ronni's heart pounded so hard her chest hurt. The blood thrummed through her veins at the feel of Hunter's fingers tangled in her hair. The way he'd said her name made her think of mussed sheets and hot bodies. He pulled her close, and she knew he was going to kiss her.

She'd seen desire and nervousness in his eyes and had purposely removed her glasses and stepped closer to show her interest and give him an opportunity to make a move, if he'd wanted it. Even so, she'd feared that her interpretation of what she'd seen might have been wrong. Apparently, not.

His lips lightly touched hers, brushing back and forth. She melted against him, even from that soft contact. He tasted hot and spicy, and she wanted more. When he gently licked at her mouth, her lips parted for his tongue.

"Hunter," a man's voice interrupted at the same time a knock sounded at the door. "Oops."

Ronni jumped back like a teenager caught necking by a parent. She shoved on her glasses and patted her hair, then rushed over to the files and pretended to search for something.

With an audible sigh, Hunter turned toward the door. "What do you want, Dex?"

"Do you have those reports?"

Ronni sneaked a peek at the man and cringed at the knowing smile on his face.

Hunter gathered the papers from his desk and shoved them at his partner. "All done. Now get out of here."

Laughter reached Ronni's ears, and she felt like crawling into the filing cabinet, right under F for fool. Now the whole office would probably know. She hated the thought of being a subject of discussion. Dex didn't normally gossip, but things like this had a way of getting out and circulating fast.

She now almost regretted taking him up on his offer to check out that fantasy resort for the company. If she left for a couple of days, it would seem like she was running from the situation. And worse, when she got back, Hunter might not be interested anymore. The timing of all this couldn't be worse.

When the door finally clicked closed, and Dex was gone, she only felt marginally better.

"I'm sorry, Ronni." Hunter's voice washed over her in a sensual wave. "I should have locked the door."

Yeah. Then they might have dropped to the rug and torn off each other's clothing. Not necessarily a bad thing. But she could imagine people with their ears pressed against the door at the sound of the first moan. And she *would* moan, if Hunter touched her sexually. "It's late." She closed the drawer. "I should go."

She really needed to talk to Hunter about being gone for two days, just to confirm, but all she could think about was getting out of there. She had to mull things over, and she couldn't do it here in the office. She'd talk to him tomorrow. There was still time. Not much, but he was usually flexible.

"Let me take you home."

She looked directly into his eyes, not about to act coy now just because she'd been embarrassed. "I don't think that's a good idea under the circumstances. People will talk."

"Who cares if people talk? Please. I don't want things to be awkward between us."

She laughed lightly. "I think—"

"Come on, Ronni." With a small smile on his face, he crossed his arms over his chest. "What's the problem? It was barely a kiss. Dex isn't going to say anything. No one will even know it happened, except us."

The challenging look in his eyes made her feel like he thought she was a scared little girl. She wasn't scared, but she was uncertain about how to handle this, even though she'd wanted his touch, and another opportunity to spend time with him. She also wanted that promotion into the research division. She had to be practical here. If she got it, she didn't want people to speculate on how and why. A supervisor needed respect to be effective. Up until now, she'd never needed to worry about appearances.

She sighed. Well, she wasn't about to stand here and have him think he'd flustered her so much that she couldn't even sit in a car with him. She was a grown woman, after all. She could handle him, as well as her own desires. Probably. "Fine. Let me put my shoes back on, and get my purse and coat."

Chapter Four

Hunter pulled his sports car up to Ronni's cottage-style home. The house looked neat and well cared for. Nothing less than he would have expected.

He'd practically dared her to let him drive her home tonight. He knew that if he challenged her outright she'd never back down. She was too strong of a woman to let some man intimidate her. The downside was that he'd had a hell of a time keeping his hands to himself on the drive over.

Earlier in the day, he'd overheard her telling one of the secretaries that her car was in the shop and she'd have to take a taxi home. So, he figured she'd have no logical reason to turn down a ride, if he offered.

Now, he needed to ask her to the fantasy resort. And if she refused? He didn't want to think about that, but he knew it was a possibility. She'd responded to their kiss, but that didn't mean she was ready for an affair.

Maybe a jaunt out of state wasn't the way to pursue things. Even under the guise of business, it might put too much pressure on her, if she really didn't want to get involved.

He knew what he wanted. He wanted to fuck Ronni's brains out. Simple. That small brush of her lips had almost floored him, and he needed more. Unfortunately, with women, nothing was so simple.

Okay, so it wasn't actually that simple for him either. He wanted more than just a physical relationship. Maybe. Taking that step was still scary for him, but he'd been alone a long time now. Lonely. And he didn't like the feeling. Ronni was a good, decent, caring, woman, with depth and intelligence. And sexy as hell, in her own special way.

He wished he'd recognized her true worth before now. She might be exactly what he needed in his life—personally, as well as professionally—to challenge him and to make him happy. Even so, no matter how much he wanted her, and wanted her to want him in return, he'd only push so far.

Ronni released the seatbelt, grabbed her purse, and reached for the door handle.

When he unhooked his seatbelt, she turned back toward him.

"What are you doing?" she asked, with one leg already out of the car.

"Walking you to the door."

"This isn't a date, Hunter."

"No, that's true. It's not a date." If it were, his hand would have already been up her skirt. Or, at least, he'd have made the attempt. Chuckling, he got out of the car.

As he rounded to her side, Ronni got out and closed the passenger door, looking at him as if unsure of his intentions. She always did have good instincts.

He held out his hand. "Come on, Ronni. I won't bite." At least not in public. In private, he'd love to tease her with small bites of pleasure. Against her clit. Over her nipples. Yep. That was definitely going on a priority, to-do list.

As if it were another challenge, she grabbed his hand and held on tight. "I never thought you would." Her slight blush said otherwise.

He couldn't stop the smile that crossed his face.

Patches of ice covered the walkway. He maneuvered them between the slippery spots, making certain she didn't skid or fall. He found a new appreciation for the slick stuff. Ronni's safety was the perfect excuse to keep his hands on her.

As they stepped up on the porch, she fished inside her handbag.

"Lose your keys? That would be a real shame. I'd have to take you home with me." Then he could tie her to his bed and test out the company's new line of erotic toys on her, everything from flavored body paint, to nipple clamps, to vibrating dildos and anal beads. He flashed his sexiest smile this time, watching for her reaction.

Another blush tinted her cheeks.

The cold or nerves? Maybe even desire? Oh, man. This was killing him. The need to sink deep inside her and make her come was growing unbearable. He'd need a *case* of condoms for this trip, if she agreed to go. If she agreed to let him between her legs.

With a look of relief on her face, she pulled out a key chain. "Here they are."

She fumbled with the lock, until Hunter eased the keys from her grasp and opened the door. He was simply teasing her, having fun, being friendly, nothing more. She shouldn't read any more into it. Yet.

He'd been curious. He'd kissed her. And that might be that. Just because he was trying to coax a smile out of her didn't mean he wanted her body.

She wouldn't set herself up for disappointment.

Of course, if she showed immediate interest in taking things further, while he was still in pursuit-mode, for real or just for fun, he might respond favorably. Then who knows where that might lead.

It would be so much easier if he weren't her boss. She'd just go for it and not worry so much about things working out. She stood inside the door and turned to face him. "Thank you for the ride. I appreciate it. Maybe we could—"

"Indulge in a nightcap?" He glanced past her, into the house.

"A drink?" *Déjà vu*. He'd given her another opening. She'd thought about suggesting dinner tomorrow after work. This was better.

"No." He smiled. "A little hat for my head. You're not going to turn me down again, are you?"

Ronni laughed. She'd turned him down once for a drink and regretted it. Turning him down again was *not* happening. Promotion or no promotion. Jobs would come and go, but a good man…

"Are you still worried about what happened at the office?"

She knew that question was coming, but hadn't quite figured out how she was going to answer it. Before she could formulate her response, he continued.

"I won't apologize for it, Ronni. And by the way, before I forget, I'm going to check out that fantasy vacation resort over this Valentine's Day weekend. I wanted to talk to you about it before time runs out."

Her heartbeat kicked up a notch. So much for the trip. She hadn't wanted to leave because he might lose interest while she was gone, and now he was leaving. "The resort Dex is looking for the company to invest in?" she asked, even though she already knew the answer.

"That's right."

"I see. Well, your going is more appropriate than me."

Hunter's brow furrowed. "Dex asked you to go?"

His question had come out casual, but he looked suddenly tense. "Yes. He said he cleared it. I haven't had a chance to discuss it with you to double-check. I was going to bring it up tomorrow."

Hunter shook his head. His partner just couldn't keep his nose out of things. Dex had done this on purpose. Trying to do a little matchmaking most likely. Certainly, he didn't think they wouldn't find out, then coincidentally meet up at the plane, and say, "oh, well," and get on the flight together, believing fate had intervened. "He never mentioned it to me."

"Well, if you're going, there's certainly no need for me to go. I'll let Dex know tomorrow."

She sounded disappointed. Or maybe she was relieved. He couldn't quite tell, and there was only one way to find out. "Actually, there is a need. I want you to go with me, Ronni." There. He'd said it.

"With you?"

"That way the company will get both a male and female perspective about the place. That's important when dealing with romance." Okay, so the excuse was a bit of a copout. But saying, *please come with me because I want to fuck you,* somehow didn't have a good ring to it. And he needed to stop thinking *fuck*. Geez. Repeating it endlessly didn't make it true. He intended their relationship to be more than that. At least, he wanted to give it a go and see what developed. "We can meet at the company airfield on Friday. I have an appointment across town that morning, so it'll be easier if we arrive separately." He stepped away from her, walking backwards toward his car. "It'll be fun. And productive."

"Wait! Don't you want to come in? For that drink."

He stepped back, closing the space between them. His mouth hovered just above hers. "More than you'll ever know," he whispered. But now wasn't the time, he realized. If he entered her home, he'd do everything in his power to stay until morning. And he wanted their first time together to be exceptional, without having to worry about getting up early and going to work the next day. He had too many important meetings tomorrow. He couldn't cancel them. His fingers stroked her cheek, and he lightly kissed her mouth, forcing himself not to lose control. A difficult feat, given the taste of her soft lips. "Goodnight, Ronni." He backed up, stepped off the porch, and retreated down the driveway. If he didn't get out of there fast, he'd be saying the hell with the meetings, and he'd end up spending the next two days in bed with her.

With her simply staring at him, her mouth hanging open, he got in his car and started the engine. He hadn't given her a chance to ask questions about his leaving or about the trip.

The next two days he had back-to-back meetings all day long, so they would only get to talk in passing until they met for the trip. That would work in his favor, he hoped. When he was extra busy, she was usually extra accommodating. He doubted she'd flake out on him. And the time apart would build the anticipation between them for the upcoming trip.

He backed out of the driveway and headed home.

Chapter Five

Everlasting Love, Inc.
Private Airfield
Just outside Chicago, Illinois

"This is not looking good." Hunter hadn't thought Friday would ever get here. Now, he stood outside one of the company's private planes, feeling like an idiot for getting his hopes up. He checked his watch. She wasn't coming. She hadn't said that she wouldn't be here. But she'd never actually said she would be either.

Maybe he should call her. If he didn't catch her at the office, he could try her at home. He shook his head. No. This had to be her decision. No pressure. He shoved his hands into his pants pockets.

"Sir," the pilot said, drawing him out of his thoughts. "We're going to need to leave in ten minutes."

He nodded. "Fine." Disappointment gripped him hard. He should have left well-enough alone. Now their working relationship would probably end up strained. He was going to have to do some major damage control when he returned.

The sky rumbled. He looked up at the looming clouds. Another winter storm. The weather matched his mood. Gray and cold.

He turned and walked up the steps into the plane. "I'm ready when you are," he told the pilot. They'd better get out of there while they could.

Hunter plopped down onto a large, leather seat. His enthusiasm was gone. This trip would be torture. Maybe he'd only stay one night, if he could get everything he needed for the company to make a final decision about the resort.

A screech of tires drew his attention out the window. A cab. His heart began to race. He switched on the intercom to the pilot. "Hold up."

The back door opened, and a woman stepped out. Hunter gulped. Ronni. Yes! Her hair hung soft and loose, as he'd told her he liked it. She wore a long trench coat and clutched a briefcase in one hand and a purse in the other.

The cab driver unloaded two suitcases from the trunk. It looked like she'd packed for a week instead of two days.

Hunter laughed. That was fine with him. The important thing was that she was here. He met her and the driver at the front of the plane, and he tried to look more composed than he felt. "Hi."

"Hi. I'm sorry that I'm late. The elevator at the office stuck between floors. I thought I'd never get out of the blasted thing. I didn't want to leave my car here, and I had trouble getting a cab. Then an accident blocked our way en route. And I lost my cell phone somewhere, so I couldn't call you. What a pain!" She took a deep breath.

Her disorganized morning had him smiling. He could imagine the hard time she'd probably given the company's maintenance team as well as the taxi driver. "It's okay. The important thing is that you're here." He felt like hugging her, but refrained. Instead, he tipped the cabbie, took her luggage, and stowed it away. "Let's go on back." He led her down a short aisle and through a curtain to the seats.

"Oh, this is nice, Hunter." Her gaze flickered over the large leather seats, separate table area, and sofa, which pulled out into a bed.

Her compliment stroked his ego, since he'd helped to design the interior. "Custom. The company has three of these. The convenience of a private jet comes in handy for business trips. And I like to be comfortable. We'd better get ourselves strapped in. If we don't take off before the storm hits, we'll be grounded." He alerted the pilot that they were ready to go.

He knew Ronni coming didn't guarantee anything, but that was all right. He was happy to see her. They'd have fun regardless of the intimacy, or lack thereof, which occurred while they were away.

Chapter Six

Not Only in Your Dreams Resort
Private Airfield
Fantasy, Colorado

The plane touched down on a small, secluded landing strip.

Ronni had thought they'd never land. She unclenched her fingers from the seat. She was a rotten traveler. Hunter had kept her distracted for most of the flight, while they went over their game plan. But landing was a terrifying experience in a small jet.

"You okay?" He unbuckled his seatbelt and stood.

She followed suit, though a little shakily. "I am now that we're on solid ground." She glanced out a window. She hadn't ever been to Colorado. It was very different from Chicago—so open. At least, the surrounding area where they'd landed was.

Hunter took her arm and led her forward. "You did great. We'll have two whole days before we need to head back. So, relax. We'll do some good work and also have lots of fun, if what Dex told me about the resort's extensive entertainment areas is true."

A classy woman, dressed in a beige designer suit, visible beneath her open ankle-length coat, met them as soon as they stepped off the plane. "Mr. Dunlap. Ms. Strickland. My name is Lanette Hamilton. I'll be taking you to the resort and showing you around while you're here. My assistant will stay behind and see that your luggage arrives safely."

"Ms. Hamilton," Hunter greeted. "We're looking forward to touring the facility and experiencing the services offered."

"I think you'll both have a good time. We're not that far from Durango. So, if you need access to town for any reason, we can charter a helicopter for you. Fantasy doesn't quite have all the amenities we'd like it to have yet. However, customer service is very high on our priority list, so just ask, if there's anything you need. We want all couples who come here to leave satisfied."

The multiple meaning of that last word wasn't lost on Ronni.

Hunter seemed so relaxed. She was shaking in her pantyhose, wondering what was going to happen between them in the next forty-eight hours. She wasn't normally a nervous twit about sex, but somehow with Hunter everything seemed so much more intense and important.

They followed Lanette Hamilton to a limousine and piled inside. Ronni watched the assistant, an older man, walk toward the pilot, apparently to retrieve their luggage.

"The resort is called *Not Only in Your Dreams,* as you know," Lanette began. "We aim to make fantasies come true for the men and women who come here."

The limousine took off, and Ronni watched the scenery go past. Mountain peaks in the distance, light snow dusting fields that would no doubt turn green in summer, and lots of foliage completed the very serene picture. The small airfield, surrounding land, and town of Fantasy, all owned by the resort, added to the company's worth and appeal.

"What's the average stay?" Hunter asked.

"Two nights. Weekends, of course, are busiest. We're a little slow right now because of the cold weather, but are still eighty-five percent booked. We'll see to it that most of the additional paperwork your company needs to see is in your room for review. We've scheduled daytime business meetings for you. But your evenings will be free to indulge in our festivities."

Ronni couldn't help but wonder if Hunter had booked them into the same room. She hadn't the nerve to ask. She was just going to take things as they came. She hoped he had. That way there would be no guessing about what would happen during their stay. They didn't have that much time here.

Uncertainties would eat up the weekend. "What's your average booking rate overall?" she asked.

"Ninety percent. In midsummer and on holidays we're sometimes as high as ninety-seven percent full. I brought along our new, promotional brochure for you both to look at." Lanette handed each of them a colorful, tri-folded pamphlet.

Ronni skimmed the contents. Her gaze lingered on a listing in the middle. "What are these fantasy communities?"

"Those are where our hotel rooms are located, divided within the resort according to fetish. A small community for each, so that everyone feels comfortable. We have specialized classes and stores, and also party areas that cater specifically to each type of clientele."

"Fetish?" Hunter asked, obvious surprise lacing his voice.

Ronni's attention had caught on the same word.

"Of sorts," Lanette answered with a smile. "We have the standard romance suites in our Romance Rendezvous community, then there's also Bondage Bay, which is along the lake, Ménage Manor, Swap Street, and our newest community, Harem Haven, located on the mountainside east of the main resort area. We also have a few more secluded areas for really unusual fetishes, for an additional fee, of course."

Ronni didn't want to know about the unusual fetishes. She couldn't even respond to the alliterations she'd already heard. She just sat staring at the woman.

Hunter cleared his throat. "Um…"

Lanette's gaze switched back and forth between them, until finally settling on Hunter. "You knew we fulfilled *sexual* fantasies for couples, right? We sent the information."

"I'm afraid not," Hunter answered. "My partner has been handling this and apparently he left out a few details."

"I'm sorry. Is this going to be a problem?"

"Frankly, Ms. Hamilton, I don't know. I'm going to need to adjust my mode of thinking here."

"Perhaps after you rest and have a look around, you'll see that we really have quite a sophisticated operation. It's nothing sleazy. Believe me. And you'll be free to explore all areas of the resort. As far as accommodations, you'll be staying in Bondage Bay #12."

"Bondage Bay," Ronni choked out, her voice barely above a whisper. The woman listed only one number. She and Hunter would be together.

"Yes. Dextor Elroy made the room arrangement. He indicated to us that our Bondage facilities would be perfect for the two of you. And that is our most popular community, so it'll give you a good idea of our client base."

Ronni squirmed on the seat. Dex had planned this whole thing. Bondage? Goodness! Did Dex know something about Hunter that she didn't? Or maybe he'd assumed something about her. Either way, if anything ruined this weekend because of what Dex had arranged, she'd give that man more than an earful when she returned.

She shifted again and glanced at Hunter, who seemed overly interested in the brochure, all of a sudden. And if she wasn't mistaken, a coat of red was creeping up his neck. From embarrassment or anger, she wasn't sure.

Chapter Seven

Hunter stood staring at the room. Every muscle in his body tensed. *Bondage.* It had been a long time since... He shook his head. He'd better control his thoughts and fantasies before he got himself all worked up.

Lanette had shown them around the grounds, while they waited for the luggage to arrive, and while the staff made final preparations to their accommodations. He'd half expected to see people running around naked or engaged in public sex after the woman informed them of the resort's purpose.

To his surprise, from the outside, the place looked about like any other high-class vacation spot, as far as he could tell. From the inside...

He vaguely heard the bellman click the door closed. Ronni moved closer beside him, brushing his arm. He itched to slide his arm around her, but instead just stood there, wondering what she thought about all of this.

Large, floor-to-ceiling windows lined one side of the room. The curtains were open and displayed a fabulous view of the lake. The sun, setting over the water, made for quite the romantic scene.

Sconces on the walls lit their immediate surroundings. A large, wrought iron bed dominated the room. Someone had turned down the covers to reveal black satin sheets.

An entertainment center sat across from the bed for easy television viewing. A sitting area, off to the side, was situated so that one could also view the television from the red and cream-colored sofa and chairs in the room.

Hunter strolled closer to the wide-screen television. Videos lined the shelf above. *The Dominatrix Strikes Back. Whip It Good. Tied & Tried…* "Geez."

"Hunter?"

He turned toward Ronni. She stood in front of a wooden armoire, the doors open. He came up behind her. One shelf contained baskets of condoms, sex toys, and edibles. Erotic books lined another shelf. Hanging off the inside of one door were whips, paddles, and chains. A small collection of colorful scarves, ties, and blindfolds decorated the inside of the other door.

"Goodness." Ronni slowly closed the armoire. She turned to face him.

Hunter didn't step back. He didn't move a muscle. He couldn't. Bondage-type images ran through his head. Tying Ronni to the bed, pumping his cock into her while she was bound and helpless. Then releasing her, and taking her slow and gentle, until she cried out his name. *Oh, yeah.*

Her gaze locked with his. "What are you thinking?"

His heart thudded, and he arched an eyebrow. "You really want to know?"

She nodded.

"It might shock you."

"I doubt it."

He hoped that meant she was feeling as turned-on as he was, because he didn't intend to lie to her. "I'm thinking that, although it's not what I expected, I'm glad we're here. I'm thinking that I'd really like to see you naked. And that I'm going to need to get my cock inside you more than once before the night is up." He felt like jerking her body against his, but he sucked in a deep breath instead.

"Oh." She chewed at her bottom lip.

Oh? The breath whooshed out of him. He'd hoped for a more enthusiastic response than that. Maybe he should have said that he needed to make love to her. Something more sensitive. Hell, he hadn't even asked if she wanted her own room. Or if she would prefer to move to another community. Or if she even wanted to sleep with him. He was making too many assumptions. *Good going, Hunter.* He might have blown his best chance. "What exactly does 'oh' mean?" With women, he'd learned to ask, rather than guess.

She lightly touched his chest. "I'm—" she hesitated. "A little nervous, I guess. But happy and…and eager."

Hope surged through him, but he wasn't about to celebrate yet. From the hesitant expression on her face, he suspected she had more to say. "And?" He wasn't used to seeing her grapple for words. It was actually quite endearing.

"And I'd like to see you naked, too, Hunter. More than you could ever know."

Wow. Great. Super. His lips twitched, but he refrained from smiling. So far, so good. "And?" He wanted—needed—to know everything she was thinking.

"And I want you inside me. I have for a long time."

Yes! Exactly what he wanted to hear. Her confession made him feel like the luckiest man alive. The impact of her exact words hit him. She'd said, "for a long time". Damn. He'd had no idea. They'd wasted who knew how long tiptoeing around each other, when they could have already been involved. Of course, that was his fault. He'd always liked Ronni, but hadn't seriously looked at her in a sexual way, until Dex had put the idea into his head. He'd have to thank his partner.

"I'd like to clean up first. If you don't mind."

Momentary disappointment hit. The need to rip off her clothes and get between her legs was so strong that it was painful. But he supposed he should be more considerate of her desire to start slow. "Whatever you want, Ronni." He stepped back. "The bathroom is yours. I'll order us something to eat."

They had all night and tomorrow night, as well. And maybe some time between meetings, if they could sneak away.

He'd make the time count, so she would want to continue seeing him after they returned to Chicago. This was not a one-night or even a two-night stand for him, and he hoped she felt the same.

* * * * *

Ronni leaned against the black and gray marble counter in the bathroom. The large shower with two sprays and an even larger, sunken tub caught her eye. Decadent.

She turned and looked at herself in the mirror. She'd never gotten around to buying new glasses, so she still sported the black atrocities. Hunter didn't seem to mind.

This Valentine's Day would be memorable, that's for sure. She hadn't lied when she'd told him that she was nervous. But even if their relationship didn't work out in the end, she wanted to go for it.

Bondage Bay #12 might be the perfect way to show Hunter that she was vulnerable and open to a relationship with him. Not that she knew anything about bondage. She hoped she didn't do anything to make herself look foolish.

He was most likely expecting her to appear in something silky and romantic tonight. And she would. She'd brought the perfect robe. But under the robe, romantic would be too tame a word to describe what she'd be wearing. She didn't want a nice, neat affair with him. She wanted something hot and wild, and she wanted her outfit to reflect that.

A smile spread across her face at the thought of what Hunter's reaction would be when he saw her. She didn't know how she was going to keep her mind focused on work during the day. Especially if tonight turned out as she expected. Though she'd better not allow her expectations to soar too high, just in case.

She took a quick shower, looking forward to a more leisurely one later...with Hunter washing every inch of her sensitive skin. She dabbed on some lip-gloss and blush. Nothing more. Caked or smeared makeup later wouldn't look very enticing. She slipped a long, red cover-up over her sexy new underwear. The silk robe looked exceedingly good with her brown hair, brown eyes, and light complexion. She put on her glasses, so she wouldn't trip over the furniture, and then fluffed her hair. "Okay, I'm ready."

After one last check in the mirror, she stepped out the door. She could hardly believe that her fantasy of making love with Hunter was about to come true. Her gaze fell on a cart with food on top. Fruit chunks, slices of cheese, crackers, chocolate squares, and a bottle of white wine. That was fast service. Although, she'd probably taken a bit longer than she should have in the bathroom.

She snatched up a strawberry and popped it into her mouth. The drapes were closed, the lights had been dimmed, and music played in the background, low and sultry. Hunter had prepared the room so nicely.

A light snoring drew her attention to the sofa, where he lay sprawled. Sound asleep and still fully dressed. Momentary irritation hit when she realized he'd nodded off, but he looked so handsome and sexy that she couldn't stay upset at him. His features had softened in his relaxed state, and his hair looked slightly mussed. Ronni's heart melted.

She knelt beside him. "Hunter?" she whispered. He couldn't sleep like this. The sofa was too small for him. Come morning, he'd be too stiff to walk.

"Hmm?"

"Come to bed." She shivered at the provocative sound of her words.

"Yes, Ronni," he muttered, but didn't move.

The fact that, even in sleep, he knew she was the one with him warmed her heart. She stroked his brow and kissed him lightly on the lips.

He stirred and wrapped his arms around her. "Mmm. Strawberry."

"Good guess." Sensitive to taste—she liked that, an oral man. Her lips lingered on his a moment, enjoying the feel of his mouth against hers. She maneuvered out of his embrace and stood up, giving him room to rise. He was probably exhausted from a long week at the office. She had looked forward to them making love tonight, but she didn't want him to fall asleep right in the middle of things. That would be a letdown.

Hunter stretched and opened his eyes. A slow, sexy smile spread across his face. "Hey, beautiful."

Ronni's heart tumbled in her chest. It had been a long time since a man had called her beautiful. And Hunter seemed to mean it, as opposed to simply feeding her a line. Tonight was, after all, a sure thing for him. He didn't need to give false compliments.

"Sorry for drifting off."

"That's all right. Let's not worry about tonight, Hunter." Her disappointment grew with each word. "We can get a good night's rest, so we're sharp for the meetings tomorrow." Not that she'd sleep a wink with Hunter next to her in the bed. She needed him inside her.

He stood up, a serious expression on his face. "Forget it, Ronni. I'm ready to go." He paused, and his voice softened. "Unless you're too tired?"

"Me? No. No, I'm fine." In fact, she felt like ripping off his clothes to see what kind of body was under those suits he always wore. She knew from his muscular frame that he'd look fantastic naked, but she wanted to see for herself…now.

His eyes filled with desire. "Come here."

Ronni slowly shook her head. She smiled and crooked her finger. "You come to me."

Hunter laughed. He stepped forward and swept her into his arms.

She squealed and laughed.

He kissed her cheek, lingered on the side of her mouth, and finally covered her lips warmly with his.

When coaxed, she sighed and opened her mouth to him.

Hunter plunged his tongue inside.

Slipping one arm around his back, she clung to him, needing to get closer. He tasted like hot cider with spice. She wanted everything he had to give. When their tongues touched, her whole body trembled. She craved the feel of his tongue on her breasts, between her legs, making her crazy with desire.

His palm slid underneath her hair. He angled her head, exploring her mouth thoroughly. She imagined him exploring her pussy the same. Her whole body shook in need. She touched his neck, fingering the soft strands along his nape.

She loved the taste of him, the way he took control.

Suddenly, he pulled away and stepped back. "Drop the robe, Ronni." He practically growled the order.

She'd never known a man so sexy and commanding, who wasn't also a jerk. Hunter excited her more than she ever could have imagined—both physically and emotionally. She didn't shake her head this time, willing to follow wherever he would lead her. She pulled open the robe's tie, slipped the silk from her shoulders, and let it pool at her feet.

Hunter's dick jerked and hardened. The rest of him froze. *Wow!*

Ronni's hair hung over her creamy shoulders. The black and red silk bra she wore barely contained her breasts. The matching, high-cut thong accentuated her legs, making her look sexier than he'd expected. The black glasses added to the erotic mix. She looked like some naughty schoolteacher out to seduce the principal. The X-rated thought made his dick grow harder than stone.

"Turn around," he croaked out, needing to see the ass he'd been fantasizing about for far too long.

She turned, and to his surprise, bent forward and rested her palms against the doors on the armoire. Her position caused her butt to thrust back toward him, and he couldn't stop the groan that rumbled up from his throat. She glanced over her shoulder and smiled.

The little seductress…

Ronni was obviously far from the conservative woman she projected at the office, otherwise she wouldn't be offering up her ass like some sexual sacrifice. And that suited him just fine. He approached her from behind, his heart hammering. He settled one palm on a bare ass cheek and felt her tremble in excitement. His fingers curled against her soft flesh. "You're perfect, Ronni," he whispered close to her ear. He pressed against her, letting her feel his cock.

She hung her head. A barely audible moan escaped her lips, but he heard it. He toed off his shoes, then peeled off his jacket and let it glide to the floor. "Don't move." He flicked the closure on her bra, and it popped open.

A quick tug loosened his necktie. He wrapped an arm around her waist and a hand around her arm, then pulled her up against him, back to chest and butt to groin. He held her like that, loving the feel of her body against his. Her skin was soft and warm, and she smelled like peaches. His lips brushed her shoulder. "Put your wrists together in front of you. I'm going to bind you."

She stiffened. "Um, bind me? I've never—Hunter, I don't know."

He slowly pulled the bra from her body. No matter her words, he heard the curious interest in her voice. "Bondage Bay, Ronni. We're going to experience it as intended." He understood her apprehension about giving him total control, but that also added to the excitement. "It'll be all right. I promise."

She relaxed against him and tentatively held her wrists at chest level. "Okay." She turned slightly, looking him in the eyes. "Bind me."

Hunter's heart pounded. He took the tie and wrapped it around her wrists, securing them together, not too tight, but enough to restrain her. Even though the armoire in front of them had numerous bindings, using his tie made it more erotic. He cupped her bare breasts and tweaked her nipples.

"Oh!"

He loved the feel of her tits, so full and soft. Her fleshy nipples would make a delicious suck. He intended to pay them proper attention soon. "Put your hands back against the armoire like before, Ms. Strickland."

She visibly gulped. "Yes…Mr. Dunlap."

Perfect. Control. In the bedroom or in the boardroom, he got off on it. His fingers slid slowly down her body, and he held her around the waist as she leaned forward and braced herself on the armoire. "Good." He rubbed his pelvis against her ass.

She pushed back against him.

"Yeah, you want it. Don't you?"

"Yes, Hunter. Please." Her voice was soft, and a little shaky.

He began to unbutton his shirt. "Do you want me to do something nice or something nasty to you, Ronni?"

"N-Nasty."

A smile tugged at his lips. He pulled the shirt off his shoulders and dropped it to the rug. His hands tangled in her hair. The long strands softly caressed his fingers. "What do you want?"

"I want you inside me."

"That's not very nasty, Ronni. Be explicit. This isn't the time or place to hold back." His voice hardened. "I want to hear you say what you need. Beg for it."

"Please. Please…"

His hand tightened in her hair. "Say it!"

"Fuck me, dammit!"

Yeah. That's what he'd wanted to hear. Nothing could stop him now. He stepped back and ripped the scrap of underwear from between her legs.

She inhaled sharply.

He reached between her thighs from behind, and stabbed one, then two, fingers into her pussy, making sure she was wet and ready for him.

"Ah!"

She was more than wet. She was soaked. He finger-fucked her, until she whimpered and squirmed in need. He pulled out and sucked her juices from his fingers, getting every drop. "Delicious, Ronni. Now let's see how you handle my dick up your pussy." He reached into his back pocket for his wallet and took out a condom.

"Hurry, Hunter."

The need in her voice spurred him on. He didn't bother taking off his pants. He simply unzipped and released his dick. After rolling on the rubber, he positioned himself and pushed slowly into her pussy, one thick inch at a time.

Ronni moaned. Hunter's cock felt better than she'd ever imagined. Certainly better than the Dunlap Dildo. The dildo was slick and smooth. Hunter's cock had more texture and moved erotically along her sensitive flesh, making her pussy clench in response. Her fingers curled against the armoire. She pushed back against him, encouraging him to fill her completely.

He clutched her hips and pumped into her. "Oh, yeah."

She was so primed for him that she knew she wouldn't last more than a few seconds. "I'm going to come."

"Not yet, Ronni." He slowed his movements. "If you come, I won't be able to hold back, and I don't want to stop fucking yet. This is too good." He stroked her back with one hand, keeping the other hand on her hip.

"I have to come." Her whole body screamed for release.

"No." He slapped her butt.

"Oh!" Surprise struck harder than his hand. She hadn't expected that from Hunter. The sting distracted her, keeping her body on the edge without tumbling over.

He rubbed the cheek. "Do you need another one?"

"No—No."

"Too bad. You're getting it anyway."

Hunter smacked her ass again, easier this time, and the opposite cheek.

She twitched and moaned, surprised by how much she enjoyed the spanks. They excited her, but allowed her to maintain control at the same time.

He caressed the fleshy roundness of her butt. He pushed his cock deep and held it within her hot, wet folds. "You're so fucking good, Ronni. Hold your orgasm. Delay it."

She nodded. He knew just how to handle her. Just what she needed. Unlike any other man ever had.

He leaned over her back. "Use your internal muscles. Squeeze my dick."

Oh, goodness. She couldn't. She'd come if she did that.

He reached around and pinched her swollen nipples. "Now. Do it."

The slight pain was just enough to hold off her orgasm. She clenched him, released, clenched, and released again. His cock felt made for her body. A perfect fit, stretching and filling her completely.

"Oh, yeah." He released her nipples, straightened, and gripped her hips. "Let me pump you a few times. Then you can come."

He stroked her vaginal walls, back and forth.

"Your pussy is so tight. It feels great wrapped around my dick! I've got to get deeper."

Deeper? She didn't see how. He was all the way in right now.

He pushed her back lower and altered his stance. He started out moving his hips slow and easy, then pumped harder and faster within her.

Because of the new angle, he was able to bury his cock deeper than she'd imagined possible. "Please. I have to come," she practically sobbed.

Hunter's body slapped against her ass, as he fucked her harder. "Okay. Now! Come now, Ronni."

Completely tuned to his demands, the orgasm shot through her body. "Hunter!"

"Yeah!"

She felt him stiffen and come right along with her. Their sounds of pleasure mingled, and she came longer and stronger than she had with any man. Her pussy contracted wildly around his cock. She never wanted the ecstasy to end.

Finally, after they both stopped trembling, he gently kissed her back and pulled out of her. He disposed of the condom, while she leaned against the wooden armoire, barely able to stand. That had been more incredible than anything she'd ever experienced.

Hunter returned and took her into his arms, cradling her against his heart. She felt almost…cherished. He dragged her back to the sofa, and they both collapsed. She slid to the rug at his feet.

His fingers stroked her hair. "That was so great, Ronni. Even better than I expected."

She glanced up at him and frowned. "What?" Hadn't he thought they'd be good together?

He raised his hands in a defensive gesture. "I meant that in the best possible way. You are a man's fantasy come true. Give me your hands. I'll untie you."

"Not yet." She knew being bound, spanked, and made to submit to Hunter had added to the explosive nature of her orgasm. She didn't want that feeling of sexual vulnerability to end.

For a long moment, he said nothing, and then, "You like being bound and controlled?"

"By you."

He reached out for her glasses and eased them off her face. "I'll take good care of you, Ronni. Sexually, and every other way."

"I know."

His heart expanded in pleasure. He set the black-framed glasses on the side table. Ronni sitting naked and bound at his feet, so trusting, caused unexpected emotions to flow through him. He *did* want to take care of her. And so much more.

He was amazed at how intense his climax had been. His legs were still shaky. Because it had been so long since his dick had been inside a woman's pussy instead of his own fist, or because it was specifically Ronni, he didn't know.

He had a feeling that Ronni was the reason. Her allowing him complete control of her body was a major turn-on.

And something more tugged at him, and at his emotions. This woman was soft and willing to yield, but smart and capable at the same time. He found he liked that combination. "Have you ever been involved in bondage, Ronni?"

She shook her head, then glanced up at him. "Have you?"

"A little." Okay, maybe more than a little. But he didn't know her tolerance level and didn't want to scare her. "Will you—will you allow me to take things further?" He held his breath, waiting for her decision. If she agreed to submit, he had plans that would blow her mind.

"Yes, Hunter. I'll allow you anything."

The air whooshed out of him. "Do you want a *safe* word?" he whispered, eager to show her pleasures she wouldn't soon forget.

She chewed at her bottom lip a moment, then released it. "Will I need one?"

He leaned down and brushed his lips across her cheek. "Not with me."

Chapter Eight

Ronni's lips brushed Hunter's muscled thigh. She felt so alive right now, that it was almost scary. She pulled his pants and white briefs off, wanting him as she was.

She'd never thought of herself as the submissive sort, in the bedroom or out. But something about Hunter made her want to give in to his desires and let him guide her sexually. She kissed his bare thigh again, allowing her tongue to touch his warm skin.

He softly stroked her hair. His tender touch encouraged her trust in him.

She pulled off his socks and tossed them aside. He had a great body, firm and fit. A flat rippled stomach, muscled biceps and thighs, and a wide chest with just a sprinkling of dark hair. The kind of body that any woman would find hard to resist.

Hunter's fingers laced through her hair, and he tugged lightly. She complied with his wishes.

With his guidance, she shifted her weight and moved between his spread legs. Even flaccid, his cock was impressive—long and just the right thickness, with a large head.

Her hands, still bound, moved over his skin, and her fingers grazed his balls, eliciting a sharp intake of air from him.

His cock began to harden, as did his gaze, which she noticed when she glanced up at him. But the intensity of his brown eyes weren't what kept her attention.

Amazed, since he'd just come not long ago, she watched his cock grow longer and thicker. His shaft rose—the purplish color deep. That and his dark thatch of hair fascinated her. Ronni couldn't look away.

She'd always been fascinated with the male body, and Hunter's was exceptional. "Tell me a fantasy to fulfill for you. Something wicked and wild."

His nostrils flared. "Ronni, you're going to kill me."

"Tell me." She watched his pupils dilate.

"Okay." His voice lowered to a husky tone. "Lick and suck my dick. Explore every inch with your tongue, then inhale me deep. I want to come in your mouth. I want to watch you swallow everything I give you, and I want you to beg me for more."

She chewed on her bottom lip and eyed his cock as she contemplated his words. After a moment, she leaned forward and licked the underside of his thick shaft with one long swipe.

"Ah..." His hips pushed up toward her.

The musky flavor of him spread along her tongue, and she wanted to taste more of him—but on her terms, not his. She sat back on her heels. "What's my incentive for swallowing you?"

The surprised look on his face made her smile. He'd thought she was simply going to follow instructions. Well, things weren't quite that simple, and she wanted him to know that.

"Pleasing me would be your incentive, Ronni."

"And what else?" She tried to tame her smile, but it was impossible. She was having too much fun.

"Isn't that enough?"

The grin on his face showed her that he was enjoying their little game, too. Now to see where he'd take it. She wrapped her fingers around the wide base of his cock and licked the tip. Her tongue swirled through the beads of moisture at the top. She loved the taste of him. She sucked the bulbous head into her mouth. The erotic act seemed more intimate with Hunter, and she felt an immediate deeper connection to him.

He groaned. "Yeah, do it for me, Ronni."

She pulled back and licked her lips, taking time to calm her pounding heart. "Still seems like I should get something first."

This time he groaned in frustration, instead of pleasure. "Who's bound here?"

"And who's probably going to be too spent to continue after I drain you a second time?" Though she wondered about that. His virility seemed boundless.

Hunter surged up from the sofa, and Ronni tumbled backward on the beige carpet, not expecting the move. Maybe she'd pushed him too far. His look of intensity gave her pause.

He grasped her arm and pulled her to her feet. He wrapped his other arm around her waist. "You want something? An incentive?" He dragged her to the bed and tossed her on the mattress.

"Hey!" She bounced on her back.

Hunter rolled her onto her stomach, then secured the end of the tie still around her wrists to the wrought iron headboard.

"Wait!" She pulled, but couldn't get loose.

He stalked over to the wooden cabinet.

If she hadn't seen the small smile tugging at his lips, she'd have been scared to death of his sudden change. As it was, she only felt mildly concerned.

Something on his butt drew her attention. A tattoo? She couldn't quite make out what it was. She hadn't thought Hunter the type, but then realized she still didn't know a lot about him.

He opened the armoire and plucked several items from the baskets and off the inside doors.

His body halfway blocked her view, so she couldn't quite tell what he was grabbing. "What are you doing?"

"You'll find out."

Maybe she'd been wrong about that smile she thought she'd seen on his face. She wasn't certain what she'd gotten herself into. Maybe she should have agreed to a safe word after all. She knew Hunter would never hurt her, but he might demand things that she wasn't accustomed to allowing.

Hunter stalked back to the bed and dumped the items at the foot. Because of her position, she still couldn't see what he'd brought over. He situated a silk-covered pillow under her head, and she automatically rested her cheek on it to relieve the muscles in her neck.

He grabbed another pillow and shoved it under her hips. "I'm going to wring every ounce of cum out of you, Ronni."

Oh, my! Her heart leapt in her chest. She felt something soft wrap around one of her ankles and realized that he was going to tie her feet to the wrought iron bed. She'd be completely helpless. Her heart rate shot up even more. "Hunter?"

Without responding, he spread her leg wide and secured her to one of the foot posts, then did likewise with her other ankle. His hand glided up her thigh to rest on her butt.

Ronni's pulse raced. For a few moments, heavy silence filled the room as he simply stood there. She realized that he could do anything he wanted to her now, and she'd be powerless to stop him.

"You okay?" he finally asked.

She relaxed a little at his softly spoken inquiry. "I…guess."

Something soft and satiny fell across her face. He was blindfolding her. "No, I—"

"I want you to feel, Ronni. And not be influenced or distracted by what you might see."

Her other senses immediately sharpened, and her skin tingled. She'd never been more aware of her own body. She felt him move away, then one palm covered her ankle, holding it against the mattress. Her breathing increased as she waited.

The tip of his tongue brushed her sole.

"Oh!" The sensation shot through her body. Her pussy throbbed, and her nipples tightened from the moist contact.

He licked the bottom of her foot. The contact caused her to squeal and squirm. His tongue slid between her toes, then back along the center of her foot again. She cried out, half-sobbing and half-laughing from the intense feeling.

When he finally stopped, she breathed a sigh of relief. She'd never been very ticklish, but something about being blind, bound, and helpless made her extra sensitive.

"Just some delightful torture to see how responsive you are to my tongue."

Ronni had always loved a man's tongue on her. She didn't know if he expected a response or not, so she decided to keep quiet. She'd given him enough control for now, without exposing the depth of her feelings.

Hunter's hand moved along her thigh, over her butt, up her back. "You're all mine, Ronni. That means I'm going to take your body to the edge, and I expect you to hold nothing back from me. Do you understand?"

"Y-yes, Hunter," she barely managed. She sensed him picking up an item from the bed. Or maybe she heard the movement. She wasn't certain which. Multiple, semi-soft strands slapped lightly against her upper back. Some sort of whip? She trembled at the realization.

The strands tickled her skin as Hunter dragged the object down her body. A soft cry of anticipation escaped her right before he struck her thighs, a little harder than her back, leaving a slight sting. She tried to shift, to pull away or to expose herself even more, she wasn't quite certain. But she couldn't move enough either way.

"Stay still, Ronni. I don't want to accidentally hurt you."

He brought the whip down, low on her ass. Several strands curled between her legs and flicked her labia.

"Oh!" Her pussy contracted, and she almost came right there. No one had ever spanked or whipped her. This was a new experience, and she wasn't quite sure what to think of it. She certainly enjoyed it more than she ever thought she would.

The strands slapped her ass again, the middle of both cheeks, very lightly. Except this time, Hunter didn't stop. He continued to make contact, varying his strokes from light to the occasional sharp slap, bringing a gasp from her whenever he struck her with more force. Her whole body tingled. After a couple of more slaps, her ass began to feel warm and too sensitive. She couldn't take much more.

"Is that enough?" he asked, as if reading her mind and body's needs.

"Y-es." For now.

He slapped the strands against her ass again. "Say please, Ronni."

She jerked, not having expected another strike. "Please, Hunter."

Quiet filled the room. He left her for a few moments, then she felt a cool cloth cover her butt. The relief was instantaneous. The fact that he cared enough to see to her comfort pleased her. Before she got too relaxed, he gripped her hair, and lifted her head from the pillow.

"Did you like having your ass whipped?"

Admitting the truth would expose her completely to him—physically and emotionally.

After a moment of silence, his voice hardened. "Answer me. Did you like it?"

"Yes." There, she'd admitted it. She was so wet and achy. She needed to come soon, or she'd go crazy.

His mouth slashed across hers, and his tongue pushed between her lips. He kissed her like a man ravenous for a woman. She kissed him back, their tongues mingling and exploring each other's mouth. Using the whip on her had obviously gotten him excited, too.

He pulled away and shoved a second pillow under her hips, jackknifing her up higher. She was ready and willing to do anything, as long as he made her come. His fingers pulled open her pussy, and his tongue touched her from behind.

She jerked against the ties. *Yes!* "Lick me!"

He growled, then licked, sucked, and ate at her pussy. She pushed back against his mouth, needing more. It wasn't a gentle taking, but one of hunger that demanded a response.

She screamed and came hard.

He kept at her, not letting up. Only after she came three times did he finally stop and allow her to rest.

Hunter had never enjoyed making a woman come as much as he did Ronni. His dick was aching, but he wasn't through with her yet. Neither of them would ever forget this night. He'd see to that.

Against the black sheets, her pale skin looked extra soft and creamy. He hadn't restrained a woman this completely for sex in a long time. He liked the vulnerability, and his freedom to do what he wanted. He removed the cloth and spread her ass cheeks. "No man could resist this ass, Ronni." He lowered his head and licked at the small, puckered opening.

She gasped. "Hunter!" She squirmed and whimpered.

He loved making her squirm. "Has anyone ever licked your asshole, baby?"

"No."

He didn't think so. "Did my tongue feel good inside you?"

"Y-Yes."

Just as he thought… He lowered his head and reamed her good, taking his time and getting her well lubricated. This woman was the perfect partner for him. He felt like he'd broken the bank in Monte Carlo. Her hips moved wildly beneath his thrusting tongue. Now, he'd blow her mind. He raised his head. "I want you to stay relaxed." He picked up a string of anal beads. Slowly, he began to insert them, one at a time.

"What—"

"Shh. They're anal beads. You're doing great, Ronni. Stay relaxed." He reached underneath her and thumbed her clit.

"You're going to come again. I love watching you, especially when you come hard and completely lose control."

She moaned and pushed against his hand.

"I'm going to pull out the beads now. Trust me. You'll love this, Ronni." He pulled gently on the string.

One blue bead popped out, stretching and vibrating the skin around her asshole.

"Oh!"

"It's an intense feeling, isn't it?" And only the beginning. He tugged on the string, pulling out one bead after the other, while he continued to rub her clit.

Ronni came, screeching and thrashing on the mattress. Her juices covered his fingers as he kept up the stimulation.

"Yes, Hunter! Yes! Yes!"

After the last bead popped out, she collapsed.

Ronni sighed. She couldn't believe what was happening to her. She could get used to being Hunter's sex slave. No man had ever taken such good care of her. Or given her such incredible orgasms.

He'd gone into the bathroom. She heard the water running in the sink, and then the faucet turned off. Moments later, something tugged at her ankle, and she realized he'd returned and was untying her. She was almost disappointed.

After loosening her ankles and wrists, he pulled the pillows out from under her hips and rolled her over onto her back. She waited for him to remove the tie from her wrists, but he pushed her arms up and reattached her to the headboard. *Ooo, goodie. More.* He pulled the blindfold off her eyes.

Without her glasses, she couldn't see that well, and it took a moment for her eyes to adjust. She gulped at the large, fully erect man, staring down at her, desire etched on his face.

He sat beside her and leaned over, cupping her breasts and massaging them lightly. His tongue grazed one of her nipples, then he sucked it deep.

At the tug of his lips, she arched and moaned. First one nipple, then the other, got Hunter's special attention, until Ronni thought she'd come just from her nipples being sucked.

"Did that get you hot, Ronni?"

"Oh, yes."

He reached up and tugged her wrists loose, while he kept one hand tangled in her hair. "Time to suck my dick. I'm going to come in your mouth." He discarded the tie.

After propping up a pillow, he sat back against the headboard and guided her head. She didn't need any encouragement. Her lips slid over his cock, and she bobbed her head up and down, swallowing more of him each time into her mouth. Her nostrils flared, taking in air and his special scent.

"Oh, yeah. That's good."

She gripped the base of his cock and pumped. He was too big for all of him to fit into her mouth without gagging, but she doubted Hunter would mind, as long as he came. She sucked a little harder, eager to get him off.

Hunter's hips rose off the mattress. "Geez. You can suck."

Her tongue glided down the underside of his cock, then back up. She licked around the bottom of the head, then over the top, and finally flicked her tongue against the sensitive nerves on the underside.

He bucked on the bed and moaned her name. "Ronni…finger your pussy, baby. I want you to come, too."

She sank her mouth as far down on him as she could, and her fingers lightly caressed his balls, remembering how he'd enjoyed that when she touched him there earlier. "Mmmm."

At the vibration against his cock, his fingers twisted in her hair. She could tell he was close to coming. She prepared herself, ready to swallow whatever he would give. One of her hands slid between her legs, and she rubbed her clitoris.

She allowed moisture to escape her mouth and coat the little finger of her free hand, then she slid that hand under him, when he moved his hips. Very carefully, she found the opening of his anus and pushed her wet finger inside.

Hunter's entire body tensed. "Ronni!" His fingers tightened almost painfully in her hair. Then his cock exploded, shooting cum down her throat.

She rubbed her clit hard and rough, while sucking him furiously.

"Ah! Oh! Yeah!" He bucked and thrashed beneath her, shouting loud enough to wake the dead.

She swallowed all she could, but it was too much, and some trickled out of her mouth and down her chin. She worked her little finger deeper into his asshole, curling it inside him.

"Damn!" He kept coming and shouting, until finally, he'd spent everything he had and collapsed on the bed. His fingers loosened in her hair, and his hands fell to his sides.

Her fingers continued to work her pussy. She let his cock slip from her lips as an orgasm shot through her. "I'm coming!"

"Do it, baby. That's beautiful and so hot."

She laid her cheek on Hunter's stomach, until her body stopped twitching. His breathing still sounded harsh, and she could feel his heart pounding.

"Where did you learn to do that with your finger?" he asked.

She brushed her tongue along his stomach. "Do you really want to know?"

"Hmm," he grunted. "Probably not."

*****

Ronni yawned and stretched. She didn't remember falling asleep. She rolled over to glance at the clock—7:14 a.m.

She turned toward Hunter. He wasn't beside her. Disappointment hit. She'd wanted to wake up in his arms.

Then she heard the water. He must be taking a shower. She'd love to join him, but didn't think her body was up to another round.

Hunter had woken her up around 2:00 a.m. He was already between her legs with his cock inside her, before she actually realized what was happening. They'd made love slow and gentle, and he'd said such beautiful things to her that she had cried.

She didn't think he'd noticed. She hoped not. She'd tried hard to cover her emotions. She didn't want him to freak out.

Men sometimes scared easily if they weren't ready for emotional commitment. Hopefully, if he had noticed, he'd thought the tears were simply from the intensity of her orgasm, which was at least partially true.

The water shut off in the bathroom.

She needed to take a shower, too, and get ready for their meetings. It was going to be a long day. She wanted to lounge around in bed with Hunter, not discuss numbers, marketing strategy, and corporate needs.

But they needed to take care of business first.

* * * * *

"What a day." Ronni collapsed on the sofa. She didn't know where the time had gone. She watched Hunter empty his pockets and place his keys, wallet, and some coins on the dresser. Something was wrong. He'd been acting strangely. Distant.

The meetings had gone well, so that wasn't it. Besides, he'd been weird even before their meetings started.

She knew he'd enjoyed their sex together, so that couldn't be it.

"What's wrong, Hunter?" She hated to ask, but his attitude was putting a damper on the weekend. It was Valentine's Day, after all. They'd had a wonderful time yesterday. Today was their last night, and she didn't want to waste it.

He turned toward her. "Wrong?" His brow furrowed. "Nothing's wrong." He shoved his hands into his pockets.

"Something is obviously bothering you."

"Obviously, huh?" He slowly approached, then sat down beside her. He let out a long sigh. "I'm sorry, Ronni. I just didn't expect this. Us."

"What? That we were going to sleep together. I thought that was the whole point of you asking me to the resort."

A small smile tugged at his lips. "So, you knew that from the beginning?"

"Well, duh." Actually, she'd *hoped* from the beginning, but that was close enough.

He shifted toward her. "That's not actually what I meant about not expecting this."

"Just tell me, Hunter." She waited for the bad news. The "let's be friends" speech. The typical, "better not let the woman cling too much" conversation about how he wasn't ready for a serious relationship right now.

Hunter took his hands from his pockets. "We need to talk."

Here it comes.

"We make a good team, Ronni."

"Yes, we've always worked well together."

He nodded. "And I don't want that to change."

She couldn't take this. "Oh, for crying out loud, Hunter. If you're trying to give me the brush-off, the 'let's keep our relationship all business and remember this as just a fun time' speech, then get to it."

His eyes widened. "No! Is that what—" He clutched her arms, then ran his hands down her blouse sleeves. "I'm sorry. That's not what I meant at all."

She relaxed a little, the tenseness in her muscles easing, and the throbbing in her head lessening. Still, she was wary. "Then what's wrong?"

"I need to know how you feel about me. When we made love this morning, you…cried. What was that about, Ronni?"

"Hunter, I—"

"Let me finish saying everything first, before I lose my nerve. I'd like to continue this. Continue us. I mean, I want us to have a long affair, more than just this weekend, and even think you'd be good in my life right now. But I didn't expect to feel so much, so soon. I don't know what the future holds, but I'd like to explore the possibilities of something maybe even permanent."

Her heart pounded. "What are you saying, Hunter?"

He released her and raked a hand through her hair. "I guess, first off, I'm asking if you want to pursue this relationship after we get back to the office. And then, if you'd be open to a relationship as a real couple, wherever that might lead?"

A smile eased across her face. "Yes. I'd like that."

"Really?"

"Really." She stroked his cheek. "I think we'll be good together, too. You're a very special man, Hunter."

He grinned and shrugged. "Well, I don't know about that. I think you're the special one. I've never known anyone so trusting and vulnerable, yet as strong as you are. You amaze me, Ronni. I wish everyone could see you as I do." He cocked his head. "Why do you hide your beauty so much?"

"What do you mean?"

"Well, the way you dress at the office, it's like you're trying to hide yourself from society."

She immediately tensed. "Excuse me?"

"You're so different from that image…naked, you're gorgeous, and even here, you're dressed differently—"

"You can stop right there. Let me lay it out for you, Hunter. What I wear and who I am are two different things. I don't wear tight clothing at the office because it's uncomfortable. I don't wear a skirt that barely covers my ass, because it's not professional, in my opinion. I wear glasses because contacts irritate my eyes, and I wear my hair up to keep it out of my face while I'm typing. Is that what you wanted to know? Are you satisfied? I'm not trying to hide."

"Yeah, um..." He hung his head. "I'm sorry, Ronni. I didn't mean to offend you. Really, I didn't." His gaze met hers. "I'm just used to a different kind of woman, I guess, women who always have some ulterior motive for everything they do." He reached over and clutched her hand. "Forgive me for being stupid."

He looked so pathetic that she had to laugh. "Okay. This time. But please don't lump me in with other women, okay?"

"Okay."

"Is it my turn for a question now? A serious one?" One she really needed an answer to.

"Shoot."

"What happened between you and your wife? I mean, I know she left you for your assistant, but I imagine the marriage must have been in trouble prior to that."

Hunter sat back and let out a deep breath. "You sure don't pull any punches."

"Well, if we're going to continue seeing each other, I'd like to know."

"Want to make sure I'm not some psycho who drove his wife nuts?"

"Hunter..."

"Okay, okay. You deserve an explanation. It's nothing that shattering. We wanted different things. She needed more time and attention than I could give her. She wasn't interested in the business, other than the money it brought in. And I wasn't interested in all the traveling that she wanted to do. We were okay in the beginning. There wasn't a lot of money, but we were happy. Then when the business came along, it ate into our time together, the money started coming, which was great, but it actually ended up driving us apart."

"I'm sorry."

He shrugged. "It could have been worse. We didn't have any children, which I'm grateful for now. I wouldn't have wanted them to go through the divorce. In the end, I guess we both got what we wanted. She got a lot of money, and someone to pay a lot of attention to her, and I got time to devote to the business."

"Sounds lonely."

"Yeah. That, too."

Ronni wrapped her arms around Hunter. She lightly kissed his cheek and rubbed his back. She needed to lighten the mood. They could talk more later about the serious issues. "What's that tattoo on your butt?"

Hunter laughed. "You sure know how to change a subject."

"I thought so." She tugged on his arm. "Now, what's the story on that thing?"

"You noticed it, huh?"

"Just barely. I didn't see what it was exactly."

"A diamond."

"A jewel?"

"No. Like a baseball diamond. I used to play baseball in college. One night after a particularly satisfying victory, three of us went out and all got one put on our butts." Hunter laughed and shook his head. "Stupid, I guess, but it was kind of a symbol for us. Those guys and I still get together every year. In fact, we have another reunion coming up in a few weeks."

"That's nice that you maintained those friendships."

"They're great guys. But you know what?"

"What?"

"We're talking entirely too much, when we should be touching a whole lot more." He pulled her close.

She laughed. "No, wait a minute." She pulled back. "It's Valentine's Day. I know, don't cringe. I'm aware of the significance of that date. But from now on, it can mean something different for you. For us."

"What did you have in mind?"

"Let's change, and go to that fancy restaurant downstairs and have dinner, then take a stroll along the lake and spend a little time in the hot tub. After that, we can see what kind of kinky trouble we might get ourselves into."

A smile tugged at Hunter's lips. "Sounds good." He caressed her cheek. "I do so like a woman who knows what she wants." He leaned in for a long, lingering kiss.

Chapter Nine

Four Weeks Later

"Sure, I'll bring Ronni," Hunter said into the phone.

Ronni turned from the file cabinet and arched an eyebrow at him. He winked at her and grinned, his eyes sparkling.

She couldn't help but grin back. She'd never been so happy.

After returning to the office, she and Hunter had continued to see each other. Most of their time they spent at her home. Hunter had moved in a few things to make it easier on him. His condo was closer to the office, but he'd said that he didn't feel right about taking her to the place where he and his ex-wife used to live. As soon as his realtor found something appropriate, he planned to move.

"Okay, Brian. We'll be there." He hung up and wrote something on his desk calendar.

"What was that about?"

He tossed down the pen. "You remember those baseball buddies I told you about?"

"The reunion guys?"

"Right. We're getting together in a couple of weeks, and Brian and Paul want me to bring you along."

"You told them about me?" She could hardly believe how comfortable she'd become with Hunter. Like their relationship was meant to be. Okay, so that sounded over-the-top romantic. But that's exactly how she felt.

He circled the desk and pulled her into his arms. "You bet. You're the best thing in my life." He lowered his mouth for a kiss.

The door swung open. "Oops." Dex laughed.

Hunter pulled away and scowled. "Do you have a camera in my office or something? Every time I try to kiss Ronni, you pop in."

"Hey, I can't help it if you two are joined at the lips. I have news." He stepped inside and closed the door.

"What's up?" Ronni asked. She and Hunter had spent quite a few evenings with Dex and his wife after returning from the resort. She genuinely liked the couple.

Dex turned toward her. "Congratulations. You got the promotion to the Head of Research for the erotic toy division. It's our newest line and not fully staffed yet, so the Board wants to see what you can do with it without going beyond the realm of what they consider good taste."

It took a moment for Dex's words to sink in. *I got it.* She let out a shriek and threw herself into Hunter's arms. "Oh, this is great news, isn't it?"

"Congratulations, honey." He wrapped his arms around her and hugged her tightly. "Thanks for letting us know, Dex. I hadn't heard yet."

Ronni pulled back. "Neither of you two pulled strings, did you?" She looked from one man to the other.

"Not me," Dex answered.

"All I told the Board was that you were excellent at your job and very dedicated," Hunter replied. "You must have impressed the hell out of them at your interview. Dex and I weren't even in on this decision, just to make sure that nobody could say we played favorites due to our relationship. I'm going to hate to lose you as my assistant. But I'm very proud of you, Ronni."

"It couldn't have happened to a nicer person. I'll leave you two," Dex said, backing up. "I'm sure you have a lot to talk about. Have a good one."

After the door click closed, Ronni turned to Hunter. "I'm so excited. We have to celebrate." She glanced at her watch. "It's after five. Most of the office personnel are probably gone or soon will be. I have an interesting idea."

"I know that look, Ronni. I'm almost afraid to ask. What do you have in mind?"

She waggled her eyebrows. "A little private office party. That's always been a fantasy of yours, right?" She couldn't get enough of Hunter. She'd become insatiable where he was concerned.

"Seems like I should be fulfilling one of your fantasies."

"You will be, oh hunk of mine." She laughed. "Now lock the door."

A grin lit his face. "Yes, ma'am." Hunter moved around her and locked them in. When he turned back, his smile faded, and a serious expression crossed his face.

No desire shone in his eyes, as she'd expected. "What?"

He leaned against the door. "I meant what I said. It's not going to be the same without you here."

"I'll just be downstairs."

"I know. But it's not the same. I was thinking, Ronni..."

She cocked her head, wondering at his hesitancy. He seemed glad for her promotion, but still, something was making him tense. "What is it, Hunter?"

"What would you think about us moving in together? My realtor called today with a place she wants me to look at. I know you're concerned about how things look, and your position in the company, and it's still somewhat soon in our relationship, but I want to come home and know you're there. I want something more permanent for us."

Her heart leapt in her chest. Moving in together was a big step. But then, they already were used to spending their days and nights together—or at least several nights a week. Maybe it would work. "I think I'd like that, Hunter. I really would."

He stepped forward and pulled her into his arms, then spun her around. "Great!"

Ronni laughed, until he set her down. He kept her locked in his arms. She loved being held by him. "There is one condition, Hunter."

"Uh-oh. What's that?"

"If anyone says anything catty to me because I'm living with the boss, I'd like permission to toilet-paper their head."

Hunter laughed. Ronni was one in a million. She'd worked her way into his heart and taken up residence. "I'll see what I can arrange." He covered her lips with his. The taste of her sent him reeling. His fingers lowered to her blouse, and he worked frantically at the small buttons, needing to feel her soft skin.

When Ronni didn't try to stop him, his body went on full-scale, sexual alert. He pulled back and pushed the blouse off her shoulders, revealing a black lacy bra, which barely contained her ample breasts. He was still amazed at how hot a body she had. Her pale skin looked smooth and more tempting than ice cream on a summer's day. Every time he looked at her, it felt like the first time he'd noticed her as a woman, and not just his assistant—the same excitement rushed through him.

He reached behind her and undid the button on her skirt. His lips were only a breath from hers, but he didn't kiss her. He simply stared at her luscious mouth. The exotic taste of her lips always aroused him to near bursting. He lowered her zipper, taking his time to draw out the moment.

Hunter stepped back. The skirt slid down her legs to puddle at her feet. The vision of Ronni standing before him in her black bra, lace panties, sheer stockings, and heels wiped all rational thought from his mind.

Slowly, he nudged her backward until he'd trapped her against the conference table. She slid up onto the wooden top, sitting with her legs dangling off the end. She reached for the buttons of his shirt, but he brushed her hands away.

"Nope."

"What? Why not?"

He liked the sense of power he felt with her naked, while he remained dressed. "Shhhh." Hunter teased his fingertips across her skin. He slowly rolled off one stocking and shoe, then the other. Early on, he'd discovered that she hated pantyhose, so he'd convinced her to start wearing stockings, even at work. Stockings were much sexier and turned him on just knowing she wore them under her skirt. He spread her legs and stepped between her silky-soft thighs.

With an urgency he desperately tried to control, his fingers traced their way up her body to work the clasp on the front of her bra. The lacy garment popped open, and in an instant, her breasts filled his hands. "Oh, yes." He loved her tits. He swallowed hard and rubbed his thumbs across the rosy nipples. They immediately hardened at his touch, and he felt a shaft of male pride at being able to arouse her so easily. "Beautiful."

Ronni moaned and tossed her head back, exposing the creamy column of her throat. She pulled the pins from her hair, letting the long strands flow down her back.

He groaned. *So damn sexy.* It was an invitation Hunter couldn't resist. He pushed her down on the table and trailed wet kisses along her neck. Her skin tasted of peaches and cream, and he couldn't get enough.

Her fingers laced through his hair, and Ronni guided him to her breasts. "Lick my nipples," she half-begged, half-ordered, her voice quaking.

"My pleasure, Ms. Strickland." Hunter's tongue flicked across one fleshy bud, then the other. He rolled and batted each nipple, scraping his teeth along the sensitive nubs. He concentrated on one tip, nibbling gently until she squirmed beneath him.

"Ah, ah..."

He drew the distended nipple into his mouth and sucked it deep while Ronni continued to moan. She pushed her hips up against him. *Yeah, baby. Show me how much you want it.* He loved making her crazy.

Stepping back, Hunter slid the panties down her long legs. He kissed his way back up the inside of her leg, letting his tongue slide along her flesh. This would be the first time they'd actually had full-out sex in the office—a fantasy he'd had for a long time. His tongue flicked at the juncture between her thighs, and she opened herself to him, offering her pussy.

At her responsiveness, Hunter's heart pounded against his ribs, and desire rushed like a flood through his body. He stood looking down at her, lying naked on the conference table—ready for him, wanting him.

She reached for a bottle of pop he'd set on the table earlier and brought it to her mouth. It was almost empty, but a drink wasn't her intent. She slipped her tongue into the hole at the top of the glass, flicking it in and out.

Hunter couldn't look away as she wrapped her lips around the head and gradually took the length of the neck further into her mouth, sliding it in and then pulling it back out again. Her seductive performance fueled his body's growing need, and he imagined the bottle gone, her lips wrapped around his cock, her mouth sucking, her tongue licking. She gave head, and loved doing it, like no other woman he'd ever known.

Ronni pulled the bottle from her mouth and dragged it between her breasts, smiling up at him the whole time. Hunter covered her breasts with his hands and his fingers squeezed her flesh around the glass as she pumped the bottle back and forth between them. A line of clear, bubbly pop splashed out onto her chest, as if the bottle had climaxed. She ran the fingers of one hand through the sticky liquid, then licked them clean. Hunter moaned, remembering the many times she'd licked him clean, after he'd come.

When he released her, she dragged the bottle down her body—over her ribs, across her stomach, between her legs. Hunter practically choked on his own breath when she began to rub the bottle along the outside of her pussy.

He covered her hand and felt along the bottle for any rough edges. When he found only smooth glass, he spread her pussy lips and gently guided the cool tip to the moist, rosy flesh between her legs.

Ronni moaned, and her eyes locked with his. He held his breath, waiting.

Her eyes dilated. "Do it to me, Hunter," she whispered, her voice husky with desire. She spread her legs wider.

The breath rushed out of him. He inserted the tip of the bottle right up into her pussy. The sight was so erotic and nasty that he thought he'd come in his pants.

"Deeper," she begged, arching her hips.

"Damn, Ronni." He pushed the neck deeper inside her, until she'd taken several inches.

"Now fuck me."

Oh, man. He fingered her clit and fucked her with the bottle, back and forth, faster and faster, until she came, thrashing wildly on the table.

"Yes!" she screamed. "Don't stop. Keep fucking me!"

Holding her down with one hand, Hunter leaned over and licked her clit, as he continued to pump the bottle into her. He sucked on the fleshy bud of nerves, drawing it between his lips.

"Oh, Hunter!" she screamed and came again.

He couldn't take any more. He eased the bottle's neck out of her pussy and yanked down his zipper.

Ronni reached out to touch him. "I need your cock. Now!"

He grabbed her wrists. He leaned over her, pushing her arms down to the table. "You're about to get it, baby. But I'll do the touching. You just lie there and come." He pushed his dick inside her rougher than intended, but he was crazy with lust.

"Yes!" She lifted her hips to accommodate him.

Hunter closed his eyes at the sensation of her tight flesh wrapped around him. She was so hot, so wet, and so eager for him. He pushed deep inside her, and a jolt of pure pleasure rocked him to the core.

She pulled her arms from his grasp, then reached down and clawed at his ass, wrapping her legs around him. "Hard! Hard!"

His fingers curled over her tits, and he squeezed her flesh, pinching her nipples. "Ronni... Geez!" Totally consumed by desire, he pounded her pussy, unable to hold back. He came inside her, moaning her name. He'd spent what felt like a lifetime looking for someone like her. Ronni's pussy contracted and milked his dick until she'd completely drained his body.

He collapsed, covering her trembling body.

"Oh, Hunter." She trailed her fingers up and down his back. "That was incredible."

He realized that she was shaking from coming again. She was phenomenal. "Ronni, *you* are incredible." Now that he'd found this woman, he never intended to let her go.

Epilogue

Valentine's Day, One Year Later
Not Only In Your Dreams Resort
Bondage Bay #12

Ronni stood looking out at the sun setting over the lake. Still as breathtaking as the first time she had seen it. While she waited for Hunter to come out of the bathroom, she smoothed her hands down the deep blue dress that she'd purchased especially for this trip. *Everlasting Love* had finally acquired the vacation resort, and they were here to see to some last details.

The acquisition had taken a lot longer than expected, but the Board of Directors wanted it done right to make sure the company's reputation wouldn't be tarnished. The "playground for adults" spin she and Hunter had put on it had finally convinced the Board that they could sell these erotic vacations to their customers without compromising their more romantic image.

She was glad they'd finally agreed. She feared their erotic toy division might be at stake, and her position, too, if they decided to pull back on erotic products. Now, she was due for a promotion to take over the entire erotic line, which was a job she looked forward to getting. Testing out the new products had proven a great side benefit for her and Hunter. Her new position, if she got it, would also put her in charge of the erotic vacations, erotic greeting card line, and a segment of the lingerie division.

The door to the bathroom opened. Hunter strolled out, perfectly dressed in a black suit.

"You look good enough to eat," Ronni said, a smile spreading across her face.

"I'll quote you on that later tonight."

If they didn't get going soon, later would come sooner than expected. "So, where are we going for dinner?"

"Right here."

"Here? In the room?"

"Yep."

"We got all dressed up to order room service?" She could have been comfy in her underwear—and had Hunter tied to the bed by now.

"It's a special occasion."

Oh, he was trying to be romantic. That was nice. After a year together, they'd settled into a nice life with great sex, but sometimes the actual romance took a backseat to the realities of the day. "Valentine's Day is special. You're right."

"That, too."

Too? Now she was perplexed. "Um, our one year anniversary of seeing each other." That must be it. And it was so sweet of him to want to make it special.

"That, too."

Hmm. "Okay, I give up. What are you talking about?"

Hunter took her hand and interlaced their fingers. He dropped to one knee and took a small black box out of his pocket.

Ronni's breath caught. She gripped Hunter's hand tightly.

He flipped open the box with his thumb to reveal an oval diamond atop a gold band. "I love you, Ronni. I can't live without you. Will you marry me?"

Her heart pounded, and tears rolled down her cheeks. She'd dreamed of this moment, but was afraid Hunter would never be ready to marry again.

"Please say something. You're scaring me, Ronni," he choked out. "Are those good tears? I can never tell."

She barely managed to find her voice. "Yes, Hunter. They're good tears. I love you. And, yes, I'll marry you."

A smile spread across his face, and joy leapt into his eyes. He released her hand long enough to take the ring out of the box and slip it on her finger. "I love you so much." He stood up and pulled her into his arms. "Happy Valentine's Day, my love."

She choked back a sigh. This was a fantasy come true. "Happy Valentine's Day."

Last Valentine's Day was a day of discovery and wonder for her. This Valentine's Day was the beginning of a new life with the man she loved.

She glanced over at the armoire. "I wonder what toys they have waiting for us this time."

About the author:

Ruth D. Kerce got hooked on writing in the fifth grade when she won a short story contest—a romance, of course. And she's been writing romance ever since.

She writes several subgenres of romance—historical, contemporary, and futuristic. Her books are available online in many internet bookstores. Her short stories and articles are available on several websites. She has won or placed in writing contests and hopes to continue to write exciting tales for years to come.

You can visit her website at http://www.ruthkerce.com for free short stories and excerpts, or email her at RDKerce@aol.com—she loves to hear from fans.

Ruth welcomes mail from readers. You can write to her c/o Ellora's Cave Publishing at 1056 Home Avenue, Arkon OH 44310-3502.

Also by Ruth D. Kerce:

Xylon Warriors I: Initiation

Diamond In the Snow

Diana Hunter

Chapter One

"All right, everyone. Last bus just called in. All the kids are safely home. You're dismissed…and drive carefully! See you tomorrow. Maybe."

Carolyn Brooks had her coat on at the first sound of the monitor's crackle. By the time the principal finished speaking, her hat and scarf were in place and her gloves in hand. Snuggling her laptop into its black cloth case and slinging it over her shoulder, she scooped up the pile of uncorrected papers and dropped them into the outside sleeve of the case before heading out of her classroom.

All down the hall, teachers emerged. Some grinned, some threw worried glances at the snow falling fast and furious outside the school's windows.

"Couldn't have cancelled school when we're all still home, could he?" Carolyn turned, the voice belonged to one of the school's known grouches. Another voice assented and Carolyn felt obliged to speak up. "You know how it is around here. With lake effect, one town could be buried, and another five miles away not get even so much as a flake."

"He knew, just as we all did, that there was a very good chance of it hitting us today."

Carolyn shrugged and kept walking. Having been through administrator training, she knew the weight of the decision the superintendent faced when snow was forecast. Cancel, and parents scrambled to find daycare for their kids. If it snowed heavily, you were a hero. Cancel and have the storm miss you? Grumbling parents were much worse than a few grouchy teachers.

"Well, none of us have crystal balls," she thought to herself as she brushed six inches of new snow off her car. And it was falling faster now. Latest weather report had warned of at least an inch an hour. They'd been in school almost four before the busses collected the kids, and another two waiting for the all clear. Looked like the weather guys got it right.

By the time she finished brushing off the back window, the front one was covered again. At least the rear defogger was doing its work. Getting in, she set the wipers to clearing a spot for her to see by and put the gear in first. The tires spun as she tried to climb out of her parking space over the pile of snow. The six inches of snow on the ground plus the six she'd brushed off made quite a mound around her little island of a car.

But then someone pushed her from behind and she was clear. Glancing in her rear mirror, she saw two of the male teachers grinning and waving as she slowly drove through the narrow strip the school's plow had been able to clear. Honking once as a thank you, she drove into the storm.

*****

"Damn it!"

Carolyn slammed on both the brakes and clutch, desperately trying to downshift and steer at the same time as a huge buck bounded across the snowy road. She got as far as third before the front corner of her bumper tagged the hind leg of the magnificent deer, sending her into a spin across the slippery surface. Without thinking, she changed tactics, steering into the spin. But keeping two hands on the wheel and one on the stick was a feat worthy of a prestidigitator. Her sleight of hand wasn't up to par; the engine stalled.

"Damn power assist!" she shouted as the wheel locked up on her. Out of the corner of her eye, she saw a snowbank approaching. Although she ducked more out of a sense of self-preservation than anything else, her body still flew left and then right as the driver's side of her car buried itself in the soft snow.

Quiet descended and Carolyn blinked several times as her brain tried to register what had just happened. Automatically, she turned off the already stalled engine, dropping the keys into her coat pocket even as she mentally checked all her parts. No injuries.

Her father's warnings of old sounded in her head. "In any accident, get out of the car immediately. You never know what damage has occurred to the gas line." Had she done any damage to the line? Almost in a panic, she clawed at her seatbelt with one hand while fumbling for the door handle on the other. Why wouldn't the damn door open? The seatbelt went flinging past her face, but the door remained shut.

Carolyn held a long-standing pride in her ability to handle any situation. A ten-year veteran of the elementary grades, she dealt with bloody noses, missing backpacks, wet pants and even arguing divorced parents with a calm aplomb that won her the respect of fellow teachers and parents alike.

"Unflappable and capable" her principal had written on her end-of-the-year report last June. So why was she now pounding on the door like a deranged lunatic?

Because enclosed spaces always made her nervous. Ever since she was a child and had locked herself in a trunk, she had suffered from the phobia.

Just as it had when she was little, time stopped again. The snowbank rose against the door, preventing her from opening it. In her welling panic, she frantically rolled down the window. A scream formed, and she fought it down. She was an adult now, no child to scream at phantoms. Scrambling to kneel on the seat, she stuck her head out the open window, her eyes closed as she fought to breathe.

* * * * *

Paul Anderson followed the car ahead of him as it pulled out of the parking lot. The woman in the car was one of the elementary teachers, but even while one corner of his mind searched for her name, the majority of his thoughts centered on the sight of her brushing off her car wearing that short little winter jacket that was more for show than warmth.

He supposed a gentleman would have offered to help, but in truth, he was no gentleman. Women wanted equal rights, then they could brush the snow off their own cars. Besides, he was having too much fun watching the way her ass filled out those slacks. Every time she reached forward, she came up on her toes and her pants stretched across an ass he would definitely not mind getting to know. Driving down the road, he imagined that ass naked on his bed, raised to receive the flogging he so longed to give. Ashamed of the thought, he squashed it down as he tried to figure out just whose beautiful ass he admired.

With her hat pulled down around her ears and a scarf covering the rest of her face, he had to fill in the blanks with his memory. Problem was, he didn't see her often enough for the details to stick in his head. Each year the entire district faculty met on the first day of school. Since he taught in the high school building, this was often the only chance he had to meet the rest of his teaching partners. Several years earlier the district had gone to a unified campus, which simply meant all the separate buildings were now located in one central court. Territorial wars, however, still reigned. The elementary teachers resented the middle school teachers telling them what to teach, the middle school teachers, in turn, resented the high school teachers. As head of the high school English department, he was often on the receiving end of many dirty looks from those who perceived his comments as directives.

Red brake lights suddenly lit up in front of him; lights that first swung right and then left as the car crossed the road to bury itself in a high snowdrift. This was a little-used back road, and Paul suddenly realized that perhaps today the two of them should have remained on the better-plowed main roads.

Letting the antilock brakes do their work, he slowed his own car and put on his hazards. The wind had kicked up and snow swirled around him as he got out of his car, listening for oncoming traffic, since visibility was so poor. Nothing but the silence of snow…and the pounding of the woman on the window of her car.

"Hey!" he called out to her, but obviously she couldn't hear him. By the time he trotted across the snow-filled road and opened her passenger door, the woman was halfway out of her window.

"What are you doing? Come out this way."

She turned and stared at him, uncomprehending. Unconsciously, he went into teacher-mode, his voice soft and calming as he realized her panic. "You're okay. You just need to climb over the seat and come out this door. Your door is blocked. But this one isn't. See?"

He backed out of the door, keeping his eye on the scared woman. Flitting through his mind went the thought that her eyes were brown…and she was beautiful.

There wasn't time for such off-topic thoughts. The woman had come back into the car, but hadn't yet moved to leave. Her breath came in heavy gasps; her coat, buttoned against the cold, heaved with each one.

"Come on, Miss…" Damn! Why could he not remember her name?

"Brooks." Her voice was breathy. He watched as she closed her eyes; her jaw set and she forced them open again, this time focusing on his face. "Brooks, Carolyn Brooks." The hand she held out to him shook, but her voice was steadying. "I'm all right. I'm not hurt."

Paul took her hand and pulled gently as he shook her hand. Keeping her hand in his, she climbed out of the car to stand in the wind and the snow. Paul watched her movements, looking for any sign of injury, but the petite woman seemed to be fine. Physically fine, anyway. The way she kept clenching her fists inside the leather driving gloves clued him in to the fact that she was still shaken up by the turn of events.

The woman's eyes, round and still a bit unfocused, looked dark compared to the paleness of her skin. No makeup enhanced her beauty; Paul decided she didn't need any. There was a natural redness to those slim, perfectly shaped lips that made them look as if they had just been kissed. Her rather thin nose canted straight down to the tip; nothing pug about it. Yet it had a charm of its own and he wondered if its arrow-straightness might be a clue to her personality. He didn't know what grade she taught, but if the stereotypes were true, then she taught one of the lower grades.

Carolyn took a deep breath and used the biting cold and stinging wind to dull the edges of her panic attack. Her head clearing, she took a good look at the man who had stopped to help her. She had to look up into the swirling snow to see his face several feet above her. A knit cap covered his head, and a neatly trimmed beard stood in for a scarf. A dark beard now covered with snow and frost. Realizing some of his tall height came from the fact that he stood above her on the hill made her feel a little less like a naughty child caught in her own incompetence. But then Carolyn recognized him as one of the high school teachers who always made her feel inferior. As if teaching elementary school was nothing more than sand tables and finger-paints. And now he had witnessed her panic attack. The man must think her a complete idiot.

"Thank you." She could not keep the frost out of her voice. "I don't believe there was any damage, other than what the deer might have done to my bumper, so once I can get out of the drift, I'll be fine."

He had to give her credit for spunk, even if she was completely wrong. Still, best not to say that out loud. "Is that what happened? There was a deer?"

She nodded even as she moved to the front of the car to inspect the damage. But snow covered the entire front of the car, and more kept falling. Already the hood had a half-inch of light, fresh snow and twilight was coming. Her shoulders sagged. This needed a tow truck.

Even as she dug her cell phone out of her pocket, she knew there would be no signal here. Damn back road. What had she been thinking? She knew to stick to main roads in a blizzard. The blank screen of her phone confirmed her guess and she dropped it back into her pocket.

Paul didn't bother to check his. He knew there was only one course of action. While he might not be a gentleman, he also wasn't a cad. He called out to her over the increasing wind.

"Let's get your window rolled up and lock up the car. I can give you a ride home. It's getting worse."

Briefly she considered refusing, but another blast of arctic air made up her mind. Although she wore winter boots, they were no match for the depth of snow and already her toes were cold. The short pea coat was warm enough, but didn't cover her legs; her thin slacks wouldn't keep her warm at all. Accepting his offer was the better option. Nodding her assent, she picked up her laptop from the passenger floor and stared at the driver's seat, now covered in a fine layer of wet snow. Setting the laptop down again, she knelt on the seat to reach for the window crank. Understanding that the car was not about to explode gave her the courage she needed to roll it up and back out without another panic attack.

Paul quickly scooped the junk from his front seat and dumped it into the back to clear a space for her. Almost demurely she seated herself, pretending not to see the McDonald's bags littering the car. As he started the car and pulled away from hers, she glanced back to be sure it was not in any danger. It wasn't. Completely off the road and now covered with snow, she wondered if she'd see it again before spring.

"My name's Paul. Paul Anderson." Since he hadn't remembered her name, he decided she might be in similar straits.

She wasn't. "I know. Thank you for your help, Mr. Anderson."

He laughed and she was surprised at the rich baritone sound. "Please," he begged as he slowed for a particularly nasty curve, "only my students are allowed to call me that. I'm Paul."

She smiled. "Well, then, thank you, Paul. I'm Carolyn. But I told you that, didn't I?"

Out of the corner of his eye, Paul saw her pull off her winter hat and run a hand over her dark gold ponytail, smoothing it into place. His answer was cut off when the car started to slip; he found himself thankful for antilock brakes a second time. The plows evidently had given up on the deep snow of the back roads. At least eight inches of the stuff was under the tires and they still had three miles to go to get back to a main road.

"Where do you live, Carolyn?"

She sighed. "Small town called Phelps. I'm sure that's out of your way, so you can drop me at the nearest gas station and I'll call for a tow truck from there."

He spared an incredulous glance at her. "What kind of a louse do think I am? I'm not leaving you at a gas station. Besides, there's no truck driver in his right mind that's coming out in this weather. I can hardly see as it is."

Carolyn hadn't been paying attention to the worsening storm. She'd been much too conscious of the handsome man beside her. He'd also pulled off his cap in the car, tousling his light brown hair in a most rakish manner. Did he know it made him more attractive? She barely knew him. So why did she have the sudden urge to smooth it down?

But at his mention of the storm, she turned her attention out the front window. Less than twenty feet visibility. After that, a wall of white obscured their vision. "There's no way we'll make it to Phelps in this. You have to take me to a garage."

"I'm taking you home. To my place."

In spite of the no-nonsense tone of his voice, Carolyn felt obliged to protest. He held up his hand to forestall her. "I can't take you all the way to Phelps. This is the turn to the main road, and look, I can barely see past the intersection."

It was true. The world was closing. If this wasn't the worst of it, then there was a good chance she'd end up in another snowdrift. The thought gave her the grace to accept his invitation.

"How far do you live from here?"

His grin was more a grimace as he eased the car onto the main road. Even here, the plows seemed to have given up and inches of snow covered the pavement. Only the telephone poles at the side of the road guided him as he drove at a crawl towards home.

"Not far."

The answer was terse, but Carolyn saw the lines of concentration that creased his face. He was worried and didn't want to say so. That was all right. She understood the need to appear calm in a crisis. As long as she didn't have another attack, she could maintain the same façade.

* * * * *

Paul didn't so much drive the car into his driveway as slide it in. Actually he guessed at the approximate location of the drive, gunned the motor to get over the hump of snow at the bottom of the drive and slammed on the brakes when the house came dangerously close. Too bad the place didn't come with a garage. He didn't relish having to dig out later.

Carolyn tried to get an idea of what the house looked like, but dusk had fallen and the world was a blur of grey and white. She felt Paul's hand in hers and she let him lead her along a path only he knew existed. The deep snow soaked her legs; her wet pants clung to her and any warmth she had in the car disappeared.

Leading her in through the back door wasn't the best way to make a good impression on her, Paul realized as he kicked aside an old boot in the mudroom. Skis and poles stood in the corner, a bag of trash ready for the landfill beside them. But then they were through into the kitchen—a safer place. Until Paul flipped on the light and remembered the three days worth of dirty dishes piled next to the sink.

"I suppose it's a sexist comment to make, but I'm guessing there's no 'Mrs. Anderson'?"

He shook his head and smiled ruefully. "No. And I'm not usually so much of a slob. Got involved in another project and let the housework slide, I'm afraid."

She had not moved far into the kitchen. Far from looking like the stereotypical bachelor pad kitchen, the room's tasteful decorations made the place quite homey. Not much in the way of knickknacks, but clean and simple lines. Hunter green throw rugs on the floor offset the light cream walls; checked curtains at the windows picked up both colors. Glass front cupboards above showed neat rows of glassware and dishes stacked by size. Without looking, she knew the pots and pans below would be neatly ordered as well.

In spite of the warmth of the house, she shivered in her wet slacks. Paul saw her shoulders shake and shook his head. Some host he was. So embarrassed about his dishes, he forgot simple things. Like not letting your guest get pneumonia.

"Here, come into the living room. There's a gas fireplace there. I'll turn it on and you can warm up in front of it."

"My boots are still on. Let me just…" Her voice trailed off as she toed off each boot and sighed. Of course. Her big toe stuck out through a hole it had carved in her stocking…and her dress shoes were still back in her car, stuck in a snowdrift.

Paul saw her grimace and looked down. Such dainty feet. He laughed as he saw her toe glaring through the hole. No nail polish, he noted, and wondered if she wore it in the summer. He glanced at her hands. Pale pink polish glimmered on shapely nails at the end of long, slender fingers. Reaching out, he took her hand, stifling an inner sigh. This one was too delicate for his demons.

"This is an ice cube! C'mon." Paul pulled her into the living room, warming her tiny hands in his big mitts. In seconds, he had the gas fireplace on and its soft light filled the darkened room. "Sit right here."

Carolyn felt his caring warm her insides as her skin began to thaw. When his hand enfolded hers in the kitchen, her first instinct had been to pull back. She barely knew this guy. She'd seen him at meetings on occasion, yes. Yet that was a far cry from knowing what sort of man he was. But Paul hadn't given her time to protest before pulling her into the darkened room. And he didn't expect her to protest when he commanded her to sit before the fire, either.

So she sat. In the firelight, she saw the concern on his face as he bent to feel her toes. The touch of his hand warmed her and her stomach fluttered. She dampened the thought immediately. She had come to an understanding of what she was, and there was no way the head of the English department was going to find out. With an effort, she did not pull away, but let him check for frostbite. Stockings did not give much protection from a boot full of snow.

"Your feet are freezing, too. Better get rid of those wet clothes. Take them off and I'll find you something to wear."

Before she could tell him she was already drying, he had disappeared into the shadows. Light shone in from the kitchen, but it did not extend all the way across the room, and he vanished into the gloom like a specter.

Carolyn considered. His bossy tone should have gotten her back up. Ever since he'd pulled her out of the car, he had been telling her what to do and she had been doing it. Like a little child who couldn't think for herself. She tried to get angry with him for it, but the problem was, every one of his "orders" were right on target. If she had stayed with the car, she would be stuck there all night long...and who knew how long into tomorrow. And her feet were cold. And her clothes were wet. Nothing he had said was out of the ordinary. Yet something pulled at the back of her mind...

Okay, she should take off her wet pants and pantyhose. Still Carolyn hesitated. To strip off the wet clothes would leave her wearing nothing but her panties from the waist down. She couldn't just sit here, half naked, and wait for his return.

She chewed on her lower lip as she stood and surveyed what she could see of the room. With her back to the fire, she felt the heat warming her rear end and stood still for several moments, simply enjoying the heat and staring at the chair she had just vacated. A crocheted afghan folded against the back was just what she needed.

"Perfect!"

The word fell into the empty room and Carolyn wondered where Paul had gotten himself, even as she was glad he took his time. Quickly, she stripped off the pants and ruined pantyhose, using the afghan to both dry her legs and then cover herself as she sat again in the overstuffed chair.

*****

Paul rummaged through a plastic bag on the floor of his bedroom. He'd cleaned out his drawers and closet weeks ago, but kept forgetting to take the bags of clothes that he no longer wanted down to the church drop-off box. Now he was glad he'd forgotten, as he remembered a pair of sweatpants that were too small for him. He'd bought them last spring when winter clothes were on sale and hadn't discovered 'til this past fall that someone had mismarked a pair of short-legged sweatpants as "talls". Too late to take them back, he had simply thrown them in one of these blasted bags.

"Ah-ha! Found you little suckers." He pulled out the short pair of navy blue sweats and held them up. Probably still too long for that diminutive woman in the other room. God, but she was cute. He didn't normally go for cute…his tastes ran to drop-dead gorgeous and he'd had his share of them. Unfortunately, his private demons made them all run screaming into the night. But there was something about this woman. Something that pulled at the demon he kept locked inside.

Once in the kitchen with the light on and her hat off, Paul had gotten a better look at her. Still cute. Probably not more than twenty-five. And he was an old man of thirty-one. Paul shook his head. The ass he'd studied in the parking lot was definitely a spankable one. He thought of the feel of her tiny hand in his and pushed the demon down. Time to rein in those thoughts; this one was too young and too delicate. Mentally, he threw her back.

Digging through the bags once more in search of a sweatshirt that she could wear, he came up empty-handed. He didn't wear sweatshirts as a rule. T-shirts, yes. And a long-sleeve, button-down shirt over them. But sweatshirts were just too warm for him.

With a start he remembered his sister's Christmas gift to him just last month. Dragging open a drawer, he found the red sweatshirt with the white heart glaring like a bull's-eye on the front. The words "Be mine" blazoned a path underneath the heart. His sister had a sick sense of humor. Had told him to wear it on Valentine's Day and maybe he'd get a date.

He hefted it in his hand and started out the door. It was more a girl's shirt, he decided. If it fit her, Carolyn could have it. Then he could safely tell his sister he hadn't given it away to charity, but had given it to a girl. He grinned at the look he envisioned on his sister's face. There was no need to tell her it was just an emergency shirt and nothing more.

"Found some dry clothes for you." He hurried into the living room and stopped at the sight that met his eyes.

Carolyn had taken down her ponytail, letting her dark golden hair spread over her shoulders. It waved and curled around to frame her face, her cheeks still reddened from the cold. Mischievous, sultry eyes gazed steadily into his; his mother's old multicolored afghan pulled up to her chin. Not an inch of her showed, yet Paul had the distinct impression there was not a stitch of clothing on that sure-to-be-beautiful body.

His mouth hung open. Carolyn tried very hard not to giggle and didn't succeed. She couldn't help herself. Flipping her hair over her shoulder and fixing a pouty smile on her lips, she purred, "Haven't you ever seen a woman before?"

He shook his head, trying to clear his thoughts. His eye fell on the kitchen chair that had been pulled up to the fire. The thought of this woman going to the kitchen totally naked, getting a chair and bringing it in to the fire to dry her clothes on, all while he was rummaging for clothes, gave him a hard-on. A good, old-fashioned hard-as-an-anvil, erect-as-a-flagpole hard-on.

Carolyn chewed her lip again, suddenly thinking she had perhaps gone too far. Not everyone appreciated her sense of humor. She let the blanket drop although she couldn't help grinning at his gasp. Her blouse, still completely buttoned, covered her from the waist up.

"Sorry. I shouldn't play like that. You don't know me and might get the wrong impression."

Paul doubted his impression was incorrect. She was a tease. He understood that now. He tossed the sweats at her without a word, dropping his rehearsed explanation for the shirt. "I'll put the water on while you change," he tossed over his shoulder as he headed into the kitchen without another look at her.

"Damn." Carolyn muttered a few other choice words under her breath as she pulled on the pants. He had taken her Hollywood siren for real and now was mad that she wasn't one. Not a good way to start this enforced togetherness.

The pants were a little long, but the elastic at the bottom would keep her from tripping over them. She held up the red sweatshirt and saw the heart. It still had that brand-new feel to it, so she surmised he had never worn it. Turning it toward the firelight, she read the words under the white heart. "Be Mine." Was this a gift from a girlfriend that he'd hidden in a drawer? Come to think of it, Carolyn realized, she had no idea as to this senior teacher's personal life.

Folding the sweatshirt, she laid it on the back of the chair. She just didn't feel comfortable wearing it. What if it was from a former girlfriend and would remind him of her? And why should she care if it did? Running her finger idly over the visible part of the heart, she sighed. Valentine's Day was less than a week away and she had no one special in her life. Hadn't had anyone for quite some time now. Tilting her head, she considered Paul. A bossy know-it-all who made her feel like a child? No, her plain old white button-down blouse would do just fine.

A pole lamp stood beside a couch positioned against the far wall of the living room. But she didn't turn it on. There was something very soothing about a room lit only by the light of a gas fire. Kneeling on the couch, she pulled back the curtains and stared at the winter storm outside.

Wind still buffeted the house with sudden gusts that kicked up small tornadoes of snow and sent them scurrying across the street outside. She supposed there must be other houses nearby, but could not see them in the storm. Might as well face it. She was not getting home tonight. With a sigh, she dropped the curtain and headed for the kitchen.

"Mind if I make a phone call?"

Paul glanced up from the stove, where he adjusted the flame under the teakettle. He nodded toward the phone on the back wall near the door where they'd entered and Carolyn crossed the room to pick up the receiver. He noted she wore the pants but not the shirt. Frowning, he hoped she didn't think he meant anything by it.

He knew polite behavior dictated he leave the room so she could have privacy for her call. He didn't feel like being polite. Instead, he got two cups out of the cupboard and pulled out a tin of teabags and a carton of powdered cocoa mix. He'd give her her choice when she got off the phone.

"Dad? Yes, I'm fine. But I'm not going to make it home tonight. The car's in a snowbank...it's fine. I bumped a deer. No, I really am fine. I'm at a friend's house and I knew you'd worry. Dad, I'm fine. I'm spending the night here and will deal with the car in the morning. It's not going anywhere. Yes, I know the number for the tow truck.

"Okay, Dad. I'll be careful." There was a pause and Paul glanced at her, concerned. But Carolyn only smiled at him before speaking again. "Yes, Dad. I love you, too."

She hung up the phone and turned to him. "I'll pay you for the long-distance call."

His brow furrowed as he spooned cocoa into his cup. "It isn't a long-distance call from here to Phelps."

She laughed, the first real laugh he'd heard from her. A deep-throated laugh that showed she was relaxing in his company.

"My father doesn't live in Phelps. He lives in Florida."

Paul stared at her, trying to understand the enigma before him. There was no doubt in his mind. Tease or no, this woman had surprised him several times now. And women rarely surprised him.

"My mom died just after Thanksgiving. I'm an only child, so I'm all my father has now. We talk just for a few minutes every night." She gestured to the cups. "I'll have cocoa, too, if I may?"

Startled, he turned back to filling the cups with the premixed powder and pouring water. Out of habit, he only filled them two-thirds full, filling them the rest of the way with milk to cool it down. His mind turned over the fact that this very cute woman, who managed tiny little rugrats all day long, who could be a vixen one moment and a "normal" woman the next, was also a woman who cared long-distance for a lonely father. Which was the real woman? Or was each side a piece of a very complicated puzzle? And why was he even thinking these thoughts? Damn it, she was getting under his skin and he didn't like it one bit.

Paul stirred the cups and picked them up. Holding hers out, he noted how slender her fingers were as they took the cup from him, cradling it between her hands as if she were still cold.

Carolyn accepted the mug, careful not to let her fingers touch his. He scared her enough as it was. Standing beside him now, she realized he really was almost a foot taller than her. And teachers who taught high school always made her feel inferior. Two strikes against him. She dropped her eyes and studied the rim of the cup as she took a sip, considering her own sexual proclivities. Men in the past always thought her crazy or tried to take advantage of her when she told them what she liked. No, her own desires pitched the third strike. No matter how handsome he was, no matter how polite and noble in bringing her home with him, he was not for her. If only he didn't look so damn sexy…

"How about we go sit in front of the fire for a while?" He nodded toward the door; she had an odd look in her eye, as if she were weighing him on some scale known only to women. He hated that look. Always felt he must come in somewhere near the bottom. Every relationship he'd ever had ended in disaster; he wanted too much, too fast. He liked having the last word. And then there was…no. Better to head this one off before she got started.

He saw the sweatshirt neatly folded on the back of the easy chair; he didn't blame her for not wanting to wear it. Ugly thing. Never should have tried to pawn it off on her. But then his thoughts were distracted by the easy way she folded into the chair, one leg tucked up underneath her, the other swinging casually in front. She leaned to one side and rested her head on the wing of the out-of-date piece of furniture, and the thought ran through his head how much she looked like she just "fit" there.

"Let me get the light." He ignored her little sound of protest. He did not like at all the direction his thoughts were heading. No romantic lighting. Bright lights. That's what they needed.

The light showed Carolyn a room less tastefully decorated than the kitchen. Early Garage Sale period, she decided. The overstuffed chair she snuggled into did not match the sofa, which did not match a recliner in the corner or the smaller chair he now slid across the floor to share in the fire's heat. No two tables in the room matched, either; nor was there even a unifying color to bring the pieces together. Definitely Early Garage Sale. Male Early Garage Sale at that.

Paul sat and sipped his cocoa, at a loss for words. He wasn't sure how to proceed with a woman who, under other circumstances, he would have no qualms about wooing. But this was a teaching colleague, they both had reputations to worry about, and besides, he didn't want her complaining about his hospitality during the storm. He could just see it now, being called into the Superintendent's office on charges of misconduct with a fellow teacher…where he was at fault for taking advantage of her during unseasonable weather.

Nope. He wasn't going there. He'd just sit here and drink his cocoa and be boring.

Carolyn wondered at his protracted silence. She smiled. His weak smile in return showed his unease. Had she said something wrong? He had seemed so easygoing in the kitchen. But now he was buttoned up tight as if a sudden draft had chilled him to the bone.

Figures, she thought to herself. *Just as I relax, he tightens up.* She sighed and closed her eyes to hide the pain the irony brought.

Her parents had been so much in love. All her life she had watched the two of them, their *pas de deux* well-rehearsed with years of familiarity. And now her father danced solo. Separated by over a thousand miles, Carolyn was glad he was so far away. Otherwise she knew he would transfer the love and caring energy he'd had for his wife, to love and caring for his daughter. And she was so lonely, she would let him.

No, it was better he was down south where both of them could make a life without Mom.

Paul glanced over at her and saw her open her eyes to stare into the gas flames. They shone with tears, and with sudden insight, he understood she still grieved for her mother.

"I lost my mom about five years ago," he volunteered, careful not to make eye contact. "Car accident," he added when he saw her start of surprise. Keeping his eyes neutral, he looked at her, judging her emotional state.

"I'm sorry, Paul. It must have been very hard on you to have her go so quickly. Not even a chance to say goodbye."

"Actually, it was the way she wanted to go. Always said, 'I want my death to be quick. No muss, no fuss. Here one minute, gone the next'." He smiled to show her it was okay for her to laugh at his imitation of his mom.

Carolyn couldn't laugh. Not yet. But she smiled out of politeness, since it was obvious he was trying to help.

"My mom died of pneumonia; complications from diabetes. She knew…heck, we all knew she wasn't going to bounce back from this one. So many times she cheated death…just not this time."

"Even after all this time, I still miss my mom. You'll find it easier to bear, but every once in a while, it sneaks up on you and you go all to pieces. At least, I do." He couldn't look at her. What had prompted him to make such an admission? Those tears were shed in private; why was he telling this stranger?

Carolyn studied his face for signs of artifice and saw only open vulnerability. He covered his lapse by draining the last dregs from his cup, but she had seen enough. Enough to know there was more to him than her professionalism would allow her to know.

He stood suddenly, the vulnerable child hidden again. He could not let that happen again. What was there about her that made him want to share all his secrets?

"If you're done, I'll take your mug to the kitchen." He knew his voice was rough, but didn't try to soften it.

Carolyn tilted her cup and forced a smile to her lips. "All done!" She handed over the mug. Their fingers touched and the world went black.

Chapter Two

"Well, so much for the house tour I was about to propose!"

Carolyn's eyes blinked several times, adjusting to the sudden loss of light. The fire still glimmered and after a moment, she could see Paul standing there, both cups in his hands and a grin on his face. On safe ground again, she grinned back.

"Got any candles?"

"Are you kidding?" Paul turned and headed to the kitchen, moving partly from the small light of the fire and partly from memory. "I'm a high school teacher. I buy everything those kids sell to support band, art club, new cheerleading uniforms, the freshmen class, the sophomore class and the junior class!"

Laughing, Carolyn called after him. "What, you don't buy from the senior class?"

"Seniors don't sell stuff. Only magazines at the beginning of the year. Perk of being a senior." He came back, two jar candles alight in his hands. Setting one on each of the small tables, he returned to his chair. "Don't tell me you've never been approached by a senior selling magazines!"

"Nope. Never."

"Well, that will change. I run the darn thing and every year I tell them to be sure to hit up…er…offer magazines to every teacher in the district."

Carolyn laughed again, the same easy laugh she felt in the kitchen. School was probably a safer topic for them…as long as he didn't try to tell her how to run her classroom.

He didn't. For the next two hours they talked shop, exchanging stories from both ends of the educational spectrum.

He shared his frustrations with parents who had given up; she shared her techniques for getting parents involved. She shared her joy when a student learned to read; he shared his excitement when a student gained a love of literature.

Only when one of the small candles guttered and went out did they notice the time.

"Oh, my! It's almost seven already." Carolyn smiled and realized she was getting hungry.

"Humph! So much for the twenty-four-hour candle that was supposed to be." Paul stood and stretched. They needed to think about supper, he supposed, making a mental run through the food stored in his larder.

Carolyn also stood, walking to the window to peer into the darkness beyond. She closed the curtain again with a sigh. "Can't see a darn thing. I don't even know if it's still snowing."

"Let's check."

"What?"

"Come on, let's check." Paul crossed the room to the front door and turned the lock, yanking it open. "Bring the candle over here."

Carolyn picked up the glass candle from the bottom; the sides were too hot from the flame; deftly she crossed the room as if she'd been walking with only a candle for guidance all her life. Paul pushed on the storm door, intending to step onto the stoop, but the door did not budge.

"Uh-oh." He peered out the door, but it was still too dark to see. Taking the candle from her, he held it low. Against the glass at the bottom was a wall of white. He moved the candle up, still white. Further, still white. A drift of snow buried half of the door.

"Not getting out this way."

Panic clutched at Carolyn and she fought it down. There was still a back door. Trying to keep her voice steady, she questioned him about it.

Paul remembered the look of utter panic she'd had in the car. Was she claustrophobic? He wasn't too fond of it himself. Always wanted a way out. But it didn't bother him the way it apparently bothered her.

"Come on. Let's go see about the back."

She followed closely, no longer quite as assured as she had been.

The drift here was less, only about a foot and a half. Enough to make him realize he'd better go out and shovel. He held the candle out the door; the snow was still falling.

"Better to shovel it now and clear a path." He reached for his boots.

"I'll help."

"No, you won't. You'll stay in here where it's warm and dry."

"I'm perfectly capable of shoveling a walk, Paul."

"I know you are; I'm not saying you aren't. Don't worry, I'm not being chivalrous, only practical. Get those sweats wet and I don't have anything else for you to wear. Besides," he added as he saw her resolve weakening, "I'm going to need another cup of cocoa when I come in." He pulled on his coat, ignoring the fact it wasn't quite dry. "The matches are on the table; you'll have to light the stovetop."

He pushed out the door before she could protest.

Carolyn shut the inside door, checking carefully to be sure it wasn't locked. One candle did not give a whole lot of light. She'd feel better maneuvering around a foreign kitchen if she could see better.

The matches were easy enough to find; lighting a stove didn't bother her at all. She remembered when her grandmother's old stove finally wore out and the old woman was forced to get a new one. How she complained about the awful clicking sound of the new electronic ignition, and how she didn't see what was so hard about lighting a stovetop with a little match.

Immersed in her memories, Carolyn lit the flame and set the teapot on top of the stove. Enough water remained from their first cups; it was still warm. Probably the water would be ready before he finished clearing a path.

The thought calmed her. No need to get all antsy about being closed in, she told herself. Paul was out there right now taking care of the matter. Somehow the thought of a man taking charge not once, but twice in one day should upset her. Since her parents moved away two years ago, she had shown herself to be perfectly capable of handling every emergency.

Until today. She knew full well where her fear of being closed in came from. Although she didn't remember the specific incident, her mother used to recount the story with tears in her eyes of the time Carolyn crawled into the antique trunk her parents had just brought home. She couldn't have been more than four; just the age when kids get curious about the world around them. Apparently she had fallen into the trunk and the lid slammed shut. It didn't lock, but the little girl wasn't strong enough to lift the lid, if she even understood that was what she needed to do. According to her mother's telling, Carolyn was in the trunk no more than five minutes…an eternity to a four year old. Ever since then, closed spaces had become her phobia.

To take her mind off her memories and the panic that threatened to rise, Carolyn went exploring through the cupboards for more candles. The one on the table still burned brightly, but if it were the only one, they might have a problem.

She found dozens of them. Apparently Paul was a soft touch when it came to buying from students. Two shelves, solidly packed with all sorts of candles, filled the greater part of one cupboard. She chose two pillars of dark green, setting them on small plates to catch any wax drippings. Lighting them made her feel more comfortable in a strange house.

The kettle whistled and Carolyn turned it down to simmer until Paul came back. She really should be out there helping him. Deciding she really didn't need to be coddled, she headed for the door.

Throwing her coat over her shoulders, she poked her head out to see how much progress he had made. But the total darkness of the night plus the now softly falling snow made it difficult to find him. Going back to grab one of the green candles, she slipped her feet into her still-wet boots and stepped into the night.

The path was easy to follow; the sides were up to her knees. Ahead of her, she heard the shovel slide on pavement and heard Paul's grunt as he lifted too much snow.

"Paul? I came to see if I could help. I feel useless in there."

He turned around and caught his breath. An angel stood in the path he just shoveled. The warm light of the candle lit her face with a golden glow; the snow dusted her burnished gold hair in a halo of white. Her dark eyes glimmered in the candlelight and captured his soul. With a clarity he did not understand, he knew his spirit was tied to this woman with a bond stronger than their short acquaintance could explain.

The angel stepped toward him and his arms dropped to his sides, barely grasping the shovel in hands gone suddenly limp. His shoulders straightened as he watched the vision approach him.

Carolyn was aware of a sudden stirring in the center of her being. The light of the candle reached his eyes and reflected back to her depths she could not fathom. He straightened and it seemed as if he were clothed in armor in the golden light. Tall and commanding he stood before her, his bearing regal, but not aloof. Her knight protecting her from harm.

The knight waited for her approach; she stepped into the protection he offered. Barely breathing, she saw him bend, his lips coming closer to hers; she lifted her face and felt the soft kiss of snowflakes on her cheeks. A sudden wind lifted her hair and the candle went out.

She froze. Disoriented by the vision she'd had and by the sudden darkness, she was afraid to move. She felt Paul move back and took a step backward as well. Soft light glimmered from the open kitchen door; light that on a normal night the electric streetlights would have swallowed. But tonight, when the bright lights were gone, magic ruled the earth and soft light guided their steps.

"You should be inside where it's warm." Gentle caring smoothed his voice, loath to break the spell.

"Come with me?" Not a command, but the request of a woman falling in love.

Her hand slid into his as a child might take the hand of a parent, yet Carolyn led the way along the path that already filled with a cushion of fresh snow.

The kettle sang as they entered and she toed off her boots and hurried to turn it off. Setting the candle on the table, in the light, she noticed his pants were soaked all the way up the thigh. And higher? She didn't want to embarrass him by staring.

"How did you get so wet?" The outside magic disappeared from her voice, replaced now by concern as she saw him shiver in his wet clothes.

"One of these days I'll think ahead and put the shovel closer to the door where it might be useful. I had to wade through the snow to the shed in the back to get it out. Got pretty wet in the process, I guess." He was soaked right through and didn't want to tell her he'd tripped into the snowbank when wrestling with the door to the old, badly built lean-to that served as a shelter for his outside tools.

"Take them off. No, take them off right there. No sense in making a path of wet snow from here to wherever." She deliberately turned her back on him and busied herself with the cups, spooning in several tablespoons of the cocoa mix as he undressed.

There was a note in her voice that brooked no-nonsense and Paul realized it was her school tone. Deciding to call her bluff, he stripped off his shirt and pants and then his briefs as well. But the air hitting his damp skin was cold and he shivered again.

"Throw me one of those hand towels, will you?"

Two kitchen towels hung neatly on a rack to her left. Pulling one down, she held it out behind her.

"I don't bite, you know."

His voice was almost in her ear. She jumped as he took the towel from her outstretched hand to dry his thighs…and his very cold cock. Grinning, he chose not to move from behind her, instead baiting her by remaining where he was.

She knew he was there…and that he must be naked. A smile playing on her face, Carolyn considered. It had been a long time since she'd seen a naked man. And the memory of him in the snow, standing like a knight in armor, stirred her deeply and in places that had not been moved in quite a long time. Her head dipped as the smile deepened into a grin and she slowly turned around.

Out of the corner of his eye, he saw her movement. The golden light of the candles deepened the dimples in her cheeks as her eyes sought his. Briefly tempted to cover himself with the small scrap of cloth, he decided two could bluff. Throwing the towel to the corner, he straightened, completely naked in the center of his kitchen.

Carolyn's breath caught as she stared at the knight without his armor, still strong and invincible before her. Strength emanated from his broad chest, the powerful muscles at rest, yet still striking in their potency. No hair marred the perfection of smooth skin that glimmered in the candlelight, the line of his chest leading her eyes down past his narrow waist to his cock that nestled in a tuft of dark hair.

She should pull her eyes away; she blinked and tried to move her head, to turn aside. But her body did not obey, instead looking its fill at him. Runner's legs, with strong thighs, stood braced against the night and her gaze lifted, again stopping at that tuft of hair. Although soft, his long cock peeked out at her, the pink tip sliding out from under its protective covering even as she watched.

From deep inside her, a yearning formed and blossomed, to flip her stomach with the force of a small boat overturning.

Paul felt himself respond to the appreciation and hunger in her eyes. His cock stiffened, turning the tip from pink to dark purple as it grew. He was not a small man, and the sight of his length had scared away at least one girlfriend in the past.

But Carolyn did not flinch, nor did she stare at the evidence of his growing desire. Her breath quickened in response. She felt poised at the edge of an abyss. If he stepped toward her, she would fall into it. Tearing her gaze from his cock, she sought refuge in his eyes. But there was no solace. Desire burned in them and reached into her soul.

Her hands went behind her, holding onto the counter to prevent herself from falling into the chasm that opened before her. For a brief moment she felt as if chains held her hands behind her back and fear stabbed her in the belly. Wasn't that what she'd wanted? She had been the one to tell him to undress here in the kitchen. She was the one who couldn't stop teasing him. Every time she looked at him, her fascination with him multiplied. Now his power dominated the room and threatened to overwhelm her. For a moment she could not breathe.

Paul read the fear and uncertainty in Carolyn's eyes and his own gaze fell to cover his disappointment. For a brief moment, he hoped she might be different from the other women he knew. The strength he radiated grew from a firm understanding of who he was…what he was. He accepted his demanding passions even as he was ashamed of them.

But his intensity scared women; if only she hadn't called his bluff by telling him to take off his clothes right there. If the darkness hadn't worked its magic outside in the snow, he never even would have considered rising to her challenge. But the night cast its spell and his hopes had risen along with his cock. Both now deflated at the look of indecision and fear in her face.

A balloon losing its air might be a cliché, but Carolyn could think of no other metaphor for Paul's sudden withdrawal.

Suddenly shy again, confused by her own reaction, she dropped her eyes to the floor, trying to sort out what had just happened.

Paul turned away, the moment gone. What was he thinking? Making a face, he reminded himself that Carolyn was a fellow teacher and that he had just brought her home with him because they were in the midst of a blizzard. Sexual thoughts about her had to be nonexistent if he intended to be able to go back to work and face her at school-wide faculty meetings.

In the candlelight, a dark patch on his rear caught the light and Carolyn squinted as if she wasn't sure she saw what she thought she saw. She tried to salvage the moment of magic. "Paul..." She saw him hesitate on his way to retrieve his clothes. "You have a tattoo?"

He straightened, the load of clothes in his arms. He'd forgotten all about the blasted thing! Small, about the size of a half-dollar, a red diamond graced his right cheek.

He twisted around as if he could see it, turning himself to face her again as he did so.

Carolyn laughed and the tension between them lessened, but did not disappear. "You look like a dog wanting to catch his tail!"

Paul's eyes glimmered with mischief. Teasing they could handle. It was seriousness that made them both nervous. "I'd rather catch someone else's tail!"

The kettle whistled and Carolyn spun to shut off the noise. Out of the corner of her eye, she saw him blur past her and into the darkened room beyond. Alone, she savored the memory of his nudity and tried to figure out what had made him pull back before she could decide what she wanted.

There was the companion question, of course. Forget what he wanted, what did she want? Certainly making love with a handsome colleague had not been on her mind when she slid into that snowbank. She wasn't a prude, but she wasn't easy, either. Still, the memory of him clothed in the snow...and then again clothed in nothing but candlelight, his eyes burning with an inner passion…she certainly was tempted.

Sighing, she eyed the cups and decided she didn't really want another cup of cocoa. Her stomach growled and she glanced at the wall clock, but its blank face reminded her that the storm had thrown them back into another century. Suddenly dinner became complicated.

His emotions and his clothes all neatly tucked in, Paul sauntered back into the kitchen, rubbing his stomach as a sudden hunger hit him. Carolyn had pulled out a kitchen chair in his absence and now sat at the old oak table, toying with one of the candles by rimming the wax around the glass jar so the light would burn brighter. The light filled her face and Paul stopped a few steps into the room as she looked up at him, glowing with sweetness…and temptation.

"How about some dinner?" He clapped his hands together to banish the desires he thought he had put away and busied himself rooting around the kitchen to cover his unease. Pulling out two pots, he held them up, twirling them to catch the light and toss it around the room. "With the electricity out, only the stovetop works…pasta sound good?"

Carolyn wondered what his sudden antics hid. Grinning to hide her own confused feelings, she nodded. "Pasta sounds wonderful. Do I dare hope there's stuff in the fridge for a salad?"

Paul snorted. "You can hope, but there's nothing green in there." He stopped and thought a moment. "I take that back. There *is* green in there, but I'm not sure I'd eat it."

Carolyn laughed, relaxing into the stereotype. "I think I'll take your word on it and not go looking."

"Smart woman."

"So how long have you been teaching?"

"Seven years this year. You?"

"Seven. So this is your vesture year? Making it into the big time, now." She opened the box of pasta he pulled out of the cupboard, noticing the little bowtie-shaped macaronis. What was that about being able to take the man out of the little boy…?

You've been teaching seven years already? How old are you?"

Carolyn grinned. She considered it a compliment that she still got carded at the liquor store. Apparently Paul had pegged her as young as well. Perhaps that accounted for his sudden withdrawal. Tempted to tease him about not asking a woman her age, she decided it might be in her best interests to just tell him.

"Twenty-nine. And you?" Turn about was fair play.

"Thirty-one. That makes me two years closer to retirement than you are."

Laughing, she handed him the box of pasta and watched him pour it into the pot.

* * * * *

They stayed on the safe topic of school all through dinner. As long as he thought of her as the first grade teacher, he could keep her sex appeal in its place. And when she reminded herself that this man had made some very unpopular decisions regarding elementary education, it was easier to forget the knight in the snow.

"We'll have to leave the dishes," Paul informed her as she set about cleaning up afterward.

"Why?"

"No hot water. It runs on electricity. The water in the heater downstairs will stay plenty hot for quite a while, but I don't want to waste it on dishes. Besides, there are too many."

Carolyn shook her head. "No problem. Just fill up the teakettle again. Not-so-instant hot water, but it will do. And ignoring them won't make them go away." She grinned and rolled up her sleeves.

Paul brought the teakettle to where she stood at the sink. Carolyn moved a candle from the table and set it by the faucet so she could see to wash up and the soft light accented her delicate features. He was too close, he knew. But he couldn't resist the urge to be near her; desperately he tried to think of her at school, but the candlelight had a magic of its own. Even as he reached around her to fill the teakettle, he leaned forward to breathe in the scent of her hair.

Carolyn's hands gripped the faucet as she froze in the act of turning on the water for him. Slowly she turned her head toward his presence, leaning back into him and bringing her face up. Closing her eyes, she breathed deeply, inhaling the scent of his cologne, sending tingles to the center of her stomach.

Cold water splashed unheeded over his hand as he set the teakettle in the sink and bent down to meet those beautiful lips. Ever so gently, their lips brushed, their breaths soft and hearts yearning. Which of them leaned in first neither of them knew; it didn't matter. Their lips touched and the yearning spread.

Neither of them moved as each savored the kiss. Pasta sauce and his cologne mixed with her perfume in a heady scent that made the mind reel with desire. When her lips parted, inviting him deeper, he entered gently…probing, tasting, wanting.

And still neither of them moved, so caught up in the passion of the kiss that movement and time faded. Their tongues entwined, separated, entwined again until they broke apart, both with a gasp and fighting for breath and control.

"Wow." Paul pulled back half a step. "I'm sorry, I shouldn't have done that."

"I think you need to do it again." Her voice was raspy with the emotions he ignited in her. Was it fate that caused her car to go off the road? Kismet? She didn't care. She was here, and falling in love.

Paul balled his fists at his sides. "Carolyn, if I do it again, I'm not sure I could stop. And that's not fair to you. To either of us."

The knight was clothed in his armor once more…armor that encased more than his body, Carolyn realized. She was the damsel in distress and the knight's chivalry had a code to live by.

"Paul, perhaps I'm not interested in fair. And maybe I don't want you to stop."

Torment flashed through his eyes. "Carolyn, you don't know what you're asking. You don't know what I am…what I like to do to women. I can't do that to you. You're too soft, too sweet…" His voice trailed off as he struggled to hide the flaws that made him imperfect…damaged.

Carolyn's eyes flashed in anger, but she bit back her retort when she saw the pain in his eyes. Whatever he was hiding, it was something he was deeply ashamed of. It couldn't be his body; she had already seen that and to her sight there was nothing there that didn't fit. And from the blossoming of his cock earlier, she knew that its workings couldn't be the problem. So what was?

She backed down. Whatever it was, he would tell her when he was ready. Or he wouldn't. But the memory of his kiss still hung on her lips and she knew she needed to try. Later. When his guard was not so formidable.

Turning her back to him to give her time to school her features, she tried to lighten the mood. "Well, since creating heat with a kiss won't heat this water, why don't you try putting it on the stove?" She filled the kettle and handed it to him, hoping the twinkle in her eye would mask her desire and her clumsy attempt at humor.

Banter. Banter was safe; kissing was not. Paul forced a grin, his shoulders relaxing as he took the cold water to put on the stove. He didn't even realize she had been very careful to hand it to him in such a way so that their fingers did not touch.

In short order the dishes were done and the kitchen tidied. Both talked and joked to hide their sudden nervousness; both soon were tired from the effort. Although it was still early,

Carolyn couldn't suppress a yawn as Paul put away the last dish.

He saw her cover her mouth and fought not to catch the yawn. He had no idea what time it was since he'd taken off his watch when he changed his clothes, and the kitchen clock was no help. Something about her brought out the hidden gentleman in him; he would give her his bed and he would sleep on the couch.

"You take the bed upstairs, I'll take the couch down here."

"I can take the couch, Paul. It's your bed."

They stood before the beat-up, garage sale couch. Clean, but a bit worn, it certainly looked broken in.

"Yes, it's my bed and I'm loaning it to you for the evening. Come on, I'll show you the way."

The little house had been built years earlier as a "starter" home for a young couple just beginning their lives together. Downstairs were the kitchen, the living room and a dining room Paul closed off during winter to save on heating. Upstairs was the bath, and two bedrooms. Carolyn only got a glimpse of a small second bedroom as they passed it on the way to Paul's room, but it appeared to be empty except for a weight bench in the middle of the room.

The double bed in Paul's room took up most of the space. A neat dresser tucked into the corner took up more room; to her right, Carolyn noticed a closet door, partly opened.

"Here you go. Bath is around the corner, although showering in the morning will be tricky with the electricity out. But we'll figure something out. Need anything?"

He was talking to keep the awkwardness at bay. The candle he held in his hand flickered and caught his eye. Almost out. Good excuse to leave and go back downstairs while he still had candle left.

"Paul," Carolyn set her candle down on the nightstand beside the bed and turned toward him in the small space. He seemed so vulnerable, so lonely. Or was she only seeing in him the loneliness she felt inside? Her hand went out to touch his arm.

Her light touch spread its warmth through his sleeve and Paul pulled back. "Carolyn, no. You don't know what I am."

She stared at the hunger in his eyes and saw the romantic knight stripped away to show the primal urges underneath. And something more…whatever he could not express, it seemed to be something he hated.

Her heart stirred with a mixture of pity, caring, and friendship that took another step toward love in spite of her own misgivings. Should she instead show him what she was? How could she do that? It wasn't in her to take the first step and it wasn't exactly something that one just blurted out. For a moment, indecision made her bite her lower lip. But the night had worked its magic and the forces between them were too powerful. She needed to find out what troubled him.

"What is it, Paul? How can I help?"

Carolyn's voice whispered into the night and into his soul. Damn her. She just wouldn't leave him alone. She wanted to push him, then he'd show her. Let her see the monster he was. Only one way she was going to understand that she really didn't want him. He let the demon out.

"Turn around." His voice was raspy with pent-up emotion and a change came over his entire being. He straightened, his shoulders pulling back and his muscles tightening. A strange light glimmered in his eyes. Carolyn watched, entranced by the transformation. One moment he stood there as Paul, the teacher with a tortured soul, the next he was…someone different. Stronger. More powerful. A force to be reckoned with. Not the white knight, but the black.

She turned her back to him as he commanded, a sudden fear tightening her belly. What had she unleashed?

"Bend over and put your hands on the bed."

Blinking and trying to figure out what was happening, she did as she had been told. A sudden slap, hard and forceful on her ass made her gasp in shock.

He had slapped her ass. And slapped it again…hard.

"Do you like this, Carolyn?" Slap. "Do you like to have your ass spanked by a man?" Slap. "Does it turn you on the way it does me?"

He pulled his hand back and turned away from her, a cry strangling his throat. Carolyn did not stand; she was too shocked by his actions…and too aroused. How often had she dreamed of being spanked…not knowing if she would enjoy it or not. His touch on her came as a shock, but it also thrilled her, making her pussy wet with excitement. This is what she'd hidden from so many men in the past, and Paul had given it to her without her asking. She knew she wanted more, but first she needed to know what he meant by it.

Paul's fist hit the closet door, slamming it shut; Carolyn jumped at the sound. Slowly she stood to face him struggling to keep her voice from trembling and her emotions under control.

"Paul, I need to know. Do you like to hit women for hitting's sake? Or because you know that a good, well-delivered spanking, or flogging for that matter, can bring a woman to orgasm all on its own?"

She spoke with a nonchalance she did not feel. Hours spent pouring over Internet sites reading about the line between Dominance and abuse haunted her mind. Where did Paul fit on that continuum?

He turned, shame filling his eyes. "Carolyn, I would never hurt you. Not how you mean. I could never hit a woman in anger." His eyes dropped as he searched for the words. "But what kind of a man am I that I want to turn your ass red and then fuck the hell out of it?"

His eyes sought an answer from her and her heart understood. Her own eyes glistened as she caressed his cheek with the back of her hand. "Oh, Paul. You're the kind of man I have been searching for!"

Chapter Three

"What?" Paul's heart jumped at her words, but he couldn't believe she meant them.

"Paul, I'm a submissive. I've known it all my life. And you're a Dominant, if I'm not mistaken." Her heart beat hard to be on such dangerous ground. Never had she expressed her "fetish" as some websites called it; her "kink" as others referred to it, her "real self" as she considered it; never had she told anyone as bluntly as she told Paul now. Her knees trembled to hear herself make the admission.

"Yes, I am dominant in the bedroom and have been for many years. But Carolyn..." His voice trailed off. How could any woman want to submit to what he wanted to do to them...for them? Every attempt he'd made in the past had ended in failure.

"But what?" Carolyn saw the war going on inside him and understood it. How many hours had she argued the need to be submissive against her independent, feminist nature in the darkness of her room? "Paul..."

He held up his hand to stop her and she fell silent. Paul gestured to the bed and she sat on the edge. He came and sat beside her, taking her hand in his.

Paul's touch excited her in a way she'd never felt with any other man. The fact that they were colleagues drifted into unimportance as she watched his fingers trace the outline of her hand against his.

"Carolyn, I like to have women do what I tell them to do. I like to flog them. In that closet, I have several floggers and a suitcase filled with many different ropes, each for its own purpose. Yes, I am a Dominant. I don't know why or what's wrong in me that I like those things, but that's the way I am.

"I have to admit, I'm a little surprised to hear you understand the term…and call yourself a submissive. Do you truly understand what a submissive is?"

Carolyn started to speak, but her emotions got in the way and her voice cracked. Taking a deep breath and clearing her throat, she started again. "Yes, I do understand. I am not a doormat, Paul. I'm an independent woman who knows what I want out of life and out of my career. But a part of my psyche is completely different. I am a submissive." She grinned, more comfortable each time she said the words. "I am submissive in the bedroom…and it's okay for me to be that way. It's the way God made me, just as being a Dominant is the way God made you. Society doesn't want us to be that way, but I cannot believe it is wrong."

Paul looked at her with respect. "You've come further in your acceptance than I have in mine. I still struggle with the whole 'cave man' mentality it seems to represent to me." He turned to face her on the bed. "Carolyn, no more beating around the bush. I want you tonight. But I don't know if it's the romantic candlelight or my own feelings. Feelings that are a little confused right now."

A small disappointment bloomed inside her stomach. The spanking had sparked a desire in her that she did not want to quench, and yet it seemed Paul was not ready to go further. "I understand," she told him. "I find you're not the Big Bad English Teacher I always thought you were; you're warm and funny, and caring…and a Dom." She bit her lip as she considered saying what was in her heart. Well, she wasn't going to get anywhere by just sitting here. Being submissive did not mean being a doormat, hadn't she just said that?

"Paul, I think it might be fate, not the candlelight. But you must take the lead in this. Running away from your feelings…from our feelings…will not make them go away."

"Are you telling me you want a spanking? A real one?"

Her stomach flipped over so hard she couldn't breathe. It was time to put up or shut up. "Yes, I want a real spanking."

Paul studied the woman before him, so petite and yet so strong in her convictions. Convictions he never would have suspected if the storm hadn't put their paths together for the night. Challenge lit her eyes as she called his bluff; did he have the courage to take her at her word and spank her? Confidence in his voice, he made his decision, standing as his eyes and manner changed. "Stand up."

Trembling with anticipation and sudden fear, Carolyn did so. The black knight stood before her; the thought of obeying his command caused her pussy to clench and her knees to turn weak. But she mastered both and stood with a mixture of strength and humility.

Paul tightly controlled the demon inside, the one that wanted to let go and give this woman who would not let well enough alone, a lesson she would not soon forget. But the gentleman side she awoke in him insisted on keeping the demon on a tight leash. He would only go so far…but he did intend to teach her a lesson.

Not moving from where he sat, Paul gestured for Carolyn to step closer. The small intake of breath she made as she did so was not lost on him. Keeping his attention on her waist, he slid his hands under her blouse, enjoying the softness of her skin. Keeping his touch light, he skimmed over the smooth skin of her belly and around her waist, pulling her another half-step closer.

Desire smoldered in her body and in her mind. When his rough hands cupped her breasts, her lips parted as her breath caught. Relishing his touch, her eyes closed and her head fell back as she let him explore. When he undid the clasp of her bra and his warm fingers traced along her side to cup her breasts, she leaned toward him to kiss the top of his head as her arms came up to caress him.

"Put your arms at your sides."

The command in his voice was unmistakable. With an effort, Carolyn lowered them, letting Paul touch her as he saw fit. Her pussy contracted and she knew her panties were now soaked. To stand so, not allowed to touch him, was to put her in her place. She became nothing more than an object for him to explore. The thought thrilled her.

He put his hands on her shoulders, moving her back so he could stand and unbutton her blouse. His cock, rock-hard from her reactions, strained against the sweatpants he wore, but he ignored it for now. Taking his time was such sweet torture, he prolonged undressing her for his pleasure.

He slipped the blouse and bra from her shoulders and bent down to taste her delicate breast. So dainty, just like the rest of her. A champagne glass full—round and small and perfect. His lips closed over her nipple and he was rewarded with a small gasp that turned into a full moan as he sucked the delicious morsel deep into his mouth.

Carolyn felt her knees giving way, but Paul was there to steady her, to hold her. She made no movement to catch herself, instead leaning into her knight's arms as his mouth left her nipple to close over her lips. She felt him press against her, his lips brushing hers, their breaths entwining…sharing…teasing…his tongue brushing against her lips. She parted and let him plunge into her, his tongue encircling hers in a dance of passion.

"Turn around," he whispered into her mouth, and Carolyn turned toward the bed. Her mind swimming from his kiss, she forced her hands to remain at her sides.

But oversized sweatpants still covered what Paul was sure was a perfect ass. Taking his time and drawing out her anticipation, he slid his hands under the waistband to cup each cheek, squeezing slightly…just enough to make her gasp. Stepping in, he moved his hands around the front of her thighs, bending down to lightly brush her mound of dark golden hair.

"Spread your legs for me, Carolyn. Let me feel how this excites you."

He knew he was pushing, but when a moan came from the depths of her throat and she opened her legs, he knew she granted him permission. Taking his time, he pressed his body against her from behind as his fingers inched closer to her pussy.

Carolyn thought she would go mad…how could he know just how to touch her…just how to turn her into a puddle so quickly? His hard, muscular body molded itself around her. Instinctively, she pressed back into him, feeling his arm around her waist supporting her even as his other hand teased her. She felt his hard cock press against her ass and her pussy flooded with her need. In a few breaths, he would touch her and she would explode.

Paul could tell she was ready. Her dampness extended down along her leg and she was having trouble standing. All good signs of her willingness to submit to him. Pushing down her pants, he helped her to step out of them and turned her to face him again.

Naked in the candlelight, her emotions raw from his touch, Carolyn stood silent, waiting as Paul stepped back and looked his fill. The graceful curve of her neck gave way to the rise of her delicious breasts. A delicate waist he could put one arm all the way around, perfectly balanced the broader sweep of her hips. But as his gaze lowered, he focused on the mound of dark golden, curly hair that hid her sex.

With an effort of will, Carolyn did not move her hands, even though the strong urge to cover herself stirred her arms. But she liked the way his eyes feasted on her, as if her body were a banquet for his pleasure. Still trim and fit, she smiled shyly under his gaze.

"Turn around and put your hands on the bed."

The Spanking. With deliberate movements, Carolyn did as he instructed. Almost defiantly she raised her ass, waiting for the first slap.

But he wanted time to study the body before him. From her posture, he knew she wanted to be on the receiving end as much as he wanted to deliver. His hand brushed over the smoothness of those rounded cheeks that dipped together to make a perfect heart in the candlelight.

Paul tapped her bottom with the palm of his hand. He did not hit hard and Carolyn did not move. Gradually, he increased the strength of his taps until they became true slaps on her ass. Changing his tactic and running his hand over her smooth skin, he felt for the small temperature change as her skin began to warm under his touch.

Pausing to reposition the candles so he could better view her rear end and the marks he would leave on her skin, he took a moment to appreciate the view of the naked woman bent over his bed, her back rising and falling with the short breaths that belied her arousal.

His hand on her bottom was all that mattered and when it stopped, she tried to get herself under control again. But that control was in tatters and had been since they first started this discussion. How often in her dreams had she been in just such a position? And now here she was for real…and on a night when she least expected it. Carolyn began to lose focus.

From the stories she had read, she knew there were women who could come just from a spanking alone…was she one of them? Paul's hands caressed her cheeks again and Carolyn stopped trying to think.

From the closet, Paul ignored the rubber and hard leather whips, choosing instead a long suede flogger…one with wide deerskin tails that caressed the skin. Now, lightly brushing the ends over her warmed skin, he let the softness stroke along her back and over her beautiful ass

"Do you like this, Carolyn? Gentle and soft, almost soothing."

The sensuous feel of the suede lulled her along and Carolyn's body began a slow dance in response. Rocking on her hands in time with her breaths, all that mattered was the touch of the leather on her skin. When Paul switched from a gentle brushing to a more forceful blow, her body's dance matched the change. Eyes closed, she raised her head, reveling in the light stinging of the flogger against her skin. Her moan was her only answer.

A sharp crack split the air as Paul brought a flat-tipped crop to bear on her pink cheeks. More sound than fury, Carolyn still gasped at the sharp retort made by the crop hitting her skin. Paul's hands worked in tandem now…sometimes using the deerskin, sometimes the crop…each blow driving her need higher and higher.

Her body reacted to his changes with a mind of its own. Balling her fists into the comforter covering the bed, she willed herself to remain still as the sharp slaps forced moans and whimpers from her throat.

He watched Carolyn's dance beneath him and listened to her song. He watched her arch her back and put her ass up for more only to then bow her head as her ass cheeks quivered from his use of her. As her moans grew deeper and more feral, he knew the flogging carried her mind into places hidden inside her, places she rarely shared with anyone.

"Paul…" Carolyn's voice was almost a whisper.

"Yes, Carolyn?" He did not stop, but dropped the deerskin flogger for one with stiffer thongs. This one required a lighter touch to get the effect he wanted—a caress with a small sting at the end.

The new sensation made it difficult to keep either her dance or her voice quiet. She withstood several blows before begging him. "Paul, please, oh please. Paul, I need to come!"

Urgency filled her voice, yet the fact that she had asked permission was not lost on him. "I will count, Carolyn, and you will come when I say 'three.' Do you understand?"

The flogger was relentless, brushing her back, her legs, her increasingly sensitive rear end. Gasping for breath, Carolyn nodded, her voice ragged with need. "Yes, I understand!"

"Then one..." He landed a blow between her legs, the tails of the flogger lightly brushing along those twin lips that swelled with her need. Her body stiffened and she cried out, but then she grabbed control again and did not come.

"Two..." Along her reddened ass, several times...taking his time and drawing out his counting, until he heard her moan and saw her knees buckle. With an effort, she straightened again and Paul knew she could not hold out much longer.

"Three... Come for me, Carolyn, come hard!"

Both knees gave way as her body bucked and she fell to the floor, spasms radiating through her. Paul's arms were around her, holding her tightly as she came. Hot waves came fast, too fast—she had no control. The orgasm ran through her entire being to shake her to the core until at last, she collapsed in his arms, her body trembling as she fought to catch her breath.

Carolyn pulled in great gasps of air as her body continued to twitch with echoes of her orgasm. Paul knew he could force more out of her, but decided that was enough for their first time. First time...as if she'd ever want another after what he had done to her.

She was on the floor, but safe in Paul's arms. His arms held her tightly and Carolyn breathed into his chest as the world came back into focus. The strong muscles surrounding her comforted her and she knew she was safe. Even after she managed to get herself under control again, she didn't want to move from his embrace. Instead, she simply rested there until she could form words and breathe them into the night.

"Thank you."

Paul looked down at the top of Carolyn's head where it nestled against his chest. Surely he hadn't heard her right. "What did you say?"

"Thank you, sir."

"No, that's not what I meant..." She nestled more firmly against him and he smiled, gathering her close. Never mind, there would be time for that discussion later.

One of the candles went out; the flame on the remaining one dimly shone in the room. A blast of artic air slammed against the house sending a cold draft along the floor to remind them of the storm raging outside. Carolyn shivered.

"Come, into bed where you can be warm." Paul helped her to stand and pulled down the covers for her.

The cool sheets soothed her hot ass, but Carolyn knew they would warm up fast. Especially once he joined her. She slid over to make room and pulled the cover down so he could lie beside her.

Paul hesitated. There was no doubt if he climbed in that bed he would take full advantage of the situation.

Carolyn saw his hesitation and smiled in the dim light. "Paul, may I remind you this is your bed? Please come share it with me."

Pausing only to blow out the candle and drop his sweatpants on the floor, Paul lay beside her, warming her as she snuggled into his arms.

"What are you thinking?" he whispered into her hair.

"That was the most incredible thing ever to happen to me." She lay her head on his shoulder and spoke softly as the wind rattled the window. "To submit to your touch…to allow you to flog me…gave me such a feeling of completeness that I'm not sure I can describe it."

When Paul didn't answer right away, she continued. "My glory, Paul! I never thought it would be relaxing…but it was. I found myself just wanting to float along as the leather hit me. I always thought it would be painful…but it wasn't. It started to sting a little, right at the very end, but I think that sting is what sent me over the edge."

Paul could not see her face, but he could hear the wonder in her voice. "That's what a true flogging is…not pain for pain's sake, but for the mental as well as physical caress of the leather." He put his fingers under her chin and pulled her face up toward his, tasting her lips again in a deepening kiss.

His scent surrounded her; on the pillows, the sheets, in his kiss. Masculine. The way his lips closed over hers as if he belonged beside her. She shifted position to let the kiss deepen and the sudden warming of her bottom along the sheet reminded her of Paul's fascination.

She was falling in love, of that there was no doubt. The strong command he had at school that she'd thought of as the haughty demeanor of an upper-level teacher, was the very command she desired in the bedroom. As the kiss deepened, she stopped trying to analyze it and just started enjoying it.

In seconds, Paul was on his feet, but the cold night air was not enough to get rid of his hard-on. "Carolyn, I can't do this to you. You're very vulnerable right now, and if I stay here I will do something we will both regret."

"Paul, I'm a grown woman and I'm no virgin, if that's your concern."

"That's not what I meant. You said it yourself, you're a submissive and I'm a Dominant. I just thrashed the hell out of your ass, and watched you reach one heck of a climax. You're riding an emotional high right now and it's too easy for me to take advantage of that."

"So you're saying you don't really want to have sex with me?" Anger built inside her.

"No!" The word exploded out of Paul in frustration. "That's just it! I'm saying I really, really, really want to have sex with you…just not under these conditions."

"So you get me in the mood, give me an orgasm better than anything I've ever known and then just walk away?"

He knelt on the floor, wishing he hadn't blown out that candle. If only he could read her face, then he would know what to do. Sighing, his shoulders sagging, he spoke to her.

"Carolyn, I'm finding it hard enough to believe you liked what I did to you. It is very possible you are the girl of my dreams, and I don't want to risk any future I might have with you because both of us let the romance of being stuck in a snowstorm get to us."

The ice building inside Carolyn's heart melted at the honesty in his voice. She couldn't read his eyes, but she could feel him trembling with pent-up passion at her side. He was right. In her current frame of mind, she would let him do anything he wanted to her if it resulted in more orgasms like that one. But more importantly, he was considering a future with her. A future she very much wanted to explore.

"Well, when you put it like that..." She reached out and found his face close to hers. Gently she caressed his cheek with the back of her fingers, feeling the stubble of a day-old beard. "Thank you, Paul. I would not say no to you tonight, but in the morning I wouldn't know if what we had was real or just loneliness and romantic light. You're right."

Paul kissed her lightly on the lips and whispered without pulling away, "I want us to be together, Carolyn Brooks. Know that I am falling in love with you and will be downstairs waiting for you in the morning."

She kissed him in the darkness and felt him move away from her. Listening to his steps as he found his way back down the stairs, she sighed. Damn. The black knight had a conscience.

Chapter Four

The phone woke her in the morning. Forgetting where she was, Carolyn rolled over to answer the ring. But her hand fell to the floor. The nightstand wasn't there. Opening her eyes to Paul's room, the events of the night before came flooding back. For several moments, her mind reeled with the sudden change her life had taken. Rubbing her eyes, she tried to focus on the fact that it was morning.

The wind had died down. Or changed direction. Listening to it howl was what had finally put her to sleep last night. Too many thoughts, doubts, desires crowded her mind, and she had tossed and turned for over an hour after Paul left her, finally falling into an exhausted sleep until the phone's ring awakened her.

It must still be early. Paul's step on the still-dark stair, accompanied by approaching candlelight informed her he was headed in her direction. Pushing herself up onto her elbows, she grinned at his disheveled appearance. His light brown hair stuck up at all angles and the stubble on his chin gave him a rakish look. A gleam in his eye told her he had good news.

"That was school. We're cancelled. And people think only the kids want snow days."

"Is it still snowing?" She watched him cross the room to the window and peek out through the blinds.

"Yep. Not much. We're back to the big flakes. Weatherman says it'll stop by midmorning. So far it's dropped over four feet. It'll take all day to dig out of this one." He dropped the blinds again and looked at the beautiful woman in his bed. The thought of her submissiveness had kept him awake half the night. That and the hard-on that wouldn't go away. Until he'd taken care of that, he hadn't been able to sleep at all.

Seeing her now, tousled from sleep and a bit bleary-eyed, should dampen the romantic thoughts in his head. It didn't. He wanted her more than ever.

"Power back yet?"

He shook his head. "Not yet. Which means showering is going to be tough for the two of us."

She giggled and then bit her lip, looking at him with that impish grin on her face. He knew right away what she was thinking.

"Before we go where you're going in that mischievous little mind of yours, we need to talk, young lady."

Her stomach rumbled. "I guess I can wait to shower until after breakfast. If you can stand to look at me like this."

"I think I can put up with you for a little while," Paul teased, sauntering out the bedroom door. "Put some clothes on, woman and come downstairs."

Carolyn grinned. He hadn't meant it as an order, she was sure. But it didn't hurt to pretend he did.

Remembering the night before, she ran her palm over her naked rear end, feeling the smooth contours and enjoying her memories. Flogging was just as erotic as she'd always hoped it would be. No residual soreness either. With any luck, she could get him to warm her backside again today.

Pulling on the same sweats and blouse from yesterday, she decided to forego the bra and panties. Both smelled a bit strong and if they offended her, they would be sure to ruin his appetite.

Downstairs in the kitchen, knowing he needed to use up the eggs or lose them, Paul cracked the four he had left into a bowl. He poured in a small amount of milk; only a quart remained and he wanted enough for the two of them to have several more cups of cocoa. Remembering how beautiful she looked in the snow reminded him of her submissiveness again.

For all his inward debating last night as he tossed and turned on the couch, he still wasn't sure where he was on this whole thing.

Yes, he was a Dominant. All his life he'd wanted to be in charge. Probably why he went into teaching. Sure, he had principals and superintendents who set a tone and path for the district, but Paul couldn't be content unless he put his two cents in. Thus, he became one of the youngest department chairs in the district.

Outside of school, his need to control life and relationships had gotten him in considerably more trouble. He didn't need to have his way all the time, but the demon inside of him wanted total control when it came to sex.

And he liked flogging women. He liked touching them with his hands, his fingers trailing over an arm in a soft caress. He liked kissing their soft mouths and nibbling on their hard little nipples. Most of all, he liked the way they melted into his arms when he did all those things.

But that was where the trouble usually began. The woman would melt, he'd think they were on the same page and suggest something; she would consider it "kinky", "perverted", "disgusting", or "sick", all words that had been thrown at him at one point or another. Even though the Internet suggested he was not alone, he had yet to meet an unattached woman who liked what he did to the extent that Carolyn seemed to.

He got no further in his debate when the woman in question came through the door. With her dark golden hair brushed and neat, and her face pink from dashing cold water on it to wake up, she looked radiant.

Carolyn grinned as she peered over his shoulder at the twin pans on the stovetop. "Scrambled eggs and sausage? I rarely eat this well in the morning!"

"Gotta use up the eggs, and, well, you can't have one without the other!" Paul scooped the eggs into a pile in the pan and nodded toward a cupboard. "Plates and cups in there; silverware in the drawer behind you."

The teakettle whistled, so Paul poured water into the cocoa cups as Carolyn bustled behind him setting the table. "Truth be told, this is a lot more breakfast than I usually have as well," he admitted. "Couple of pieces of toast and a glass of orange juice and I'm out the door." He put the filled cups onto the table. "Sorry no orange juice this morning, I'm all out. And I have no coffee to offer you…don't drink it myself."

"I don't either! Love the smell, hate the taste. Cocoa's much better." She pulled out a chair and watched as Paul slid the eggs onto the two plates. Putting a plate of sausage between them, he sat opposite her at the old-fashioned oak table and grinned.

"Here's to snow days!"

With a celebratory clink of cocoa cups, the two dug into the homey breakfast. While they ate, they discussed the storm, comparing it to past ones and reliving favorite snow days of the past. An easy camaraderie grew as they exchanged stories and fell further in love.

No mention was made of last night's activities; as long as they stayed away from the topic, their conversation remained pleasant. Neither one wanted to be the first to bring up the topic.

Instead, Carolyn brought up a safer one. "I want to know about your tattoo, Paul."

He snorted and shook his head. "Forgot all about that blasted thing. Got it after a college ball game. My two best friends pitched a no-hitter to win the championship."

"And what did you do during the game?"

"Someone had to catch their pitches."

"So naturally you three had to get tattoos to celebrate."

"Of course."

"Of course." She grinned. "I'm afraid it's just not something I expected to see on the rear end of the head of the English department."

He drained the rest of his cup and winked at her. "Oh, great. I've given you ammunition you can use to blackmail me."

"Hadn't thought of that, but now that you mention it…"

"You want that last sausage?"

Tempted as she was to use this question as a straight-line, she refrained and shook her head. Instead she asked him about the snow outside the door. "Suppose we ought to get to clearing out a path for ourselves, even if it is still snowing a little."

Paul remembered her dislike of being closed in. Although she said it nonchalantly enough, he heard the edge in her voice and hastened to reassure her. "I cleared it twice last night. Not far, but enough to get the door open anyway." He didn't tell her it was his way of channeling his energy. If he didn't shovel, he just might have climbed those stairs. "I suspect it's all filled in again, though."

His rueful face made her feel bad. Here she'd spent the night in his comfortable bed while her black knight had slept on the couch and kept the door clear.

"Do you have only the one shovel? I can help."

"Only the one. Tell you what…" Paul took his dishes over to the sink and piled them neatly. "…you do the dishes and I'll shovel the walk."

"Deal." While suspecting she was still getting the better end of the bargain, there was a glint in his eye she decided not to argue with. He seemed to like the idea of taking care of her and she found it endearing.

Paul suited up, bracing for the cold outside, and stepped into a silent world of white. No wind blew this morning and only a few flakes drifted down like lazy feathers to add another layer to the snowbanks. Without the wind, the door remained clear; the path he'd shoveled, however, had another foot of snow inside it.

At least it was light and fluffy this time and it didn't take him long to reach the street. No snowplow had been along yet. Paul widened the path knowing full well he'd be shoveling again once the plows got out and filled it in once more.

The air was cold, but not biting, and Paul found relief in the heavy physical labor. If he was working, he wasn't thinking about her…or about what he'd like to do to her. An image of Carolyn, her body bound in an intricate web of rope, laid out on his bed like a morsel for his consumption, blindfolded and ready for him… He shook his head and shoveled twice as fast to rid himself of the tempting picture.

Inside, Carolyn put on the water and filled the sink as she waited for the kettle to whistle. Her hand strayed again to her rear end, probing more deeply to find any trace of soreness, but not one bruise marked her skin.

Obviously she accepted her submissiveness more than Paul did his dominance. Long ago she had gone through the guilt feelings, then the feelings that something was wrong with her, and then, after much soul-searching, acceptance. It had not been an easy time; the boyfriend she had been with when she'd first started her journey had left her when she admitted she wanted to be tied up and taken. The online chat rooms proved to be filled with men who just wanted a quick thrill; for every man who was absolutely wonderful to talk to, there were at least a dozen slimeballs.

In desperation, she turned to self-bondage…well, what she could manage of it. Trying out things she saw in pictures educated her as to what she liked…and what she didn't. 'Course she couldn't do it all; to be truly bound and at a man's hand still remained her heart's desire. Just as wishing to feel the caress of the flogger had been before last night.

Having decided Paul was at the "something's wrong with me" stage, she set about coming up with a plan to help him past it. The weather and fate had combined to give her a wonderful opportunity and Carolyn did not intend to squander it.

*****

Paul managed to shovel about half the drive before giving up for a while. Just as he leaned the shovel against the house, he heard the rumble of the snowplow and watched the monster machine create another three-foot high wall of snow at the end of his driveway.

With a shake of his head and a sigh, Paul went back in. The temperature was warming as the flakes stopped falling; the sun tried unsuccessfully, however, to poke through the clouds. Inside, he stripped off his winter gear and looked for Carolyn.

She wasn't in the kitchen, although the dishes were done and neatly stacked in the drainer. Nor was she in the living room where the afghan was now neatly folded and back in place. Heading up the stairs, he paused at the bathroom; her bra and panties hung drying over the shower rack. The girl had been busy.

But the sight in the bedroom made him stop in his tracks. The closet door was open and Carolyn sat on the bed, stroking the soft deerskin thongs of the flogger he had used in his weakness the night before. His hopes that she would ignore the incident dashed as shame colored his cheeks.

"Um, Carolyn, about last night…"

The wide-eyed, trusting, intelligent gaze she turned toward him made him stammer like a schoolboy. "I don't know why I did that and I'm really sorry. I hope you'll be able to forgive me at some point and I won't do it again. I promise. As long as you're stuck here, I won't touch you again."

She frowned. This wasn't going according to plan. He was supposed to be thrilled that she was submissive. "But I want you to touch me again. Paul, I told you last night, I like it. I like bondage and whips and chains and all that stuff people call 'kink.' It took me a long time to accept it and I won't pretend I understand it all, but I know I liked what you did last night…"

Paul held out his hand for the flogger and obediently Carolyn put the handle in his palm. Whirling it around his head, it whooshed through the air and he slapped it against his palm. The soft thongs wrapped around his hand in a tight caress that immediately loosened as the tails followed the handle.

"I like bondage, and whips and chains too, Carolyn, but that's because I'm a perverted and depraved man. I want to control a woman, not to rule over her or anything like that, but to use her body like a canvas, painting her with ropes and turning her skin pink. Or maybe like an instrument that sounds when I want it to, how I want it to."

Tightly controlled passion flared in his voice and in his eyes, Carolyn's stomach flipped over in response to the latent power emanating from his being.

"Exactly! But you cannot have that unless a woman first gives you her submission." Carolyn's cheeks colored. "I know you brought me home just to be polite, and I know I'm being tremendously forward, but do you know how hard it is to meet someone sexually compatible?" She shook her head. "Can you just see it? Me having a nice conversation with an attractive man and then saying to him, 'So I like to be tied up and treated like a sex object, do you mind?' It's not exactly an easy position to be in."

Paul looked at her, clearly not understanding her point. She tried again.

"Whether it was the darkness or the candles or the romance of being stuck in a snowstorm, it doesn't matter. Last night you and I showed our true selves to each other…the selves we protect and hide because society frowns on our peculiarities. It took me a long time…a *very* long time…to accept that my desires to submit in the bedroom are not abnormal…that I'm not a freak. It took even longer to reconcile my need to be seen as a competent professional and independent woman, with my need for a dominant male to balance me." Her explosive sigh gave away her frustration. "And now I find that a man whom I respect and am attracted to, has that dominant gene in him and he thinks it too perverted to let it out. Despite the fact that he has a closet full of those whips and chains he professes to despise!"

Paul's shame at his needs flared into anger. "I have a closet filled with those things because I dream of someday using them again. I've gone to workshops and met others like me; I'm no novice, despite what you think. I've flogged women to orgasm…and I've hurt them as well. That doesn't change how I view my own behavior last night. I had no right to do what I did when we've known each other such a short time."

"Paul, you are confusing the hell out of me. One minute you're ashamed of being a Dom, the next you're telling me you've taken lessons in how to be a good one!"

"I *am* ashamed of it. I went to those workshops at the local Kink Society…yes, miss-know-it-all, there is one. That was several years ago when I went through the same struggle to understand as you did…only at the time, I embraced it wholeheartedly. Dominating women, subjugating them to my will was a very heady experience to a kid of twenty-five.

"And then I grew up." He shrugged and tossed the flogger into the closet in frustration. His shoulders sagged as he sat on the bed beside Carolyn, the fight gone out of him. "Talk about how you can't just say, 'I want to be a sex slave'. Imagine me moving to the next stage with a woman I'm interested in and telling her, 'By the way, I want to tie you up and beat you silly, then fuck your brains out.' Not exactly good for relationships."

He looked so forlorn, Carolyn's anger dissipated. His hands lay loosely on his lap in defeat. She took his hand in hers, twining her fingers with his in sympathy.

"You must have been burned pretty badly."

He nodded. "I was. Even asked her to marry me. Then she found the whips. And the chains. And the rope."

"And she didn't understand."

"That's an understatement."

"And somehow she convinced you your needs were perverted and disgusting."

A grimace crossed his features. "That about sums it up, professor."

Carolyn sat back and considered, still keeping her hand in his. She wondered if he even knew her hand was there. "Well, if a woman you loved convinced you that you were sick, perhaps another woman you respect might convince you otherwise." She shrugged, keeping the tone in her voice light. "'Course, that presumes I'm a woman whose opinions you respect."

"What?" Paul came out of his reverie. "Of course I respect you. Which is why I shouldn't have done what I did last night."

"Damn it, Paul!" Carolyn dropped his hand and stood. "When are you going to get off that kick? Get it through your head, you did not do *anything* to me last night that I did not want!"

She retrieved the deerskin flogger; the symbol of their discussion, and held it in her hands, the sensuous softness of the tails causing an immediate reaction in her pussy. Ignoring it for the conversation at hand, she tried one last time.

"I don't want you telling me what to teach. I don't want you making career decisions for me. But to know that a man who's starting to steal my heart is also a man who could give me my sexual desires? Paul, can't you see I'm falling in love with you? The real you…and you're not perverted and you're not disgusting, and I want you to do those things to me. I wanted them last night and I want them again today."

She held the flogger out, handle first, in challenge. Paul looked up, his eyes narrowed as he struggled with her request. A small hope bloomed in his heart where despair had lived for the past several years.

"Carolyn, you cannot toy with me on this. I admitted last night I am attracted to you, but I don't want to get burned again when you realize this is no game."

She still held the flogger in her hand. Dropping her arm to her side, she knelt before him, letting her emotional intensity shine through her eyes. "Paul, I don't want it to be a game. Last night you told me we might have a future together. I feel the same way. I've met the man of my dreams. Please don't shut me out."

His eyes searched her face for any trace of deceit; there was none to be found. Only honesty shone in her soul…honesty and pleading. He touched her cheek and caught a tear as it fell. She had opened her heart for him to read and he believed her at last.

"Carolyn."

His voice whispered her name and she saw the acceptance in his eyes. Turning her face into his hand, she kissed his palm, closing her eyes to revel in his touch.

"This will not be an easy journey; there's a lot of exploration ahead of us." The chivalrous side of Paul warned her even as the sensuous beast inside him watched her reactions, marveling at the curve of her neck and the softness of her winter-white skin.

"The journey *is* the destination. It's exploration that makes life worth living."

"And what about your claustrophobia? I want to wrap your body in rope, tie you so you cannot move. You panic when snow blocks the doorway." His fingers traced the line of her throat, brushing against the softness of her lips, caressing her cheek.

"That's because there is no escape."

"And there will be no escape when I bind you." He wanted her. Yet even as his body responded to the warmth of her skin under his fingers, he threw the last roadblocks before her.

"Yes, there is. You are there to protect me." She turned her face to kiss the palm of his hand where he cupped her cheek. "I trust you, Paul. I am safe with you."

Their minds traded words, yet their bodies behaved with wills of their own, beginning a dance that would move them for the rest of their lives.

Chapter Five

"Stand up."

No mirth shone in Paul's eyes as the black knight took his place. Pretense and banter dropped away; shoulders straightened, his demeanor grew serious. Carolyn's stomach flipped so hard it sent shivers straight to her pussy, making her tremble. She had seen this very same look in his eyes the night before. Just before he flogged her. Standing, she took a deep breath and cleared her mind, immersing her being into the dance as Paul methodically stripped off the clothes she wore as if she were a doll to undress.

Going to the closet, Paul unzipped a duffle bag on the floor to choose the rope he would use to bind her body, confining her in a web of ropes woven to capture her mind. Such a delicate creature, and yet a willing partner to his artistry, deserved a special kind of binding.

Feeling the dark rope caress her skin urged Carolyn's mind into a blissful state where the everyday noise of life faded and only sensation mattered. Paul had chosen heavy coils of a soft, thick rope; the weight of it draped across her shoulders bound her to the ground so she would not float away.

Paul raised her arms and twined the rope around her body, lightly binding her champagne glass breasts in a framework of black rope. Once around, then twice, the pressure changed their shape into small balloons of need. Carolyn closed her eyes briefly, enjoying the sudden tightening in her pussy. Crisscrossing her torso, he worked the web down to her waist, knotting and weaving them into a mental state of togetherness.

When he bound her arms and hands behind her back, restricting her movement and making her vulnerable, Carolyn shivered in anticipation. She did not see Paul behind her, who paused the weaving to be sure she was with him. When her head turned and he saw her eyes closed and a small smile playing on her lips, he continued binding her body.

"Spread your legs for me."

The air caressed her pussy lips and Carolyn felt them part when she shifted her stance. Paul knotted a shorter rope in several places before tying it around her waist and bringing it between her legs; the dampness he found gave him all the permission he needed to continue. Centering the knots in position, he brought the rope up to her bound hands and tied it off behind her.

"Walk forward a few steps."

Carolyn took only one step and felt a knot rub on her clit, making that tiny organ swell with desire. A second step and she became aware of a second and third knot placed near on either end of her vagina. In three steps, she was ready to come.

"Oh, Paul…"

Immediately he stood beside her, holding her tightly in his arms. "Do not come, Carolyn. Do not come until I give you permission."

She nodded and struggled internally for a moment, letting the tension in her loins fade before she stood on her own feet again. Paul let her go and stepped back towards the closet again. "Walk to me, Carolyn. But do not come."

Focusing on his face, she crossed the space, determined not to come, even though the need grew at every step. Almost collapsing in his arms, she fought for breath as she fought to control her body so that she would not disappoint him.

"Someday you will wear this harness out in public, under your clothes." His mouth near her ear whispered the scene into her head. Her knees grew weak; she barely held her orgasm in check.

"No one will know what you have on; it will be our secret. But you will walk and come in public at my command."

She moaned and nodded her agreement. "Please let me come, please, Paul..."

"You want to come now?"

"Yes!" Her being shouted it, but her voice only whispered into the abyss.

"Then I will count to three and you will come when I tell you. Are you ready?" He prolonged the torment, knowing her body would respond harder for the wait.

"Yes, I'm ready."

"One...do not come yet." He tightened his grip on her, holding her in a safe place as her body shifted and the knots did their work.

"I'm holding it. Oh, Paul!" The plea in her voice was unmistakable.

"Two...almost there." He listened to her ragged breath, elated to feel the power in his hands.

"Three...come for me, Carolyn. Come hard."

Her body contracted with a powerful wave as she let go. His voice coached her, caressed her; his arms encircled her and protected her as her mind and body exploded. Each writhe made the knots brush against her sensitive spots and the orgasm continued, enveloping her mind as the world ceased to exist. Only Paul mattered. Paul who held her in her arms while her body was torn apart.

The tightness of his arms around her comforted her and she leaned against him, letting him hold her up as her body recovered. Once the world came back into focus and she no longer gasped for breath, Paul stood her on her own two feet and brushed her hair from her face.

Shyly she grinned up at him. "Thank you. That was incredible."

Her voice still held a dream-like quality; Paul's movements seemed slow to her; she watched, fascinated, as he stepped beside her to untie the rope that went between her legs. She didn't know whether to be relieved or disappointed.

"You liked the knots?" He threw the short rope onto the bed.

"Very much."

Good, her voice was steadier so Paul knew he could continue. "Come over here and take a look at yourself."

A long pier mirror hung on the wall on the other side of the room and Carolyn let him lead her to stand before it. The sight in the mirror made her breath catch. Black ropes encased her body like a spider's web, the whiteness of her skin shone through the diamond pattern he'd created across her abdomen. Twisting to see herself from the side, she caught a glimpse of her arms folded behind her, also tied with the black rope. Her back arched where her arms rested, pushing her breasts into the framework the rope supplied for them. Gently pulling to test the strength of the knots, she smiled at her reflection, caught fast in the webwork of his hands.

"You like looking at my creation, don't you?" Forming a woman's body into beautiful shapes made him proud. "You have become something more than yourself, tied in such a way. It is a position you could not achieve on your own; a position I could not create without you."

"You have made me greater than myself." Awe at his handiwork softened her voice and she gazed at him in wonder. "Let me be your canvas. Please?"

He smiled at her eagerness. "Not all in one day, nor all at one time. But I think we can take this picture further if you wish."

She nodded and he went back to the closet for something, leaving her to admire his work in the mirror. When he returned, he held some small coils of rope in one hand. By the side of the bed sat an old-fashioned straight-backed chair. He pulled it around so she stood behind it, yet could turn her head and see herself in the mirror. Grabbing a pillow from the bed, he set it over the back of the chair and gently leaned her forward.

With her arms bound, Carolyn had no balance; she placed her trust into Paul's strong hands as he bent her over the chair. The back was low enough that she didn't have to stand on tiptoe even though her head came down almost to the seat. Behind her, she felt Paul's hands reach for one of her ankles and she shifted her weight so he could move her foot, tying it to the leg of the chair. With a second rope, he tied her other leg and she was caught.

Now he ran a hand over her bare ass. With a blush, Carolyn realized how open she was to him, how vulnerable. He had access to every part of her pussy in this position and there was nothing she could to do stop him. In the mirror, she turned to watch his hand slide along her back and down over her bottom, inspecting her much as a buyer might inspect a thoroughbred before purchase.

Even though she saw him raise his hand, she still jumped when his slap connected. But a full spanking was not what he had in mind today. Just enough to turn her cheeks pink; to remind her how much she enjoyed his touch.

And she did. Watching him in the mirror, Carolyn's heart soared to see the black knight use his bound slave girl. Her pussy cried out for his cock…if only he would take her this way! His hand beat a rapid tattoo on her skin until she could bear it no longer.

"Oh, Paul, please! Take me…let me feel your cock inside me. Please!"

Ever since last night, when he'd first glimpsed that beautiful pussy with its twin pink lips, he had wanted to sink his cock deep inside her. Agonizing over his sexual preferences didn't change the fact that he was falling in love. Now their twin passions built to create an inferno between them. Her pleas called to him and he answered.

"Do you really want this, Carolyn?" His hands softly stroked her naked ass, the skin warmed by his touch. His cock, long and hard, aching to bury itself inside her, pulsed with a life of its own.

"Yes, Paul. Please. Oh, God, please take me!"

"And you will not come until I tell you to."

She shook her head as the caress of his fingers on her ass caused thought to recede. "I won't come until you tell me to."

Paul stripped off his clothes, dropping them in a pile on the floor. Parting her cheeks with his hands, he held her ass firmly as her muscles quivered in his palms. Her pussy gaped open, the white juices heralding her arousal pooling just inside. Resting his cock against that opening, he teased her, waiting for the moan she would make when he did not immediately enter her.

She did not disappoint him. "Please, Paul! Let me feel you inside me." Straining against the ropes, Carolyn tried to push back onto him.

"I like it when you beg." The surge of power that filled him throbbed in his cock. Her body, bound and helpless before him, waited for his taking. Slowly, he pushed ever so gently, barely entering her before pulling out to rest his cock at the opening again.

"Oh, yes, oh, Paul, please!" Humiliation at having to beg threatened her self-control. His teasing drove her mad with desire and again she strained against her bindings, trying to push back and take him in. But his knots held fast and she could not move.

Another long, slow thrust, this time going in deeper before pulling out to tease the sensitive spot right behind her vagina; his cock, slick with her juices and dark with desire, throbbed for release.

But the torture was too sweet and the release would be greater for the teasing. Entering her again, he pushed himself all the way in until his balls caressed her clit and she cried out. He felt the muscles of her pussy twitch once before she regained control of them; she could not hold out much longer.

"Do not come, Carolyn. Hold it." Warning sounded in his voice as he asserted his control over her.

She could not answer him. Focusing all her energy on not coming took every ounce of strength she had. Tension built inside to burn between her legs. She could barely breathe. From some depth, she found the willpower to nod her understanding and did not come. The tension receded.

When her body relaxed, Paul increased his tempo, hammering deep inside her, slamming against her in a steady tattoo designed to make her beg for real. Could she? Would she be able to give him control when she had none left of her own?

His cock hit her G-spot repeatedly and Carolyn cried out, a wordless cry beyond the capability of speech. Her body was not her own. Paul took it, seized it, played with it as he saw fit. Whimpers forced from her by his thrusts filled the room. The tension in her body grew again and from the depths of her soul, she moaned, "Please, let me come, oh God, please!" A sob escaped as his continued thrusts used her body.

Pulling completely out, Paul took pity on her. She couldn't take much more. And neither could he. His cock, swelled and purpled with ridges of need, ached for release. For the past several thrusts, he barely held himself in check. Poising himself again at the entrance to her pussy, he let himself sink into the desire that swept them both.

"When I get to three, you will come, Carolyn? Do you understand?"

She nodded and tried to speak in assent, but only whimpered. No longer trying to push back, she hung limply, giving Paul control over her body. All she could do was clench her pussy tightly and hold onto the edge until he gave permission for her to fall off the cliff.

"One..." Paul thrust in deep, letting his own need drive him now. His cock touched the back wall of her vagina and the wet caress threatened to overtake his control.

"Two..." Guttural and feral, his voice rasped out the number. Several thrusts as her tight pussy caressed him. He glanced in the mirror and the sight destroyed the rest of his control.

Carolyn's body, encased in black rope bent over the straight-backed chair, pushing her ass into the air. Her arms bound behind her and her legs tied to the legs of the chair, made her vulnerable to his every whim. Her face—turned toward the mirror—grimaced in pleasure/pain as he thrust into her. His own naked body, muscular and trim, slammed into her open pussy.

"Three..." With a groan, Paul emptied himself into her as her orgasm contracted around his cock. The muscles in his groin snapped as the tension coiled in his cock released his seed to spurt into her.

Carolyn's body, bound and helpless, racked with the contractions of her orgasm. Anchored with ropes, her soul flew between the clouds as each spasm rocked her body. Paul's cock inside her formed a link between them. Together they dipped and flew through the clouds. The artist and the canvas became one. Their spirits soared together to create a new masterpiece.

Paul came back to earth first, his cock softening inside her. Loath to pull out, he knew he needed to; she was in his care. Although still tied to the chair, he helped her to stand so he could embrace her as she continued to shake with the aftershocks of her powerful orgasm.

Carolyn felt his arms around her; the knight protecting his beloved slave girl. After several moments, her breathing slowed and she nodded. "I can stand." Her voice a whisper in the room.

Kneeling behind her to untie her ankles, Paul could not help caressing her legs. He hadn't noticed how beautiful they were before. Especially the little hollow behind her knee. Gently he placed a kiss in each hollow before he stood to untie her arms.

Floating in the haze of their coupling, Carolyn smiled a lazy smile. As her hands came loose, she stretched them slowly, allowing the cramped muscles to return to normal. The webwork did not take long to dismantle and in only a few moments, the two of them nestled together under the covers of the bed, entwined in each other's arms as their hearts entwined with love.

*****

Sunlight streamed through the unshaded window; its brightness woke Carolyn from a very contented dream. The particulars faded, however, when she opened her eyes and saw Paul sleeping beside her. One arm curved protectively around her waist; his other rested under her head. The softness of his skin brushed her cheek and she turned to place a delicate kiss in the crook of his elbow.

Her movement stirred him and he opened his eyes, finding a beautiful woman in his arms. Stretching, he pulled her close; she rolled over to face him and fit her body to his, embracing him for what he was.

For several long moments, they lay entwined, not speaking. The afterglow of their lovemaking still wrapped them in a haze and neither wanted to peel it away. Only after several moments did Paul realize the red numbers on the bedside clock blinked off and on.

"Power's back." He made no move to get up.

"Good." Carolyn rolled onto her back. "We both need showers. Especially after our…workout." The impish smile he loved the night before was back.

"Don't want to take one together?" He couldn't help teasing her.

She cocked her head sideways. "Go take your shower, my black knight and perhaps your slave girl will join you. And perhaps she will not!"

Paul's laugh, genuine and heartfelt, gave Carolyn a thrill of satisfaction.

"Black knight, hmm? Well, perhaps this 'black knight' will command his slave girl to give him five minutes and then come wash her master!"

"Your command is my wish!"

She watched him saunter off to the bathroom, admiring the taut muscles of his rear as he walked away. The broad sweep of his shoulders tapered quite nicely to that ass, she decided as she lay on her side, enjoying the view. His diamond-shaped tattoo darkened the one cheek, but she decided it accentuated the curve of his rear end rather than marred it. She would have to ask him for more details about that later. Paul turned the corner into the bathroom and her analysis of his physical attributes was cut short, so she fell back onto the bed in utter contentment.

The sun still shone in her eyes, however, so she got up to look upon the winter wonderland outside. Deep snow covered the landscape, smoothing out the lumps of everyday life. Although Paul told her the snowplow had been along the street earlier, apparently not much else had disturbed the snow. And the small amount that had fallen after the plow left had softened even the piles pushed up by the blade.

The room's temperature, colder than the warmth she shared under the covers with Paul, worked on her bladder and she made her way to the bathroom. Hearing the shower turn on, she crossed her legs and waited until she heard the shower curtain pulled into place before entering quietly.

The toilet seat was up; she grinned and put it down for her own use. Once her needs were taken care of, she stepped to the small shower stall and peeked in. No tub graced this tiny room; behind the curtain was just enough room for one person.

Paul grinned and stepped into the corner, making room for Carolyn to squeeze in, but she shook her head. Instead, she stepped up and balanced on the ledge that separated the shower floor from the bathroom floor and motioned for him to hand her the soap and turn around.

Facing the back of the shower, Paul enjoyed the feel of the slippery bar of soap as she ran it over his back and shoulders. While he knew what he wanted of a woman in the bedroom, what he wanted from her the rest of the time was still murky. She said she wasn't a doormat; he doubted he would have given her a second glance if she were. Clearly she was in charge in this shower. The thought made him grin as he realized he liked the switch.

Rubbing the soap over his skin, first with one hand, then with two as she leaned against him for balance, gave Carolyn the thrill of exploration. Where he had explored her body fairly thoroughly, she had not yet had that opportunity. When he didn't object, she traveled further.

The broad expanse of his smooth back tapered nicely to a trim waist. Small, fine hairs softened the touch of his skin. Standing on the ledge, the top of her head came to the top of his shoulders, so she leaned in, letting her cheek rest on the damp skin as her hands wrapped around to explore his chest.

In the candlelight the night before, she had gotten a glimpse of this strong chest, but in truth, her attention at that time had followed the line of his chest hairs to a spot somewhat lower on his body. Now, however, she dwelt on his upper body, exploring the ridges of his muscles, finding tiny, hard nipples that she could tease with the soap, all the while listening to his heartbeat where her ear pressed against his back.

Paul's cock grew at the sensuous movement of her hands over his body. In all his life, with the few girlfriends he had gone to bed with, never had any one of them come to the shower with him. Had he known just how erotic getting washed by a beautiful woman could be, he would have done this a long time ago.

Carolyn's hands slid down, satisfied by their exploration of his chest and ready to find more information. She circled around his waist, coming back to feel the smooth curves of his ass…an ass she greatly admired up close as well as from far away. Tight muscles held the cheeks firmly in place, muscles that relaxed under her touch. Lightly she traced the dark diamond shape with the tip of her finger and when he reached out for the bar on the other side of the shower to steady himself, she grinned in satisfaction.

His leaning pushed his ass toward her and threatened to unbalance her. In self-preservation, she grabbed hold of his waist. Her fingers brushed his erection when she did so and her grin deepened. Steady once more, she purposefully ran her hands down the backs of his thighs, coming around to the front and moving up along them…being very careful not to touch his cock or his balls. Two could tease at this game.

But when his hand came down and guided her to his erection, she knew he was taking charge again…and she loved it. Taking the lead for a while was fun, but she was more than willing to let him bring them home. The soap dropped from her hands as she caressed his cock, feeling its wet, velvety-soft skin under her fingers. He moved forward and she stepped into the cascade of water and explored his cock with her hands.

She had seen his cock under candlelight, now she closed her eyes and imagined it as her fingers ran along its length. Wrapping both hands around still left a full inch of his cock in the cold. She moved a hand up to cover the tip with her palm.

Leaning against the bar, Paul endured her explorations, even though his cock throbbed with need. Her fingers found the ridges made by the veins and traced along them; he resisted the urge to take care of matters himself and bring things to a quick conclusion. Instead, he savored her touch and the flames she set burning inside him.

But when he could take it no more, he turned to face her, taking her petite and beautiful face in his hands to kiss her under the stream of water. Their bodies pressed together and she felt his hard cock stabbing into her belly. His hands reached down to squeeze her ass, and with a sudden movement that made her squeal, Paul lifted her up and put her against the wall of the shower. She wrapped her legs around him and held on tight.

"Tell me you want me," his voice growled over the shower.

"Oh, yes, Paul. I want you. Please take me right here."

"Beg me."

Her need grew with his words. He demanded of her; her heart soared as she complied.

"Please, Paul, oh God, please take me…let me feel your cock buried inside me. Please!"

His voice softened and he eased her down so his cock just touched her skin. "I love you, Carolyn. You give me what I need without hesitation, without fear."

Carolyn looked into his eyes, at the passion tempered with kindness and wonder. "Paul," her voice a bare whisper above the sound of the water. "I love you, too. Now please fuck me!"

Laughing he obliged, his cock entering her in one swift motion. She rode him, holding onto for dear life as the orgasm reached its peak, her muscles contracting around his cock caressingly. He closed his mouth over hers as she came, breathing in her essence, sharing her moments in the clouds as his own orgasm shook him.

And when they were spent, he let her down carefully, making sure she could stand before gracefully conceding the shower to her so she could wash her hair.

Listening to her hum a tune in the shower while he dried off, Paul was struck by the contentment he felt. He couldn't remember the last time he had come twice in one day. His watch lay on the sink; already it was noon and neither of them had eaten. While sex all day was an intriguing prospect, reality had to set in sometime. They needed to eat, and Carolyn's car was still buried in a snowdrift. Whistling something tuneless, he sauntered out of the bathroom to get dressed.

Later, while pulling on her borrowed baggy sweatpants, Carolyn looked at the mess they'd made of the bathroom. Water puddled in several spots where the curtain had been pulled aside when their minds turned toward other pursuits. Quickly she cleaned up, rehanging her still wet panties and bra before going to the bedroom for her blouse.

But she couldn't wear it…not having worn it all day yesterday. Scanning the room for that hideous sweatshirt he had given her to wear, she remembered it was still downstairs by the chair. Naked from the waist up, she ambled down to retrieve it.

Paul heard her come down the stairs and poked his head in from the kitchen. There stood his angel, his slave girl, her wet hair combed back from her face and bare-breasted. All she wore from the waist up was a frown.

"What's the matter, my naked slave girl?"

"That red sweatshirt with the heart on it? I thought I left it down here last night."

"You did. I put it over on the far end table. That's it."

She picked it up. The white heart practically glowed against the red background. Sliding it over her head, she stuck her arms through and pulled it into place. "It says, 'Be Mine.' Are you asking me to?"

Though her eyes teased, the question was serious and Paul knew it. He set down the pan he had in his hand and crossed the room. Standing before her, he traced the heart with his finger, feeling the curves of her breasts under the shirt.

"'Be Mine.'" He gave a wry grin as he said the words. "You know, my sister gave me this shirt at Christmas. My married sister who thinks I'm long overdue for a wife." His manner was suddenly shy again and Carolyn's heart grew tender as he made his confession. "She told me if I wore it for Valentine's Day, maybe I'd get a date. I don't know what she was thinking."

Carolyn grinned as he tugged on the shirt and pulled her into his arms. "I suppose you've already got a date for the school dance?"

He laughed. "Oh, I think I might be able to rustle up someone. Someone who looks much better in that shirt than I would." He bent forward and kissed her lightly.

"I am not wearing this sweatshirt to the dance at the high school, Mr. Anderson!" She affected a shocked expression.

"Fine, I think you'd look much better in nothing at all…" He ducked as she swung playfully at him, then pulled her into his arms. "All kidding aside, Carolyn…"

The seriousness in his tone caught her attention. "Yes?"

"Will you be mine? I won't pretend to know where our relationship is going, but I do know my life would be empty if I didn't explore this with you."

She didn't hesitate. "Yes, Paul, I will be yours. I'm not sure what exactly that means yet, but I know I want to find out."

"Then it sounds as if we're both in the dark on this journey."

"As long as you're there beside me…or should that be one step ahead of me?" Her eyes twinkled as she teased him, yet there was an underlying unease in the question.

"Perhaps I'll keep you barefoot and pregnant, too." He bent to kiss her again just because she looked so adorable in that hideous sweatshirt.

Carolyn snorted and put her hand up to stop him. "Not on your life, buster. Well, barefoot, maybe. But kids? That's a long way into my future yet."

Paul smiled and the black knight peered out. "Mine as well. For now, I can be perfectly satisfied getting to know my slave girl cum teacher."

She giggled. "Hmmm… I think I know a slave girl cum teacher who has already come numerous times today!"

Laughing, Paul took her hands, holding them behind her back so that he could get the kiss he wanted from the petite woman before him. She obliged by standing on her tiptoes, meeting his lips with hers in a warm touch. Out of habit, she moved her arms to bring them around his neck, but he held them fast. Smiling in the kiss, she let him know how his hold on her made her tingle all over. Her lips parted and he took her invitation, letting his tongue gently brush against her softness before entwining deeper to caress her very being.

The teakettle whistled and both of them jumped back as if they were children caught doing something naughty. Carolyn giggled first, and Paul laughed as he took her hand and they headed into the kitchen to eat.

Chapter Six

The afternoon deepened into twilight and Paul enjoyed the warmth of the woman who snuggled with him on his hideous couch. No doubt tomorrow they would have school; the plow had been down the street again and traffic had already begun moving around the neighborhood. A tow truck had been called and Carolyn's car should be uncovered soon. Which reminded him; his own car still sat where they had left it the afternoon before, two feet of snow piled up on top of it.

After a late breakfast, the two of them had snuggled together on the couch and talked away the lazy afternoon. From time to time, the hum of a snowblower alerted them another driveway or sidewalk was being cleared; but both felt more inclined towards the simple enjoyment of each other's company. Now, however, Paul stirred, sighing over the inevitable.

"I suppose I ought to go dig out that car in the driveway if we're to get back to school tomorrow."

Carolyn sat up, reluctant to give up the comfortable pillow of his chest. "I know. I've been thinking about it, too. The garage will call when they have my car dug out; I can pick it up there first thing in the morning. But I haven't any clothes and I really should go home to change."

"Your classes start later than mine tomorrow; why don't I drop you off at the garage early and then you can go home and do what you need to do?"

"You do start an hour before we do…that would work." Stretching out, she flexed her arms and arched her back; snuggling with Paul all afternoon made her feel slow and lazy. But he was right; they really shouldn't be idle all day, not if they had school tomorrow. She brought her hands down to slap her thighs and stood with resolution. "Come on, lazybones. Let's get that driveway shoveled out. Doesn't look like the snow fairy is going to come and do it for us."

She laughed as she pulled him up off the couch. How natural it felt to slide her arm around his waist as the two of them walked toward the kitchen. "I think the snow fairy brings the snow, not takes it away," he whispered in her ear.

Twilight was fading fast; the winter days weren't very long this time of year. Carolyn slipped her arms into her short winter coat and slid on her too-fancy boots. The job wouldn't take them long with both of them working on the car, so the boots would do. Paul headed to the shed in the back for an old broom while Carolyn pulled on her hat and gloves. Satisfied she could keep the cold at bay, she ventured out into the evening.

The crisp air felt good on her face after all that time inside. Breathing deeply, she watched the sunlight fade to twilight; the few wisps of clouds turning rainbow colors of pink and purple before fading into gray. Thick snow still clung to the trees, outlining the branches in the stark relief of black and white.

Paul came from behind the house to see her standing in the cleared part of the drive, an angel in snow clothes. Her hair spread over her shoulders like a mantle of golden warmth as the streetlight shone on her upturned face. The fact that this petite beauty, this heavenly yet earthbound angel, could love him, could embrace his demons, humbled him, shamed him. Whether he deserved such a gift was a debate for a later time. For now he simply sent a silent "thank you" heavenward. Her presence in his life was enough.

She heard his step on the crunchy snow and turned to see her knight, armed with a shovel and a broom and ready to do battle with the elements. Over the past twenty-four hours, she had studied his face in many types of lighting and in many moods, from commanding to shy and everything in between. He stood in the shadow of the streetlight now, looking handsome and brave in the dim light. When he beckoned to her, she went with a willing step.

Paul gave her the broom to push the snow off the car; he shoveled what she pushed off. In relatively short time, the car was cleared and he attacked the bottom of the drive where the plow had filled it in. Since he only owned the one shovel, Carolyn couldn't help, but it was too nice an evening to go inside just yet. Through the trees with their laden branches, she could see the full moon rising. The snowblowers had long since stopped their incessant hum and quiet descended on the street as neighbors moved back into their own homes for another night of peace.

With a final heave, Paul cleared the last of the snow and turned toward Carolyn. But she wasn't there. Where could she have gone? The broom leaned against the side door and he decided she must've gotten cold and gone back inside. Carrying the two tools back to the shed, he whistled something tuneless as he sauntered along the side of the house.

She waited for him in the postage-sized backyard. As soon as he came into view, she grinned, threw her arms out wide, and fell backwards, flat against the snow. The day's sun had tamped the snow a bit, but she still landed pleasantly deep. With quick, strong movements, she flapped her arms up and down along the snow, her hands making small plows. Opening and closing her legs, she felt the snow slide into her boot, but she didn't care.

Paul's laugh started as a chuckle and grew into a full belly laugh as he realized what she was doing. Leaning the tools beside the dilapidated shed, he trudged into the snow to stand off to the side. But when he turned to make his own angel, she cried out to stop him. "No, Paul! You can't fall yet, you have to get me up first!"

Grinning, his cheeks reddened with the cold, he stood in front of her and held out his hand. Grabbing it, Carolyn felt as if she flew up and into his arms. He stepped back and they admired her perfect angel in the snow. The moon slid over the top of the shed and its light bathed the angel in white.

"Oh, look! The moon's given her diamonds!"

"What?"

"Diamonds in the snow…see? The way the moonlight makes the snow glitter? My father used to call that 'diamonds in the snow'."

It was true. The moonlight on the angel sparkled like tiny white diamonds.

Paul gazed at his real-life angel in amazement. "Carolyn, I cannot believe I have lived all these years without the poetry you have brought to me in the past twenty-four hours. You've given me your body to wrap in rope and flog with my whip; you make me snow angels and give me diamonds where I never expected them. You are incredible."

Carolyn blushed, her cheeks warming at his words. "You bring out the poet in me, I guess. For the first time in my life, I don't feel I need to watch my words, or temper my reactions to anything. You accept my passion and just let me be me…that makes you pretty incredible, too."

"But one snow angel isn't enough. I want two angels made of diamonds in my backyard." With a spin, Paul flung himself into the snow, making the wings of his angel brush against hers. Waving frantically, plumes of snow flew into the air as his legs and arms created the image. Laughing, Carolyn stood at his feet, putting out her hand to help him rise.

Except that her small frame was not strong enough for his larger bulk. As Paul struggled to rise without damaging the angel, her feet slipped in the snow. With an oath, he fell backward with Carolyn landing on top of him, gasping in surprise.

They erupted into laughter. His angel ruined, Paul threw caution to the wind and rolled Carolyn over, creating a new impression in the snow. She squealed and he put his hand over her lips to shush her. A furtive glance to be sure the neighbors weren't watching assured him of their privacy. He looked down to see Carolyn's wide eyes dissolve into giggles.

"A real angel and a snow angel in my backyard. What more could a man wish for?" He cupped her face in his hands. "I love you, Carolyn Brooks. I love your angels and your poetry, and the gift of submission you want to give me."

"And I love you, Paul Anderson. I love you for the passion you show for life and for the ugly couch you own, and for the gift of dominance that scares you, and yet you give it to me anyway. You and your tattoo are my very own diamond in the snow."

He kissed her hard and deep and passionate. Her fervor matched his as she opened her very being for him to claim. The warmth of their fervor fueled their need, the coldness of their bed forgotten in their revelations of love.

Until snow slid down Paul's pants. With a start, he sat up, eyes wide. "Damn, that's cold. Really, really cold!"

Carolyn leaned on her elbows, the mischievous look back in her eyes. "Then let's go undress you and get you warm again."

Paul kissed her again and struggled to stand in the deep snow. After a few false starts and a push from Carolyn, he made it to his feet. He looked down at the woman he loved, still on her knees. "Perhaps I should just have you come into the house that way."

She looked up at him and grinned to see the black knight before her. "What ever you desire, dear Sir." With a catlike grace, she crawled through the snow, her clothes already drenched from their playing. Mischief glittered in her eyes…mischief intensified with challenge.

Paul waited until she had cleared the snow and knelt in the shoveled driveway. "Stand, my slave girl."

How she managed to be subservient without being servile astounded him. Carolyn rose to stand before him, eyes downcast, chin held high. A small smile played on her lips as she acquiesced to his commands. The little minx loved this and Paul again sent a thought of amazed thanks heavenward.

And then she shivered in the cold and all the protective fibers of his chivalry gathered in concern for her welfare.

"I'm not the only one who's cold. Inside and undress now."

The small smile turned to a grin as she darted through the door, kicking off her boots and stripping off her coat at the same time. "I'll beat ya!"

Paul yanked off his coat even as he hollered. "No fair…you had a head start!"

Giggling, she pulled her sweatpants down and off in one fluid motion. As Paul tangled himself in his bootlaces, she crossed her arms and grabbed the bottom of the red sweatshirt, denuding herself in record time.

"Ta-da!" Pirouetting in the kitchen, she gloried in her nudity. The light under the stovetop dimly lit her with its fluorescence. She turned, and turned again to be sure Paul had an eyeful.

His wet pants still clung to his legs, chilling him even as his heart beat faster at the sight of the naked woman dancing around his kitchen. Sliding them into a heap, he kicked the entire soggy pile into the corner. The clothes could wait until later. In two strides, he crossed the space between them and scooped his dancing angel into his arms.

"Make love to me, Carolyn. Right here, right now."

For answer, she stood on tiptoe and kissed him.

Soft lips closed over his as he bent down to meet them. Her tongue flicked out to brush against his; they met, entwining as the kiss deepened and passion ignited. Encircling her waist with one hand, he caressed her breast with the other, not needing to tease awake a nipple already stiffened with desire, but rather enjoying the feel of the hard little nub under his thumb.

Carolyn moaned as his hands slid over her body, awakening every nerve ending. "Please, Paul, take me. Right here in the kitchen."

He loved the power she gave him. "Beg me, slave girl."

For a moment, joy lit her eyes. But as she knelt, urgency replaced her contentment. Her begging pushed her need.

"Please, Paul…please take me. Take me right here and now. I beg you. Please take me?"

"And what should I do with you?"

Her cheeks flamed with heat as she realized what he wanted her to say. Embarrassment flared into full arousal as she swallowed hard and forced the words out. "Fuck me. Please, Paul. Fuck me right here in your kitchen."

He raised an eyebrow at the proper woman who now knelt in his kitchen using gutter language to beg him for what she so desperately wanted. Power rushed through his being, power channeled into his rising cock. She had begged; he would oblige.

Reaching down, he took her hands and lifted her up so she stood before him. The rise and fall of those wonderfully pert breasts quickened as he stepped nearer. But instead of embracing her, he lifted her up and set her on the old oak table.

"Spread your legs for me, slave girl."

Leaning back on her hands, she spread wide, feeling sluttish and wonderfully free as she did so. Open and vulnerable to his gaze, she gloried in his use of her.

A small tuft of darker hair covered her mound, the last sentinel of her modesty. Lightly he tugged at it, watching her melt as he did so.

Each hair felt as if it had its own nerve ending and his touch enflamed every one of them. Grinning seductively, she arched her back and pressed her mound into his palm.

Sliding a finger between lips already swollen with desire, Paul was not surprised to discover a fair amount of wetness had already prepared her for his entrance. But he was not one to rush. Slowly sliding one finger inside, he bent to pull a delicious nipple into his mouth. Sucking it hard, he pushed against her clit with the palm of his hand. The deep moan from the back of her throat was music to his ears.

"Remember, don't come until I tell you." Keeping his palm centered on her clit, he slid his finger all the way out before plunging in again. He loved the way she wiggled under his touch as he lightly bit her nipple and increased the tempo of his finger.

She nodded, not trusting her voice as he changed from one finger to two pumping in and out of her vagina. The nerve endings sent ripples from her breast to her pussy. Each time a wave of arousal passed through her abdomen, her stomach tightened and her breath quickened. Wrapping her feet around the table legs, she fought against the rising orgasm, willing herself to not give in.

He liked the look of utter concentration she had on her face. Eyes closed and brow furrowed as she bit her lower lip. As his palm pushed against her with more force, her body swayed in the dance with him. Yet still she held and her muscles did not contract around his fingers.

His cock throbbed. Paul knew he could not hold out much longer himself. Feeling her sensuous dance beneath him, watching her breasts rise and fall faster and faster tightened the muscles in his chest 'til he felt he could hardly breathe. He needed her. But he needed her submissiveness more.

Putting his hands on her tush, he pulled her toward him so that she just hung on the edge of the table. Leaning forward to balance himself on one hand, he positioned himself at the entrance to her pussy. His voice raw and commanding, he ordered her one more time.

"Beg me, Carolyn."

Her eyes flew open and struggled to focus on his face. "Oh, Paul…please fuck me now!"

With a slow and steady thrust, Paul pushed his cock inside her. Carolyn cried out, her legs wrapping around his waist, encircling and encouraging him. With her head thrown back, she arched her spine, wanting to feel his cock deep inside.

He obliged, relentlessly pushing against her as her body accepted his intrusion until the full length of his cock buried itself in her tight warmth. Gathering her in his arms, he whispered in her ear. "Hold onto me, Carolyn. Hold on tight."

She wrapped her arms around his neck as his cock slowly moved in and out. His lips nipped at her ear and she whimpered as her body responded to his touches.

"I want to own this, Carolyn." He squeezed her tight. "I want this body to belong to me."

"Oh, Paul..." Her voice was little more than a whisper in her need. "Yes. Take it and use it."

He thrust in again and she cried out. "Paul, I can't hold it. Please let me come!"

"Tell me you want to come, Carolyn."

"Yes, please! I want to come!" The words ripped from her soul. How could he be so maddeningly deliberate? She held tightly onto him, as if her very being were being ripped from her. The tension in her body would overwhelm her at any moment.

Increasing the pace of his thrusts, Paul's need threatened to overtake him as he held her close to his chest. Faster and faster they danced together, their bodies arching and crying out for release. Barely able to force the words out, Paul commanded her. "Come for me, Carolyn. Come now!"

Their voices joined in a feral chorus as passion erupted, waves of warmth radiating from their joined bodies. Over and over Paul thrust into her as his body emptied its fury, his groans filling the air. He clung to her, desperation replaced by fulfillment as the world faded and then slowly returned.

Carolyn hung limp in his arms, her breath coming in great gasps. He felt her leg muscles loosen and shifted her to lie back on the table. Her eyes opened and looked at him as if she still floated in a dream.

And it was a very nice dream, Carolyn decided as she looked at the concerned face of the black knight above her. Lazily, she reached up to caress his face with the back of her hand, idly running her fingers over his jawline as contentment settled upon her.

"Thank you."

Her simple words touched him. Never before had any woman thanked him for the sex they shared, but then, it had only been sex with them. With Carolyn it was so much more. For the first time, not only his hormones were involved. This woman had touched his heart with her acceptance of his "kink". Bending over the table, he kissed her lightly and brushed an errant hair from her face.

"I love you, Carolyn Brooks." He scooped her into his arms and carried her out of the kitchen.

Carolyn knew she should at least make some token protest. At least, they always did in the movies. But then again, that would take too much energy and she loved how she fit in his arms and the strength that surrounded her. Putting her arms around his neck, she nestled her nose against his neck as he carried her up the stairs.

"You gave me diamonds in the snow tonight, Carolyn," he told her as he lay beside her in the bed. "Someday soon, I will give you a real diamond."

Such an earnestness shone in his face, Carolyn smiled. There were times he looked so much like a little boy in a candy store…and times when the darkness of his soul made her quiver. "Perhaps it should be a diamond-studded collar instead of something more conventional."

He kissed her. Hard, and long, and deep. How could she set off such fires in him? Turning toward her and pulling her into his arms, he knew acceptance of his nature for the first time in his life. As he felt her fingers drift over the diamond tattoo on his ass, he sighed in total contentment, and began to mentally design the slave collar he would fasten around her neck. This woman who reveled in his sexual domination and set his demon free. This woman who made him whole.

Epilogue

Carolyn stretched and yawned when the alarm went off, Paul was out of bed and on his way out of the room before she even remembered where she was. His absence left a warm spot in the bed and she curled into it, thinking how nice it would be to have this luxury every morning.

"Come on, lazybones. Time for school."

Paul's voice cut through her dozing and Carolyn blinked and yawned again as she rolled over. Beside the bed, Paul rummaged in the closet, pulling out clothes and tossing them on top of her where she lay. Trying to get her body moving, she pulled herself up and paused to watch him dress. Quite a pleasant sight to wake up to, she decided.

Pulling on a white T-shirt, he poked his head out to give her a mock frown. "Out of bed, slave girl. We have school today."

Poking out her lower lip, she flounced out of bed and headed for the shower. By the time she finished, Paul was already downstairs. The clothes she had been wearing when her car went into the ditch were neatly laid out on the straightened bedclothes.

The sound of the teakettle greeted her as she entered the kitchen, dressed and ready to leave. Paul had two cups out, the hot chocolate all ready for her. Grinning she accepted both the cup and the quick kiss he gave her.

"I wish I had time to tear off those clothes and make mad passionate love to you, but..." Paul checked his watch. "I have exactly twenty minutes to get you to the garage and myself to school."

Downing her cocoa, Carolyn watched as he pulled on his coat, the professional demeanor of teacher coming as naturally to him as the role of dominant had been denied. An unexpected qualm made her put down her cup harder than she intended.

"Paul..." She stopped, unsure how to express her sudden unease.

He saw the uncertainty in her face. Dropping his briefcase, he crossed the room and took her face in his hands, bending to kiss her as his heart wanted to—long and deep and filled with love. And when he finished, he held her close and whispered in her ear, "I am not the same man taking you back to your car that I was when I picked you up. You have changed me, Carolyn. I don't know where this is going, but I do know I want you beside me."

He felt her relax in his arms and stepped back so he could look into her eyes.

"Thank you, Paul. I just needed a little reassurance, I guess."

"I'll give you all the reassurance you need. Because there will be times I'll need it too, I'm betting."

She grinned. "We'd best be getting you off to school, my dear sir, or it's more than reassurances we'll be needing!"

"Nice English, Teach." He swatted her playfully on the rear as she walked past him to put on her coat and boots. Her eye fell on her laptop, still sitting where she'd left it when she'd first walked in the door. She groaned as she remembered the pile of papers she had thrown in just before leaving school.

"What's the matter?" A frown crossed Paul's face and Carolyn hurried to reassure him.

"Just uncorrected papers that the kids will have to wait for."

He grinned. "They won't care. Getting them back fast matters more to us than to them. Come on, let's get rolling, Cato!"

Wrinkling her nose at him, she walked into the cold, dark morning. The sun wasn't quite up, but would be soon; dim light shone on the horizon. To her amazement, his car started right away, even after having been ignored for so long in the cold.

All too soon, Paul pulled into the garage's parking lot. Her car sat in the middle of a row of several others, all of which bore evidence of having been dug out of snowbanks. When she hesitated before opening her door, Paul put his hand out to her and she slipped her gloved one into his.

"Carolyn, after school today...would you mind if... Oh, never mind. I'll call you tonight."

Carolyn grinned and kissed him soundly. "Yes, Paul, you may stop by my room. Or, if you'd rather not be seen together yet, call me later. But you'd better get going now if you don't want to be late!"

Paul watched her as she threaded her way through the towed cars to the attendant. Satisfied she was in safe hands and able to take care of herself, he pulled out of the parking lot and headed for school. The roads were crowded as life returned to normal. School buses and minivans jockeyed for position in the drop-off zone at school and a seemingly unending line of students trudged into the building.

Paul parked in his regular spot, grabbing his briefcase before shutting and locking the door. Halfway to the building, he stopped as the sun came over the horizon and glimmered on the snow. He stood still, grinning like a lunatic, staring at the sight until a student bumped him on the arm.

"What's so interesting, Mr. Anderson?"

"Just looking at the diamonds in the snow, James. Just looking at the diamonds."

About the author:

For many years, Diana Hunter confined herself to mainstream writings. Her interest in the world of dominance and submission, dormant for years, bloomed when she met a man who was willing to let her explore the submissive side of her personality. In her academic approach to learning about the lifestyle, she discovered hundreds of short stories that existed on the topic, but none of them seemed to express her view of a d/s relationship. Challenged by a friend to write a better one, she wrote her first BDSM novel, *Secret Submission*, published by Ellora's Cave Publishing.

Diana welcomes mail from readers. You can write to her c/o Ellora's Cave Publishing at 1056 Home Avenue, Arkon OH 44310-3502.

Also by Diana Hunter:

Ellora's Cavemen: Tales From the Temple III anthology

Irish Enchantment anthology

Learning Curve

Secret Submission

Table for Four

Diamond In the Rough

Ruby Storm

"Oft have I heard both youth and virgin say
Birds choose their mates, and couples too, this day;
But by their flight I never can divine,
When I shall couple with my Valentine."

Herrick

Prologue

Claire Holliday rolled slowly to her back, cloaked by the heavy darkness that surrounded her body. Where is he? Just minutes before, Scott had cradled her in his muscular arms, pressed a deliciously wicked kiss to her already swollen mouth, and then carried her down the hallway to her bedroom.

Her fingers fluttered across a bare breast. The feel of warm, naked skin surprised her. When had he removed her clothes? Claire had no time to ponder the situation, however, because her attention instantly returned to the masculine hand that touched her midriff with light, feathery strokes as its counterpart glided over the soft curve of her hip. He was back! Her body surged against the pressure of searching fingers between her thighs.

The mattress dipped beside her. Those masterful fingers now rustled through the downy pubic hair surrounding her pussy, then traveled a delightful path to her breasts, paying no heed to the fact that Claire had just arched her mound against his hand, signaling her urgent need. Her heart beat rapidly when he took a breast in each hand, squeezed the generous mounds together, and then tweaked her rigid nipples.

"Scott…" she whispered.

He bent forward and leisurely kissed her full lips. A hand traveled back between her legs to toy with her frustrated emotions. "What do you want, Claire?"

"I want you," she moaned. "I want you to fuck me. Please don't make me wait…"

A light gasp left her lips when a finger slid teasingly through her wet slit. The tip flicked her clit, worked its way back between her labia to be moistened, and then returned to torture her throbbing bud.

"Please, Scott…" Her body jerked with desire when his teeth nipped at a swollen breast. Her mind jumped from the sensation of his moist tongue at her nipple to follow his one wayward finger as it circled her clit, and then swirled through her pubic hair again. The sexual tension heated her blood. Her vaginal muscles clenched with the aching desire to be fucked. She had to be fucked…

The heat of his naked skin warmed her body as he slid between her open thighs. Claire spread her knees wider and pressed her pubic mound against his erect cock. She bucked beneath him, her body searching for his penis, ready to capture the velvety length and suck it inward.

Hot breath heated her neck; the wetness of his tongue dampened the inside of her ear.

"I'm going to fuck you." His murmured promise echoed around her head where it lay on the pillow. He shifted above her body and reached down between them.

Claire's heart pounded quicker as she followed the motion in her head. Maybe now he would stick his cock inside her. Instead, the round head of his penis rippled through her moist folds as he held them open for entry, but still refused to enter her heat. She squirmed and arched her hips yet another time when the pressure of his hard cock left her gasping in the dark. The heat continued to build in her lower body. Hot sparks in her groin intensified when the full, hard length of his cock pressed against her mound once more.

"Oh, God…I'm going to…"

Instantly, the tip of his cock circled her throbbing clit…teasing, promising that soon she would tremble with sexual release. She was powerless to stop the aching waves of pleasure building in her womb. Claire groaned as the first burning spark of an orgasm ignited in her belly. The tip of his cock continued to coax her further into the fire as it bounced against her clit. The orgasm exploded through her belly, heating her breasts as masculine lips suckled one nipple, and then the other. She bucked and gasped for air; the intense feeling suffocated her as she mindlessly searched for something to fill her…

"Oh…" she gasped as her body throbbed with the intense orgasm. Her body arched on the bed as her fingers curled around the soft pillow beneath her head. The shudders slowed and perspiration dotted her forehead; a single tear slipped down Claire's cheek.

She was alone in the bed and had only dreamed once more.

Chapter One

"Hurry, Larry! We're gonna be late!" Rosebud beat her wings crazily as she darted through long green stems that supported bright yellow peonies. Her shimmering pink tights reflected the Miami midday sunlight, sending out a beacon to any human enjoying a late afternoon lunch in the park. No one took note, however, as she buzzed past two women who ate from plastic containers. She really didn't have to worry about being seen anyway; humans didn't believe in fairies. Therefore, the only thing Rosebud needed to worry about was if someone mistook her for a small irritating bug and tried to flatten her with a rolled-up newspaper.

Larry zipped across the concrete sidewalk and tried to catch up to his dearest friend in the world. A deep scowl lined his forehead just beneath the brim of his black felt derby. Rosebud always did this to him. From the time they were fairylets and just out of diapers, he'd spent most of his days watching her pixie ass bounce in front of him, because before Rosebud finished one thing, she was on to the next, leaving him spinning in her fairy dust.

He grabbed his hat just before the wind whisked it away, flew between two thick stalks in the peony garden, and hollered to get her attention. "Slow down, Rosey! I'm getting airsick!"

He nearly smacked into her ass when Rosebud skidded to a stop and hovered in place while glancing over her shoulder with a harried look in her soft brown eyes. Her little breasts swelled and contracted from her speedy flight across the park. "Do you realize how important today is?"

"Of course I do," he scoffed. Larry automatically timed his wing beats to keep himself hovering. "We'll get to our meeting in plenty of time. Slow down, hey? You're gonna give me a fucking heart attack."

Rosebud clapped her hands together and a ruby-red smile creased her elfin face. "I'm just so excited! I've been waiting for this day my entire life. Just think, Larry, Valentine's Day is right around the corner and we'll be off and flying to our first assignment. We're finally gonna get our Gold Wings!"

Larry watched her execute rolling somersaults through the air with joyful giggles, before she stopped to hover smack-dab in front of him. Her slanted eyes shone with suppressed energy and blonde ringlets fluttered on a breath of wind. He couldn't help but respond to Rosebud's enthusiasm with a rare smile of his own. "You're a real nut-cake, Rosey. All right, let's keep moving." He grabbed her hand to assure she would stay beside him. "But let's keep it at a steady pace." With transparent wings beating in unison, they continued their flight above the curving sidewalk and headed for Cupid's office.

*****

Cupid flipped open a red, embossed folder on his desk. His blue eyes thoughtfully scanned the list of this year's human names of lonely, forlorn people who needed to discover love in their lives. It was his job to pair a human female and male, forward their names to the recruits, let the magic begin, and hope like hell it worked.

Tilting his head slightly to the side, he gazed over the thin wire rims of his bifocals and pursed his lips. The two before him, however, had Cupid somewhat apprehensive in regard to the poor humans who would be assigned to this rather young and overexuberant team of fairies.

Realizing that their boss scrutinized them, Rosebud squared her slender shoulders, elbowed Larry to the side despite her petite stature, and took a dainty step forward. Darting her thick-lashed eyes sidelong, she cringed when Larry puffed up his cheeks and noticeably blew the edge of her wing from the side of his face where it poked one brown eye. A second later, a slight jab to her rib cage signaled his reaction to her stepping front and center stage.

Cupid's eyebrows lifted as he watched their antics and his eyes rolled heavenward before he brought his gaze back to their resumes. "Rosebud Kisses and Larry L'amour. I see this will be your first mission. Do you think you're ready?"

"Yes, sir!" the two shouted in unison.

Cupid put a finger in his ear, wiggled the tip to stop the ringing, and shook his head. "Rather enthusiastic, aren't you?"

"Yes, sir!"

Cupid winced. "You realize that if you accomplish the mission, you both will be granted your Gold Wings for permanent fairy status?" His hand shot up as the two before him opened their mouths again. "No need to answer. I see that you've both finished at the top of your classes. That's very good. The only thing left is to see how you work out in the field."

Rosebud dipped forward a step, clasped her tutu's gauzy short hem and curtsied over her pink slippers. "You won't be disappointed, sir."

Not to be outdone, Larry scuttled forward, tipped his derby to his boss, and smiled. "We'll do a wonderful job, sir. When we're done, there will be one more couple on this earth madly in love."

One thick brow cocked over Cupid's eye. "Well, yes…we'll see about that." Studying the names scribbled across the paper, his fingers shuffled across the surface of his desk to grab a red pencil. He closed his eyes and let the tip of the pencil drop haphazardly to the paper. Peering beneath one eyelid, he drew a red heart around two names.

God help them – and I don't mean these two in front of me…

* * * * *

Larry and Rosebud sat cross-legged on her grass couch, but only Rosey stared reverently at a shiny metal box given to them by Cupid. Nestled inside was an inventory of Valentine weapons for them to either use or discard in their effort to generate an amazing love between two humans.

"Who's gonna open it?" Rosebud breathed quietly.

"Why in hell are you whispering?" Larry boomed out.

His loud voice startled her. "You don't have to holler, Larry."

"I wasn't. It just sounds like I was to you because you're…ah, hell, forget it. I wouldn't get anywhere anyway. Go ahead. You're the one that's so damned fired up. You open it."

Rosebud rose and cautiously approached the box as if it were a land mine ready to detonate. Her gossamer wings accordioned beside her body with uncertainty.

Larry placed his slippered feet on a small rock coffee table, crossed his ankles, and looped his fingers behind his head. "You crack me up, Rosey. It's not going to explode. Just open the damn thing."

Gracefully, she sank to her knees and, with trembling hands, gingerly turned the key to open the lid. "Oh, look Larry," she gasped. "Arrows. Two of them." She gasped louder and spun in one quick movement to stare up at her friend. "These are the arrows Cupid told us about."

"No shit."

Her eyes bulged, and she gulped once, ignoring his flippant response. Her voice returned to the whisper. "They're magic…"

"They'd have to be in order to work."

Pivoting on her ass, she gazed into the box again. Her eyes darkened to a soft, doe-like brown as she smiled, deep in thought, but talking aloud nonetheless. "Just think. Because of these arrows, we can help two humans to fall in love." She clasped her hands together and rested the back of one against her cheek. "How romantic is that?"

Larry observed her theatrics. Rosey was pretty fucking cute. Funny, it was the first time he'd noticed that. Well, maybe not the *first* time. Lately, fixating on her firm little ass was starting to give him half a hard-on more often than not. His brow wrinkled. Rosey was his bud for chrissakes, his pal, his amigo and nothing more.

Suddenly, he bounded up from the couch to get his mind off the strange excitement he felt at times when he thought about her. "Okay. Let's just get this over with. Where's the list with the names? If we don't haul our asses out of here, we'll never get our two humans to fall in love by Valentine's Day." The sound of her soft, happy sigh floated past his ears. He stared at the glazed look in her eyes. "Sheesh. This is our job, Rosey. You can't get so mental over a mission or about the humans involved. I really want my Gold Wings, so quit the mushy shit." His eyes narrowed when she spun three circles in the air and landed on her tiny feet with her back to him. "What are you doing now?"

Rosebud's perky little ass pointed straight up to the heavens as she dug around inside the box. A second later, she yanked out a wrinkled paper and waved it about in the air. "Ha! Here're the names of our humans and all the pertinent information." She plopped onto the couch, her lips silently moving a mile a minute as she read.

Larry just shook his head again as he noted how her chin moved like the carriage of a typewriter as she read line after line. He bent over, pushed his hat further off his forehead, and tapped her shoulder none too gently. "Are you going to share that?"

"Oh, sorry. Yeah, you can have it in a sec. You're not gonna believe this," she beamed. "Our lady's name is Claire Holliday and our guy…well, this is absolutely marvelous. His name is Brian Valentine. How cool is that?" She continued to read, but second by second, the upturned corners of her red mouth sagged until finally, her lips parted and a tiny moan escaped past their fullness. Her tiny brow creased in a sudden frown. She glanced up, surprising Larry with glistening tears.

He rested his fists on his spandex-covered hips. "What are you crying about now? I thought you were happy about this?"

Rosebud clutched the paper to her small bosom and took a deep breath. She blinked her big eyes, her long eyelashes spiked with tears. "Our humans? Oh, Larry, it's so sad." She clutched at his arm and clamped onto his hand. "We can't make a mistake. We have to get them together. No matter what, our Gold Wings won't mean anything if we can't make this first one work."

"Let me see." Snatching the paper from her fingers, he shook out the wrinkles, held it up to the light, and began to read. "Brian Valentine and Claire Holliday hmmm addresses yadda…yadda…ya…" His voice lowered as he met Rosebud's sad gaze, his eyes as serious now as his best friend's. "I see what you mean. Okay, I think we definitely need to use the arrows, don't you?"

Rosebud's small head bobbed in instant agreement.

Larry tipped his head toward the box. "See if there's anything else we might need from in there and let's get going."

"Where do we start?" she asked as she dug around. "We never received any directions about the first step—just the expected end result."

Larry spun his hat into the thinking cap position. One furry brow dipped over an eye and one finger came up to tap his cheek thoughtfully. "Let's see. First off, we need to familiarize ourselves with our subjects."

Rosey levitated with beating wings. "Oooo! Good idea. I can't wait to see Claire. She sounds so pretty. And Brian's description said he's got a great butt. Okay, then what?" She did a loop and nearly knocked Larry's hat off his head.

He straightened the derby with an irritated smile. "Son of a bitch! You gotta stop doing that."

She spun once more and hovered upside down in front of his face, waiting for his answer. Her brown eyes blinked innocently. "Doing what?"

"That!"

Chapter Two

Claire Holliday sat back on her heels, pulled off her dirty work gloves, and brushed auburn tendrils from her forehead, picturing in her mind what the beautiful perennial garden in her backyard would like when another year passed. Preparing the flowerbed was something she'd wanted to do for over three years, but she'd always been too busy—or too heartbroken to even be interested.

"Too busy taking care of a lowdown scoundrel who couldn't have given a shit less about me," she muttered quietly. Her dog whined beside her when she spoke. Claire tipped her head and ruffled the lab's ears. "Not you, Buddy. I'm talking about—" Her lips snapped shut. Claire wouldn't say Scott's name aloud. She had actually thought at one time that he was the man she would spend the rest of her life with. The two had met through a mutual friend and, after three months of dating, her new boyfriend had moved into her house. That's when the misery started.

Once the bastard realized that living with someone meant at least some sort of commitment, he'd turned sullen and surly. Claire finally realized Scott would never provide her with the emotional support she needed. The sex that had once stolen her breath away had turned stale early on. When she tried to discuss it with him, he took offense and soon looked elsewhere for quick sexual gratification. Claire discovered his transgressions and it was only a matter of hours before he quietly stuffed his belongings into a few suitcases and left without a word. She hadn't heard from him since. That was nearly two years ago.

Claire grabbed the edge of a nearby bench to lever herself to her feet. "Come, Buddy." She waited with her hand dangling at her side until the dog brushed against her. Waving her hand until she found the lead strap, she clasped her fingers around the soft plastic handle. "House, Buddy."

The dog turned with her and slowly led her to the back door. The fingers of Claire's free hand found the doorknob, turned it with familiar ease, and stepped inside the kitchen. Just in time. The phone began to ring.

Feeling along the counter, she hurried to pick up the receiver. "Hello?"

"Hi, Honey!"

"Hi, Mom. What's up?"

"Well, that's what I was wondering. I called earlier. Did you and Buddy go for a walk?"

"Nope." Claire's hand swished through the air until she found the back of a kitchen stool. She slid easily onto the seat while her fingers searched for the dog to scratch the thick fur covering his neck. Her companion whimpered beside her. A second later, his front paws were on the surface of the snack bar. "Why are you whining?"

"What are you talking about?" Her mother's confusion was evident in her voice.

"Down, Buddy," Claire ordered the dog. "Sorry, Mom. I was talking to the dog. He must hear your voice over the phone. What were you saying?"

"I asked if you and Buddy were out walking."

"No. We were out back. I finally started my perennial garden." The silence on the other end of the line was deafening. "Mom? Are you still there?"

"Yes, dear." She paused. "Claire, isn't it a little weird for you to be planting a garden?"

"Why? Because it's such a visual thing? You know blind people can smell even if they can't see."

"That's not what I meant. I just worry about you out there alone."

"I'm not alone. Buddy is with me every minute."

"Give me a break. Now you'll have to relearn the mapping in the yard again. What if you forget a shovel lying around and trip over it? All right, forget it. I don't want to fight with you. I know you don't want to hear this, but you really need to listen to me. Your dad and I gave you the freedom you wanted. Now that you've proved you can do it, why don't you sell the house and move back in with us? We really want you here."

Claire clutched the phone with white fingers. "I really don't want to discuss this, Mom. I'm twenty-six years old—a fully capable adult who can live on her own."

"Honey..."

"I know you and Dad want what's best for me. This house and my independence is it. Dad understands that. Why can't you? I really have to get going. I want to get to the nursery and pick out some plants."

"You're going to the nursery yourself? Why don't you wait? I'll drive over and take you. Besides, you can't even see what you're buying."

Claire slid off the stool and struggled to keep her anger at bay for a mother who only said thoughtless things out of love. "Gotta go, Mom. Love you!"

"Claire! Don't—"

"Bye!" With a sigh, she placed the phone back into the cradle and turned. "Buddy? Want to go for a walk?"

*****

Brian Valentine moved about the greenhouse pruning plants, and rearranging partitioned trays to fill in any empty spots. The morning was busy, and he'd run flats of greenery back and forth from the back lot for hours to assure his customers had everything they needed. The season had started off well and, hopefully in another week, every beautiful rose he'd tended would be sold for Valentine's Day. The Valentine Shoppe was known statewide for the thousands of roses sold every year on that special holiday.

He shook his dark head at the very thought, and his own wry chuckle echoed around him. Why did most husbands scramble to buy their wives roses only for Valentine's Day? If he were married, his wife would receive one fresh rose every day of their married life. An ironic snort replaced the chuckle. *What the hell am I talking about? Who'd want me anyway?*

At one time, he'd had a great girl. He and Kristen had been high school sweethearts. They'd broken up during their college years, but after running into one another at a mutual friend's party after graduation, both had immediately rediscovered the sizzling passion that still burned just beneath the surface. That night, he'd offered her a ride home and ended up in her bed.

Brian's hands stilled as he thought of the hot sex they'd shared that first year. But, when he'd asked Kristen to marry him, she'd only laughed—probably for the first time since his accident—and then had stated that she didn't love him anymore as a woman loves a man. Instead, she had found herself in the comfortable place of being a good friend who supported another in a time of need. She didn't care to be his lover any longer. Kristen was gone the next day. It was then that Brian realized the titillating sex had been the only reason they were together. Even if she had said yes to a marriage proposal, it never would have lasted.

He took a deep breath to take control of the anger threatening to rise up, surprised because usually he had a pretty good handle on his emotions—something that post-accident therapy had helped him with.

Sex. What was that anymore? *A quick jerk of my dick in a hot shower?* At thirty, life sucked and Brian's was defined by two specific segments of his existence—before the accident, and after the accident.

Shaking off the old baggage he usually kept at bay, Brian glanced up at three women who worked their way down the crowded aisles, each dragging a red wagon behind them. His blue eyes automatically scanned the contents of the cart. They chattered and laughed as they pulled pots from the loaded tables and placed them beside others in the wagons. An older couple argued two aisles away about whether to plant hostas or some other sort of flowering perennial beneath their front porch alcove. His seven employees were busy helping others make decisions as to what to buy, and the cash register drawer opened time after time.

His broad shoulders rose and fell with the huge sigh that left his lips. Brian loved the shop, but he couldn't wait for the end of the day. Nothing gave him more pleasure than to sit quietly at its end among the many pots, listen to the hum of the giant fan installed in the far wall, and enjoy the tranquility of total solitude behind locked doors. Only at those times could he be the person he once was, the laughing young man looking to the future without fear of being alone forever.

Hunkering down, he examined a leaking irrigation hose, noting that the black rubber hose would probably have to be changed out in the next day or so. A small crack caused a shallow pool of water to build beneath the table. He knelt down on one knee and followed the length of hose with his hands to discover if there were any other problem spots.

"Excuse me? Could you answer a question?"

Brian gritted his teeth, straightened his back, and rose to a standing position. This was the part that was the hardest—the part when a customer saw him for the first time. He turned with a forced smile. "How can I help you?" He heard the instant intake of breath from the woman's lips. She juggled two pots in her hands and looked everywhere but at the lean, muscular man before her. "I'm…I'm trying to decide what would work best for a ground cover. Could you tell me which of these blooms the longest? I really love to have color all the time."

"Nothing really blooms twelve months out of the year, but if I were you, I'd pick this one." He pointed to the pot in her right hand. "It has pretty reddish-pink flowers that look great against a backdrop of green."

"Thank you." She spun and hurried down the aisle.

Brian watched her return one of the pots to the table after sending him a quick, flustered glance. He turned back to disconnect the hose.

* * * * *

Larry and Rosebud dipped and glided their way across Miami. She giggled incessantly, filled with the exhilaration of their first mission. Larry cursed. He had to get his set of Gold Wings. After all, isn't that what fairies strove toward? He just hated all the Valentine's hoopla and crap that had to be accomplished in order to get them. Although, after reading Claire and Brian's bios, he had to admit he'd softened slightly.

Earlier, he and Rosey had both agreed that to begin with, they would find Claire and discover what she was like. From there, they'd head out to find Brian's flower shop.

Larry adjusted the archer's quiver on his back and shot Rosebud a pointed glare. To get her to shut up before they left her house, he'd finally agreed to take along the arrows even though this was just a fact-finding mission.

She grinned at him now as if everything was…rosy with the world. "Want me to carry the arrows for awhile? Huh, Larry? Do you want me to? You seem out of breath."

He hiked the quiver more securely against his shoulder. "I'm not out of breath. Besides, they're too damned heavy for you. Although, that might slow you down a bit. Why in hell do we have to do everything at breakneck speed?"

She disappeared from his line of vision as she darted to his other side, took his hand, and kept flying. "Because we only have one week until Valentine's Day. We can't afford to miss one minute." Dragging him forward, they rounded a corner of one of the residential sections in town. Her eyes shone brighter while she counted aloud as they passed the homes on the block. "One-hundred-one, one-hundred-three, one-hundred-five. Ah-ha! There it is! Larry, look! There's Claire's house! One-hundred-seven." She yanked him to a halt and hovered with him over the front sidewalk. "Where do you think she is?"

Larry adjusted his hat with a querulous look. "You're whispering again. Let's fly around and see if there's anyone outside. If not, we'll go under the door and check out the house. Stay behind me." He didn't stop to think about the sudden urge to keep her safe and fluttered past the front of the house while she breathed down his neck. When Larry slowed down to peek around the corner, Rosebud slammed into him, knocking his hat into the wind.

In a flash, she dove to retrieve it, and then perched it back on the point of his head with brown eyes rounded in fearful expectation when he opened his mouth—most likely to reprimand her. Thank goodness Larry just shook his head and nodded to keep going.

Rosebud curbed her enthusiasm at the opposite corner of the house and put on the brakes early. They peeked around the corner. A woman rested comfortably on her knees as she dug around in the dirt. A yellow dog sat close and observed her progress. When the woman stood and headed for the house, Rosebud grabbed Larry's hand with a tight squeeze. "It's her! It's Claire. Isn't she gorgeous?"

Larry stared at the human, suddenly overcome by the vision of bright sunlight filtering through the auburn waves that hung down past the woman's shoulders, turning her hair to the color of glowing embers. The sheer feminine grace of her rolling hips as she walked toward the house made his tiny heart thump a little quicker. Coming face-to-face with one of their subjects who, up until now, was just a simple written name, made him shift uncomfortably on the breeze. Claire was so…so vulnerable, yet so beautiful. Instantly, another rare jolt of protectiveness raced through his blood. His little partner, Rosey, wasn't the only female he was responsible for anymore. Larry straightened with sudden purpose. This Brian Valentine, whoever the hell he was, damn well better treat her like a lady when he and Rosey got them together or there'd be hell to pay.

"Hurry, Larry! She's going in the house." Rosebud grabbed his arm, flapped her wings crazily, and tugged with all her might. She dragged him along on the breeze as he used his free hand to keep his hat on his head.

"Hey, don't think I'm going to shoot any arrows yet. Cripes, we can't do that until she and Brian are in the same room."

"I know that! But I just want to watch her for a little while."

"Ah, hell..." He darted across the lawn in her jet stream. They just made it into the kitchen before the door slammed shut. The whoosh of air that smacked the two fairies sent them rolling across the brightly lit room. Larry's arm shot out, and he managed to catch Rosebud's foot before she sailed too far away. When he set her upright, he let go and dusted his hands together. In a blink of his eye, Rosebud flew away to perch atop a sugar bowl, closer to where Claire sat at the snack bar, chatting on the phone. "Son of a bitch," he muttered as he flew to her side. "I don't know why I let you talk me into these things..." A second later, his arm snatched his friend's waist, and he yanked Rosebud down behind the bowl as the huge snout of Claire's dog appeared over the edge of the counter. The dog snuffled loudly before a whine rumbled in his throat.

Rosebud peeked up from behind Larry's shoulder. "Oooo, isn't he cute?"

Larry secured his hold more firmly on her arm. "Cute, my ass."

Claire ordered the dog down.

Larry inhaled deeply to slow his pounding heart, loosened his hold on Rosebud's arm, and wiped the perspiration from his brow. "Rosey, you gotta be a little more careful."

She darted upward to sit on the sugar bowl cover. A giggle preceded her next words. "Loosen up, Larry. All he wanted was a little pat on the nose."

"Pat on the nose, my ass." Larry climbed up beside her and adjusted his damned hat again. It refused to sit straight atop his pointed little head. "He was looking for a treat, and you and I would have been it. I sure as hell don't relish the idea of seeing what a dog turd looks like from the inside."

Rosebud rested her elbows on her knees and plopped her chin into upturned palms. She gazed at Claire and hardly heard Larry's mutterings. "I just know in my heart that Brian's going to fall instantly in love. She's the prettiest human I've ever seen."

"Speaking of him, don't you think we should take a flight down to the shop before it closes?"

"Oh, my gosh!"

"Rosey? Cripes, Rosey!" He grabbed the quiver of arrows and raced after her. "That's it. I know I'm going to have a fucking heart attack."

*****

Twenty minutes later, they waited above the door of the flower shop. When a customer exited, they darted into the building and had a look around. A large crowd of customers moved about the interior and flowed into the greenhouses set up in the back lot.

"I don't see him, do you?"

Larry recognized instant panic in Rosey's eyes as she spun circles to search every corner of the shop. "Calm down. Don't get your tights in a bundle. I'm sure he's here. His bio said that working in his store is all he ever does."

Rosebud chewed on a silver fingernail. "Do you think we'll recognize him?"

"What do you think? You know how he was described."

"Oh...yeah... I don't care. He sounds wonderful. Do you think we should check the greenhouses?"

"I suppose. Just stay by me and don't get in front of one of those fans or you'll get a free ride to the Caribbean." Taking her hand, they sailed through the many hanging pots and headed for the hot houses erected behind the store.

Rosebud knew instantly that the man who quietly watered plants on a far table with his back to the customers was Brian. Tightening her grip inside Larry's hand, she silently led him to a hanging ivy. They settled softly onto a shiny leaf and waited for him to turn around.

Brian straightened and glanced about. The customers continued to meander through the aisles. No one was looking at him. *Funny*...he thought...*I could've sworn someone was staring at me*...

Larry placed an arm around Rosebud's shoulders for moral support as quiet tears rolled down her cheeks. It hit him how great it actually felt to have her little body cuddled beneath his arm.

"It's not fair," she whispered as she watched the man who stood within a human arm's reach. Her brown eyes took in the horribly fire-scarred skin. Red, wrinkled blotches disfigured one entire side of what was once a devilishly handsome face; the raised scars extended down into the neck of his T-shirt. One muscular arm possessed the same patchy blemishes almost to his wrist. A shock of wavy dark hair curled over his ears. Rosebud swiped the tears from her cheek. "He's a wonderful man—his bio said so. If it wasn't for firefighters like him, an entire family might have died." She rested her head against her friend's shoulder. "We can't fail, Larry. Claire and Brian need to find one another."

Larry gently rubbed Rosebud's satiny bare arm as he watched Brian move away to another table. Rosey was right. The world would never be right if their mission failed—no matter what his personal feelings were in regards to this mushy Valentine's shit.

Chapter Three

"Come on, Rosey. Let's go get something to eat and get our plan figured out."

She nodded quietly as she watched Brian move about and finally followed Larry out onto the street. He hovered above the sidewalk, looking both ways and trying to figure out what he was in the mood for. Spotting a pizza shop with outdoor seating, he took her hand and headed back over the same route they'd used earlier. Perching on an overhead sign, they surveyed the various choices on the different tables.

"Hmmm…you pick, Rosey. What looks good?"

She leaned precariously over the edge and spotted a couple munching on a plain cheese pizza. "Let's get some of that. I'm not in the mood for anything too heavy."

Larry stood and heaved the quiver of magic arrows from his shoulder. "Good choice. Here, you watch these. I'll be right back." He flitted away only moments later.

Rosebud cupped her hands around the edge of the sign and crossed one knee over the other, thinking about the mission while she waited. Only six and a half days. That's all they had left to get Claire and Brian together. How were they going to manage it? Poor Brian wasn't the sort of person to be out and about in public. Rosebud knew he hid most days behind the cover of his plants and flowers. And Claire? Neither Rosebud nor Larry knew if she left her house much because of her blindness.

She rested her chin in her palm over a bent elbow, pursed her lips and scanned the many patrons who ate their food. Rosebud leaned slightly forward and spied Larry creeping up on the cheese pizza. Her stomach growled. Larry, for all his surliness, was her best friend, but she couldn't imagine their relationship staying as it was. Rosey wanted more. Her hormones had kicked in and she was ready to find a mate, but Larry didn't seem too receptive to the subtle clues she tossed his way.

With a sigh, she glanced down the street. A woman walked toward her with a yellow dog at her side. "Hmmm...she looks just like..." Rosebud shot off the sign, hovered over the sidewalk as she struggled to hang on to the clumsy quiver of arrows, and squinted her eyes to make sure. "Oh, no!"

She darted closer to the table where Larry worked at ripping a small piece from the pizza. "Larry!" She waved her arms, flapped her wings, and hollered again. "Larry, you numskull, look up here! It's Claire!"

He glanced up from where he stood on the surface of the table, held out his hands in supplication, and mouthed the word "what".

Rosebud frantically pointed down the street. "It's Claire! She's coming this way. What are we going to do?" She spun in a circle and nearly dropped the quiver. *Oh no, oh no, oh no. She's getting closer!*

"What did you say?" Larry hollered up again as he adjusted his hat.

"Open up your fucking ears! Look, you idiot!"

Larry flew to her side with the stolen pizza and spun to follow the direction in which she pointed. His face paled when he saw Claire and her dog. "Ah, fuck!" He tossed the small tidbit of pizza into the air. It sailed down and landed on the cheek of the woman sitting at the table—who proceeded to chew out her husband for spitting on her.

"The arrows! Take the arrows, Larry. We've got to get back to Brian's shop. We've got to shoot him first. Here's our chance. Oh, my gosh, here's our chance!"

Larry fumbled with the quiver as Rosebud shoved the strap over his shoulder. "Why do we have to nail Brian first?"

"Because! The directions said the male human has to be darted first. Come on. We've got to be ready if she goes into his shop." Rosebud stopped on a dime. "Wait a minute! She will go in there. Remember when she said she was going to buy some flowers? Oh, holy cow, this is it. *This is it*!" She pirouetted through the air, clapping her hands and waved her legs about. "What luck! What luck!"

"Rosey," Larry admonished. "Get hold of yourself." The reprimand was instantly forgotten, though, as he watched her flutter about. "Did you swear before?"

She looked at him as if he'd grown a second head. "What?"

He waited for her to float down beside him. "I thought I heard you say a swear."

"A *swear*? You mean the word *fucking*?"

"Sheesh, Rosey, you've never said that before."

"You've never listened before. I'm not a little fairylet anymore. I'm grown up. Maybe it's about time you noticed."

Claire and Buddy passed directly below them. Suddenly, the remembered task had both Rosebud and Larry gasping when Claire's lilting voice drifted up as she spoke to the woman who wiped pizza from her cheek.

"Excuse me. I heard your voice and need a little help. I just got off the bus. The driver said that The Valentine Shoppe was the sixth building on this block. I'm not quite sure if I passed it or not."

"She's going in!" Rosebud screamed with joy. "Oh, holy cow, she's going in!" She and Larry waited for Claire to thank the woman for her help. They followed immediately over her shoulder as she urged Buddy forward, passed the restaurant completely, and came to Brian's shop.

Claire opened the door and walked in.

Rosebud and Larry completed a high-five, darted through the open door before it swished closed, and flitted around her shoulders to wait and see where she would go next. Claire stopped at the front desk.

A young woman looked up from the cash register. "Can I help you?"

"Hi. My name's Claire Holliday. I'm putting in a perennial bed and, if it's not too busy, do you think you could help me pick out some plants? As you can see…I can't."

Dead silence.

Claire leaned forward slightly. "That was a joke." Her face split into an amused smile at the continued silence. "Maybe I should come back another time?"

"Oh, no," the woman responded. "You just caught me off guard." She glanced around. "Everyone working here looks pretty busy, and I'm not supposed to leave the front counter. I'll tell you what, though. I don't think the owner will mind if I'm away a few minutes. Why don't you come with me and we'll go find him out back? I'm sure he would be plenty happy to help you."

Claire smiled again. "Thank you."

Larry and Rosebud flipped in the air, and then raced to find Brian.

*****

Rosebud's little body trembled as she waited for Claire to enter the attached greenhouse. Larry glanced down at her, refusing to let on that his blood probably pumped as fast as hers. "You're vibrating like a bad tire."

"I'm so excited," she gasped loudly, and then did a back flip. "Oh, my God. There she is. There she is! Get the arrows ready. I'll tell you when to shoot. Hey!" She spun around. "There's no one else back here. Just shoot Brian now and get ready again for Claire."

"I don't know. I think we should wait…"

Rosebud's delicate brows slanted down over her eyes. Her lips formed a straight line as she glared at him, totally out of character. "I said *shoot* the *fucking* arrow. Now! If you can't follow a simple order, then give it to me. I'll shoot the damned thing myself. We're not going to miss our chance."

Larry stared at the heightened color of her cheeks and noticed how dark and glittering her brown eyes had become. His pixie penis poked against his green tights. Never had he seen his Rosey in such a state. If she wanted him to shoot the fucking arrow, well then, he'd shoot the fucking arrow—anything to keep the sexy look blazing in Rosebud's eyes. He turned, aligned it against the bowstring and took aim at Brian's heart.

Zing…

Whap!

Brian scratched his chest.

"You hit him!" Rosebud darted closer, grabbed Larry by the shoulders, yanked him forward, and planted a wet, sucking kiss on his surprised lips. "Okay, get the other arrow ready."

He was absolutely stunned. Rosey had never kissed him. Well, she'd kissed him, but never on the mouth. Larry kept his eyes on her when she flipped around and hovered in the air as Claire approached. His gaze followed the tiny outline of her small jutting breasts and perfectly rounded ass encased in the pink tights. Her tutu framed the small firm globes. Taking in her long slender legs, the only thing he could think about was having them wrapped around his waist. *Fuck me. Where in hell did that come from?*

"Larry! Shoot!"

He shook his head to clear it, waiting for Claire to get closer, knowing he couldn't make a mistake—their Gold Wings depended on it. He'd think about his hot new emotions later on. Larry pulled back the string, took aim, and let go of the arrow just as Rosey darted across the aisle. The arrow hit her square in the chest.

Her little body rolled wildly past a row of hanging plants. Her arms and legs twisted and turned as she struggled to catch her balance, and then her body went limp. Larry dropped the bow, mortified by what had happened. His little wings flapped as fast as a hummingbird's when he took off after her.

"Rosey! Rosey!" Her silence panicked him further, but finally her spinning slowed enough to give him a slight advantage. Larry stretched out his hand, missed her foot once, and then flapped his wings harder. He caught hold of her hand on the next try.

Yanking her to his chest, he cupped her small heart-shaped face with a shaking hand, and flew up to sit on an overhead beam. "Rosey! Oh my heavens!" He gently patted her cheek. "Please wake up. Are you okay? You gotta be okay. I'll never forgive myself if something happens to you. Rosey, come on, wake up!"

Her long lashes fluttered against her cheek as she struggled to open her eyes and focus on her surroundings. She stared up at him. Then she grabbed him by the front of his shirt, yanked his mouth to hers, opened her lips, and sucked his tongue into her mouth.

"Rosey! What the fuck!" he mumbled incoherently against her seeking lips.

Her head lolled back to rest on his arm, and she gazed up with eyes glowing and her pink little tongue now running across her upper lip. "Mmmm…you taste good. Yes, sweetheart, I'd love to fuck."

"Oh, my aching cupids…the fucking arrow…" Larry dropped Rosebud like a hot potato and slid further down the beam to lean against the wall. Beads of perspiration instantly dotted his forehead beneath the brim of his hat. Grabbing the hankie from his front pocket, he dabbed at the moisture. From his vantage point, he saw Claire and Brian talking, but he couldn't worry about them now. Rosebud was up on her feet and swaying toward him with uninhibited lust. He jumped to his feet, pressed his body against the wall behind him, and stared unbelievably at the come-hither heat glowing in her eyes.

"What's the matter, big boy?" Her finger beckoned him closer, but Larry stayed glued to the wall. His eyes darted about. She wasn't the cute little pixie he'd known since they were fairylets. The mishap with the arrow had turned Rosebud into a horny wanton sprite who looked like she could slurp him up in one gulp. She stopped only a petal width away and ran the same finger across his heaving chest while running her tongue across her lips again.

Larry winced and flattened himself further against the wall, which knocked his hat down over his eyes. Scrambling for the brim, he bent it back so he could observe the little wanton with a skeptical eye. "Knock it off, Rosey. Do you remember what happened?"

She swayed forward. "Yeah, I hit a little turbulence." Her palms slid upward until she locked her fingers around the back of his neck. "I think you should hang on. It's going to be a rough ride out tonight." Her wings trembled with passion.

Larry's hard-on shot heavenward when she rubbed her flat little pubic area against his crotch.

*****

Brian straightened and brushed his palms together as he stared at the new water connection. Things seemed to be working. Nothing leaked to wet the floor beneath him. He turned to head for the door. His eyes widened when he glanced up and saw a beautiful woman enter the building with his employee, Kate. No, not just beautiful...she was... *Christ, she's the prettiest thing I've ever seen...*

Kate lifted her hand and waved to get his attention. "Brian! I need your help."

He spun to face the wall, knowing there was nowhere to escape. Panic combined with thick dread to send a sick jolt of nausea through his stomach. He wanted to imagine from afar what it would be like to speak with the woman—not have her see the ogre he'd become. The woman walking toward him was beautiful. Just before he'd spun away, he had spied her auburn curls swaying gently around her face and shoulders. Her tiny body didn't look to have an ounce of fat on it—probably from all the hours she spent in a gym. He didn't get a chance to see her eyes because of the sunglasses she wore. *Probably some little rich princess who will have a great time telling her sorority friends about the horribly disfigured man who sells flowers…*

"Brian?"

They were right behind him. He swiped at the beads of perspiration that dripped past his temples and wondered if he'd ever get over the sensation of wanting to find a hole to crawl into every time he met someone new—especially a beautiful woman. Taking a deep breath of courage, he turned and looked down at the most gorgeous set of lips he'd ever seen.

"Hi, Brian," Kate smiled. "This is Claire Holliday. Everyone is really busy up front. Claire's putting in a new perennial bed at home and needs some help picking out plants."

So, why in hell did you bring her to me? What does she think now that she's seen my face? And then his gaze lowered. Stunned, Brian couldn't take his eyes off the seeing-eye dog at her side—the one that was hidden by the tables of plants as she'd walked toward him only a moment earlier.

"We're really busy up front. Do you have a few minutes to help her? Brian?"

"Ah…sure."

Kate's relief was instantly evident. She turned to Claire and laid a hand on the woman's arm. "Okay, I guess you're set. There isn't a thing that Brian doesn't know about gardening. You're in good hands." A second later, she turned and hurried back to the front of the store, never noticing how awestruck Brian was as he stared at his customer.

Claire wondered at the silence. She wasn't alone because the hint of his cologne still wafted past her nose. She held out her hand. "Hello? Are you still there?"

Brian blinked, and then hesitantly took her fingers in his. A spark of heat radiated up his arm. He shook off the insane urge to pull the woman into his arms. *Where in hell did that idea come from?* Letting go of her hand, he cleared his throat. "Um, hi…I'm Brian."

Her grin widened. "I know. Remember? We were already introduced."

Brian could have kicked himself for acting like an adolescent boy, but he couldn't think of a thing to say—he simply stared at her, amazed by his hot physical reaction to her quiet beauty. His jeans tightened between his thighs.

Claire's smile filtered away to nothing. "Maybe this isn't a good time…"

"Oh, no! It's a perfect time…I mean…I'm sorry. It's just that—" *think of something!* "I was keeping an eye on your dog, wondering if he might bite…" *Jesus…that was anal!*

"Buddy?" Claire's smile reappeared as she lowered her hand to rest on the dog's thick neck. "He might lick you to death, that's all. He's very gentle. So, you're the owner of Valentine's?"

Brian nodded, and immediately realized she couldn't see his response. "Yup. Which brings us to the reason you're here. If you'd like to give me an idea of what size bed you're putting in, I can show you—" *Shit!* "*Tell* you about some plants that would work."

Claire caught his little faux pas in regard to her blindness, but let it pass. Most new acquaintances stumbled over their words with the same problem until they realized she really wasn't any different than any other woman. She reached out with her hand to feel the table beside her. Presuming that it was sturdy enough, she leaned her hip against it, crossed one ankle over the other, and tucked her fingers into her jeans pocket. "Well, I've got a high fence on the north side of my backyard. I know the sun shines there most of the day because I can feel the direct heat on my face when I'm working in that area. I want plants that have a strong aroma—you might have noticed that I'm blind…" *There, it's out in the open so we don't have to worry about it coming up later on,* "but, I can still smell." Her lips turned up in a crooked smile. "Think you can help me out?"

Claire's comical grin made Brian's heart knock against his ribs. "Roses…I think you need roses. I'm sure you would enjoy the smell of lavender, too. Should we take a walk out back and you can decide for yourself?"

Claire straightened. "That sounds great. Would it be too much trouble if I held onto your arm? It just makes things easier for me, rather than try to follow the sound of your voice."

Brian quickly swiped his sweating palm across the front of his jeans, took her hand, and tucked it into the crook of his left arm so she wouldn't feel the scars on the right. "At your service, Mrs. Holliday."

"Miss Holliday. Claire would even be better."

"All right, Claire, let's go play with the plants."

Chapter Four

Larry tried to keep one eye on Brian and Claire, and the other on Rosebud's hand as the little sprite ran her fingers across the front of his chest again. "Hey! Hey, Rosey." He grabbed her hand and stopped it from slipping inside his tights. "They're leaving!"

Rosebud swayed against his quaking body. "Who?"

"Claire and Brian! They're heading down the aisle."

She closed her eyes, swayed closer, and breathed in Larry's cologne. "Hmmmm…that's good."

He reached up, clasped her gloved wrists with both hands, and forced the little wanton to step away. "Snap out of it. We've got to follow them. Do you even remember that we're on a mission here?"

"Oooo, yeah…I'm on a mission, all right. I'm on a mission to get fucked silly!"

Larry wheezed, nearly choked on his tongue when he turned her to face the door, then took one slender arm in his grasp. "Okay, missy, that's about enough. We've got to follow them. There are only a few days left until Valentine's Day and our mission is to get those two together. Now, you're either going to keep your hands off and listen to me, or I'm going to take you home and do this myself."

Rosebud glanced over her shoulder, batted her long eyelashes, and winked. "I love a take-charge man. Okeydokey, I promise to be good—but only until we get back to my place. Then, I can't promise anything."

Holy shit! I gotta get hold of Cupid and find out how long the arrows work. Until then… He would have to put up with hiding his erection from Rosey's wandering eyes—and fingers.

*****

Brian's skin was warm to the touch. As they walked through the sunshine to another greenhouse, Claire could feel the slight bunching of a well-muscled arm as it flexed slightly with each step. She swallowed and wondered what it would be like to touch the rest of his body. Her eyes widened with shock behind the dark glasses at the mere thought. *He'd probably laugh his ass off thinking I'm some kind of poor little blind girl who's never been with a man…*

Brian's head swam with the scent of her light perfume. He pushed aside the urge to lean close to her body for a sweeter sniff and concentrated instead on how well Claire moved beside him, though he was the one leading them through the maze of tables. Every step she took exuded confidence even though her hand rested lightly in the crook of his arm.

"We must be near the roses."

His eyes swung in her direction. "You've got a pretty good nose."

Claire grinned. "I depend on my other senses to 'see' for me. I hope this doesn't sound too forward, but I love the scent of your cologne. It's even better than the roses. You wouldn't by any chance have any plants with the same fragrance?"

A chuckle burst from Brian's mouth. Not just a forced laugh to make a customer feel at ease, but a real laugh for the first time in a long time. "Thanks for the compliment, but I can't think of one flower that would help you out."

"Well, then, you'll just have to come and sit in my backyard." Claire gasped inwardly, wondering why she had just spouted the uncharacteristic response.

Dead silence—for the second time that day.

"I'm…I'm sorry, Brian, if I made you feel uncomfortable just now. I don't know where that came from. My mom has always said I speak before I think."

Brian stared at the soft curve of her cheek, wondering what Claire's skin would feel like beneath his fingertips. "Don't apologize. In fact, I just had a great idea. I have a proposition for you. I'd like to offer my services to help you plant your garden if you don't have anyone else in mind. If you're serious about something that looks great, then I'm your man." A twinge of instant sadness rippled through his mind. *Well, something other than a great-looking man…* The fact didn't discourage him, though. For the first time in years, Brian was able to be himself in a woman's presence, feeling secure in the fact the she couldn't see the horrifying disfigurement on his face.

Claire stopped beside him and tilted her head. "Honestly? You'd really do that?"

"Sure, why not? I love to dig around in the dirt. It would be fun and give me something other to do than maintenance and shop setup." He waited, hoping like hell that Claire's other senses wouldn't pick up the rapid beating of his heart.

Claire's lips widened to a radiant smile. "I think I like the sound of that. I was already wondering how I was going to keep everything straight. Are you sure you have the time?"

"Of course. I have a great staff—" *Who are going to kill me when I leave during the busiest week of the year.* Brian gently clasped her elbow and led Claire forward. "Okay, let's get some teamwork going here. You do the sniffing and I'll do the visual. Sound like a deal?"

Claire's smile widened further.

*****

Larry observed Rosebud from the corner of his eye. The petite sprite absolutely would not pay attention to Claire and Brian's conversation as the couple selected one plant after another. An entire hour had passed and Larry was the only one gathering information. Brian offered to go to Claire's. The plan was falling into place and he and Rosey weren't even trying!

When Rosebud wiggled beside him and let out another breathless sigh, Larry reached up, grabbed the top of her head with one hand, and swiveled her face in the couple's direction. "Would you quit sighing and take note of what's going on?"

Rosebud's eyes rolled as she tried to capture a sidelong glance of the fairy who had her pink tights all moist between her legs and her nipples nearly engraving permanent dents in her spandex blouse. She wanted him. She wanted his sweet fairy ass. Tired of wondering about the sexy things her girlfriends whispered about, she yearned to feel the thrust of Larry's hard cock that was outlined beneath his tights. Hell, Larry even had his hat resting on his lap to cover his swollen penis—and Larry rarely ever took off his hat.

Her smile widened just thinking about what his cock would feel like pounding inside her. She swayed in his direction, but his fingers only tightened around her scalp, forcing her eyes to stay front and center. "It seems like they're hitting it off. Let's just let nature take its course for the next few days. Come on, Lar. I'd rather you take me home."

Larry's brow furrowed with indecision. They had a mission to accomplish and it looked like he was going to have to become the guiding force. It was bad enough having to hide his hard-on, but now he had used his best hat to hide the wet spot just below his waist. His dick was dripping like a leaky faucet—all because Rosey had become all horny-like and crazy to touch him. They were friends, weren't they? He was in one helluva quandary. And all because of the damned magic arrow, she wanted to climb up him now like an English Ivy.

His mind jumped forward to when he would drop her off at her house. What would the rest of the night entail?

They were both virgins—or at least he hoped Rosey was. The way she'd acted over the last hour, however, had him second-guessing his innocent little friend. The only thing Larry knew about making love was the fairy fuck flicks he'd watched on guy's night in the back room of Pixy's Porno Hut. Now, envisioning some of the positions that the actors performed while screwing each other senseless, his cock was throbbing to do the same. The wetness beneath his hat spread. *Son of a bitch…quit thinking about it or you're going to come right on the spot!*

"Larry?"

He darted another quick glance in her direction.

"Would you quit squeezing my head?"

"Are you going to behave?"

"Sure…for a little while at least."

He let go of her, albeit hesitantly, and gripped his hat with both hands. His attention was suddenly drawn to the humans below him. Brian held Claire's elbow and pulled a wagon filled with plants behind them. Another cart was mounded in the aisle. "Hey, Rosey, did you hear what Brian just said? He's going to Claire's in the morning. That's great!" Larry jumped up, plopped his hat on his head, and rubbed his palms together. "Looks like things are going well. Whew, with only six days left, that's a good thing." He turned to catch her staring at his bulging, dampened crotch and quickly tugged on the hem of his shirt to cover his erection. He twirled away. "Well, I guess we better get going."

Before he knew it, Rosebud flitted over his shoulder, hovered upside down, and stared directly into his embarrassed gaze. "Are your tights wet because you peed them?"

His jaw sagged just before he quickly recovered. "I beg your pardon! I quit wearing diapers years ago."

Her gossamer wings fluttered slightly and her head lowered until she was eye level with his crotch. "I know what your problem is! You've got a boner. I've heard about those. That's why you're wet, isn't it?"

"Chrissakes, Rosey, would you knock it off!" When she simply smiled and continued to hover, he grabbed her waist, flipped her right side up and set her on her feet. "All right, so I have a boner. Fairies my age get them sometimes."

Rosebud licked her lips. "Do you have one because of me?"

Larry fiddled with the brim of his hat.

Rosebud stepped closer. "Can I touch it?"

A snort erupted from his throat. "Fuck no!"

She sidled closer. "You can touch mine."

His eyes bulged at her audacity. "Don't be an idiot! Female fairies can't get boners."

Her chin rose, she cocked one leg at the knee, and jutted out her lower body in his direction. "I know that. What I *meant* was do you want to touch my *pussy*? Go ahead…I won't mind."

Larry's Adam's apple bobbed when he gulped. Touch Rosey's pussy? He glanced up at the blatant lust burning in her eyes. He suddenly remembered watching the flicks one night and thinking about Rosey—not one of the actresses, but Rosey. His thoughts scurried around like a frightened mouse. What were the rules as far as friends went? Did they take a chance to deepen a relationship as the humans did, or would they just hump like a couple of dogs?

She wanted him to touch her pussy…*her soft, downy pussy. Shit! I've never touched one before!* Just thinking about it now almost made him come. He couldn't. He wouldn't. Well, it was wise to never say never—not until he'd at least checked out a sex manual that he had hidden somewhere at his house.

Rosey swayed closer, her little breasts titillating to say the least. The heat of her sweet breath whispered across Larry's cheek. God, how was he going to say no?

"I want to touch you, Larry. Just once. Please?"

He gulped again, sounding like a dying fish in his own ears. "Rosey girl, we just can't—"

The words died in his throat when she traced a finger up the throbbing distance of dampened spandex from the base of his fuzzy nuts to the tip of his dripping cock. His ears buzzed. Larry almost toppled to the surface of the wooden beam.

Rosebud's eyes were wide as she stared at him and continued to trace a tickling path up and down his covered shaft. "Oooo, I can't believe how hard it is. Does it always get this hard?"

Larry opened his mouth. One hoarse squeak was all she got for an answer.

Her delicate fingers stretched around his cock that throbbed beneath the green tights. "It feels like a big, hard hotdog." She licked her lips, something she was doing at a steady pace since the arrow whacked her one in the first greenhouse. "Oooo, Larry, I *love* hotdogs."

He yanked her hand from his cock just as spoonfuls of come shot inside the tights. He spied the look of incredulous wonder in Rosey's eyes as sweat poured down his round cheeks. His breath came in strangled pants. Larry bent at the waist, grabbed his knobby knees, and sucked in air as he waited for the orgasm to run its course. He couldn't think, he couldn't look at her. He could only shudder in pleasure as his cock pulsed in the tight space between his legs.

"Fuck…me," he breathed out finally and shook his head in astonishment.

"Well, it's about time you asked—"

His hand shot into the air. "That's not what I'm talking about." God, it felt good to shoot a load because someone else had played with his dick instead of having to jerk it. He had to get his ass home and get some reading done.

"Come on, Larry. Let's go back to my place. I want to do it."

He straightened, a huge sigh belting out of his mouth. One hand kept the hem of his shirt pulled over his deflated cock and soaked tights. The other adjusted his skewed derby. "Rosey, we ain't doing it tonight."

Before he could move, she wrapped her arms around his neck and stared into his heated gaze. "Could you at least kiss me then? Come on, Lar. I've never kissed a guy before you. I want to try it again."

His fingers tightened around her tiny waist. He searched her pleading gaze. *What will one tender little kiss hurt? I'll be gentle with her so she doesn't get frightened. The fairies in the movies are always gentle…at first…* He firmed his stance, lowered his mouth, and touched his lips to hers.

Rosey grabbed him by the ears, yanked his head closer, and plunged her tongue halfway down his throat. Her petite size belied the strength of *amour* that raced through her veins. She held him in place and sucked on his tongue, wrapped a trim thigh around his, and ground her pink-tights-clad crotch against his shriveled penis.

The brim of his hat flattened against his forehead as he struggled for air. Hot bolts of lightening sparked in his groin once more as she continued to thrust against him. "Ros…mmm…hey!… I need…my fuckin'…ears!" he babbled against her demanding lips. He worked a hand up between them to break the suction of her mouth. "Rosey! Fuckin-a, Rosey!"

Finally, he managed to break the hold she had on his ears and leapt back, sucking air into his lungs like he'd been under water for the last ten minutes. The heat blazing in her eyes almost lit his tights on fire.

"See? Just one little kiss. That's all it was."

Larry yanked his hat down over his aching ears just in case she tried to snag him into another lip-lock. "I told you it ain't gonna happen tonight."

An impish smile turned up the corner of Rosebud's mouth. "Maybe not tonight, big boy, but soon…very soon…"

Chapter Five

Claire huddled in the center of her double bed that same night. Her fingers gently scratched Buddy behind one ear as he snored beside her. For the umpteenth time, she slid her hand across the mattress until her fingers found the clock. Pressing a button, she waited for the mechanical response.

"It is now four twenty-one a.m."

Almost four-thirty in the morning and still, she hadn't been able to fall asleep. All she could think about was the few hours spent in the company of a very nice man, and the fact that he would be at her house in less than four hours. Claire rolled to her side, stuffed the pillow more firmly beneath her head, and wrapped a loving arm around Buddy's neck as she cuddled his warm body.

The day had been like no other, and Claire had found herself stalling her departure from Brian's store. She had never met anyone quite like him who told dumb little jokes just for the sake of putting her at ease. Yet, she couldn't quite put her finger on some remote attribute of his personality. Brian was a man who seemed tenderhearted and giving one moment, and then untouchable the next. He was, for the most part, all business, but by the time she'd finally left the shop in order to catch the last bus home, she'd felt like they had been friends for years. Her attraction to him had grown by the hour.

"Buddy?" she whispered. "Are you awake?"

The dog instantly bounded up and stood on all fours, ready to do her bidding.

Claire giggled. "Sorry, old man. I didn't mean to wake you." The dog whined quietly. She patted the mattress beside her. "Down, boy. We're not getting up yet."

Buddy instantly lay beside her, but his ears stood at attention as he waited to see what would happen next.

"I just wanted to know what you thought of Brian Valentine. Is he handsome?"

The dog woofed.

Claire giggled louder. "That's what I thought. He sounds handsome, doesn't he? Did you catch that gravelly laugh of his?" Her airy sigh ruffled across the dog's fur. "I'm so excited, Buddy. For the first time in a long time, I'm excited about spending the day with a man. I just hope he's not coming here out of pity, because I won't put up with that. I had enough pity dumped on my shoulders by that rotten Scott. There isn't much I can't do that a woman with sight can. Does that make sense?" Buddy laid his snout across his paws and heaved a tired sigh. "I suppose I should let you go to sleep. It's almost morning." She listened to the familiar sounds of the night, feeling secure behind the locked doors with the dog's presence by her side. "It's just that I get so lonely in this house without someone to talk to. Even so, I'd never tell my mom because she'd harp on me something awful about selling our house and moving back in with her. Can you imagine that? I know my parents wouldn't mean to, but they would treat us like a couple of preschoolers." Claire sighed again and rested her cheek against the dog's shoulder. "You know what? I'll take the loneliness over being treated like a small child. Since I lost my eyesight, not very many people include me in on things. That really sucks. It's as if they think I've lost my ability to have fun. Boy, are they wrong. We're fun to be around, aren't we? Just because you're my eyes now, doesn't mean that I've lost my sense of humor." Claire's next words died momentarily until the lump in her throat disappeared. Every once in a while, the blindness she lived with daily overwhelmed her soul until she was able gather her wits and rise above the regret of being unable to see the world around her. "Dammit, I'm fun, Buddy. And from what I remember, I'm not too horrible to look at." Her fingers stroked the soft fur of her best friend. "I wonder if he thinks I'm pretty.

You know what? This is what we're going to do. We're going to get up early because we've got company coming. We're going to prepare one helluva a lunch and blow Mr. Valentine out of the water with everything we can accomplish. And maybe…just maybe…he'll see me for who I really am."

Buddy wiggled, laid a paw on Claire's chest, and sighed heavily. A second later his tongue gently licked her hand.

"Thank you for loving me, Bud. At least I know you'll always be here for me." Claire wrapped her arm tighter around the dog. Soon, she entered a world where colors were vivid and images were clear. A gentle smile touched her lips when a handsome, sexy man came to visit in the foggy aura of her dreams.

* * * * *

Brian sprawled naked across the mattress with his long legs entangled in the sheets. His bedspread lay in a heap on the floor at the end of the bed, evidencing his restless slumber. He lifted his head and squinted at the clock. It was five minutes to five. He dragged his hand from beneath the pillow and turned off the alarm button before the clock radio buzzed beside his ear.

Rolling to his back, he stared at the ceiling and thought about Claire Holliday—something he had done most of the night. He couldn't get the picture of her full smiling lips or her willowy body out of his mind.

Spending time with her the day before had been wonderful. Acting like the man he really was and not worrying about any sidelong glances was like a breath of fresh air. Because of the comfort level Brian had instantly discovered, he'd found himself laughing at the airy giggle that was her constant response to the jokes he continually cracked. Thinking on it further, spending those few hours with her was the most relaxed he'd felt in a long time, because being friendly with a woman was a part of his life he had buried away not long after the accident.

Brian squeezed his eyes tightly and winced as the memory of those horrible first days shot through his brain. After the fireball nearly engulfed him, he had been in so much physical pain that he hadn't even thought about what a third of his body looked like beneath the bandages that were changed daily. It wasn't until a month had gone by, that he finally came out of the morphine haze long enough to demand a mirror. The doctor argued with him but Brian was insistent to evaluate the severity of his burns…

Brian shot up and dragged his legs over the side of the mattress, mentally preparing himself to wander further into his memory. His lips drew in a straight line, his jaw firmed, but he still winced against the instant sting of unwanted tears and fought against the ache of constant loneliness that fate had dealt him by forcing him to survive the convalescence after the explosion. Back then, all Brian wanted to do was simply die rather than live with the fire's disfigurement. A shaky hand swept through his tousled hair as he stared across the room that became lighter by the minute. The memories returned…

That day when he had stared at himself in the mirror was the last day of Brian's life, as he had known it. What Brian saw staring back at him was the face of a monster, not a man who was in his early twenties ready for a long, proud life as a professional firefighter. If only he had taken the advice of his best friends, Paul Anderson and Hunter Dunlap, who after graduating thought he was crazy not to pursue a professional career in baseball. But Brian had remained firm to do the thing he had always wanted to do.

And look where it got me…

Now, he simply existed because he had no other choice. Fate had forced him to live through the agonizing pain of physical therapy, through horrible bouts of depression, and more surgeries than he cared to count. And, even though he was touted as a hero for saving an entire family from dying, the honor fell flat. Since the day he'd left the hospital, his life had become someone else's. Everything had changed the minute that gas hot water heater exploded.

Brian glanced at the clock again out of habit, wondering if it was too early to call Paul or Hunter. They were great friends. Both men had flown into town when word of the explosion reached them and had stayed by his side for weeks. When Brian felt the cloak of depression descending upon his shoulders, the two could always be counted on to bring some sense of sanity back into his lonely life.

His existence was lonesome because there were no more invitations to so-called friend's parties, no more days at the beach, and no more sex. Even Kristen, who'd wept beside his bed in the hospital, telling him that his disfigurement meant nothing, had hit the road as soon as possible. Brian had sworn then to never let a woman hurt him like that again. No, he had learned early on that not many acquaintances could be depended upon—especially women.

The experts had told Brian he was lucky because he'd only lost a part of one ear and growing his hair slightly longer could easily cover that up. He still had his eyesight and fingers. They'd told him his body would heal enough to allow him to move without pain.

"For what?" Brian murmured quietly into the room. "So I could spend my days being lonelier than a person ought to be?"

Meeting Claire, however, was the first good thing to happen to him. She would never be judgmental because she couldn't see him. He rose from the bed and headed for the shower, actually excited about spending the day at her place. The offer to plant her flowerbeds was spur of the moment, but now he was glad he had opened his mouth. With Claire, he could be himself. With Claire, he could pretend the accident had never happened.

Heading for the bathroom, Brian had the shower on seconds later. He stepped into the hot stream of water as his thoughts moved to the day ahead. Her plants were carefully packed in the back of the shop van. His gardening tools were in place. All he needed to do was buzz down to the store and make sure things were set for the day. Kate planned to meet him early…and then? He would probably drive around for an hour waiting for the clock to strike eight so he could pull into her driveway and get the day going. Hopefully, there would be a lot of work. Brian wanted to stay as long as possible.

*****

Larry spent the entire night turning his apartment upside down as he looked for the damn book about sex. Once Cupid's secretary returned his call and stated that the effects of the magic arrow would never really disappear, he quit fighting the urge to have sex with Rosebud. Dammit, the little sprite wanted him, and when Larry was really honest with himself, there wasn't a thing he could think of that would be better than having her beneath him with her legs straight up in the air. Besides, he'd learned a long time ago that when Rosey wanted something, she eventually got her way.

Disheartened because he couldn't find the book and the sun was already rising, he plopped down on the couch, scowled intently, and looked at the mess he had created, still finding it unbelievable that he planned to screw the hell out of Rosebud. "Where in hell did I put that thing?" He needed to do some studying. If he was going to do this thing right, he needed to be suave and sex-polished like the guys in the flicks.

Straightening his tipped hat, he leaned back into a soft cushion and closed his eyes, amazed that he had gotten away from Rosey the evening before with his dick in one piece. The horny little imp had done everything in her virginal repertoire of wanton acts, but Larry had stayed firm.

"My…where in hell did she find all those moves…" he mumbled to the untidy room. Just thinking about her wandering fingers and arching crotch caused his tights to tent up between his thighs. Opening one puffy lid, he scanned his lap and eyed his hard-on. "I wonder what it'll feel like to slide into Rosey's pussy?" His cock bobbed once against the spandex. *Rosey!* He bounded up and raced for his bedroom. *I know where I put that damn book!* Dropping to his bony knees by the side of his bed, his ass stuck up in the air as he shoved about old magazines, rotten banana peels and apple cores, and finally pulled out a tattered shoebox. Rolling to his butt, he flung the cover across the room and dug through some old Valentine's Day training papers until he found what he was looking for. "All right!" he exclaimed excitedly and held the manual in the air. Larry scooted to his feet and flopped onto his stomach across the unmade bed. Flipping the book open to the first page sent him into a slather of instant arousal. He stared straight into the open vee of a female sprite's thighs. He studied all the intricate pink parts of her anatomy. "Man…females got more things hidden than what you could find in a squirrel's nest. Hmmm…clitoris. Rub until wet. Vagina…hmmm…so that's what that thing is really called. I like pussy better." His finger dropped to the italicized index at the bottom of the page. "Vagina…other names…pussy, snatch, beaver, twat, schnutka, pooter…" He nodded his head. "Hmmph. Pooter…" He flipped to the next page and started reading physical terms that outlined other various areas of female genitalia. "Sheesh. I didn't think this sex stuff was going to be so technical." He ruffled through the pages again. "Let's get down to the real business…pictures, I need pictures."

Another fifteen minutes passed. He studied one picture after another of the naked female bodies, wondering why he had ever hidden the book in the first place. He was having the time of his life! It wasn't long before Larry was flat on his back, tugging on his cock like a dog fighting over a bone while he studied the many various sexual positions. Soon, the book went flying to the floor as he shoved his tights down, used both hands to whack his cock while visualizing Rosebud in his head, and jerked like crazy until cum spurted from his tender violet-colored tip.

Chapter Six

Larry hovered in front of Rosebud's heart-shaped door, trying to control his pounding heart. She had called him every ten minutes from the time she supposedly woke up, demanding that he get his ass to her place. They would do the deed today or, Rosey announced, she would not help him with Cupid's mission—screw the Gold Wings is what she had stated. Then she stated, quite graphically, what she was going to do to his cock as soon as she had it in her hot little hands. And, because of her declaration, Larry still sported a boner.

He fluttered down to the rock stoop, quivering in his pointed slippers. A quick dart of his eyes around the leafy porch assured Larry that he was, as of yet, undetected. With the quickness of a lightning bug, he shoved his sex manual behind a planter in case he needed it for further reference. Lifting his arm to rap his knuckles against the door, his fingers stopped in midair. Quickly, to take on a mysterious aura, he adjusted his hat low over one eye and yanked on the hem of his shirt to cover his swollen dick, then jutted out a knee to strike a pose. *Good…okay…now you're looking a little James Bondish… This is it, big guy…just don't shoot your load prematurely. Be cool…be calm…be suave…and knock on the fucking door.* He adjusted his cock first.

Rap, rap, rap…

The door swung open. He was yanked right out of his slippers and jerked inside. Rosebud grabbed him by the ears and planted a kiss on his lips that sucked the air from his lungs. When she finally let him come up for a breather, his heart banged against his rib cage and his cock thumped wildly against his belly.

"Okay, how do you want to do this?" Rosebud's fingers worked the buttons at the back of her neck.

If Larry didn't do something immediately, his plan for a long, sensuous seduction was definitely headed for the shitter. His fingers instantly stayed her hands. "Okay, Rosey. I've agreed to do this, but let's take it a little slower. I haven't even had a chance to kiss you."

"You just did."

"No…*you* just cut off my air supply."

Rosey spun in a circle and ended upside down as she hovered before his face. "I like a take-charge man, Lar-bear." Her wings sent a warm rush of air past his cheeks. "I'm so excited." She popped a little closer. "Are you excited, Larry?"

He stared into her brown eyes and swallowed. How could he not be? He was finally going to have sex for the first time in his life. His fingers fidgeted with the brim of his hat ready to pull it down over his ears if she made a grab for them. His excitement was laced with a bit of apprehension, however. What if he couldn't get his cock to do what he wanted it to do?

Rosebud flipped right side up and fluttered to the floor. "I'm ready, Larry. My friends told me that when fairies have sex for the first time, it doesn't hurt like it does to a human."

"*What!* You told people that we're going to do it?" The pressure was on. He had better perform like a champ.

"Oh, yeah. I'm the only virgin left in our group. They want me to call them as soon as we're done fucking." She stood before him like a horny sacrificial lamb. "Let's play a game." She darted to a counter, grabbed a small glass of toothpicks, and hurried back. "See these? Some of the sticks are painted with red fingernail polish. Let's play 'strip toothpicks'. We'll take turns. Whoever gets a colored tip has to take off a piece of their clothing. Oooo, this is going to be fun."

Larry eyed the twenty or so picks. Playing the game would rid him of the task—and his nervousness—of getting her naked.

"Come on, please, Larry?" She had the cutest little pout on her mouth.

"Oh, all right," he agreed.

"Oooo! I'll go first. Let's sit on my bed."

Just the word "bed" made his cock jump. Larry sailed after her until they reached her room. He settled as far from Rosebud on the mattress as possible, his eyes rounding when he took in the feminine trappings of the sprite's room. Everything was neat as a pin—a far cry from his own room a few blocks away. Pink and lilac ruffles abounded in the cozy space. Pictures of the past adorned every table, but the one on Rosebud's bed stand made his heart rap. It was a picture of him! "You have my picture?" He turned back to study her smiling lips. "Why?"

"Because you've always been special. You've always been my best buddy—now you're going to be my best lover."

Rosebud placed the container of picks on the table and daintily withdrew one from the center. The tip was blood red. Her eyes instantly darkened. "Looks like I get to take something off first." She leaned back on her elbows and waggled a slippered foot in the air. "Would you like to help?"

"I... I guess..." Taking a deep breath, Larry reached up, grasped her shoe with both hands, and yanked. The motion threw Rosebud off balance, and she sprawled flat on her back. "Oh, shit, sorry, Rosey."

She scurried up and whisked strands of blonde hair from her eyes. "That's okay. All right. You pick one."

Please no polish...please no polish...please no polish... Fuck! The tip was painted.

"What are you going to take off, Larry?" Syrupy sweetness laced her words.

"Well, it ain't gonna be my fuckin' shoes. You pulled me right out of them. I ought to get a free pass because they're both on the porch outside."

Her head wagged back and forth. A sly smile appeared on her red lips. "Uh-uh, Lar. If you didn't get them before, it's too late to do anything about it. Now, what is it going to be?"

A cantankerous sigh raised his shoulders. "I guess my shirt." Reaching for his hat, he set it beside him, crossed his arms and yanked the garment over his head and tossed it toward the floor. The derby was immediately perched back in place.

Before the shirt even fluttered to the ground, Rosebud's fingers poked at the fuzz on his chest. "Oh, Larry, your chest hair is so cute. Can I rub my cheek against it? And look!" she exclaimed while pointing at his crotch. "Your pecker is hard!"

His hand swiped at his hat, and an instant later, he smacked the derby over his cock and pushed her fingers away. "Hey, that's cheating. If I don't get to touch, then you don't either."

She pushed her breasts forward. "So, go ahead and touch."

"Rosey..."

"I want you to. Just see what they feel like—and then imagine them naked."

Larry stared at the jutting mounds beneath her lacy blouse. Each had a tight little nipple darting against the material. Man, he'd never felt up anyone before. Wiping the sweat from his palms, he reached up tentatively.

"Go ahead," Rosey whispered. "They won't bite."

Slowly, he cupped the small swells, letting his fingers slowly glide over the rise of her chest.

Rosebud's head lolled back when Larry's thumbs brushed across her pointed nipples. Fairy juice leaked into her panties.

Larry stared at his fingers. Her tits felt great in his hand—they fit perfectly into his cupped palms. A small spark of excitement rushed through his groin. He was starting to enjoy himself. He continued to fondle her chest even when she opened her eyes and reached for another toothpick. Their gazes locked. She held it up. The pick was bare.

Rosebud's eyebrows bounced over her glazed eyes. "Looks like it's your turn again. Larry? *Larry?* You can let go of my breasts now. Your eyes are rolling back in your head."

He jerked back to the present, yanked his hands away and placed them on his knees. "Oh…sorry." He reached for the glass and pulled out a red-tipped pick.

Rosebud giggled at the sarcastic twist of his lips. "Looks like your belt's gotta go…"

"This isn't really fair, ya know. I've only got a hat, shirt, belt and my tights. That's it." His eyes raked down her slender body. "You got all the damn trappings on of three fairies."

She crossed her arms in a slight huff. "If you don't take off that damn belt, I'm gonna do it for you. And put that damn hat back on your head. You're not fooling anybody. I know you got a boner under there."

"Sheesh!" He shook his head. "All right!" He smacked the derby down over his brow in a show of courage even though he wanted to hide his hard-on with his hands.

Her frown turned to a leering grin. "That's better. I think your boner is so cute."

"Boner's aren't supposed to be cute…they're supposed to be sexy and mysterious."

A high-pitched laugh bubbled from Rosebud's throat. "Mysterious? Okay, Larry, your boner is sexy and mysterious—and I can't wait to feel it slide into me."

He gulped when she selected another pick. Once again, it was plain and unpainted. She simply tossed it to the floor, tilted her head, and smiled.

Larry's lips drew in a straight line when he silently took his turn. "What the fuck?" he questioned and held up another red tip. "This must be a conspiracy."

Rosebud rubbed her hands together, lay back on one elbow, and waited for the show. "Okay, stand up. Let's see your cock, big boy."

Larry winced. He'd never shown his penis to anyone, let alone a girl fairy. "Close your eyes first."

"No way!"

He sighed as a stalling tactic. "You have to close your eyes, Rosey. It's kinda embarrassing to just drop my tights and let all my jewels hang loose."

Rosebud levitated off the mattress. Her wings beat silently as she crossed the room to the door. A quick flick of her wrist, and the lock clicked.

She returned and floated down to the bedspread. "Just making sure you don't bolt when my eyes are closed." Her lids fluttered shut. "Okay, go ahead. Tell me when you're ready."

The mattress jiggled when he stood. Larry hooked his thumbs inside the spandex waistband. "Keep 'em closed. No cheating. Fuck. I can't believe what I let you talk me into." Even though irritable, he was instantly aware of how it was a little more difficult to keep his breath even. The elastic waist got hung up on his hard-on the first time. He finally managed to work the material over his swollen cock without snapping the band against his violet penis head. He shimmied the tights over his knobby knees. His next mistake was to try and slip the tights over one foot when they were stretched around his ankles. Two clumsy hops and he was flat on his wings, rolling with his legs in a knot.

Rosebud's eyes snapped open. Larry lay on his back with his feet tangled in his stretchy tights and his fuzzy nuts bouncing between his legs. He jerked like crazy, trying to free his ankles. She took advantage of his position and was beside him in an instant, fondling his balls and sliding the fingers of her free hand around his cock. "Ohhhh, Larry."

He still fought the winding tights and tried to see beneath the brim of his hat that was smashed across his lower brow. "What the hell are you doing?" he squealed.

"I'm trying to help you get loose." Her hand stoked his shaft. She continued to cup his balls. "Man, for a little guy, these things are pretty big."

Despite his embarrassment, Larry couldn't discount the heated sparks that intensified in his groin. His thighs spread with a will of their own despite the imprisonment of the material wrapped around his ankles.

Rosebud licked her lips as she caught her first full view of his penis. Larry's cock was huge! The end had a sweet lilac-colored head that smiled all on its own. This was the thing that her friends' giggled over all the time—and she had it in her hot little hand. His little ass began to pump, making his cock slide faster inside her cupped palm.

"Is this what we're supposed to do, Larry?"

His face had turned red and his eyes bulged. "I'm gonna... I'm gonna...tug harder..." he panted.

Rosebud planted herself over her knees, wrapped both hands around his dick, and jerked like crazy as she watched his face screw into...she didn't know how to describe it because she'd never seen anything quite like it in her life. She waited breathlessly to see what would happen. Liquid bubbled over her hand, thicker and thicker with each stroke. His lilac tip turned purple. All of a sudden, white cum shot straight up into the air at the same time that Larry let out a yodel.

"Ohhhh, Larry!" she shrieked and jerked harder as the streams of milky liquid slowed, excited that just watching her friend made her own tights hot and wet between her legs. "Do it again!"

His bony butt began to slow with the dwindling rhythm of the spurts, but Rosebud's fingers continued to haul ass.

Larry's cock tingled with the heat of his spent orgasm. The slurping sound of her fingers sliding the length of his wet, half-hard cock, made him realize somewhere in his foggy brain that his dick was going to turn to hamburger if he didn't do something quick. He reached up, flailed until he had a firm grip on her wet fingers, and managed to take control of the situation. "Rosey…you can stop now! It's gonna fall off if you keep doing that."

"Can I play with your nuts? They're so darn cute, although they seem a little smaller now." Her wings fluttered crazily.

"No you can't play with my nuts," he stated while he adjusted his hat and sat up. He dragged his tights over his ankles and tossed them to the floor. "And they're only smaller because I— Never mind. What about you? When are you going to get naked? We may as well shitcan the game."

She sat back and crossed her arms. "I'm not taking anything off until you tell me what it felt like to shoot that white stuff…that cum…all over the place. Did it feel good? Be honest—and lose the crabby attitude for once in your life."

Larry hooked his elbows across his raised knees, gazed at her, and heaved a sigh. "All right, you really want to know?"

"Uh-ha." Unexpectedly, she watched his mouth spread into a wide grin. Soon, a booming laugh followed. He fell to his back and rolled back and forth. "Larry? Are you okay?"

He wiped his watery eyes. "Okay? I'm fucking fantastic! That hand job was fucking fantastic! I can't believe we waited so long to get this far." He reached out. "Come here, Rosey. I want to kiss you."

Chapter Seven

Claire had everything ready for lunch, had cleaned up the dishes, and now perched on a stool in her kitchen. The radio was loud enough to hear the time, but low enough that she wouldn't miss the sound of a slowing engine as it turned into her driveway. Every vehicle that had passed the house so far had just kept going. Her fingers drummed against the countertop.

It was almost eight o'clock when the sound of a vehicle slowing on the street outside filtered through the window screen. Her head tilted as she breathlessly leaned forward and waited. An instant later, Buddy's woof signaled a visitor. *It's got to be Brian!* "Buddy, come!" The dog was at her side in an instant. Claire grabbed the plastic handle, placed a hand over her chest, and took a deep cleansing breath. "Well, Bud, this is it. Now, let's make a good impression so we don't scare him away." Claire rounded the corner of the house just as Brian alighted from his van. He glanced up when Buddy barked and saw her standing in the morning sunlight with a bright smile of welcome. Seeing her in person again was far better than imagining the sight of her through the long night.

"Is that you, Brian?"

"Good morning, Claire. Finally got here. Hope I'm not late." *Yeah, right. I've been circling the block for the last twenty minutes…*

Claire's beaming smile widened across her face. "Oh, no! You were so great to offer your help that you could have showed up this afternoon and you still wouldn't have been late." *But I would've been devastated, thinking that you weren't coming…* "Tell me how many steps to your van and I'll help you carry plants to the back."

He didn't want to look at the sidewalk and count steps; he wanted to look at her. This morning, the sunglasses were gone. So instead, he used the distance between them to study her face—and the burnished russet-colored curls lifting in the wind—and the way her breasts pressed against her tee shirt as he strolled to the side of the house.

"Brian?"

"I'm right here." *Green eyes...she's got green eyes...beautiful green eyes...* He reached out and took her hand. "I figured I'd just come and get you. Are you sure you want to help with the load?"

"I'm blind, Brian, not an invalid. Lead the way."

"Sorry, Claire. That's not what I meant."

She shrugged her shoulders apologetically. "I know you didn't. I guess I just get a little defensive at times. It's a standard trademark of the handicapped."

Brian had absolutely no rebuttal. He lived the emotion daily.

"Brian?"

He tossed away his angst and tugged on her hand. Damn, he was excited about the coming day. "Come on. We'll take one load around back and then spend some time mapping out your garden."

* * * * *

After spending an hour laughing and discussing the layout of Claire's flowerbed, both she and Brian were now side by side on their knees, ready to begin the planting. He was always careful to keep her to his left so she wouldn't feel the raised ridges of his scarred right arm if she happened to reach out. Buddy lay contentedly in the shade of a maple tree, but his eyes followed Claire's body as she moved about with her hand tucked in the crook of Brian's arm.

Brian shuffled the first set of potted roses into separate groups. "I think what we'll do, Claire, is divide the gardens by scent. That way, it'll be easier for you to distinguish what you have growing."

As he continued to plan aloud, Claire sat back on her thighs and listened to the steady cadence of his voice. The distinct, husky tone rattled her insides as each minute passed in his company. She could listen to the sound forever. Even discussing flowers, Brian sounded sexy as hell. She was already willing to bet she could pick him out in a loud crowd. And his laugh—it was a slow, easy chuckle that started deep in his chest and became more resonant as it worked its way up his throat and across his lips.

"In addition, there's the attar, which is how you describe the true rose or spicy scent of the blossoms. Some roses produce an apple or fresh green scent from their leaves and braces. The morning dew will encourage the strong scent to be carried all around your garden and right through an open window. That's why we'll plant this group right under your kitchen window. That way you can enjoy them when you're having your coffee in the morning."

"You amaze me, Brian, with all your knowledge. When did you learn all this stuff? I've never even heard of the word 'attar'."

Brian's hand paused for a moment to rest on the edge of a pot as he glanced her way. How could he tell Claire that out of boredom and because he was bedridden for months that he had picked up one of his mother's gardening books that she'd accidentally left at the hospital? One magazine led to another when he realized he wouldn't be lucky enough to die. Reading killed the monotony of his long, painful days and made him forget about the flames that had turned his world upside down. It was when he'd read an article stating that growing fragrant roses was a form of natural healing that his interest was actually piqued. Brian would never be able to face a burning building again. He was forced to come up with an alternative way to make a living. Gardening happened to be the first choice presented. Not caring one way or the other what he did with the rest of his life, his resilient mind soaked up the information he read.

Brian shook off his melancholy and forced a chuckle. "Lots of reading. I guess I discovered that I wanted to be in business for myself and not have someone telling me when and what I had to do next." His heart did a tiny flip when her cheeks dimpled in response. "Do you work?"

"Doesn't everyone?"

"Yeah. But are you on vacation or something? It's the middle of the week."

A soft giggle floated past his ear. "I guess you could say I'm on a small vacation until the end of the month. I teach Braille at a school for the blind, and the students are on an early spring break. I could have volunteered for some extra time in the office, but I enjoy being home." *Even though it's lonely at times.*

"How long have you lived by yourself?"

"Too long, according to my parents. They're really uptight about me being here by myself. But I'm not really alone. I've got Buddy." The dog's head came up instantly and he padded across the lush grass to sit beside his master.

Brian observed the two as Claire's fingers scratched the animal behind one ear. The dog cuddled closer to her side. It was crazy—it was if they had a secret language all their own. "You can't blame them, Claire. Even though you're an adult, you're still their child." A quick flash of his own parents' pain while he lay half-dead in the hospital raced through his mind. "So, how long have they put up with your willful independence?"

"Ha! Is that how you see me?"

How did he see her? Brian studied her beautiful green eyes, the gentle curve of her slender neck, and her full breasts beneath her cotton tee. Instantly, he was ashamed of himself for leering at Claire just because she couldn't see what he was doing. "I see a beautiful woman who must have a pile of courage stored up inside her. Living here alone as a sighted woman would be difficult at times. Would you be upset with me if I asked you a personal question?"

She shrugged her slim shoulders. "Go ahead, but I think I know what you're going to ask. You want to know how long I've been blind and what happened."

His eyebrow rose at her intuitiveness. "Busted. You don't have to answer if you don't want to."

But Claire wanted to. She wanted Brian to know everything about her—well, except for her lousy relationship with Scott. "I have what's called retinitis pigmentosa. I started having symptoms like night blindness, problems with peripheral vision—things that wearing glasses couldn't help even when I was thirteen. A lot of people who have the same thing retain some of their vision most of their lives. The pattern and degree of visual loss is different for each individual."

Brian's heart went out to the woman beside him when she winced and didn't even realize it.

"I wasn't so lucky. Everything finally went black when I was twenty-one. That was five years ago. It was horrible at first, but my parents were there every second of the way. My dad was the one who insisted I get into a seeing-eye dog program. Thank God I listened to him. I discovered that I could still do a lot with Buddy by my side—including living on my own."

"You're amazing, Claire. I give you a lot of credit." *You're a lot braver than I was…*

Her cheeks stained a light pink. "Why, thank you, Brian." She leaned in his direction and reached out until her hand found the base of a plastic pot. "I'm not so amazing though as I am excited to get these flowers in." Sliding her hand further, her fingers unexpectedly came in contact with his. They were long and slender and, out of nowhere, Claire wondered what they would feel like against the naked skin of her breasts. That thought immediately led to the idea of them sliding inside her. A rush of heat laced through her belly. Her hand jerked back, and she covered the motion by quickly scratching her arm.

Brian felt the instant scorch of her touch—a searing heat unlike the flames that had enveloped him years earlier. Instead, the feeling was like a slow, sweet burn that promised immense physical pleasure. He shook his head to rid himself of the picture of Claire naked in his arms. *It's been too long…*

"I want to help with the garden, Brian. But I'm a little unsure of what to do. Have any suggestions?"

His dark eyes rested on a small hand spade. "Want to turn over the dirt a little more while I get the pots ready?"

"Sure. What do you want me to use?"

He reached for the spade, took her fingers in his, and ignored how much he simply wanted to sit in the bright sunlight and hold her hand. The emotion startled his brain. Brian was too accustomed to forcing women away, and the emotions Claire created had his head whirling. Gently, he placed the spade into her palm and guided her hand to the black dirt. "Just do this." He kept his hand over hers as he showed her the motion. Claire's face was so near to his that all he would have to do was tilt his head slightly and he would be able to press a kiss to the soft skin of her cheek. "Just put it in the dirt, pull it out, and pile it over here."

Claire's breath caught in her throat at the vivid picture his innocent words evoked. *Put it in and pull it out… Oh, my God…I've been without a man for far too long!*

They worked like that, sharing past experiences of youth and feeling as if they'd known one another for years. Finally, Claire sat back and peeled off the gloves Brian had found for her when she heard the city's noon church bells ring. "Okay, I'm the foreman on this job and I declare an official lunch hour."

Brian swiped his forearm across his brow and surveyed their work thus far. "We've done pretty good this morning. Only one more bed to go." *I wish it were yours…with satin sheets and fluffy pillows…* He shook his head. All morning long, thoughts of holding Claire in an intimate embrace bombarded his mind until he quit fighting the lurid ideas and simply went along with them. He was infinitely happy she hadn't seen the many times he had leaned in close to quietly sniff her sweet-smelling hair. *She'd probably call the cops and have my ass hauled off somewhere...* He reached for her arm and gently helped her rise to her feet. "If you want, I can help you to the door. Then I'm gonna go grab something to eat at home."

Claire's heart sank. He was going to leave. *Ask him, you ninny. You worked hard to get things ready,* a voice yelled out at her.

Maybe he doesn't want to hang around with a blind woman...

She straightened her shoulders with purpose. The morning with Brian was the best thing that had happened in a long time. "I'd love for you to stay and have lunch with me. I prepared something for us this morning. Please, say you'll share. It's the least I can do for all your hard work." She waited, listening to his breath sigh across the short distance between them.

She didn't see his slightly lopsided smile.

"Are you sure? I guess anything would be better than a peanut butter sandwich."

Claire grinned like an idiot, but she didn't care. "Buddy, come." She waited for the dog to nudge her thigh. "House, Buddy. Come on, Brian. I hope you're hungry!"

He followed her to the door, his gaze taking in the slight swing of her rounded ass as she strolled up the sidewalk.

Once inside, Claire insisted he sit after he washed his hands and let her wait on him. Brian finally gave up the argument and watched in amazement as she moved about the kitchen with ease. It wasn't long before the room was filled with the aroma of shrimp scampi. "Man, does that smell good. You shouldn't have gone to so much trouble, though. Are you sure I can't help with anything?"

"Nope! I've got everything under control. Just pour yourself a glass of lemonade. I hope you're hungry. I kind of went overboard this morning." As the shrimp sizzled, her hand glided over the edge of the counter until she stopped before the fridge. "Let's see, if memory serves me, I've got some sliced fruit…" She placed the container on the surface beside her, "and some crab salad. Ah, there it is!" Soon, Claire had everything on the counter beside a freshly baked chocolate cake.

Brian stared in wonder. "I can't believe this! It's too much, Claire. I haven't had a lunch like this for a long time."

After she scooped the cooked shrimp onto a small platter, she found the stool beside him and plunked down happily. "I haven't had anyone over for a month of Sundays. Be kind and enjoy it." She pulled the salad bowl close. "Here you go."

The next half hour was spent reminiscing about college days and Brian regaled her with the crazy antics of him and his two best friends when they'd traveled around the country playing baseball. Claire literally glowed beside him as she daintily picked at her food and laughed uproariously.

Brian had a hell of a hard time watching her as she ate. Claire had a way of opening her mouth and slowly sucking in the chunks of pineapple, melon, or strawberries that had him wiggling in his seat. He forced himself to keep his hands on the surface of the snack bar when all he really wanted to do was to have those red lips sucking on the end of his fingers. He swallowed unbelievably at how aroused he actually was with her innocent actions. After burying that part of his life, Claire had easily awakened his sexual desires.

Every so often, Brian's arm brushed against Claire's. And each time she yearned to take his hand and press it against her cheek. Her senses were clouded with the masculine scent of his cologne, the sexiness of his voice, and the warm emotions of getting to know a man once more. She missed having someone special in her life—someone other than her parents. Claire was a woman ripe with the longing to be loved. To her, Brian Valentine could easily be the man.

She stood to retrieve two plates for dessert. "I guess we should have our dessert so we can get back outside. Why don't you grab two clean forks and—" Her words were cut off when the phone rang.

"Go ahead and answer it, Claire," he said as he hopped off the stool. "I'll get the plates and serve us up some more calories. It's the least I can do."

His stool scraped across the floor as she headed for the phone. Having Brian in her kitchen and sharing a meal with him seemed...so natural and comforting. She reached for the phone on the fourth ring. "Hello?"

"Hi! Is this Claire Holliday?"

"Yes, it is."

"Hi, Claire. This is Kate from The Valentine Shoppe. We met yesterday."

"Hi, Kate. What can I do for you?" Claire heard Brian take a step in her direction.

"Could I talk to Brian? We've got a little problem here at the store."

"Um, sure. He's right here—or at least I think he is." The last comment was an attempt at humor on Claire's part when she realized the day might be done. "Brian?" She held out the phone. When his fingers touched hers she almost dropped it.

"Hi, Kate. What's up?"

Claire could hear the muted voice of Brian's employee, but couldn't understand what she was saying. She listened as he asked questions. Something with the water system.

"Just shut off the main valve in the pump room. I'll clean up here and be down as soon as possible." He paused. "No, that's just fine. I sure as heck am not going to pay for someone else to fix it." Another pause. "All right. See you shortly." He hung the handset back in the cradle before he glanced at Claire as she stacked dishes in the sink. "I guess you heard that."

Her head nodded. "Yeah, you have to go." *God, I wish you could stay.*

"I've got a broken water main that needs to be repaired." *I should just hire someone to come in. I hate to leave.*

"Well, I can't thank you enough for everything you've done already. It shouldn't be too hard to get the lavender in the last bed."

Brian stood beside her, feeling terrible. Suddenly, he jumped at the first excuse to come to mind. "I was looking at that when we were outside. You need some other plants to go with the lavender—something that will bloom opposite so you always have something flowering. How about I come back tomorrow and help you finish planting? I'll see what I have and bring a few pots with me." He actually crossed his fingers hoping that she would agree. "In fact, I insist—that is if you're going to be around. I'll even bring lunch. My treat."

Claire's heart knocked in her chest. She would get her second chance. "That sounds great! But you don't have to bring lunch. I can fix something—or maybe I'll even take you out for all your hard work."

Brian almost quit breathing. There was no way he would go out in public for a lunch and risk Claire finding out what he really looked like. "No. I'm pretty handy in the kitchen. Let's just stay here."

Claire smiled brightly. She would agree to walk through fire if it would give her another day with Brian all to herself. "Okay, then it's a deal. You're on for lunch."

Chapter Eight

Rosebud stared at Larry. "You want to kiss me?"

He nodded. "Yes I do. Come over here, Rosey." He reached out his hand and waited for her to float into his arms.

Rosebud came willingly and was quickly wrapped within his tender embrace. She tipped up her mouth.

Larry eyed her moistened lips for a second. "Now, when I kiss you, don't be grabbing my ears, okay? They already feel like someone hit 'em with a baseball bat. Just let the moment flow. Can you do that?"

Rosebud's eyes fluttered shut. She puckered up and tightened her hands around the back of his neck.

Remember how they kissed in the movies…be cool, be suave… Larry lowered his mouth and tentatively brushed his lips to hers. The intimate touch warmed his heart. This was right. This was perfect. He suddenly realized that he wanted Rosey by his side for a lifetime. Her lips were soft and wet. His cock bobbed once against her belly. They both opened one eye and stared at the other in wonder. "Sorry," he stated quickly. "Damn thing's got a mind of its own."

"Kiss me again, Larry," she breathed out.

This time, he opened his mouth and slid his tongue across the seam of her lips. A small moan came from deep inside Rosey's throat.

Confident now, Larry cuddled her closer and slanted his mouth across hers. *Okay then…it's time to bust inside.* Working his way into her mouth, instant pings of heat increased the size of his spent cock. Rosebud darted her tongue around the inside of his mouth, which increased the swelling between his legs even more.

Damn! This is damn fine! Rosey's mouth tasted sweet and delicious—just like a fresh peach in the summer. There really was something to this kissing crap, so he kept his eyes shut and simply enjoyed the moment. When she grabbed his cock, his eyes shot open, and his head jerked back. Rosebud's grin was a mile wide.

"Can I have my turn now?"

"What do you think we're doing?"

"No, you numbskull. I want my turn to strip. It's no fair that you're the only one naked."

A slow grin spread across his lips when he thought about her smooth, bare skin, and not just the skin of her face or arms. He wanted to view it all. "Good idea. I'll just sit on the chair." He pecked her mouth once more for good measure and hurriedly yanked a cushioned chair into the middle of the room.

Once he was settled, Rosebud glanced at his cock that stood proudly once more. Her eyes softened to a deep shimmering brown. She'd show him. By the time Rosebud was done teasing Larry, he would be nothing but a wet noodle. Well, that would be after he came for the second time. And then her quick mind darted to the third, and the fourth, and the fifth as she sauntered over to her CD player. "I have a little treat for you. I thought you might enjoy me stripping to some music. Are you ready?"

Larry nodded his head so quickly that the hat vibrated atop his pointed head. His wings fluffed up on his back.

"Okeydokey. Here we go!" A slender finger pressed the Play button. Instantly, the loud, lewd strains of a striptease song bounced across the room. The bass almost blew Larry off the chair as Rosebud spun around with her hips jerking forward to the beat and her fingers at the back of her blouse.

By the time she stood before him, the neckline gaped open, revealing the upper swell of her breasts. She leaned forward, waggled her shoulders and, a second later, Larry stared straight at the perkiest little pink nipples he'd ever seen. His mouth sagged open.

The music continued to blare as Rosebud floated away, tossed her blouse into the air, and reached for the waistband of her pink tights. Running her moist tongue across her lips, she winked at him. Larry's boner sprouted as each inch of her pale thighs came into view. He didn't blink. He didn't breathe. He just worried about all the blood leaving his brain and heading for his cock.

Just before Rosebud pulled her tights over her ankles, she swiveled away and presented Larry with a great view of her backside as she let her ass bounce to the music. Glancing over her shoulder, she wondered if he was going to slip right off the chair. His body sagged and he clutched the edge of the seat, but his eyes never left the satiny, firm cheeks presented to him. *Well,* she giggled to herself, *I know how to keep him in the chair...* Grabbing the tights from the floor, she turned and bounced to the beat of the music in his direction.

Oh, my God...here she comes! Larry's brain fogged as he watched her strut closer. The pink tights hung from her hand as she jutted out her breasts and kicked up her legs to give him a sneak preview of her pooter. Never taking his eyes from the sight of her naked body, he grabbed his wrist and pressed his fingers against the pounding beat of his blood, knowing his heart was gonna blow, and he would be dead before he had a chance to stick his cock inside her.

He jumped with a start when Rosebud looped the pink tights around his neck, took a firm hold on each end, and then straddled his closed knees. The music blared. The feminine scent of her perfume filled his nostrils. His heart pounded, and he nearly fainted when she squatted slightly and brushed the lips of her dripping pooter across the tops of his thighs, leaving his skin scorched and wet with her musky essence. He gulped—something he was doing a lot of lately—and continued to clutch the edges of the chair.

"Larry!" she hollered above the music as her wings fanned her body upward. "Come on! Touch my pussy!" Her head fell back as she hovered before him.

He stared in disbelief at the softly furred pooter right before his eyes. Rosebud's musky scent surrounded him, sending a jolt of hard arousal through his blood.

"Come on, big boy! Do it!"

Do it! For chrissakes, do what? Just touch it? I've never touched one before! Forcing the fingers of one hand to uncurl, he lifted his arm. His finger wavered before his eyes. Gulping, he poked forward. His cock bobbed crazily when the tip of his finger slipped through her slit.

"Oh, yeah! Larry!" Rosebud's thighs spread wider. She thrust her hips with the music's beat, and glided over his finger again and again. "Stick it to me, baby!" Her own fingers threaded through her hair crazily as she worked herself into a flurry. "Stick your finger in me! Stick your finger in me!"

Larry's blood raced. Bravely, he parted the pooter lips, eyed her glistening hole, and went for it. His eyes rounded wide when the muscles of her vagina clamped around his finger.

"Come on, big boy, move it! Move it!"

Oh, my God! It's like in the movies…only way fucking better! God, the only thing he wanted to do was stick his pecker in her as she bounced in the air on his finger. Instinct washed through him. Pictures from his sex manual ran through his brain like tickertape. His cock throbbed until he thought the violet-colored head would pop right off. "Let's do it, Rosey!" he yelled above the music. "Let's fuck!"

Retiming her wings, Rosebud let her body float to a horizontal position, but she clamped her thighs together to keep his thrusting finger inside.

Larry levitated off the chair, and he fingered her pooter all the way across the room until they settled on the bed. Rosebud's hips possessed a rhythm all their own as her feet lifted to the heavens. He had two fingers up her tunnel now as she rocked against the pressure that filled her small opening. "Rub this! Rub my clit!"

Oh, shit…that's right…rub until wet. Wet? Fuck, I could go swimming with the liquid dripping out of her – not to mention what's drizzling down my thigh… He used the finger of his free hand to wiggle her clit. Boy, this was getting better by the second.

"Something's happening, Larry! I can feel it. Hurry!"

"Okay!" He flicked her clit as fast as he could as she bounced on the mattress. "Like this?"

"No, you idiot…well, yeah, you idiot. No! Let's do it! Oh…man…something's going to blow! I can feel it!"

He rolled between her splayed thighs, rested his body over his knobby knees, and panted like a madman as his fingers slipped from her pussy and his cock knocked around between her legs. *Christ, I hope I hit the right hole!*

"Larry! Hurry, Larry!" she screamed with hot passion darkening her eyes. "Fuck me! Come on, baby, fuck me!"

Son of a bitch! I can't find the hole! Where in the fuck is the hole! He slid his fingers through her wet slit again and located his point of entry. Her hips rocked. "Rosey! You're gonna have to lie still so I can get in!"

Rosebud's yodel of pleasure drowned out the music as she ignored his directive. Her hands squeezed her breasts, drawing her nipples to hard darts.

His finger slipped inside her again. *Okay, there it is. Easy now, big boy. Easy…you can do this.* His eyes squeezed tight in concentration. He let his cock do the walking until it pressed against his plunging fingers. In a flash, he pulled them out, repositioned his cock, and… *Son of a bitch. I missed again.* He thought about the guys in the flicks who easily found the right hole. How come it was so damn hard for him?

He watched Rosey's head roll wildly on the pillow. Suddenly, her pooter lips wrapped around his cock head. He'd finally hit the mark. Heat slithered through his belly. She grabbed his hips and yanked him in.

Holy fuck! I'm in. Holy mother of… His hips jerked on their own against Rosebud's surges. Her tight pussy sucked him in further. There was absolutely no doubt—he was going to drop dead of a heart attack, but who gave a shit? He was going out in style. Remembering how the guys slammed their chicks in the movies, he bunched up the muscles in his thighs, withdrew slightly so he could dive in for the big bang, and then slipped right out of her pooter.

"Dammit, Larry, what the hell are you doing? You're driving me nuts!" Rosebud panted out.

As he scrambled to locate her hole again, his eyes narrowed in frustration. "How the hell do you think I feel? Quit jerkin' around on the bed!" He couldn't tell if it was the beat of the music's bass that pounded in his chest or his heart.

Rosebud raised her head and knew she would have to take charge of the situation as he fumbled about, or the sexual tension racing through her blood would light her on fire. She reached out to grab his cock. Before he could holler anything, she found the hole for him, guided his pecker to it, and wrapped her legs around his skinny waist. With a kick of her heels against his ass, he was back in the saddle and pumping like mad.

"Ohhhh…Laaarrrryyyy!"

Chapter Nine

Brian lifted a plastic cover, sniffed the spaghetti sauce inside, and smiled with satisfaction. As he snapped the lid back in place, his gaze darted to the counter where a key lime pie waited along with a bowl of fresh salad greens and garlic bread. Claire would definitely be impressed. He'd worked the entire night before to prepare the promised lunch, acknowledging in the back of his mind that he had enough to feed an army, but he didn't care. If the garden work was extended into the afternoon, he had made damned sure they wouldn't have to go out in public to find something else to eat.

As he gathered the lunch items on the counter and began packing them into a box, his hands stilled. Lifting his eyes, Brian stared out his kitchen window. He couldn't wait to get back to Claire's house this morning. Since the day of his accident, he couldn't remember feeling so excited about something—not even the opening of his own business. Claire had sparked an emotion inside him that he never thought he'd experience again. Well, not sparked. More like ignited. Sometime during the night, Brian had discovered a raging desire be a half of a whole. The rediscovered emotions of sexual arousal, the intense need to protect, and the longing to be physically and emotionally loved by Claire had kept him awake most of the night.

He shook his head, wondering at the fact that only over the course of a mere few hours, he had fallen in love. "Love…how is that emotion even possible in such a short time?" He shook his head happily and continued to pack the box.

And what about everything else? Just because Claire can't see you now, doesn't mean that she won't discover what happened. What then? What will you do when she runs in horror? You'll be alone again. Don't you remember what it felt like when Kristen abandoned you? The loaf of bread dropped from his numb fingers onto the counter. *End it now. Call her and make up some sort of excuse.*

Brian sank to a chair and closed his eyes as he rested his head against the wall, his excitement suddenly overshadowed by the psychological wounds he still carried. Claire had stated that she let her other senses take the place of her sight. Certainly, she would be able to feel the raised edges of his puckered skin. She had been able to see at one time. It would be easy for her to imagine what he looked like.

The constant paranoid feelings of inadequacy reared up to take hold of his emotions. How could he drag Claire into his shitty world? He knew the future still held more surgeries and pain. How could he walk down the street with her hand in his knowing that strangers gawked at the beauty and the beast?

His fingers trembled through the thick hair of his temples until they were clasped behind his neck. He couldn't do that to himself, and he couldn't put Claire through it. Sanity returned as he stuffed his emotions away, berating himself because he actually thought that, for a few short hours in the middle of the night, nothing was more important than having found someone to love again. He'd call her and tell her that he'd send someone over to finish the garden, and just go back to the greenhouse and hide behind his plants.

Brian jumped when the phone rang beside him. With a heavy heart, he reached out and plucked the handset from the cradle. "Hello?" His voice was flat and uncaring.

"Brian? This is Claire."

His heart slammed in his chest. "Claire? Is something wrong?"

Silence.

"Claire?"

"I'm still here. I hope you don't mind that I called you at home."

"No…it's fine. How did you get my number?"

"Crazy thing about these phones. You can actually call an operator and they connect you. I think it's called modern technology."

Brian couldn't help but smile at Claire's dry sense of humor. "So what's up?"

*****

Claire clutched the phone and fought for courage. Now that she had him on the line, her nerve flagged slightly. Buddy intuitively sidled up to his master and licked her hand to lend encouragement. She smiled and decided to go for it.

"I wanted to call you and say something before you came over." She took a deep breath. "I don't normally plunge in like this...well, yes I do. Remember when I told you my mother said I always speak before I think?" She heard the quiet chuckle on the other end of the line. "Well, this could be one of those situations. Although, I was up all night thinking about it, so maybe this really doesn't qualify as one of those situations..." Okay, now she was really babbling on like an idiot.

"Thinking about what?" His gravelly voice turned her inside out.

"I...I need to ask you something. Does it bother you that I'm blind?"

"What are you talking about? Why would you being blind bother me?"

"Because I wanted to ask you something if it doesn't." Claire nervously twirled an auburn curl around a finger of her free hand. "Do you think you could accept me like you would a normal, sighted woman? I mean, like someone you could have a relationship with?" Silence. "I know this is kind of forward, but when you're in a situation like mine, sometimes it doesn't pay to wait. I say that because, looking back on the last few years, I wish I would have stopped to pay more attention to the color of a flower when I could still see it. I wish I would have had the opportunity to see how clouds shade out an entire side of a mountain instead of just looking at it in a picture, or to at least, just once, have enjoyed the sight of a building storm instead of running into the house to hide from it. There are so many things I could have collected then and had as a memory now if I only would have paid attention and done something about it. Brian? Are you still there?"

He answered after a slight pause. "Of course I'm here, Claire. Don't even think that I see you as different from women who have their sight. You're pretty awesome. Look at how independent you are. You could do or have anything you want."

"I want a chance with you." Her eyelids closed when he didn't respond. "You're shocked, aren't you? Well, then I'll just keep talking until it wears off. Yesterday after you left, I kept thinking about our day together. We seemed to have so much in common. It really was a great day. When I finally went to bed, I couldn't get you or the sound of your voice out of my mind. You're the first man in a long time that has treated me like I'm worth something. I am, Brian. I am worth something. And I'm tired of being alone all the time. I know I work at the school and have my parents and my coworkers, but that's not what I'm talking about. I'm trying to tell you that I think you and I could have something special. I don't know why, but I'm afraid that you might disappear if I'm not totally upfront. I know we just met, but sometimes that doesn't make any difference either. Sometimes people just click when they're together. And yesterday, I felt that. I felt that I didn't simply want you to plant my garden and go away. And I know I'm a coward for calling you on the phone instead of telling you in person, but I didn't want to take the chance if for some reason you couldn't make it today. I don't know why I felt that way, but I knew I had to call right away. So, if you—"

"Be quiet, Claire."

"Okay."

"I'll see you in about fifteen minutes."

The dial tone sounded in her ear. Her hand shook when she replaced the phone into the cradle. She sank onto a chair—the one whose back she had clutched tightly during her speech. "He must think I'm a damn idiot." Buddy laid his head on Claire's lap and wiggled closer. She scratched his ear. "I don't care. If you snooze, you lose, Buddy. And I'm going for it. Something brought Brian Valentine into my life and I'm not going to sit idly by just because I'm blind."

*****

Larry's eyes batted open. He rolled his head and noted Rosey's sweet open mouth as she snored softly into a fluffy pillow. Eyeing the black derby dipped over one of her eyes, he had to chuckle to himself. Once they had really got going the evening before, the little imp had insisted that he give up his hat so she could wear it. Jeez, she was cute as hell with the addition.

His eyes were drawn to the sugary tips of her perky breasts. Carefully, he lifted the edge of the sheet lying across her tiny waist, raised it high enough to see beneath it, and looked at her furry pooter, amazed that it hadn't fallen off sometime during the night along with his pecker. Fucking was about the best thing in the whole world—especially with a partner like Rosey. They had both decided, somewhere between hanging from the ceiling light and doing it upside down in the air, and then trying it doggy style, that they were now an "item", and he couldn't be happier. She was his and that was that.

The morning sun shone through her window as he examined the delectable events of the evening before in his mind. The sex had been fantastic! He remembered how Rosey had clapped her hands with glee when he'd managed to finally extract himself from her clutches for a moment, unlock the bedroom door, and race across her living room. She had giggled uproariously when he held his hand over his cock in case someone spied him, flung open the outside door, and grabbed his sex manual from behind the potted plant. They had fucked their way through page forty-six. The two had tried every position up to that point. Rosey planned to get in at least another forty pages today.

Larry slipped from beneath the sheet, stretched his wings quietly, and noted how there wasn't a muscle in his bony little body that didn't ache. If he were going to keep up with Rosey and all this screwing, he'd have to start working out and build up his strength. What a boon to know that he had accomplished all the heart-hammering positions the evening before and never experienced a heart attack. That was one worry he was going to toss to the wind from here on out!

He tiptoed across the room and headed for the bathroom. Once inside, he closed the door, turned, and caught his reflection in the mirror. His chin rose. Turning sideways, he raised his arms and posed like a classic body builder, and then checked his form from all angles. His bony butt was pretty nondescript, his arms pretty scrawny, but his cock, he thought, was a champ. Now, if it would just stay as swollen as his ears, he'd be in great shape!

He reached up to touch the tender pointed tips. Somehow, he was gonna have to break Rosey's habit of yanking on the dang things every time they changed sexual positions. Still, a satisfied grin broke out across his face, and he headed for the toilet. To hell with it. Screwing Rosey was worth the pain.

Chapter Ten

Brian's white knuckles gripped the steering wheel as he drove in the direction of Claire's house, fighting the biggest battle of his life. Twice, he'd pulled over, trying to convince himself that he needed to turn around and call an immediate end to what could be a devastating day. She might want him, but she didn't understand what she was getting. Claire didn't know about the terrible scars. She'd never be able to comprehend what he had gone through emotionally after the fire—the fear of a stranger's horrified glance—the terror of being forced to live through the endless, painful therapy. She could never understand what it was like to want to end your own life because of the abject misery of your existence. It had taken years to finally find some level of comfort when he was in the company of family, close friends, and his employees. If he continued down this road, she would eventually discover the scars...and how would she feel then?

Beads of nauseous perspiration rolled down his back when he pulled into her driveway. This was his last chance to turn and run like hell. He sat with his foot on the brake, wondering if he had the courage to put the vehicle in park. At one point in his life, he had been a strong, willful man who knew what he wanted and had always strived to attain it.

A movement out of the corner of his eye caught his attention. His jaw clenched tightly when he glanced up to see Claire standing on the sidewalk with Buddy by her side. Closing his lids, he tried to force the picture of her smile away, but it only beamed brighter in the dark corners of his mind.

"Brian! Is that you?" Her voice filtered through the van's open window.

Adrenaline shot through his blood.

"Brian?"

His fingers trembled around the shifter. Buddy yipped excitedly. Brian stared at his scarred arm and moved his gaze past the raised ridges at his wrist to where his fingers gripped the gearshift. The same old wave of horrified confusion that something like this had actually happened to him made his stomach churn. He lifted his gaze. She waited, the smile now gone from her lips. Claire was so beautiful…so…vulnerable. He slammed the van into Park and shut off the engine. Brian was so weary of the constant loneliness. The sight of Claire and what he could have with her fueled his nerve.

"Hi, Claire," he said as he slid off the seat, slammed the door, and walked toward what he hoped would be a bright new future.

Her smile was back. "I was beginning to think I scared you off with the phone call."

"No such luck on your part." He stopped before her. As his gaze traveled over the soft curve of her cheek, her shimmering green eyes, and the full lips that begged to be kissed, he knew it was true. Brian had no doubt that he'd fallen in love—a heady emotion he thought he could never have again. At the moment, he wanted to pull her into his arms and feel the comforting warmth of someone who could care for him, disfigurement and all. His fingers, instead, formed into tight fists at his side.

"You're wrong. It's wonderful luck," she stated with conviction.

Her teeth nibble nervously on her bottom lip. "Can I ask you something, Brian?"

"Sure." God, he wanted to pull her close, but he couldn't. She would surely feel the scars…not yet. He needed to tell her first if he could gather the courage.

"When I was babbling on the phone, you never really had a chance to answer me. All you said was that you were coming over. As strongly as I feel about you, I refuse to believe that you wouldn't feel something of the same. Do you? Could you accept me into your life even though I'm blind?"

He reached out his left hand and took her fingers in his. "Something happened to me yesterday when we were together. Your blindness means nothing, Claire. I…I just don't know if I can be the man you're looking for. Contrary to what you think, I don't know if I'm good enough for you."

A bright smile suddenly appeared on her face. Her eyes glistened with unshed tears of happiness. "Well, how would you like to discuss it on the bench in my backyard? I'm sure I'll be able to make you see the error of your thinking."

His fingers squeezed hers. He had to hear what she wanted to say. Being with Claire felt so right…so…absolutely perfect. Brian led her around to the back of the house and it wasn't long before he settled her on the bench, sank down beside her, and kept a tight hold on her hand.

She tipped her head to feel the morning sun on her cheeks. Just having his quiet presence beside her at the moment made up for all the challenging lonely, dark days of her existence. "Okay, can I talk first?"

"Could I stop you?"

"No," she giggled, and then sobered. Her struggle whispered across her face.

"I want to tell you a little about myself. I never thought my life would end up the way it did. I always had this idea that I would go off to college to study interior design. My high school counselor did everything in her power to push me in that direction. She constantly told me I had what it took to be at the top in my field. I planned to move to New York and establish myself as one of the best in the city. I saw myself designing grand penthouses for the rich, rubbing elbows with celebrities as they begged me to work for them and, somewhere along the way, the man of my dreams would walk into my corner office, sweep me into his arms, and I would live happily ever after." She shook her head. "Life plays horrible tricks. Imagine, yearning for a job where the ability to see colors and textures and put them both perfectly together is the only way to succeed. I could have lost my hearing or the ability to speak, or I could have been paralyzed and sentenced to a wheelchair, but I still could have lived my dream to be a designer. Instead, I lost my eyesight—the one and only thing I couldn't afford to lose. Life sure has a way of pulling the rug from beneath one's feet."

I know, Claire. I know what's it's like…

Her slender shoulders sagged with a heartfelt sigh. "Do you know that just because I'm blind, people treat me differently? They're either so damned sugary that it makes me want to throw up, acting as if I'm three years old and can't do a damn thing for myself. Then there are those that go to the other extreme. My so-called friends from my old life have slowly disappeared. It was too hard for them to be slowed down with someone holding a white cane. I quit going places. I stopped doing anything that involved others. I just stayed in my room and listened to music. Hell, I wouldn't even listen to the television because I couldn't see it. TV was for the sighted."

A heavy sigh whispered across her lips. "I was so lonely." The touch of Brian's thumb brushing across the top of her hand comforted Claire beyond belief. "My dad came into my bedroom one day, made me get out of bed, and forced me into the car. Before I knew it, we were at the Center for the Blind. He put me in therapy. Man, I fought them. I hated the people there, and I hated my father for forcing me to get on with my life, when all I wanted to do was shrivel up and die."

Brian felt as if something heavy pressed against his chest. His quiet breath was strangled. He struggled for air. He knew the emotions. He understood the devastation of having your life wiped out. The handicap didn't matter. They all came with the same set of rules—the same anger and the same grief.

"It wasn't until I listened to a group of speakers who came to the Center to discuss how their lives had changed with the help of seeing-eye dogs that I finally started to pay attention." She lovingly scratched Buddy's ears. "What is it about the love of a dog that can change a person's life? Those people talked about the bond they had with their animal caretakers and how with their help, they were able to go on. They were happy and excited to meet each day. I realized somewhere inside me that I wanted to feel the same way. I found myself taking lessons in Braille and doing anything I needed to do just so I could be accepted into the Seeing Eye dog program. For some odd reason, something clicked and I didn't want to live an empty existence."

The light stroke of her fingers feathered tenderly across the top of Buddy's head. "I thought it had all come together when I met Buddy. He changed my life. I found purpose. He's the only thing that gives me complete joy. Then you drove into my yard yesterday, and I realized that I didn't have it all. You're the first person outside the Center to just let me be me. By the time I woke up this morning, I just had to tell you. I told Buddy we had to go for it. I don't want you to disappear from my life. I don't want to waste any more time being lonely. It's crazy, Brian, pure craziness, but I fell in love with you. You've got so much going for you and could probably have someone who was perfect, so I absolutely refuse to believe your comment that you don't think you could be the man I want you to be. Is it because I might stumble along the way sometimes? I can do anything I put my mind to and would never hold you back. Do you think there's any chance that we could have something? I need to know now. I don't want games. I want someone I can spend my life with."

He stared at her, his love growing by the second.

Could he tell Claire? Did he dare take the chance to let her know how imperfect he really was? She would understand. She'd been to hell and back—she knew what it was like. He had to. Brian couldn't let this wonderful woman slip from his life. He gripped her hand tighter. "It's funny, Claire. But I think I had the same kind of night as you did."

"There you are, Claire! I've been calling and no one would answer the phone. You had me worried."

Brian's frantic gaze darted to an older woman rounding the corner of the house. Insecurity slammed him in the gut. He dropped Claire's hand like a hot potato and swept his palm over the side of his face, searching for somewhere to hide.

"Hi, Mom! Come on over and sit down. I want you to meet someone."

Jean Holliday's shoes clipped across the sidewalk, the sound getting louder and louder in Brian's ears.

"Honest to God, Claire, you've got to start carrying a portable phone with you when you're not in the house. I told your father that I was coming over and, if you were here, I was going to spend the day and help you with the garden. Just give me a job and—" The woman froze when she stopped before the younger couple on the bench. Her gaze took in the man's horribly burned arm to where the marred skin disappeared into the sleeve of his shirt. But, it was when he slowly turned his head to meet her eyes that the air rushed from her lungs.

"You worry too much, Mom. I told you I've been outside a lot, working on my gardens. This is Brian Valentine. He owns The Valentine Shoppe and has been helping me with the planting. Brian, this is my mom, Jean Holliday." Claire tipped her head when the other two remained silent. "Mom?"

"Yes…yes, dear, I'm here." Her eyes evaded the right side of the man's face. "It's very nice to meet you, Mr. Valentine."

Brian stood slowly. "Nice to meet you, Mrs. Holliday." He had to get away. "Since your mom sounds like she wants to spend the day with you, I think I'll head back to the shop. We can do this another day, Claire."

"What?" she asked as she jumped up. "You don't have to leave. What about the garden? What about our…conversation?"

Rivulets of perspiration streamed down his back for the second time that day. "It's probably better that I go. I could get a lot done before we get hit full force for the Valentine's holiday." Brian nodded his head in the direction of Claire's mom, trying not to meet the horror in the woman's eyes. It was over. He was a fool to even think that he could have told Claire. He just wanted to find somewhere to hide. "Have a nice day." He turned on his heel, and struggled to keep his pace even as he strode away.

Once in his van, he swallowed the lump of sadness that threatened to choke him. Claire probably knew by now—that is if her mother had recovered from the sight of the monster sitting beside her daughter.

*****

Larry relaxed against Rosey's headboard, amazed that he wasn't totally exhausted after the rousing afternoon of sex. True to her word, they had sailed through the next forty pages of the sex manual, laughing their asses off in the process as they bumped and ground and slipped and slurped. Now, Larry was showered, had one ankle crossed over the other, and listened to Rosey's chattering from behind the ice packs pressed to his swollen ears.

She stretched out beside him and played with the thin chest hairs sprouting between his almost nonexistent pecks. "These past few days have been the best of my life."

Larry tossed the ice packs to the floor, rolled to his side, and met her sweet smile. "I have to agree with you, Rosey. It's been fun as hell."

She studied one of his swollen ears, feeling slightly apologetic for having been so rough with him.

He reached out and smoothed a long blonde curl around her breast. "I have to tell you something. I could absolutely drown in your pretty eyes. Your body just sets me on fire all the time. Rosey? I love you—not like before when we were just friends. This is something different. I always want to take care of you. I want us to be together always."

Rosey squealed with happiness. "Oh, Larry!" She made a grab for him.

"Not the ears!" he cringed and covered them quickly with his hands.

She quickly wrapped her arms around his neck and pulled him close until her lips breathed against his. "I love you, too. We're going to be happy forever, aren't we?"

Larry brushed his lips across hers. "Forever, Rosey, forever." He cuddled her close and sighed against the top of her head where it nestled in the crook of his arm. "Now that we've got us all figured out, we really need to knock off some of this fucking and get back to business. We haven't checked in on Brian and Claire for almost two days. If we don't get our Gold Wings, we're gonna be heckled like crazy by the other teams."

"I know. We've only got a few days left. Shame on us for being so selfish. You know what, Lar? I couldn't give a shit less about the wings. I mean, I know that's what this is all about, but to me it's more important just to get the two of them together. No one should be that lonely."

"Yeah, I know. How are we gonna do it when we've used up our arrows already?"

Rosey studied her best friend and decided to go for it. "The arrows were duds, so the point is moot."

"What do you mean, duds?"

"That arrow didn't do a thing to me."

He shot up. "What are you talking about? After it hit you, you wanted to suck me dry on the spot."

Rosey flopped to her back and howled. "I'm a pretty good actor, hey? That arrow hitting me was the one opportunity I've been waiting for to make my move on you."

Larry snorted in disbelief.

"Really! I've wanted your skinny little ass for a long time, but I know how you can be." She giggled quietly. "You're so gullible that I figured I'd take the first chance that was presented—so I darted in front of it and the rest is history. You're not angry, are you?"

"Angry? After the way you've acted?" A slow smile broke over his lips. "You've wanted me? Hell, here I was feeling bad about watching your ass bounce around in front of me when we were flying from one place to another."

"Shit. I did that on purpose, trying to get you to notice me."

Larry rolled over her body and pressed his growing cock against her pooter mound. "You're fuckin' something, Rosey. I love you."

Her fingers stroked his smooth cheek all the way to the top of his pointed head. "I love you, too, but we'd better get going."

Chapter Eleven

The two sprites decided to check on Brian first. After discovering that he wasn't at the flower shop, they headed back to Rosebud's apartment, looked up his address in the papers they'd received from Cupid, and headed for his house. Not seeing him anywhere in the yard, they entered the home via the crack beneath the front door.

Once in the living room, they stopped to view shelves lined with pictures of Brian's high school and college baseball days. Team photos, pictures of Brian on the mound, gold trophies, and sports paraphernalia finished out the display. From there, they moved on to a lone picture of Brian in his fireman's gear on the day of his graduation. "He looks so proud..." Rosebud whispered. "He's such a handsome guy. I could cry for him, but I know that's not what he wants."

Larry placed his arm around her shoulders. "He's still the guy he was, Rosey. He just got lost for a while. Think about his bio. We're gonna help him find his way back. Claire is the key. I think we've got our work cut out for us—especially now that I know those damned arrows are a pile of crap."

"And she needs him. Beauty isn't only on the outside, Larry. Why can't Brian understand that he's the same man...probably better because he doesn't even realize the strength of character he possesses to have made it through all those horrible times?"

"That's where we come in. Claire is the one who will make him shine. And he'll do the same thing for her. Nature is going to take its course. It just needs a little help, and then they'll do the rest. Okay, let's go find Brian. If he wasn't at the shop, I'm sure he's in the house somewhere."

They buzzed about the house, coming up empty until they reached his bedroom. Cautiously flying through the open doorway, they discovered him lying on his bed with the shades closed. His unscarred forearm rested across his eyes. Strange. It was past noon and, instead of working at his shop, he was home on the bed. Glancing at one another, they floated closer and perched on a shelf above where he lay.

"What are we going to do?" Rosebud asked while keeping her eyes on his still form.

Larry's thin shoulders shrugged once. He spun his hat into the thinking position. "I'm trying to come up with a plan," he responded.

The sound of the phone ringing on the bed stand startled them both. Brian straightened his arm and let it fall to the mattress as it continued to ring. Finally, the answering machine picked up.

"Brian? This is Claire. Please. Pick up the phone. I know you're home because Kate said you were." A pause. "Brian."

Rosebud and Larry watched him reach up and wearily rub his face with both hands, but he didn't make a move to pick up the receiver.

"All right." Claire's voice sounded tired. "I can't understand why you won't at least talk to me. If you're really not home, I'm sure you'll eventually get all the messages I've been leaving. As you know, I've been trying to get hold of you since yesterday. I can't understand why you thought you had to leave. Did I do something? I got rid of my mother right away and tried to find you so we could finish off the garden. Although, I guess that was only an excuse. I just wanted to be with you and hear the sound of your voice."

Larry nudged Rosebud when he thought Brian was going to answer the phone. Instead, the man only rolled to his side and stared at the answering machine.

"I've been thinking about us…"

* * * * *

Brian swallowed back the lump in his throat. He wanted to hold her. He wanted to say to hell with what everyone thought, but the look on her mother's face continued to haunt him. "I've been thinking about us, too…" he whispered.

Rosebud and Larry floated off the headboard and hovered closer to hear his quiet murmurings.

Claire's voice filled the room. "Yesterday when you were holding my hand, I was the happiest I've been in a long time. You must have been trying to let me down slowly, though. That's the only thing I can figure out. I wish my mom hadn't showed up, because you were really listening to me. You said you had the same kind of night. I felt you really understood when I was talking about my initial reactions and emotions as far as being blind. I don't know, maybe I was wrong about you. Maybe it would be too difficult for a man like you to love a woman like me."

Brian shot up and hauled his feet over the edge of the bed. The air movement sent the two little fairies into a spin until Larry was able to right both of them. They sailed back to the headboard to safety.

"That's not true, Claire. How could any man not love you?" Brian clasped his hands together and let them hang between his knees. She sounded so hurt.

"So, I guess I've bothered you enough over the last few days. I'm a little dense at times when it comes to taking a hint. Either that or…well, you know the problem I have with keeping my mouth shut. Thank you, Brian, for helping me with my garden. Please have Kate send me an invoice and I'll get a check sent to you right away. You're a wonderful man. I wish you the best. Goodbye." The machine beeped once and the room went quiet.

Both fairies gasped when Brian snatched the answering machine from the table, yanked the wires from the wall, and heaved it across the room. When it hit the wall, it broke into pieces. A second later, Brian's chin sank to his chest.

Larry grabbed Rosebud's hand and headed for the door.

"Where are we going? Oh, no, this is terrible! What are we going to do, Larry?"

"We're going to Claire's." He pulled her across the living room and dipped beneath the door.

Rosebud stared at the look of determination on his face. "Did you come up with something?"

"Of course, I did," he stated as they hurried over the sidewalk. "Christ. How can anyone blame Brian for thinking he's sparing Claire a whole bunch of heartache by walking out of the picture? Look what he's been through. But, that's bullshit. We know it, Claire's going to know it, and Brian's gonna finally discover that he's got life by the nuts when he's got her by his side." He glanced at Rosey and felt the instant warmth of loving her rush through his blood. And it wasn't that his loyalties had switched—he still felt very protective as far as Claire was concerned, but dammit, Brian was going to have the same thing that he did. Love was grand. Love was wild. Love was...indescribable. He tightened his grip on her fingers. "Strengthen up your shoulder muscles, Rosey girl, because you're gonna be sportin' Gold Wings before you know it."

*****

They arrived at Claire's within thirty minutes. Rosey did her best to keep her hand in Larry's in order to keep up with him. Hot streaks of excitement pinged through her limbs. This new persona of his had her trembling. He wasn't the crabby, indecisive shit he'd always been. Now, he took control of the situation like it was second nature. He was alpha-cupid, the fairy of her dreams, and she couldn't be happier.

She smacked into him when he stopped short as they rounded the corner of Claire's house. Instead of the usual complaint that poured from his mouth, he instantly turned, set her upright, and studied her face with concern in his eyes.

"Oh, my gosh. I'm sorry, Rosey. You didn't get hurt, did you?" his hands floated over her body, checking for injuries. "I'll give you better warning next time."

Rosey blinked—and her blood heated further. "I'm…I'm okay. I wasn't paying attention. I was thinking about…I love you, Larry."

He gave her a quick kiss. "I'm gonna make you prove that when we get home. Until then, Claire is sitting on the bench with Buddy."

They hurried across the yard and perched on the wooden arm of the garden seat. When Buddy woofed and sniffed in their direction, Larry popped to a standing position and pointed his finger. "Sit down, you fucking bag of hair. I don't have time to be worrying about you." The dog quickly smacked his ass to the ground and swished his tail happily across the grass.

"What's the matter, Buddy?" Claire said. "Did you see something?" Her fingers ruffled the hair at his neck. "It's just you and me again, baby." Her head tipped to the side. "Well, that's a dumb statement. I guess it's always only been you and me since Scott left. Brian wasn't really a part of us, yet, was he? I don't know why, maybe wishful thinking, but since yesterday, I didn't see just you and me anymore. Brian was there already." A heavy sigh left her lungs. "Even if he doesn't want to be here with us, I still love him. Crazy, irrational love, Buddy. The type that makes me yearn for the touch of his hand against my skin, the sound of his voice in my ear…his presence beside me when I'm old and gray…"

Larry gently pushed Rosebud in Claire's direction. "Okay, this is where we come in. Get over there and start whispering in her ear. Just make sure you don't touch her and get flattened when she thinks a bug is after her."

"What am I suppose to say?"

"You're going to be her inner voice. The power of suggestion, Rosey. Just keep telling her she can't give up. I can't do it with my male voice. I'll take care of Brian if the need comes up. We can't let her give up. Brian just needs a little push, and I plan to shove him good if necessary."

Rosey hovered in the air above the bench, figured out how she would start, and then fluttered closer to Claire's ear. Larry gave her a thumbs-up for encouragement when she glanced over her shoulder.

Claire sighed again. "I just wish he would have at least picked up the phone. I know he was home."

"Go on, Rosey!" Larry urged.

Rosebud cupped her hands around her mouth and floated close. "So, Claire, don't give up on Brian."

Claire straightened on the bench. Her brow furrowed slightly.

Getting the hang of it, Rosey darted nearer. "I love him. There's a reason why he left. Maybe I should ask him what it is." She bounced away when Claire lifted her hand and rubbed her neck as if listening to something.

With another glance in Larry's direction, Rosey moved closer to Claire once more. "I know he feels the same. There was a spark between us. I love him. I should fight for him."

"But, he left," Claire muttered.

"But why did he leave?"

Claire's shoulders raised in a small shrug. "I can't keep begging."

"Yes, I can. If I love him, and I think he feels the same, why shouldn't I give it another try?"

Larry's head nodded wildly. Rosey was doing a great job.

Claire rose from the bench. "Come, Buddy." Her fingers clasped the plastic handle. "House, Buddy."

Rosebud's smile disappeared as she watched them leave. She met Larry halfway to the bench's armrest. "Now what? I don't think it's working."

"Hell, we just began. We'll work on her all day. If she doesn't do anything, then I'll head for Brian's. Trust me, Rosey. By Valentine's Day, this is gonna be all over."

*****

They kept it up all day. Whether Claire was taking a nap, preparing supper, washing the dishes, or back outside enjoying the warm night in her garden, Rosey kept talking in her ear until her voice grew hoarse.

Taking a break, she headed toward Larry where he slumped against a blade of grass poking up between two brick pavers.

"I don't know, Larry. Every time she starts to agree with my whispers, she comes up with another reason why she might not be good enough for Brian. I'm really starting to worry."

He pulled her close and gently rubbed her back as he stared at Claire. "I know. I think I'm gonna have to go to Brian's and work this relationship from that angle."

Rosey pressed her breasts against his chest and hugged him close. "Does this mean that we're not going to make it home tonight? Can we take a break, go in the house, and screw a little. I miss the feel of your boner."

"Rosey, there ain't anything else I'd rather do than stick my pecker in your pooter, but we're running out of time. Once this is finished, I'm going to haul your sweet ass back between the sheets, and there won't be a page in the sex manual that isn't wrinkled."

"Oh, Larry, I love how you've changed. You make me horny simply with your new take-charge attitude."

His chest swelled with pride at her words. If his Rosey thought he was something now, just wait…

They both glanced up at the sound of a car pulling into the driveway. Rosey wanted to swing around to the front to see if Brian had finally come to his senses, but Larry stayed her with his hand. Claire continued to sit on the bench and he didn't want to leave her by herself. His gaze dropped to Buddy's wagging tail.

It wasn't long before the back door opened and Jean Holliday stepped onto the patio. "Hi, Claire."

"Hi, Mom. I recognized the sound of your car. I figured you'd find me out here."

Jean sank to the seat beside her daughter. "Dad is watching baseball, so I thought I'd take a ride over. Honey, I want to talk to you about something."

Claire crossed her arms. "You're not going to give me a speech again, are you? Mom, I've had a shitty day and a half. Please don't start."

"That's not why I'm here." Jean hesitantly smoothed the front of her pants even though they were perfectly creased. Claire's situation broke her heart. She hated the fact that her little girl had suffered so terribly over the past years. And, then, there was Scott, who broke Claire's heart. Something had been missing from her daughter's step after she was abandoned by the good-for-nothing. Yesterday, however, there was a glow on Claire's face when she had discovered her sitting in the backyard with Brian Valentine. When the man left in a hurry, most likely because Jean had let her shock shine out, Claire insisted she leave because she needed time by herself. Claire hadn't said why, but Jean instantly understood. She had gone home, told her husband, Ted, about the horribly burned man, and discussed Claire's odd attitude toward him. Ted had known exactly whom Jean spoke about. He had remembered the many articles of one of Miami's finest and how the man was injured while saving a family from burning to death in their home.

Jean stared at Claire, knowing that it was time to let Claire's free spirit fly on her own. "I can't quite put my finger on something, so I thought I'd come over here and ask you straight out. The minute I saw you yesterday with Mr. Valentine, your change of attitude hit me. You literally glowed, Claire. Did I interrupt something? Is this Mr. Valentine someone who you've been seeing?"

Claire's lips parted in wonder as she turned her head in her mother's direction. "Seeing? That's the first time you've used a word like that when you're talking to me. Normally, you do your best to avoid any reference to sight in that context. You don't realize it, but I do. You always watch your words very carefully. I can't believe you're talking to me like you would anyone else. Thank you."

Jean clasped Claire's hand and tucked it close. "I'm sorry, honey. I've been so angry about you losing your sight. You're my baby." She sighed heavily. "Dad and I had a long talk last night. He always was so strong through all of this. I apologize that I haven't been the same way. I want to change that. He made me see that you're a big girl and that, despite your blindness, you're living a completely independent life of your own and making it work."

Claire nestled into her mother's embrace when she felt the comforting arms encircle her. "Thanks, Mom. You don't know how much that means to me. It's been hard, but Buddy has changed everything."

They leaned in unison against the backrest and Claire rested her head against her mother's shoulder.

"So, Claire. What about Brian Valentine? I'm sure I saw a spark of something when I interrupted the two of you."

"He's a wonderful man, Mom… Can I tell you something? I haven't known him long, but I fell in love. I don't know what it is, but I sense a kindred spirit when I'm with him. Here's this handsome, great guy that's got everything going for him, yet I felt a strong connection."

Jean's heart quickened as she gently rubbed Claire's shoulder. *She doesn't know. She can't or it would have come out.* "So, are the two of you dating?"

Claire snorted. "I thought something was happening. I'm so confused. He made mention more than once that he didn't think he could be the man I wanted him to be, but he's wrong. When we were together, he treated me like he would any other woman. I don't know. Maybe he's afraid that my handicap would be too much of a problem. I told him I loved him—yesterday—just before you came. I thought he was happy about it. Then suddenly, everything changed. He got up and left in such a hurry." A sad laugh left her mouth. "I think you scared him away—something did. I've tried to contact him, but he won't pick up the phone and he won't call me back. I made my last call this afternoon and told him goodbye. It stinks. It really stinks."

Jean closed her eyes for a moment. She understood Claire like no other person in the world. If she told her what she knew, she would lose her last protective hold on her daughter. But Claire deserved her own life—and if she knew Brian most likely walked away because of a horrible accident from the past, Claire would go after him. She would meet his problems head-on like she had everything else over the past few years. She tightened her hold and took a deep breath. "I think I know why your Brian left, and I think I understand why he won't call you back."

Claire straightened and turned her head in her mother's direction. "What are you talking about? How do you know anything about him?"

"Honey, did Brian tell you he was a firefighter before he owned his own business?"

"A firefighter? No. How do you know that?"

"It was in the papers some years ago. Your father remembered and told me about it last night. Honey, Brian was injured while helping an entire family out of a burning building. The city even gave him an award for being a hero."

Claire suddenly found it difficult to breath. "How? What happened to him?"

Jean took a deep breath. "He was severely burned and almost died."

Claire's hand rushed to her trembling lips.

"Honey, I think I scared him away yesterday because he didn't want me to see him. If I ever run into him again, I plan to apologize for my initial reaction. I couldn't sleep last night just thinking about how I must have made him feel."

"Where was he burned?" Claire's hand dropped limply to her lap.

"The entire right side of his face. From what I could see, most of the right side of his body."

"Oh, my God…" Claire covered her face with both hands as instant tears rolled down her cheeks. That's why he insisted on eating in. When she thought about it now, Brian always kept her to his left. "Oh, my God. He must have gone through hell." Her face lifted. "That's it, Mom. That's why I feel such a connection with him. You know, today I thought I was going crazy. I kept hearing this voice telling me that I loved him—that I couldn't give up."

Jean clasped her hand. "So, what are you going to do? Honey, I've always tried to dictate your life since you became blind, but I saw your face yesterday. I saw how happy you were. If you think Brian feels the same about you, go to him. All I want for you is your happiness." She smoothed the back of her daughter's hair. "Beauty is in the eye of the beholder, Claire. You have innate ability to see people from your heart, a far better way than most."

Claire flew into her mother's embrace and hugged her tightly. "Thank you, Mom. Thank you for telling me. I'm going to go tomorrow and tell him I love him again."

Larry and Rosebud twirled through the air as they cuddled and laughed crazily.

Chapter Twelve

Claire entered The Valentine Shoppe the next morning, glad that she'd waited for the city bus rather than accept her mother's offered ride. She wanted to be alone to think about all the things she would tell Brian, even though she'd been awake most of the night going over it in her mind. Larry and Rosebud hovered directly over her shoulder, just about bursting with excitement. The clock was ticking. Valentine's Day was only two days away.

Kate glanced up from where she stood behind the cash register, and quickly rounded the counter. "Hi, Claire. It's me, Kate. Glad to have you back. Are you and Brian still planting?" She leaned over and patted Buddy's head. "Hi, boy. Your mom must have one heck of a garden."

Claire swallowed bravely and forced a smile to her face. "Hi, Kate. Is Brian here? I hoped to have a chance to speak with him."

"Yeah, he's out back closing up a greenhouse. With Valentine's Day almost here, he's moved everything up front. Boy, has it been busy. Want me to show you the way?"

"Could you? If you just get me close, I can take it from there."

"Sure, come on." Kate clasped Claire's elbow and guided her to the back of the store.

"This is it!" Rosebud squealed. "What if Brian refuses to see her?"

"He'll see her, Rosey. I just gotta believe that he will. If not, then we'll have to take some drastic measures."

She flipped around and flew backward as she stared into his eyes. "What kind of drastic measures?"

"I haven't figured that out yet. But I'll think of something. I promise!"

She couldn't help herself. Careful not to grab his still-swollen ears, Rosey clasped her arms around his neck and stuck her tongue down his throat. When the embrace finally ended, Larry had a hard-on that sucked the blood from his brain.

"Larry, you make me so horny."

"Ditto…but, we've got to pay attention. Now come on, we're losing them."

When Kate and Claire stepped out the back door and the sunshine warmed Claire's cheeks, her stomach churned. They crossed through two greenhouses and finally came to the last. Claire found it hard to respond to Kate's ramblings about the coming holiday as they came to a stop.

"Okay, Claire, here it is. I'll point you in the right direction. I can see Brian in the back doing something. You've got a straight shot down the aisle with nothing in the way. I know these greenhouses like the back of my hand. You've got about one hundred steps and you'll be there."

Claire tightened her grip on Buddy's handle. "Thanks, Kate. I think I can take it from here. Forward, Buddy."

Larry and Rosebud darted past her, and hurried to sit on a beam above Brian's head.

*****

"Brian?" Claire took one last step forward. "Please. I know you're here. I can smell your cologne."

His fingers gripped the hose in his hand. His jaw clenched as he searched the beam above him—anything to keep from turning around. She knew. She had to. The horror on her mother's face a few days earlier only confirmed it. Claire knew he wasn't the handsome man he hoped she thought he was.

"Please say something, Brian."

He hooked the nozzle on the end of the hose over the lip of the wooden table. Forcing himself to face her was as difficult as if she could really see him. Slowly, he turned and stayed rooted to the spot when all he wanted to do was feel the warmth of her soft skin.

"I heard your boots in the dirt. Are you looking at me?" Claire grasped Buddy's plastic handle with white knuckles.

"I'm here, Claire."

She took another step forward. "Why didn't you tell me?"

His heart sank. "For what reason?"

Silence surrounded Claire. "Brian?"

"I'm here." He shrugged, knowing Claire couldn't see the motion edged with unmistaken defeat. "It happened. I'm scarred. There's nothing else to say."

"You could have told me because I understand, Brian. Because I know what it's like to exist in a world where you're forced to wake up every morning and face your handicap." Pain clogged her throat. "Because I know what it's like to be so goddamned angry at the world and everyone around you that it consumes every second of your day." She let go of Buddy's handle and swiped angrily at her tears. "And I know what it's like when you can't talk to someone who understands, and the terror of your situation slowly begins to suffocate you." Her chin lifted slightly. Brian's cologne floated across the small space between them, surrounding Claire with its familiar essence. "You could have told me because I think you're someone special, who I want in my life."

Brian winced and sagged against the table. He clutched the edge with white fingers. "Don't. You don't know what you'd be getting into. I'm not the man I used to be."

"You're probably better than most," she returned immediately. "You went through a horrific experience and lived in spite of it. Why haven't you returned my phone calls?" she demanded.

He straightened, his eyes devouring the slenderness of her waist, her perfect full lips, and her beautiful green eyes. Claire had fast become someone special who lived in his nightly dreams. But, the picture he had of them together was with him as an unscarred man, loving a beautiful redhead. He was selfishly thankful that she couldn't see him. Brian didn't know if he could withstand the look of horror on her features when she looked his way.

Claire held out her hand. "Come to me, Brian."

He shook his head, knowing she couldn't see the action, but needing to do it anyway. "Go home, Claire."

"Forward, Buddy."

"Don't, Claire," Brian quietly demanded through clenched teeth. He flattened himself against the table's edge, ready to glide sideways to elude her tentatively flailing. Her fingers brushed across the front of his shirt. Trapped. He quickly turned the disfigured side of his face away. "Please...you don't want to do this."

Her hand slid tentatively down the length of his chest and over his stomach as she reached out to search for his right hand. Her fingers touched his. "You always keep me on your left side. I know that your right arm was burnt. Is that why?"

Brian squeezed his eyes tightly when she lifted his hand and turned the palm upward. Sensitive fingertips brushed across the inside expanse before she moved on to his wrist. He heard the small, shocked intake of her breath when she discovered the puckered skin of his forearm. He wanted to yank his hand from hers to race down the aisle and keep Claire from discovering the rest.

Her fingers circled his forearm before slowly moving upward to his biceps. The damage to this skin was worse. Claire could easily feel the difference. The hard ridges were deeper...the wrinkled skin stretched tighter than that at the wrist.

He watched warily as her chin trembled when she slowly continued upward. No one but the doctors and nurses at the burn center, and then those who worked at the rehab center had ever touched his injuries. Not his parents, not his friends. Not Kristen. Perspiration trickled down the left side of his face. He wanted to run. He wanted to bolt from her side, but her gentle, caring touch mesmerized him. As her fingers tentatively brushed upward over the fire-ravaged skin of his neck, his lids lowered to avoid witnessing her reaction.

Claire's knees shook as her trembling fingers skimmed across his jaw. Her beautiful Brian. And that's what he was—her Brian. She would never give him up now that there were no more secrets. Taking a deep breath to rid herself of the pain that tightened her chest, she let her fingers move slowly up over his cheekbone, across one closed eyelid, and then brushed downward over his nose until her fingertips rested against his parted lips. They were warm and dry. They were perfect. He was perfect.

She stepped closer, keeping her fingertips lightly pressed against his lips while threading her other hand through the silky textured hair at the back of his head. Urging his head down, Claire replaced the touch of her fingers with her own mouth.

Brian fought the love that surrounded him. If only he dared to believe… If he took her in his arms, he would be unable to let her go. What of the future?

"Kiss me back, Brian," she breathed.

The scent of her light perfume urged him. Her breathless whisper was a plea to let her into his world. Her fingers played through his hair. Her mouth waited…

"Claire…I'm not…"

"You're not kissing me back," she cut in. "And I want you to kiss me back. Ever since you left two days ago, I've been crazy. Crazy to touch you. Crazy to feel the touch of your lips. I love you, Brian. I fell in love with a kind man who was patient and caring, not the person you believe yourself to be. And I love you more than I did yesterday. And tomorrow…I'll love you even more. Kiss me, Brian."

His heart opened. And Claire's sunshine poured inside. Trembling arms encircled her waist. The feeling of Claire sliding her hands protectively around his neck was something he would never forget. For the rest of his life, he would remember this one magical moment when the loneliness he'd experienced for so many years dropped away like the petals of a flower as a new bloom came to life. Claire's love, pure of heart, would be something he could count on forever. He was done hiding—and all because of the wonderful woman in his arms who had peered into his soul.

He tightened his embrace, and felt a rush of ecstasy race through him as he pulled her close and opened his mouth.

Claire groaned within his embrace and murmured his name as he slanted his mouth across hers.

"Oh, God, Claire…" He pulled her closer and deepened his kiss. She arched against the length of his body and clutched at his shoulders. They clung to one another, two people sharing the beauty of a world that was no longer cruel…no longer lonely. They breathed in one another's scent, memorizing it for a lifetime of tomorrows.

Tears coursed down Claire's cheeks as the kiss ended. Her hand rested lightly against his scarred cheek as she tipped her head back. "I was so afraid that you would send me away. It doesn't matter, Brian. Nothing matters except that you're holding me now. Please say that you'll never walk away from me again…"

Struggling to regain a hold on his emotions, Brian pulled her to his chest, wrapped his arms around her tightly, and rested his cheek against the top of her head. His heart thundered inside his chest. His hand shook as he stroked the slim line of her back.

Claire.

He found it hard to believe that only days earlier, he hadn't known she even existed. Now? The last two days were so horrible that he didn't even want to contemplate them. The loneliness he'd felt had nearly consumed him. "I'll never walk away again," he whispered. "I promise."

"Then take me home," she uttered quietly.

Larry handed his hanky to Rosebud who sniffed and cried silent tears beside him. He refused to look at her. If he did, he would be lost. As it was, it was all he could do to keep his own emotions from escaping. The mission was over—and it looked to be a complete success.

Chapter Thirteen

Brian held Claire's hand the entire drive back to her house. Once there, he hurried around the front of the van, opened the door, and helped her alight from the front seat. A quick pop had the side door open. Buddy jumped out with his tail wagging and, when Claire slid her hand inside the crook of Brian's arm and walked with him around the house, Buddy instinctively knew he was off-duty. The dog loped in front of them, sniffing at the trees and shrubbery with joyful abandon. With a command from Claire, however, he raced to her side as the three entered the kitchen.

Claire never hesitated as she easily led Brian down the hall. Once inside the feminine bedroom, she turned, and was welcomed into his arms.

He lowered his mouth to hers, instantly experiencing the mysterious thrill of holding someone he loved, of opening his heart to allow someone inside. Hot bolts of sexual excitement streaked through his blood as their lips touched. He waited one last time for the fear of rejection and his old insecurities to rear up...but they never appeared. In their place was, instead, a slow fire ready to blaze brightly—a magical flame that promised never to be extinguished, because Claire had handed him his life back when she'd touched his damaged body and hadn't recoiled in horror. Her gentle touch was like beautiful eyes smiling at him with love and acceptance.

The kiss ended with the sound of heavy breathing across one another's cheeks. They knew. They instinctively knew that the coming hours would be the beginning of a wonderful life.

She hugged him one more time before stepping back. "Wait right here."

"Where are you going?" he asked quietly as her fingers drifted from his.

She only smiled, and walked to the door. "Buddy? Come." She listened to the pads of his feet as he obediently crossed the room and brushed against her leg. "Come on, boy." Taking him by the collar, she led him calmly through the doorway and into the hallway. "Down. You lie down and go to sleep." Knowing the dog would obey her command, she bent, patted him on the head, and returned to Brian's side after closing the door. Pulling his mouth close, she kissed him passionately, and then stepped away.

Crossing her hands in front of her, she reached down, caught the hem of her shirt and pulled it slowly over her head.

His lips parted as the rise of her rounded breasts above her bra came into view. Lowering his gaze to her hands as she unhooked the clasp between her soft, womanly mounds, he found it amazing that the only man she desired was him. Claire dropped her lacy bra to the floor and stood proudly with soft pink nipples that puckered in anticipation.

"You're beautiful, Claire. So beautiful."

She tipped her head with a gentle smile curving her full lips. "And we'll be beautiful together. Always together. No more loneliness, Brian. We're through with that."

"We're through with that," he repeated in a whisper as her hands moved to the snap on the waistband of her jeans. He suddenly found it hard to breathe. His cock swelled against his zipper.

"Yes, we are." She slid her jeans over the slender curve of her hips and stepped out of them only moments later. Brian's body blazed with heated lust, an elusive emotion that had been absent for so many years that it now shook him to the core. Taking in the roundness of her breasts, the flatness of her belly, and the satiny trim thighs that soon would be opened in welcome, his gaze skittered to the subtle shading of pubic hair beneath the white silk of her bikini underwear. He would make love to her today. He would make love to her always…

"Life is always going to throw us curves." Claire hooked her thumbs inside the lacy waistband. "But together, we'll figure it out. Because we're through with the bad stuff, Brian."

His head nodded in agreement, even if she couldn't see it, as tears burned behind his lids. She offered him freedom…she offered him the future. He blinked away the moisture, and then saw a single tear trickle down Claire's cheek. Everything they had been through—all the fear, all the heartache—had led them to this day. To this minute. To one another's arms. "I've been in limbo Claire…until you. I never thought I could find someone to love me again."

"You were so wrong. It was me, Brian, who thought I'd be alone for the rest of my life," Claire returned quietly as she slowly pulled the panties down past her thighs, over her slender calves, and then kicked them away with a petite, feminine foot.

The air rushed from his lungs. "God…Claire…"

"Come to me, Brian." She held out her arms and waited.

His steps were steady and determined as he walked into her embrace. Letting his eyes close, he brushed his hands slowly down the length of her silky back, relishing the softness of a woman's skin…Claire's skin…and overwhelmed by the emotions of love that swelled within his heart. His palms moved to cup her firm buttocks, and gently, he pressed her body against his erection.

"Oh, God, Brian…it's been so long…" she breathed beside his ear.

He lowered his mouth and feathered tender kisses against the sweet-smelling skin of her neck, loving the feel of Claire's petite body in his arms. It had been so long since he'd had the scent of a woman in his nostrils, so long since he'd felt the rush of sexual adrenaline race through his blood. Brian could have stayed right where they were for the rest of his life, because the moment was perfect as it could be. Sighing contentedly, he continued to move his lips across the tender skin of her collarbone, as one of his hands slipped from around her waist to capture a breast. Claire groaned softly beside his ear. His fingers trembled as a thumb brushed over the crested tip of her nipple.

"It's been so long, Brian, since I was held and didn't feel fear at the coming day. You make me feel safe."

"I'll never let anything hurt you..." He bent slightly, ready to rediscover the raised dart of her nipple as his cheek slid across the warm skin of her chest. The pounding of her heart rippled against his face. His tongue circled the hard tip. His cock throbbed to be released from the confines of his jeans. "I love you, Claire...only you...forever."

Moving upward, he captured her lips once more as Claire's fingers slowly unbuttoned his shirt. Brian wasn't frightened. She loved him and he could never ask for anything more.

"I want to know everything about your body," Claire stated softly.

His eyes remained closed when her fingers slipped beneath his shirt and pushed the material aside. His emotions hung in the balance of wanting her so badly that his body ached, but needing the womanly, accepting touch of her hand even more. Brian wanted Claire to memorize the feel of his skin—the imperfections—all of it. He wanted nothing between them.

Her hands brushed across the smooth, bare expanse of the left side of his chest, across to his shoulder, and back again. The muscles were sleek and hard—muscles that belonged to a powerful man. Starting at his heart, Claire placed her hands flat against him and glided across the rough ridges that increased in severity as she moved to his opposite shoulder. It was easy to feel where the fireball had hit him that long ago day. Pressing a kiss against his right nipple, she then laid her cheek against the puckered skin as she caressed him.

Silently, she stepped behind Brian and slipped the shirt from his shoulders and down the length of his arms. Tossing it away, her hands reached up to gently knead the muscles of his neck, again finding smooth, firm skin on one side, and deep creases on the other. Her sensitive fingertips floated down the broad length on either side of his spine. One part of her mind acknowledged the thrill of the sleek, masculine line she followed. The gentler side rebelled against fate and what it had done to this beautiful man. Claire vowed silently to never impart pain or agony toward Brian in any form, no matter what the future tossed her way. She would spend the rest of her days loving him.

Her hands settled at the trim line of his waist, slowly rounded both smooth and mottled skin until she stroked the line of wiry hair below his navel. She smiled when his firm stomach muscles flinched slightly beneath their weight as she slid her fingers to the snap at his jeans, opened it carefully, and slowly unzipped his pants. The heat from his erection scorched her fingertips through the cotton briefs as they drifted the length of his cock in perfect promise.

"Claire…" His whisper floated by in Claire's darkness.

Brian kicked off his leather sandals.

A gentle smile curved her lips upward as she pressed her breasts against his back, and laid her cheek against the line of his spine while continuing to lightly stroke the covered bulge. "I love you, Brian. You're so beautiful." The muscles of her vagina clenched in anticipation.

Before he could respond, Claire worked Brian's jeans over his hips, delighting in the feel of the masculine hair of his legs against her palms as she slid the denim down over powerful thighs and firmly muscled calves. Straightening once more, her hand drifted against the skin at his waist as she stepped around him. A shiver trickled down her spine when she immediately felt his fingers cup her breasts. His hands fell away again when she tugged at his briefs and, instead, he helped to rid himself of the last piece of resistance between their naked bodies.

Claire's hand slowly encircled his rigid cock, using her thumb to tease the dampened, velvety tip. She heard Brian's slight gasp as she sank to her knees before him.

"You don't have to..."

"I want to, Brian." Her tongue licked gently at the swollen crown of his penis before she opened her mouth and slipped her lips completely over the head of his cock. Brian's soft grunt echoed around her as she worked her way down his shaft, and then back up to dart her tongue against his slit.

Feeling her softly stroking his balls, Brian threaded his fingers through her wavy, auburn tresses, and his hips followed her rhythmic motion as she repeatedly slid the length of his cock, sucking first at the tip, then swirling her tongue around it. Heat churned in his belly when her hand clamped around his thickness, building hotter with each burning second.

Brian urged Claire to her feet, struggling against the blaze of an impending orgasm, his fingers gently caressing her chin as he lowered his mouth against hers to taste himself on her tongue. The kiss was sweet with promise...secure in the truth of what was to come. Both had waited so long to experience the emotions hanging heavily in the air that time slipped away to nothing.

Claire clasped his fingers at her chin, trailing his hand down over a swollen breast, past the dip of her belly, to the moist vee of her thighs. "Brian..." She urged his hand to cup her pussy.

The air rushed from Brian's lungs as he continued to gaze at her closed eyes while tenderly parting the pink lips at the entrance of her wet heat. Her face was a changing plane of emotions...happiness, sultry passion, and acceptance. Claire's head sagged back, and she clutched at his shoulders when a finger trailed through the slick folds to gather moisture, and then slid upward to her swollen clit. Rolling it slowly, Brian gathered her closer within his embrace, pressing sweet kisses filled with love against her mouth.

Claire's head swam in the sensual paradise he created with his gentle, feathering touch. Her knees turned weak when he dipped a long finger inside her pussy and stroked the walls of her vagina, then returned to swirl the tip against her now throbbing bud. "My God, Brian..." she panted.

Goose bumps raised the hair on her arms when he sank to his knees and wrapped a supporting arm around her waist. His gentle, probing tongue against her thigh silently begged her to open wider. Sparks slithered through her womb as she was instantly rewarded when he spread her lips wide with his fingers. The heat of his warm breath as he blew lightly against her clit shook her to her soul.

He flicked his tongue against her clit, the musky feminine scent filling his senses.

Claire's hips moved sensuously with the tender, darting rhythm of his tongue, her inner muscles clenching and unclenching as her pussy waited to be filled. The heat between her thighs increased.

"Brian..." Her hips rolled to a slightly quicker beat. His fingers no longer spread her pussy wide. His lips were now wrapped warmly around her clit as he suckled and drew the bud to an even harder dart, and a tender hand massaged her ass.

Claire gripped his shoulders tightly as a low moan sounded in the back of her throat. Two fingers entered her dripping heat, filling her completely as they slid deeper and deeper, and then began to move inside her. Her head fell further back. Her hips dipped forward against the tongue that continued to tease its way through her slit, seeking, always seeking her clit as the final reward.

Her breasts ached. Heat filled her belly, radiating from the gentle tugs against her clit. She squeezed her vaginal muscles tightly around his fingers, fearing that the wondrous magic of his touch would disappear.

The pulses started from somewhere deep inside her womb, then traveled like wildfire to her breasts. Brian's fingers slid tightly against her cervix as he let her shudder around their length. He nibbled her pulsing clit, drawing an even hotter response as her body surged against his mouth. His arm tightened around her waist, his shoulder supporting her body until the waves began to slow.

Feeling her weight against him as she sank forward, Brian rose to meet her, curled his free arm beneath her knees, and lifted Claire against his heaving chest. Their lips melded, each drawing strength and life from the other. For all in life that he'd experienced so far, nothing had ever been finer than feeling the softness and warmth of Claire's naked skin and smelling her sweet sex in the air.

Claire wrapped her arms tightly around his neck when he crossed to her bed. "Brian…I love you so much," she whispered between kisses pressed against his neck. She continued to clutch his shoulders when the cool satin of her bedspread met her back, and Brian's warm body slid atop hers. As her tongue danced against his, her fingers skimmed his back.

He lay with his hard cock pressed against her wet slit, his breathing becoming more intense when she wrapped one slender leg across his buttocks. Remaining in her loving embrace, his palm followed the curve of her hip, trailed down the outer line of her leg, then whisked past the tender skin of her inner thigh until her body fell open, allowing room for his hand to find her pussy. His cock still throbbed against her wetness, but Brian pressed his finger back inside her vagina, loving how she instantly clamped her muscles around him as he kissed the soft spot at the base of her throat.

"I love you…I love you, Brian…I love you," she murmured as her body surged against the length of his finger.

Withdrawing from her pussy, Brian held his cock, guided the glistening head to her clit and began to swirl it against the pulsing bud—prodding—teasing—promising. Claire gasped beside his ear as she hugged his shoulders and her hips slanted forward, seeking more…seeking him.

He waited until the fevered pitch of her moans became as rhythmic as her thrusting hips, knowing that Claire would again climax. Brian poised his body above her and, when she spread her knees wide, he slid into her writhing heat, filling her tightly, spreading her lips wide as they stretched around his cock, using the weight of his hips to slow her thrusts and entice her to join him in the magical tempo of hot, sensual slides against one another.

Beads of perspiration dotted his forehead as she drew him in with each stroke. Her pussy milked pre-cum from his body, until the rattling blaze of orgasm began to build. The muscles in his tight ass bunched as he continued the sensuous glides to her cervix, pulled back until only the tip of his cock rested inside her dripping heat, and then slid inward once more. His cock swelled further with each erotic glide, the tip sensitized to the friction they created between them.

Claire's body jerked beneath his when the orgasm slammed through her. "Brian!"

"I'm here, Claire...I'll always be here..." His strokes instantly shortened and, only seconds later, he rammed forward and spasmed with a massive orgasm. Wrapping his arms tighter around her shuddering body, he buried his cock deeply within her.

The pulses of sexual release lessened, but their hearts continued to beat wildly. They kissed, they touched, they came to life.

Brian brushed Claire's happy tears from her cheeks, before dipping his mouth for another kiss as she lay splayed beneath his lean body. Her round breasts flattened against his chest. Adjusting his position, Brian's spent penis brushed against her silken thigh. He reached up and tucked errant strands of auburn hair behind her ears, amazed that he had never felt her presence in the world. He should have. He should have known she was out there somewhere. Whatever the force was that had brought Claire to his side, Brian would always be thankful to its intricate power.

"I love you, Claire."

"I love you, too, Brian. Thank God I found you." Her hands brushed over his back, across the dip of his lean waist, and past the firm cheeks of his ass. Her fingers returned to caress his right ass cheek.

Brian studied her furrowed brow while enjoying the light strokes against his backside. "Is something wrong?"

Her fingers continued to brush against his skin. "I didn't feel this here before."

"Feel what?"

"There's a slight difference in texture from one side to the other. I don't even know if anyone else could feel it, but I can. In my mind, it seems like a…"

Brian's smile widened as she traced the outline of a diamond on his ass with her fingertip.

"Like a diamond. Is this part of your injury?"

He chuckled as he nuzzled her neck. "Maybe an injury to my pride, once it got out."

"What are you talking about?"

"It's a tattoo, Claire."

Her eyebrows lifted in instant humor. "A tattoo? Of a diamond? Okay, come clean. I have to know." Her fingers continued to stroke the curve of his ass cheek.

"College." He shook his head. "Stupid. I was in baseball. We won the State Championship, and me and two of my best buddies who, by the way, you'll be meeting soon, decided to celebrate the win by getting our asses tattooed.

Claire belted out an unladylike snort. "Oh my God! Were you drunk?"

"Honest to God, we weren't, but I don't know what the hell we were thinking. I've taken plenty of ribbing because of it. I didn't think it was funny at the time when I was in physical therapy but, looking back, I guess I can see the humor in it now. My female rehabilitating therapists used to call me their diamond in the rough."

The smile disappeared from Claire's face. She reached up, cupped his face with her slender fingers, and pulled his mouth to hers. "Yes, a diamond in the rough, Brian." She breathed against his lips. "But a diamond nonetheless."

*****

"Now stay close to my side," Larry whispered. Clutching Rosebud's hand, they silently tiptoed past Buddy's head, rounded his snout, and scampered beneath Claire's bedroom door. Their wings beat hastily as they rose to hover above the rumpled bed.

"Oh, Larry, look at them!" Rosebud squealed with delight. Her eyes softened when Larry placed his arm around her shoulders and they gazed upon the human couple who lay sleeping on the bed. Their naked, entwined limbs were a testament to what the two had shared. A gentle smile curved Claire's mouth as her head nestled in the crook of Brian's arm.

"We did it!" Rosebud exclaimed quietly.

"Did we?" Larry wondered aloud. "Was it really our interference, or would they have found one another anyway? Humans are amazing, Rosey. Nothing can be done about the past and everything that happened to them, but when placed in terrible situations, most are able to create something of worth. Just like Claire and Brian." He shrugged and clasped Rosey's hand, thinking over the last week. Did they really have something to do with it or was it just Cupid's red pen that had done the trick? "I guess it really doesn't matter, because things are the way they're supposed to be. Brian needed Claire and she needed him." He swiveled until he was able to take both of Rosey's small hands in his so she wouldn't yank on his ears. Their lips came together. "And I needed you, Rosey girl. Yup, I sure as hell needed you."

Epilogue

"Hurry, Larry! We're gonna to be late!" Rosebud beat her wings crazily, clutched the flowers in her hands, and skidded around the corner of Claire's house. Realizing that the ceremony was just beginning, she grabbed Larry's hand and hauled ass until they were both perched on the edge of the patio awning. Their gold embossed wings shone in the bright sunlight of the Miami afternoon.

Larry sent her a querulous look, and then immediately lost it because Rosey was so fucking cute in her new flounced dress. Quickly, he straightened his brand new black top hat and adjusted his tie.

Today was Claire and Brian's wedding. Only six and a half days since the fairies had received their mission papers and, already, the two were getting married. He sighed happily, thinking about two days prior when he and Rosey had hung around, playing grab-ass on the dresser until the two humans had awakened.

At first, they were upset when Claire had started to cry. It didn't take long, however, for them to figure out that her tears were tears of happiness. Brian had just asked her to marry him on Valentine's Day, stating it was ridiculous to wait when they had lost so much time already. He was sure of his feelings and so was Claire—so why wait?

Now, Larry's gaze scanned the hundreds of roses set in pots about the patio, their heavy scent hanging in the humid air. Claire and her father entered through the decorated arbor and walked toward Brian. Buddy, who sat beside Brian with a red tie around his furry neck, happily swished his tail across the grass.

Only close friends and immediate family were in attendance, making the intimate ceremony a cherished one.

Larry leaned forward, rested an elbow on his bony knee, and plopped his chin into his upturned palm as he watched Brian take Claire's hand and tuck it into the crook of his arm. They turned to face the minister.

Maybe this mushy Valentine's crap isn't so bad after all. Love is pretty fuckin' great. I got Rosey… Tipping his head to look at her, his heart did a quick flip when she sent him a lewd wink. That damn Rosey was always up to something. Glancing back to the wedding service, a smile tipped one corner of his mouth. *Brian's got Claire, and we even got our Gold Wings out of the deal. Although, I think those two would have found one another anyway. Love's like that.*

"Pssst! Big Boy! Hey! Look over here!" Rosey whispered loudly.

Turning his head casually, Larry almost slipped off the awning. Rosey had her tights off, her dress hiked up to her chest, and her pooter was shaved.

"Want a little of this?"

Larry dove right between her legs, his hat forgotten as it tumbled to the bricks below them.

Rosey dropped the pink taffeta over his head and sighed as she felt the pressure of his tongue against her pooter. She leaned back on her elbows and darted her gaze around the perimeter to see if anyone noticed them. Her eyes suddenly widened.

"Ooohhhh, Larry…"

About the author:

Picture Ruby with her hair on fire! Yup, that's her every morning when she bounds out of bed and heads for her home office. Ruby thanks her lucky stars that she's a full-time writer and a part-time matchstick. Although, there is a hint of a bulldog somewhere in there, too. Once she sticks her teeth into something, there's no turning back until it works. Her husband says she reminds him of that little mouse who stares up into the sky at a swooping eagle (this would be the mouse with his middle finger up) daring that darn bird, and just about anyone else, to screw up her day when she's got writing on the brain.

Ruby loves to write, plain and simple. So much so that she took a leap of faith in herself and quit her 'professional' job, stuck her butt in front of a computer, and finally discovered what brings her true happiness in the wilds of Minnesota.

Some might think that the life of a writer is glamorous and enviable. This is what Ruby has to say about that: "Glamorous? Think of me in sweats and an old t-shirt just beneath that flaming head of mine, typing with one hand and beating out the fire with the other. Envious? Most times my 'new' job consists of long hours of dedication and damn hard work, cramping leg muscles from sitting too long, and a backside that for some reason is widening by the week. But I wouldn't change my life for the world."

Most people who fantasize about strange people and occurrences are sitting on the sixth floor of some psychiatric hospital. Not Ruby—she gets paid for it!

Ruby welcomes mail from readers. You can write to her c/o Ellora's Cave Publishing at 1056 Home Avenue, Arkon OH 44310-3502.

Also by Ruby Storm:

Lucy's Double Diamonds

Payton's Passion

Twilight Kisses

Virgin Queen

Perfect Betrayal

Enjoy this excerpt from

Adam 483: Man or Machine?

She often felt born into the wrong century. Fantasies of navigating the high seas before technology had taken that thrill out of man's hands, haunted her dreams.

Even more enticing, in her sea-faring fantasies she indulged every eroticism she craved. Sexy-as-sin pirates took her body and soul to sexual heights she'd never experienced.

If only those fantasies were real…

A harsh buzz snapped her thoughts back to reality. Rarely did she work or even relax uninterrupted these days. The burden of a senior officer's rank, she supposed. Her time as strictly a navigational officer with less responsibility had come and gone long ago. She pressed a button on the edge of the desk, unlocking the door. "Come."

With a light swoosh, the panel opened.

The medical officer, Lieutenant Sheera Roiya, strode inside. "Captain."

Tyree's gaze returned to her charts. "No need for such formality, Sheera. We're alone."

"I'm here on business."

Tyree paused and sat back in her chair, her interest captured. "Business? Is there a problem? We lifted off from Jenway Station without incident. The ship and crew checked out perfectly."

"While docked, your newly assigned, personal security bot came aboard."

Tyree frowned. She hated the idea of some pre-programmed robot following her around. But in the last month, ore smugglers had made three attempts on her life. After finding out about it, her brother, the Ambassador of Jenway and the one in charge of her expedition, insisted upon sending along personal protection for her.

A heated argument had ensued when she'd heard his decision. "I don't want a shadow dogging my every move." She'd made her opinion clear before leaving Jenway.

"Don't sound so disgruntled. A lot of senior officers use them." Sheera stuck her head out the door. "In here. The Captain will see you now."

The doorway filled with a large presence, and Tyree's breath hitched. "It's a male."

Sheera looked at her as if she'd lost her mind. "Of course. A male looks more intimidating to any aggressors lurking nearby and intending harm when you're off-ship."

Tyree stood and rounded the desk. She examined her new guard. Though a robot, she still felt uncomfortable with a male. Especially since regulations dictated he stay inside her quarters.

He stood over six feet, with dark wavy hair, deeply intense eyes, broad shoulders, a square jaw, and something she couldn't identify. He held himself differently than other robots, almost proudly. "He's Cyborg?" she ventured warily, because Sheera was a friend who Tyree felt would admit to the truth.

"Of course not!" the woman responded quickly, sounding full of astonishment. "You know Cyborgs were outlawed five years ago."

"That doesn't mean the Governing Council eradicated them all. This bot is not standard issue. He looks too…real." She preferred the days when a robot looked like a mechanical. At least she always knew who and what she was dealing with.

"Isn't that the idea, to blend in?"

"Perhaps, but this situation leaves a bad taste in my mouth." She circled him. Strong shoulders, tight butt. Nice. She stepped in front of him again and glanced between his legs. What started as a casual look, ended with her captured attention. He possessed a *very* noticeable bulge. Her body responded with an automatic rise in temperature.

"He seems capable, don't you think?" Sheera prompted.

At the sound of the woman's voice, Tyree gave herself a mental shake. "Mmm." *Capable of what?* Attributing her carnal reaction as simply too long without a man, she dismissed the feelings and raised her eyes to his.

He returned her stare without wavering.

A shiver raced down her spine. That direct look, as if he knew her every thought, intimidated her somehow. But she held her ground.

"What are you called, bot?"

"Adam 483," his voice rumbled in response.

Why an electronic book?

We live in the Information Age—an exciting time in the history of human civilization in which technology rules supreme and continues to progress in leaps and bounds every minute of every hour of every day. For a multitude of reasons, more and more avid literary fans are opting to purchase e-books instead of paperbacks. The question to those not yet initiated to the world of electronic reading is simply: *why?*

1. *Price.* An electronic title at Ellora's Cave Publishing and Cerridwen Press runs anywhere from 40-75% less than the cover price of the exact same title in paperback format. Why? Cold mathematics. It is less expensive to publish an e-book than it is to publish a paperback, so the savings are passed along to the consumer.
2. *Space.* Running out of room to house your paperback books? That is one worry you will never have with electronic novels. For a low one-time cost, you can purchase a handheld computer designed specifically for e-reading purposes. Many e-readers are larger than the average handheld, giving you plenty of screen room. Better yet, hundreds of titles can be stored within your new library—a single microchip. (Please note that Ellora's Cave and Cerridwen Press does not endorse any specific brands. You can check our website at www.ellorascave.com or

www.cerridwenpress.com for customer recommendations we make available to new consumers.)

3. *Mobility*. Because your new library now consists of only a microchip, your entire cache of books can be taken with you wherever you go.
4. *Personal preferences are accounted for*. Are the words you are currently reading too small? Too large? Too...**ANNOYING**? Paperback books cannot be modified according to personal preferences, but e-books can.
5. *Instant gratification*. Is it the middle of the night and all the bookstores are closed? Are you tired of waiting days—sometimes weeks—for online and offline bookstores to ship the novels you bought? Ellora's Cave Publishing sells instantaneous downloads 24 hours a day, 7 days a week, 365 days a year. Our e-book delivery system is 100% automated, meaning your order is filled as soon as you pay for it.

Those are a few of the top reasons why electronic novels are displacing paperbacks for many an avid reader. As always, Ellora's Cave and Cerridwen Press welcomes your questions and comments. We invite you to email us at service@ellorascave.com, service@cerridwenpress.com or write to us directly at: 1056 Home Ave. Akron OH 44310-3502.

ELLORA'S CAVE
ROMANTICA PUBLISHING